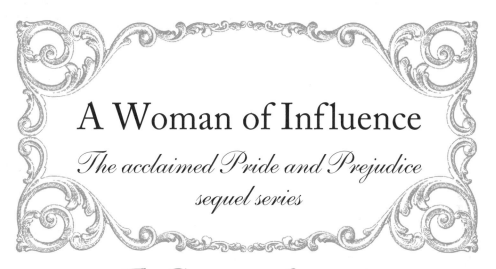

A Woman of Influence

The acclaimed Pride and Prejudice sequel series

The Pemberley Chronicles:
Book 9

DEVISED AND COMPILED BY
Rebecca Ann Collins

sourcebooks
landmark

By the Same Author

The Pemberley Chronicles
The Women of Pemberley
Netherfield Park Revisited
The Ladies of Longbourn
Mr Darcy's Daughter
My Cousin Caroline
Postscript from Pemberley
Recollections of Rosings
The Legacy of Pemberley

Published by Sourcebooks Landmark, an imprint of Sourcebooks, Inc.
P.O. Box 4410, Naperville, Illinois 60567-4410
(630) 961-3900
FAX: (630) 961-2168
www.sourcebooks.com

Originally printed and bound in Australia by Print Plus, Sydney, NSW, 2004. Reprinted October 2006.

Library of Congress Cataloging-in-Publication Data is on file with the publisher.

Printed and bound in the United States of America.
VP 10 9 8 7 6 5 4 3 2 1

6592

Dedicated to all my friends, with love

An Introduction...

BECKY TATE NEEDS NO introduction to readers of the Pemberley novels.

It may, nevertheless, be necessary to explain that this "woman of influence" is *not* Rebecca Ann Collins, author of the Pemberley Chronicles series.

Lest my readers misconstrue the situation, because I have used her name as my *nom de plume,* I should point out that the central character of this novel is the original Becky Collins, daughter of Charlotte Lucas and Reverend William Collins (from the annals of *Pride and Prejudice*), wife of the publisher Anthony Tate, and a woman of considerable standing in her community.

Her efforts at writing, however, never amounted to much more than scribbling—personal impressions that were, happily for her, regularly printed in her husband's journals and released to a captive audience.

Becky's story is interesting because, like a significant number of Victorian women, she sought to emancipate herself from a tedious and impecunious life by marrying a man of wealth and influence, not because she loved him, but for the advantages and opportunities the marriage offered. The realisation that, in attempting to escape the stifling environment of Victorian domesticity, she had foregone something far more precious than affluence and power, comes upon her gradually. While she admits her mistake and strives valiantly to make something of her marriage, its disintegration is hastened by the loss of a beloved daughter and the apparent indifference of her husband to her grief.

The disapproval of her more fortunate friends serves only to exacerbate her plight, isolating her further. Marriage had clearly brought Becky influence but little contentment and less happiness.

Many women, similarly placed, resorted to clandestine liaisons and extra-marital affairs, taking lovers when and where they could, often scandalising their families and compounding their misery. Becky Tate does not.

When, at the beginning of this book, we meet her again, she is a mature woman, who has survived the failure of her early ambitions, suffered loss and humiliation, and, having taken stock of her life, is ready to reclaim her future. The warmth of her relationship with her sister Catherine and the sincerity of her desire to help those less fortunate than herself redeem her from accusations of shallowness and prove more rewarding than the trappings of wealth and influence. It is a situation in which many modern women find themselves.

Therein lies my fascination with her.

I hope my readers will agree and enjoy Becky's story.

RAC 2004
www.rebeccaanncollins.com

For the benefit of those readers who wish to be reminded of the characters in the Pemberley Chronicles series and their relationships to one another, an *aide-memoire* is provided in the appendix.

Prologue

BECKY COLLINS WAS BACK at Hunsford, not at the parsonage, where she had spent much of her childhood, endeavouring to fulfill the expectations of her zealous father, Reverend Collins, and avoid the censure of his indomitable patron, Lady Catherine de Bourgh, but at Edgewater—the property in the county of Kent, where she now lived.

She was, of course, no longer Miss Collins; having been married before she was twenty years of age to Mr Anthony Tate, a publisher of some power and influence in the community, she had been considered to be a woman of some rank and substance.

Thanks to the generosity of her husband, who, having separated from his wife, had elected to live out the rest of his days in America, where he had recently died, she was now a reasonably wealthy woman. Having sold their house in London, Becky had acquired Edgewater, an investment that had the universal approval of most if not all of her friends and relations.

Standing at the window of what was to be her private study and work room, Becky looked out across the grounds of her new home and smiled as her eyes took in the lovely aspect across the lake from which the property took its name. There was a singular sense of satisfaction in knowing that everything in this place would be as she had planned it; she no longer took directions from nor waited upon the approval of anyone. Neither was she obliged to submit her accounts to her husband's clerk for payment.

Becky Tate was at last her own woman and she enjoyed that above anything.

For the very first time in her life, Becky had chosen where she was going to spend her time, just as she was now free to decide how that time was to be spent. It was for her an especially thrilling sensation, the likes of which she had not known in many years. Looking at the work she had begun at Edgewater, she could not resist a frisson of excitement as she contemplated the future that lay before her, a future to be determined entirely by her own wishes and limited only by her resources.

Becky was glad to have left Derbyshire. Her son Walter and his family now occupied the Tate residence at Matlock. She had been at Edgewater throughout the Winter, save for a visit to Pemberley at Christmas.

It was February and Winter had not as yet released its hold upon the countryside, though here in Kent it was decidedly warmer than it had been in Derbyshire. While many trees were still bare, but for the merest hint of tender green buds upon their boughs, the ground beneath them was broken by impatient clumps of bulbs pushing up out of the soil—snowdrops and crocuses, amidst drifts of scilla and bright wood anemones that covered the ground under the poplars in the spinney.

Becky loved the haphazard nature of the gardens at Edgewater, where large trees and evergreen shrubs, untamed by the fashionable art of topiary, held sway, while under them and along the edge of the lake, myriad wildflowers bloomed freely, unrestrained by the discipline of a formal garden.

Quite unlike the tidy beds at Hunsford parsonage, which her father had tended, or the hedged formality of Rosings Park in the era of Lady Catherine de Bourgh, the grounds at Edgewater appealed to her more spontaneous nature with their lack of orderliness and regulation.

As a young girl, Becky had hated Rosings Park with its innumerable rules and its regiment of retainers all trained to do Her Ladyship's bidding, without question. There had been so many gardeners and minions, she had been afraid to pick a bloom without permission, lest it should disturb the grand pattern of the most celebrated rose garden in the south of England!

Here, it was very different; she could do exactly as she pleased. On an impulse, she decided to go out into the garden and gather some flowers for her study. Collecting a basket and secateurs from a cupboard under the stairs, Becky went out through the side door onto a wide terrace, down the steps, and out toward the lake. There, the flowers were in abundance, stretching as far as she could see, across the water and into the meadows beyond. Clusters of blue scilla in the spinney caught her eye; they were a favourite with her.

She was about to take the path around the lake when her maid, Nelly, appeared, running towards her.

"Please, ma'am, Mr Jonathan Bingley is here to see you," she said.

"Jonathan Bingley? Are you sure, Nelly? Mr Bingley is in Hertfordshire at Netherfield. I know he is, because my sister Catherine and Mr Burnett have travelled there to visit Mr and Mrs Bingley only a few days ago."

But Nelly was adamant.

"Indeed, ma'am, it is Mr Bingley. He said he has come directly from Netherfield to see you, and he says it's a matter of great urgency, ma'am."

Puzzled and incredulous, Becky handed her basket to Nelly and hurried indoors to find Jonathan Bingley standing by the fire in the sitting room. She knew the very moment she set eyes on him, he was the bearer of bad news. Jonathan was wearing full formal black and his handsome face was unusually grave.

As she entered the room, he came towards her at once. Becky did not know what to think, but as her mind raced and her heart thumped in her chest, he took her hand. Becky's hand trembled as he held it; she knew something had happened, but she was afraid to ask the inevitable question.

When he spoke, his voice was low and gentle. "Becky, I am truly sorry to be the bearer of such sad news, but last night your mama, Mrs Collins, was taken ill suddenly and though the doctor was called to her immediately, she took a turn for the worse and passed away just before dawn. Anna has gone with Catherine to Longbourn, and I have come as soon as I could, to take you back to Hertfordshire."

He was gentle and concerned as he broke the news, and as she wept, he held her awhile. When she was calmer and seated herself upon the sofa by the fire, Jonathan offered to get her a glass of sherry or something stronger and when she refused, he went to find the maid and order some tea. All this he did as though it was quite the most ordinary thing to do.

Mrs Charlotte Collins was dead.

She had been ill, intermittently, since a bad bout of influenza in the early Autumn, but had seemed to recover her health. However, a damp, cold Winter had proved too much for her weakened body; pneumonia had set in. Her eldest daughter, Catherine, and her husband, Frank Burnett, had arrived in Hertfordshire only just in time to attend to her before her condition worsened.

As Nelly arrived with the tea, Becky's tears returned. The news had hit her like a thunderbolt. She had never been especially close to her mother, unlike Catherine, but she'd had great affection and respect for her. Her sense of shock was all the greater because the invitation from the Bingleys to Catherine and Mr Burnett to visit Netherfield had been extended to her, too. They had at first made plans to travel together to Hertfordshire and visit their mother at Longbourn, but Becky had changed her mind, deciding to return to Edgewater and supervise some of the work being done around the house and grounds. She was keen to get it done right.

She had written to her mother making her excuses and promising to visit her in the Spring. Now that promise would never be kept.

Jonathan Bingley had helped himself to a glass of sherry and waited to one side of the fireplace, while Nelly handed her mistress a cup of tea.

Becky dabbed at her eyes and apologized. "I am sorry, Jonathan, you must think me weak and silly, but I had not expected this. Had I known Mama was ill, I should never have postponed my visit. I feel so guilty…"

Her voice broke and, setting down his glass, Jonathan went to sit beside her on the sofa, attempting to reassure her, offering her his large pocket handkerchief, which she accepted with gratitude.

"My dear Becky, there is no need for you to feel any guilt whatsoever; you could not have known, no one knew Mrs Collins was seriously ill. Her companion, Harriet, assured us that when she went to bed after the doctor had seen her, she was comfortable, cheerful even, looking forward to the dinner party she had planned for Catherine and Frank. None of us could have predicted it. You must not blame yourself."

But she would not be consoled. "But I do; Jonathan, can you not see that had I thought more of Mama and less of the need to supervise the renovations to this house, I would have been there, with her? It was thoughtless of me, and I feel quite wretched!" she confessed as her tears fell again.

Jonathan could only hope that she would presently recover her composure and, despite her grief, would be ready to undertake their journey. He had a hired vehicle waiting to take them to the railway station.

They set off an hour later travelling by train to London, where they broke journey, staying overnight at the Bingleys' town house in Grosvenor Street.

Jonathan Bingley, considerate at all times, mindful of Becky's need for rest and privacy, had, during the journey, left her and Nelly together in their private compartment. Upon reaching their destination, he had instructed the house-keeper to attend to all her requirements, while he went out to his club, returning only after Becky had retired to her room for the night. He had indicated to her that they would be leaving on the following day for Netherfield, having ascertained first that Becky would be fit to make an early start.

Becky was acutely aware of the kindness and generosity of her host. Since they were children, their mothers being lifelong friends, Becky and her sisters had been close companions of the Bingleys, knowing Jonathan and his sisters well. With Cassy and William Darcy, they had played together as children at Pemberley and Ashford Park, where they had always been welcome visitors, especially after the death of Reverend Collins, when their mother had moved to open a school for girls at Mansfield.

On the long journey by train to London, Becky had remembered those days. There was some irony, she thought, in the fact that it was Jonathan Bingley who had arrived at Edgewater with news of her mother's death and had tried to comfort her. She recalled how he, as a young boy, had accompanied his parents to her father's funeral, and when, after the service was over, she had disappeared into the garden, it was Jonathan who had been sent by his mother Jane to look for her. He had found her red-eyed and tearful, behind the garden shed, among the beehives, and been sufficiently concerned to try to console her.

On that occasion too, he had offered her his pristine white pocket hand-kerchief, having assumed that she was grieving for her father. When she had confessed that she was not—indeed she was weeping because she was confused, unable, unlike her sisters Catherine and Amelia-Jane, to weep as they had done at the news, his response had surprised her.

"I am sorry," she had cried. "I wanted to feel sad, but all I could think of was how wonderful it was that we would have to leave Hunsford and Rosings Park, now Papa was dead. Jonathan, I feel wicked and terrible!"

She had expected him to look shocked, even to reproach her for such a callous thought, but he had done nothing of the sort. As she had haltingly explained how she longed to leave the stifling atmosphere of Hunsford parsonage and escape the constant scrutiny of the meddlesome Lady Catherine de Bourgh, he had looked neither surprised nor censorious.

She had insisted, sobbing, "I do not mean that I did not love Papa," and he had smiled.

"Of course not. I quite understand, Becky. It is not at all unusual to feel relief in such situations," he had said in the calmest, most grown-up voice. "You must not feel guilty; it is not your fault that Lady Catherine aroused such feelings in you. I believe it is quite natural."

He had persuaded her to dry her eyes and accompany him indoors. "Now, you must come in, else your mama will begin to worry about you, and that will not do."

He had sounded so confident, so reassuring, she had been immensely grateful, as she had written some time later in her diary:

> *Jonathan Bingley must be the best, kindest person in the world. No one, not one single person, has said anything as kind and comforting to me, ever. I wish I was Emma Bingley and Jonathan was my brother.*

And now, once again, here he was, reassuring and comforting her, urging her again not to feel guilty. He was being considerate and kind just as he had been those many years ago. As the train had rattled and swung through the Kentish countryside, it had been easy to slip into a reverie of reminiscences. Remembering their youthful association, her mind toyed with memories of Jonathan Bingley.

"He has not changed," Becky thought. "He has always been one of the best men I have ever known."

Approaching London, the train seemed to gather pace, and as it clanked and screeched over the points, she had been jolted out of her daydream. The gritty ugliness of the town had replaced the idyllic scenes of pastoral life outside. They were almost at the end of their journey, when Jonathan rejoined them to ask if all was well, and in that moment, Becky understood clearly why it was she had fallen in love with Jonathan Bingley all those years ago.

It was not just that he had been the best looking man she knew—he had an air of gravity that often made him look rather solemn—but there was also his remarkable gift of knowing exactly what to do and say when one was distressed or upset, without any trace of superiority or arrogance. After the insufferable rudeness of Lady Catherine and the obsequious manners of her father, Jonathan had been to Becky the very model of what a young gentleman should be.

After a comfortable night at Grosvenor Street, Becky was awakened at daybreak by her maid, Nelly, who brought her mistress tea and helped with her toilette, while relating for her benefit the latest news she had gathered in the servants' quarters.

She was very well informed.

"They say, ma'am, that Mr and Mrs Darcy and her sister Mrs Bingley have arrived in London and are staying at the Darcys' house in Portman Square. Mrs Darcy and Mrs Bingley are said to be very distraught, ma'am, at the sudden death of Mrs Collins. She was a very dear friend to both of them. Mr Bingley is unwell and did not accompany them, but the rest are to join Mr Jonathan Bingley's party on the journey to Netherfield," Nelly explained.

Becky appreciated Elizabeth Darcy's feelings; she had been one of Charlotte's closest friends, and Jane Bingley, tender-hearted and well-meaning, could not possibly have stayed away. Becky hoped her husband Charles Bingley's illness was not a serious one. Nelly thought not.

But, eager to be gone as early as possible, wild to see her sister Catherine and to look upon her late mother's face, no matter how much she dreaded the encounter, Becky was a little impatient.

"Oh dear, I trust we will not be delayed by having to wait for all these people," she grumbled. "I had hoped to make an early start."

Nelly was quick to reassure her mistress. "Oh no, ma'am. Mr Bingley has given strict instructions that we are to be ready to leave within the hour. He is very anxious to get you to Longbourn as soon as possible, ma'am."

"Indeed?" said Becky. "That is very considerate of him. I don't suppose he has mentioned if we are to travel with the party from Derbyshire?"

This time, Nelly answered confidently, "Indeed no, ma'am, but the footman says we are to travel in Mr Bingley's private vehicle. The Darcys and Mrs Bingley are travelling in one of the grand carriages come all the way from Pemberley. He says Mrs Darcy will not use the railway, ma'am."

Becky smiled wryly. "That is exactly like Mrs Darcy," she thought. Her mother had said as much on another occasion.

"Eliza will *not* travel by train; she cannot bear the noise and the soot and the crowds at the stations!" Charlotte had said with a smile, pointing out that it was just as well Mr Darcy had several fine vehicles and many good horses in his stables at Pemberley, else Elizabeth would not travel anywhere at all.

Becky recalled how, after her father's death at Hunsford, they, having no private carriage, had travelled everywhere on the railway. Her mother had been quite comfortable on the trains, until more recently when her painful rheumatism had made train travel difficult.

Yet, when Becky's husband Mr Tate had died and their son Walter had travelled to the United States to bring his ashes back to England for burial, Mrs Collins had braved the long journey to Matlock for the funeral.

Becky remembered again that it had been Jonathan Bingley who had arranged to have Mrs Collins conveyed to and from Derbyshire in his own carriage. Charlotte, who had been determined to be there to support her daughter, had been full of praise for the generosity and consideration shown her.

"I cannot say enough about Jonathan Bingley's kindness, Becky dear. He has not spared himself nor any expense to ensure that I had everything I needed and could make the journey comfortably," she had said. "He was most particular that we should be here to support you at this time. Even though Walter was going to be here, Jonathan felt it was important that we should be with you too. 'Mrs Collins,' he said, 'Becky needs us now,' and I agreed." Her mother had been unstinting in her praise of him.

After Nelly had helped her mistress dress and packed her trunk, they went downstairs to find that Jonathan had breakfasted earlier and was making preparations for their departure. Their trunks had already been carried downstairs. Having enquired if Becky had slept well and was ready to travel, he informed her that they were awaiting word from the Darcys at Portman Square.

"As soon as I have word from Mr Darcy, we will be on our way," he said.

Becky thanked him and indicated that she was ready to leave whenever he wished. "I am very keen to see my sister before I proceed to Longbourn," she explained, and he concurred.

"Of course, Becky, Catherine and Frank Burnett are staying at Netherfield, where we are bound first. I expect to reach our destination by early afternoon. You may then arrange to accompany your sister to Longbourn whenever you choose. I shall arrange to have a vehicle made available for you," he said and added, "I understand that Mrs Darcy is exceedingly distressed. Your mama was her oldest and dearest friend."

Becky nodded, unable to speak, as she rose from the breakfast table.

She had hoped she would not have to encounter Mr and Mrs Darcy, at least not until she had seen Catherine and they had reached Longbourn. She was apprehensive about meeting Elizabeth, in particular, being quite convinced that if she discovered that Becky had turned down an opportunity to see her mother a few weeks ago, Lizzie would be very censorious indeed. Mrs Darcy, whom she admired, had always intimidated her. Becky feared her judgment would be questioned once again, as it had been over the circumstances of her daughter's tragic marriage to young Julian Darcy.

Turning to Jonathan, she asked rather tentatively, "Jonathan, may I ask if Lizzie… Mrs Darcy… is aware that you… what I mean is, have you or Anna told her or Jane of your invitation to me last month… to visit Netherfield?"

Jonathan, aware of the strained relationship that had existed for many years between Becky Tate and his aunt Mrs Darcy, was not about to allow that particular demon to reappear. His answer was quite emphatic.

"Certainly not. I can assure you, Becky, that neither Mrs Darcy nor any other member of the family will learn of it from me or my wife. We entirely understood the reasons for your decision—there was much to be settled after Mr Tate's death and later at Edgewater; it was not a matter upon which there was any censure of you on our part. Nor will we contribute to criticism against you by any other person. I give you my word."

Becky thanked him and left to complete her preparations for the journey, while he went to summon the servants who would accompany them to Netherfield Park. Soon afterwards, word arrived from Portman Square that Mr and Mrs Darcy and Mrs Bingley had just set out on their journey to Hertfordshire.

Their luggage had been stowed in the carriage that stood waiting at the front door, and without further delay, Jonathan helped Becky in, and they were on the road to Netherfield.

Unlike their journey on the railway, this time their close proximity to one another in the carriage made some level of conversation inevitable. Becky was glad of the presence of her maid, seated beside her, assuming this would limit the topics upon which they might converse. But Jonathan Bingley appeared not to be aware of any awkwardness, nor did he seem at all inhibited by Nelly's presence, and he made conversation quite naturally as they travelled. When they stopped briefly at Barnet to water the horses and take some refreshment, he was particular to ask after their comfort and ensure that Becky and her maid were looked after appropriately, and as they journeyed on, their conversation turned mostly to Becky's new home in Kent.

Following the sudden death in America of her husband, Mr Anthony Tate, Becky had sold the house he had left her in London in order to purchase outright the property Edgewater, which she had leased the previous year.

Both Jonathan and Mr Darcy had pronounced it to be an excellent investment at the time, which accounted for his astonishment when Becky revealed that her son Walter and his wife had been of the opposite opinion and had tried quite assiduously to dissuade her from proceeding with the purchase. But Becky had determined her course of action and had said so.

"I did not intend to let Walter or his wife, who has no interest whatsoever in my existence, to influence me on a matter that was of vital importance to myself alone. I had settled upon it; indeed it was the first time in my life that I had had the opportunity to make such a decision, primarily because I wished it and not in consideration of the wishes of any other person," she said in a determined way that left Jonathan in no doubt of her feelings.

Somewhat surprised, he said, "I am truly astonished to hear you say that, Becky. I would have thought, indeed I have always believed, that you, above anyone else I know, had made every choice in your life because you wished it to be so. At no stage would I have considered that you could be easily swayed by a contrary opinion or were likely to change your plans to suit another's purpose.

"Why, Anna and I have always spoken with the greatest admiration of your independence; we have regarded you as a woman of considerable influence, who used that position to achieve much for others. Your most valuable work in the community, helping the poor, educating young women, providing for the sick and aged—in all these things as well as the active political campaigns in which you and Mr Tate were involved—I cannot accept that in all these matters, your decisions were not always your own.

"I saw no evidence to the contrary and had no doubt whatsoever that your actions were the consequence of your own judgment and determination."

He seemed confused, almost troubled, and Becky tried to make light of it.

"Ah," she said, in a voice that suggested he ought not be too concerned, "that must surely be because I am so very good at concealment, by not letting you or anyone else see the truth about myself. I have not always been such an independent woman, Jonathan, but I am quite determined to be one now."

Jonathan shook his head. "I should not think so at all. Concealment is surely not your way, Becky. Indeed, you are renowned for your openness and frankness. No, if what you say is true, then I must plead guilty to poor judgment myself. I would have said that your sister Catherine, Mrs Burnett, was more likely to be persuaded by others to adopt a particular course than you are. But I am happy that on the matter of Edgewater, at least, you have stood your ground and followed your heart," he said approvingly.

Becky's face coloured with embarrassment; his words had been too close to the truth for comfort, but she would not betray herself.

"Indeed I have," she said brightly, "my mind was quite made up. I fell in love with Edgewater—it is exactly where I wish to live and work for the rest of my life—and now I have no one else to please, I need only please myself."

Jonathan left her in no doubt of his opinion. "That is unarguable, Becky; indeed, you are completely justified in doing so, and I for one would support your decision totally."

Becky was delighted to have his approval and said as much. The displeasure of her son, whose annoyance at being deprived of the convenience of using his late father's town house in London lay at the root of his objections, paled into insignificance beside her immense satisfaction at Jonathan's words.

Like her mother, Charlotte Collins, Becky had always trusted Jonathan Bingley's judgment in many things. It was no different on this occasion, except she was absolutely determined that he would never discover that it was her youthful affection for him that had been the source of her trust.

Nothing had happened since to shake her belief in him. Yet that must remain forever her secret, for Jonathan Bingley had married first her younger sister Amelia-Jane and then, following her tragic death, their accomplished and beautiful cousin Anna Faulkner, with whom he had fallen deeply in love.

He must never learn of her own youthful, unrequited feelings.

They reached Netherfield sometime after midday and were met by Anna Bingley, who greeted Becky warmly before taking her upstairs to Catherine.

As the sisters embraced, they wept.

END OF PROLOGUE

A Woman of Influence

Part One

Chapter One

RETURNING TO KENT AFTER the funeral, Becky and her maid travelled with her sister Catherine and her husband, Frank Burnett.

Mr Burnett was a very capable man; he had organised and arranged everything about their journey to the last detail, thereby leaving Catherine and Becky with ample time on their hands, time they used to talk about everything and anything that related to their dear mother.

It afforded Becky the opportunity for intimate conversations with her sister, to whom she had grown especially close in recent years. Still troubled by feelings of guilt, she wished to ascertain if Catherine regarded her conduct preceding her mother's death as contrary or selfish. There had been little time and less opportunity to do so at Netherfield and Longbourn before and after the funeral, what with the innumerable friends, relatives, and pupils who had gathered to farewell Mrs Charlotte Collins.

Becky was anxious to discover her sister's opinion. It would not have surprised her if Catherine, always exemplary and proper in her ways, had expressed some disappointment at her decision to remain at Edgewater.

But Catherine had no such criticism to make of her sister. Happy in her own marriage to Frank Burnett and well aware of the pain Becky had endured, Catherine had understood her need to make a place of her own where she could find the contentment that had eluded her for many years.

Edgewater had provided her with just such a place, and Becky had wished to have the work of restoration and landscaping done right. Catherine had been disappointed but not surprised when her sister had changed her mind and decided not to join them on their visit to Hertfordshire.

Still, Becky's sense of guilt had not abated, and Catherine tried hard to convince her sister that it was not justified.

"Dearest Becky, why do you reproach yourself needlessly?" she asked, remonstrating as Becky confessed to feeling cold and callous.

"No doubt you will feel some sorrow at having missed the opportunity to see Mama; you would not be human if you did not. But believe me, my dear sister, Mama was not angry—disappointed a little, perhaps, but she hoped as we did that you would visit at Easter, after the work at Edgewater was completed. She did not know and you could not have known what was to come; it was very sudden," she said.

Becky persisted, "Did you not consider my action selfish and unfeeling? I should not have blamed you if you had."

Catherine was adamant. "Most certainly not, Becky; neither I nor Mr Burnett ever thought such a thing. I have not said this to you or anyone else before, but I know, my dear, what pain you have been through since Mr Tate moved to live in America."

Becky's eyes filled with tears as Catherine continued.

"It was a hard, unfeeling thing to do to you, after all those years of loyalty and hard work, when you had taken up every cause he championed and given so much of your time to furthering his ambitions. I do not mean to speak ill of your late husband, Becky, but I must admit that I have rarely seen such thoughtless conduct and nothing you have done can be considered in a similar light. I know you loved Mama and would have been with her more often, had not your life been seriously disrupted by Mr Tate's self-indulgent behaviour. I will not hear any criticism of you on that score, nor should you fear it."

Becky held tight to her sister's hand, but she could not hold back her tears.

As they journeyed back to Kent, she recovered some of her composure, and she owed most of that to the kindness and compassion of her sister.

Nevertheless, Becky could not help experiencing a twinge of regret that she had said nothing to Catherine about the true circumstances of her marriage to Anthony Tate. It was neither the time nor the place for revelations, but Becky had decided she would seek out an occasion when, in confidence, she could tell Catherine the truth she had hitherto revealed to no one else.

⁓᠎⧫⁓

With the onset of Spring and preparations for the new term at the parish school, the opportunity did not arise for quite some time. Catherine was kept busy with her own domestic concerns as well as the many new pupils admitted to the school, necessitating the appointment of a new teacher. With the help of her sister, the guidance of her husband, and the enthusiastic support of the parish priest, Mr Jamison, Catherine had taken the little parish school at Hunsford from an unlikely dream to a happy reality. Now boasting more than twenty-five pupils from the parishes of Hunsford and Lower Apsley, it was her proudest achievement.

Becky's acquisition of Edgewater had made the entire project much simpler by solving the problem of an access road, which had threatened to cause trouble for them. Her generous donations of furniture and time— volunteering to keep the books for the school and assist it with funds—had earned her sister's gratitude.

As they had worked together, both women were inevitably drawn closer, and it was no surprise that they were even more inclined to exchange confidences than before.

Catherine's were mostly about her marriage to Frank Burnett, confirming in her present happiness what she had felt in her heart to be true. Yet, knowing her sister's unhappy situation, with widowhood following upon a quite inexplicable and humiliating separation initiated by her husband, Catherine was inclined to be somewhat restrained in her expressions of marital felicity.

Becky had for many years refrained from making any criticism of her late husband; indeed she had frequently defended him from accusations of selfishness by her mother or any other member of the family. She had always claimed that he had denied her nothing in their marriage and had been exceedingly generous to her in the settlement he had made on separation.

It was therefore a matter of some astonishment to Catherine when, on a quiet Spring afternoon, with the school closed for the day, she had traversed the woods between Rosings and Edgewater, crossed the park, and entered the house by a side entrance to find her sister in tears. Seated in a private parlour looking out over the lake, Becky appeared distressed as she held in her hands a letter, recently delivered.

As Catherine entered the room, she rose, apparently discomposed, and walked about in a rather agitated manner. Inviting her sister to take tea with her, Becky revealed that the letter she had received had come from Jonathan Bingley. With it were enclosed documents from Mr Sharpe, her late husband's solicitor.

Catherine was puzzled; it was several months since they had received the news of Mr Tate's sudden death in New York. She could not understand why, after all this time, Mr Sharpe was writing to Jonathan Bingley and how this would affect Becky.

Surely, she wondered, *there cannot have been an error in the will?*

That would have been disastrous for Becky, who had been informed that she was the sole beneficiary of her husband's American estate.

When Becky handed her the letter and documents, Catherine seated herself beside the window to peruse them in better light.

Jonathan's letter was brief and clear; stating that he was writing because he had received a significant communication from Mr Sharpe, which he enclosed for her information and wished to consult her on the unusual arrangements proposed therein.

Having first apologised for any pain this might cause in re-opening matters pertaining to the death of her husband, he continued:

> *While I have always respected the late Mr Tate's business acumen and admired his political influence, I would never consider myself his equal in either of these fields. I was therefore surprised when Mr Sharpe wrote to me detailing Mr Tate's proposal that I be the principal trustee of his American estate.*
>
> *Furthermore, he has expressed a wish that the income accruing be used to provide financial assistance to any project or charity in which you may wish to invest, so long as it is, in my judgment, a reasonable one.*
>
> *You will agree that this places upon me a very grave responsibility, and I am anxious to discover your opinion before I agree to Mr Sharpe's proposition. I have spoken only to my wife, Anna, about this matter and will say nothing to any other person until I have your permission to do so.*
>
> *If you have no objection to my involvement in what must seem to you to be matters of interest primarily to yourself, I should be honoured*

to assist you in the way proposed by your late husband and shall write to Mr Sharpe accordingly.

However, should you have any objection whatsoever, you must feel free to indicate that this is the case, and I shall withdraw from the scheme immediately.

If you are agreeable, I should like to visit you at Edgewater at an early date, to discuss your wishes regarding the use or investment of the moneys.

Catherine's eyes widened as his letter continued:

I understand there will be a sum close to two thousand pounds a year available for your use. If I am to help administer this money, I should wish to consult you closely, so it is invested to best advantage for your purposes.

I trust, my dear Becky, that you will not object to my writing to you in this way and hope we may have an amicable and useful association in the future.

His letter ended with the usual warm and sincere felicitations and good wishes for her health, regards to her sister, etc., concluding:

Yours very sincerely,
Jonathan Bingley.

Reading the letter, Catherine was pleasantly surprised both by its tone and contents. Jonathan Bingley had long been a favourite of hers as he had been of her mother's, and if he had been selected by Mr Tate to assist his widow, then in Catherine's eyes, that was unarguably good news.

She could not understand why Becky was so obviously upset.

She glanced at the letter from Mr Sharpe the solicitor, but was disconcerted by the exceedingly legalistic language in which it was couched and appealed to Becky to interpret it for her.

The gist of the letter appeared to be an explanation of the terms of Mr Tate's instructions to him regarding his businesses in the United States. In an addendum to his will, added shortly before his death, Anthony Tate had instructed that the proceeds of his estate in America be held in trust and that Jonathan Bingley be asked to administer the income thereof.

The proceeds were to go to his wife, Rebecca Tate, to be used for any project she chose, so long as Mr Bingley believed it to be reasonable and worthy of support. Clearly Mr Tate had greatly valued Jonathan Bingley's judgment.

Becky laughed as she explained, "So you see, Cathy, he did not trust me to use his money wisely; fearing I might fritter it all away on something silly like gowns or jewels, no doubt, he arranges for Jonathan to be my guardian! Isn't that just like Mr Tate?"

Catherine had found it difficult to account for her sister's discomposure, until Becky made it clear she had been hurt by the proposition contained in the documents.

"You seem so distressed, Becky," she said a little lamely, not knowing quite how to respond.

"I am indeed," replied her sister, "very distressed. To think that my husband, after all these years, did not believe I could be trusted to use his bequest wisely. How would you have felt, Cathy?"

Catherine indicated that it was not a question she could competently answer, since Dr Harrison had had very little to leave to his widow—certainly nothing like the two thousand pounds a year which Jonathan predicted would flow from Mr Tate's estate.

"But, Becky," she said in a characteristically logical way, "can this not be seen as a prudent device, to ensure that the money from Mr Tate's American enterprise is made available to you, through a trust arrangement, thereby avoiding the possible unpleasantness for you, which might follow the disappointment of Walter's expectations? Just think, this way, there can be no pressure brought to bear upon you. If Walter and his wife wish to contest Mr Tate's wishes, they will have to deal with Jonathan and Mr Sharpe, who are disinterested parties, instead. I think your husband, far from not trusting you with the money, has by this means ensured that you will be able to use it for whatever projects you choose to support, without having to justify it to Walter and his wife."

Becky had listened to her sister with increasing astonishment.

"Cathy, you have an unerring instinct for making the very best of every situation, and no doubt there is some truth in what you say. I would not put it past Walter's wife to urge him to press me to part with some of this money on some pretext, despite the fact that he has inherited all of the printing business, the entire family estate in Derbyshire, and some properties elsewhere as well. They were very cross that I had been permitted to sell the house in London in order that I might purchase Edgewater—I have no doubt they had hopes of retaining it for their own use whenever they wished to come up to town."

"Well, then?" Catherine seemed unable to understand her continuing discomfort. "Surely the fact that you will now have the use of the money, without being burdened with administering the estate, since Jonathan as principal trustee will take on that responsibility, must please you. It seems a most convenient arrangement."

But, surprisingly, Becky shook her head.

"It may appear so to an observer, Cathy, but it is an arrangement that would make me exceedingly uncomfortable," she declared, and Catherine, uncomprehending, asked, "Why, Becky, do you not trust Mr Bingley?"

Becky blushed and looked anxious, but her response was immediate. "Trust Jonathan? Of course I do. I would trust him with my life."

"What is it then?" asked her sister, troubled by the apparent contradictions in Becky's attitude. "What possible objection could you have to him?"

Becky Tate sighed and sat down beside her sister. She had decided that the time had arrived when Catherine would have to learn the truth. And, in the course of a long afternoon, she told her story, prefaced by a poignant appeal.

"You must promise me, my dear sister, that no word of what I now tell you will be repeated by you to anyone. I cannot ask you to keep secrets from your husband, but if you must tell him, then I beg you to extract from him a similar promise. There are too many people who may be hurt should the truth become common knowledge, and others may use it to hurt me or Jonathan and his family for their own perverse ends. Will you promise me, Cathy?" she asked.

Still exceedingly concerned, Catherine gave her word. "Of course, my dear, if it concerns you alone, there may be no reason at all for me to divulge it even to Frank. If it is a matter of no consequence to anyone but yourself, I believe you are entitled to your privacy. There, it shall be our secret," she said, with no notion at all of what she was about to hear.

Becky Tate's story had its beginnings in the days after the death of her father Reverend William Collins, when her mother had decided that, rather than accept a paid position in the household of Lady Catherine de Bourgh, she would use the sum of money she had inherited from her husband and her own small income to make an independent living.

With the assistance and advice of her friends the Darcys and Mrs Darcy's uncle Mr Gardiner, Charlotte had set up a modest enterprise—a school for young ladies—whose parents wished them to learn to draw, paint, and read poetry, as well as acquire the social arts and graces that would enable them to take their place in polite society.

Unlike her elder sister, Catherine, who had accepted an invitation from Her Ladyship to stay on at Rosings Park, Becky and young Amelia-Jane had accompanied their mother to Mansfield, where in a leased house on the estate of Lord Mansfield, Charlotte Collins had set up her school.

It had been something of a struggle at first, with only a few pupils and some of them being of such a poor quality as to defy the efforts of even the most dedicated teacher, but Mrs Collins had persevered, and in time, the school had become a modest success.

Becky had participated actively in her mother's work, enjoying the challenge of teaching young girls, for she was well-read and educated herself and enjoyed the chance to pass on some of her skills and knowledge to other young women.

But her heart had always been elsewhere, for Becky had dreamed all her young life of being a writer, and though she was a good teacher of poetry and enjoyed reading to her students from her favourite books, she yearned to have time for her own work.

Despite the long hours she spent on preparing lessons for the paying pupils who were their livelihood, she had still found time, often after dark, when everyone else had gone to bed, to sit at the kitchen table, scribbling on scraps of paper, filling old notebooks with the words and stories that filled her head.

Unlike her very practical mother, Charlotte, and her eminently sensible sister Catherine, Becky had had romantic tendencies, which had lain dormant for years. It was not that she craved some unattainable lover or longed for some passionate romance, but her desire to achieve that which had always fired her imagination, since childhood—to see her work in print—had burned bright. She was not particularly ambitious; she did not seek fame or fortune, merely the fulfillment of a dream, nourished chiefly by her imagination in the long periods of boredom at Hunsford and Rosings Park.

She had always hoped that one day, someone would be sufficiently interested in her work to read it and want to publish it. She was determined that whatever else she did in life, she would not abandon that particular hope.

The notebooks she filled with her "scribbling," as Charlotte called it, she kept well hidden among the clothes in her trunk, afraid that they may draw adverse comment or ridicule from her sisters.

No one had read them or shown any interest in them, until, on a visit to Ashford Park, she had mentioned them to Jonathan Bingley, who was home on vacation from college. They had talked of hobbies, and he had praised his sister Emma's accomplishments in music and painting; on Becky's mentioning her love of writing, he had suggested that she send one or two pieces of her work to the editor of the *Matlock Review* in Derbyshire.

"It does no good to keep it hidden away, Becky," he had said, and when she had seemed surprised at the suggestion, he had assured her that the journal, with whose owners he was well acquainted, was keen to encourage local talent. He had gone so far as to offer to introduce her to the family that ran the business.

"The Tates are a distinguished family; they are friends of my aunt Lizzie and her husband, Mr Darcy," he had said, "and I have known Anthony Tate and his mother for some years. They are well regarded for their support of important projects in their community; the *Review* and the *Pioneer* have both been used by the Tates to champion many worthy causes, and I am confident they will pay your work some attention, should you submit it. If you choose to do so, you may say that I encouraged you in that course, if you wish," he had added.

Grateful for his encouragement, though rather overwhelmed, Becky had asked, "But how can you be so sure, when you have not read any of my work?" only to be told that he did not need to read it, although he would be happy to do so, if she wished him to. He said he could judge from her conversation that her compositions would probably be sensible and well written, and editors were always looking for new talent, because their readers demanded it.

When Becky had rather nervously permitted him to read a recent composition of hers, Jonathan had claimed that while he was no judge of literary standards, he thought it was interesting, and besides, he had argued, it was the editor of the *Review* who would decide, so it was to him she should submit her work.

"Be assured, Becky, they will not reject it arbitrarily. If it is deemed good enough to print, they will print it," he had said, adding, "Their readers are always looking to read something new."

With such encouragement, Becky had needed no further prompting. Picking out two or three compositions, she had, with Jonathan's help, composed a brief letter and dispatched them to the *Matlock Review*, but with little hope of a favourable response.

She had been unsurprised when two of them were returned almost at once with a polite rejection slip, but then, to her astonishment, the third, a short piece about the tribulations of a farmer's daughter visiting her city relatives, was accepted. Not long afterwards, a letter had arrived, inviting her to submit another piece in a similar vein.

Delighted, she had written to thank Jonathan Bingley for his assistance and had received from him a short congratulatory note, which she had folded and put away in her pocket book, carrying it around with her for years like some miraculous talisman.

Jonathan had written:

> *I will not say I told you so, Becky, but let me say how happy I am that I was right and that you have been invited to submit more material.*
>
> *I am confident that you will go on to have real success in this enterprise, and I congratulate you most sincerely.*

This brief note had meant more to Becky than praise from any other source or the small payment she received from the *Review*.

Her career as a writer, albeit under the pseudonym of Marianne Laurence, had progressed rapidly in the years that followed, when Mrs Therese Tate, who managed the printing business for her son, Anthony, had shown a particular interest in her work. A kindly and educated woman with an abiding concern for the welfare of rural women, she had seen in Becky someone who could be a useful ally.

Education for girls, the removal of women and children from underground mines, the provision of a hospital for women, these were all dear to her heart, and in Becky she had found a young person whose desire to write could be channelled into support for these important causes.

Having invited Becky to visit her at her home at Matlock, she had been so impressed by her enthusiasm and touched by her keenness to please, Mrs Tate had immediately offered her employment with the business and a regular column in the *Review*.

For Becky it had provided an opportunity to sharpen her skills and widen her horizons. She had accepted the position without delay. And so had begun an association that had changed completely the course of young Becky Collins' life.

Catherine was keen to ask a question. "And did Jonathan not write to you again, Becky?" her sister asked, growing curious about the connection with Mr Bingley, but Becky shook her head.

"No, never, nor did he ever mention it again, except one afternoon, when he was visiting Matlock to see Anthony Tate about some political matter. While Mother was spending some time with Mrs Darcy at Pemberley, Amelia-Jane and I had been invited over to take tea at home with Mrs Tate. We talked of Miss Jane Austen's book *Emma*, which Mrs Tate and I had liked very much and Amelia had not. She was too young to understand it anyway, but Jonathan, who had heard that the Prince Regent himself had admired Miss Austen's novel when it was published, said, 'And when do *you* propose to write a novel, Becky? Now you are regularly published in the *Review*, is it not time you turned your talents to something more weighty than a weekly column for young ladies? I look forward to seeing your name on the cover of a popular novel, even if you do not wish to dedicate it to the King.'"

Becky confessed she had thought at first that he spoke in jest. "But before I could answer, Amelia-Jane butted in," she said. "'But what would Becky write about? She has such a boring life! She never goes anywhere new nor meets any interesting people.'"

Even as she repeated the words, Becky blushed at the memory of her sister's cruel taunt.

"I was so mortified! I became completely tongue-tied. I think I was about to disgrace myself and burst into tears when Jonathan said, 'That does not signify at all. Miss Austen, I understand, wrote all her novels while living at home in a modest country parsonage. One does not have to lead the high life and travel the world to be a writer; all one needs is imagination and talent, and I am confident Becky has plenty of both.'

"That certainly silenced Amelia-Jane," said Becky, "then Anthony Tate came into the room and took Jonathan away, but I think, Cathy, at that moment I realised that I knew no kinder, better man than Jonathan Bingley, and I was convinced that I loved him with all of my foolish, young heart."

This candid confession so astonished her sister that she was silent, unable to respond for several minutes. While Catherine had once sensed that her sister had an interest in young Mr Bingley, she had had no notion it had become an absorbing passion. Becky had seemed too sensible, too preoccupied with her work and other interests for that.

Yet as her story unfolded, it became clear that Becky had cherished her affection for Jonathan for many years, despite the fact that he had at no time said or done anything to encourage her feelings. Indeed, it could be fairly said that he had been completely unaware of them.

Over the next few years, while Becky kept her feelings hidden, she had been given opportunities to use her talent as a writer, while working with Mrs Tate and producing regular pieces for the *Review* and the *Pioneer*.

The work had stimulated her own interest in the lives of young rural girls, who lacked any opportunity to study or improve themselves except through domestic service or marriage. The need for schools and libraries in country areas had become almost an obsession with her, and as she had grown more confident, with the blessing of Mrs Therese Tate, Becky Collins had worked tirelessly to beg, bully, and cajole wealthy members of the community and councils to support their cause.

Yet, during all of this time, she had not abandoned hope. Not even when Anthony Tate, having returned to Matlock to become editor of the *Review*, had begun to show a particular partiality for her, had she given up on Mr Jonathan Bingley. Each time he had visited the Tates and occasionally when they had met to dine and dance at the splendid parties at Pemberley or Ashford Park, Becky had found even more to admire and esteem in young Mr Bingley.

Unaware of her interest, Jonathan had treated Becky Collins as he did all young women in his circle of acquaintances—with respect. In her case, he had a very good reason for doing so; his mother and hers were close friends. It was almost a family connection.

Becky admitted that she may well have mistaken his gentlemanly conduct for fondness, but insisted that she had no reason to blame him in any way for her misapprehension.

"He neither did nor said anything to encourage my feelings; if I was mistaken, it was entirely self-deception, on my part," she said.

Catherine's heart went out to her sister. "Oh my dear Becky," she said gently, "however did you bear it when Jonathan began courting Amelia-Jane?" she asked.

"Very badly; I think I was so deeply stricken, I wept for days. Only dear Emily Gardiner, in whom I confided, knew how wretched I felt."

Becky fought back tears. "I think we comforted each other. Emily had only just lost her beloved husband, Paul Antoine, and we were both still stunned by the deaths of young William and Edward earlier that year.

"As you would recall, Cathy, it had been a wretched year for all of us and Jonathan most of all, because he had suffered great remorse that he'd not been able to prevent William and Edward riding out on those horses and getting killed on that dreadful evening at Pemberley. Mama was convinced, and she says Mrs Bingley told her so, that Jonathan often blamed himself for their deaths.

"That same year, the Bingleys invited us to spend Christmas with them at Ashford Park, and later we travelled with them to London. At first, Jonathan was quiet and withdrawn, and when we spoke together, I confess I did believe that he appreciated my company; but by the time we went to London, his spirits seemed to lift, and when he took Amelia-Jane to the *Review* and the Richmond Ball, it became clear to me that she had won his heart. She was so vivacious and pretty, and I was always so sober and serious; perhaps he needed someone like her at the time, to take him out of his melancholy mood. Besides, his mother Mrs Bingley seemed captivated with our Amelia-Jane and hardly noticed my existence at all."

"And you, Becky? How did you feel?" asked Catherine gently.

"Bereft, desolated, I thought my little world had ended."

"Was it not very soon afterwards that you became engaged to Mr Tate?" Catherine recalled.

"Yes, it was. When we returned to Derbyshire, Anthony Tate proposed and I accepted him. I had known for a while of his interest but had not taken it seriously while ever there was a hope of Jonathan. When it was clear that I had no chance with him, Mr Tate's offer seemed a good deal more attractive than before. I am not very proud of my decision, Cathy; as you know well, there was more ambition than love in it; while I knew it would please his mother and Mama, I think if Jonathan had wanted me, I would not have given Mr Tate a second thought."

Becky's admission that her acceptance of Anthony Tate had been based more on practical reality than affection did not entirely surprise her sister, especially now she had learned of her unrequited love for Jonathan Bingley. Quite clearly, the realisation that he had chosen Amelia-Jane, whose youthful beauty had outshone her sister's attractions, had resulted in the kind of bitterness that could lead to such a contrary decision.

Catherine understood now why Becky might find a close association with Jonathan Bingley, even if it was many years later, uncomfortable. Not wishing to pry, but eager nevertheless to know the truth, she asked, "And Becky, forgive my asking, but did Mr Tate ever discover that you had once loved Jonathan?"

Becky was absolutely certain. "No, he never did; not just because I was careful to conceal my feelings, but because he truly believed that his offer was one I could not resist. And it was. Not only was I marrying into a distinguished and wealthy county family, I would be the wife and active partner of a man whose influence in both business and politics was rising every day! He was a personable gentleman of substance, and he was offering me not just a comfortable home but a partnership, with a good income and the chance to have my work printed in any one of six or seven journals, which his family owned."

Typically, Becky did not seek to spare herself. "How could I, a daughter of the widow of a country parson, turn down such an offer? Besides, he had declared openly to his mother that I was his choice because, as she told it, 'She is intelligent, independent, and hardworking, just the kind of wife I need. My Mrs Tate has to be much more than a pretty face.'

"His mother liked me, and Mama was happy for me to accept him; she said he was respectable and honest, as well as generous and amiable. How could I have possibly turned him down?"

Catherine remembered well her sister's wedding in the Spring of 1835.

None of the members of the Darcy or Fitzwilliam families had attended; they had been in deep mourning for their beloved children. Emily had been there, but only at the church, to lend support to her friend.

Becky, expensively gowned and wearing a diamond necklace, which was a Tate family heirloom—a gift from her mother-in-law—had looked happy if somewhat subdued, but Catherine had put that down to the general atmosphere of melancholy that had continued to hang over the families for most of that year. She had had no notion of the true nature of Becky's dilemma.

For her part, if Becky had needed to be convinced of the material wisdom of her choice, the death of her grandfather Sir William Lucas and the marriage not long afterwards of Jonathan Bingley to Amelia-Jane were sufficient to do so. That Charlotte Collins and her daughters were no longer very welcome at Lucas Lodge had become clear following the arrival of the new Mrs Frank Lucas, Charlotte's sister-in-law.

Furthermore, the ironic realisation that when Jonathan Bingley inherited Longbourn from his grandfather Mr Bennet, it was young Amelia-Jane who would be its future mistress had served to illustrate the parlous situation in which Becky and her mother would have been placed had she remained unwed. The prospect of having to seek a home with Mr and Mrs Jonathan Bingley at Longbourn or returning to Rosings Park to attend upon Lady Catherine had made her shudder.

It had not taken her long to convince herself that her decision to marry Anthony Tate, which would obviate the need for either her mother or herself to rely upon the reluctant charity of relatives or the dubious patronage of Lady Catherine de Bourgh, was a sound one.

꧁꧂

In the years that followed, Becky Tate had fulfilled all the expectations of her husband and his family. Her son, Walter, was born, providing the Tates with an heir to their thriving business, and Becky had flung herself into every cause her ambitious husband had wished to champion.

Local councillors had learned to dread the approach of the popular and indefatigable Mrs Tate, who never took no for an answer, and businessmen could not pretend that they had left their wallets at home when Becky Tate opened the bidding to raise money for her favourite charity. Schools or soup kitchens, libraries or lying-in homes for the poor—it mattered not which cause she supported; with her enthusiasm, she carried all before her.

In matters political, too, the Tates had the power and the influence to make and unmake candidates, and they did.

When Therese Tate died, leaving her interest in the business and most of her personal assets to her daughter-in-law, Becky's role as a woman of influence in the community was confirmed.

Of Anthony Tate's commitment to his wife and family there had never been any doubt; he had shown not the slightest interest in any other woman, and his dedication to their joint prosperity could not be questioned. His portfolio of provincial journals and newspapers had grown rapidly until he was the head of a highly profitable and influential business empire.

Sought after for his influence by politicians and philanthropists alike, he was well aware of the contribution that his wife's charm and energy had made to his success.

While he had been proud of his son, Walter, who had demonstrated an early interest in the family business, it was the birth of their daughter, Josie, that had set the seal of contentment upon his life. Small, pretty, and precocious, she was, in his eyes, the perfect child, and he had encouraged, indeed some would say he had spoilt her, in every way possible. In her childhood, he had refused her nothing, going to great lengths to ensure that she had every comfort she could possibly need.

As she grew older, the little girl had learnt that she had only to ask her father nicely, and almost any wish would soon be granted, despite her mother's reservations.

Clearly displaced in her husband's affections by this tiny newcomer, well aware that Josie meant more to her father than almost anyone else in the world, Becky had devoted her time and energies to her work in the community, where she was much admired and loved.

Like her husband, Becky had loved her young daughter dearly and longed for her to enjoy life as well as succeed in her chosen field of endeavour. That Josie also wanted to be a writer, albeit of a more serious bent than her mother, had not surprised Becky, but she wanted more for her than literary achievement.

As Josie had developed into an intelligent and attractive young person and young Julian Darcy had begun to show an interest in her, Becky had seen a chance for a different type of success. She had encouraged the friendship, which had at first appeared to be mainly about Josie's writing. Julian clearly appreciated her work and wished to encourage and help her have it published.

But it had not been long before it became clear that the heir to the Pemberley estate was in love with Josie. When the inevitable proposal came, Josie, despite some misgivings, had been persuaded by her mother that her future could be secured by marrying Julian Darcy. Accentuating every advantage while denying any hindrance, including Josie's aversion to the entire prospect of becoming the Mistress of Pemberley in the future, Becky had promoted the match with enthusiasm.

Sadly, it was a decision that every person involved in making it would, within a few years, deeply regret. It transformed not only Josie's young life but that of her mother forever.

Chapter Two

ON RECEIVING BECKY TATE'S letter, Jonathan Bingley carried it upstairs to his wife's sitting room, where Anna was teaching her youngest son, Simon, to paint. The child, who was not five years old, was already displaying something of his mother's artistic talent.

As Jonathan entered, Anna looked up and knew from his countenance that he had pleasant news for them.

"Are we free to travel to Kent next week, my love?" he asked, holding out Becky's letter, "because if we are, there is an invitation to spend a week or two at Edgewater, which we might all enjoy."

Anna looked surprised, "What? All of us?"

"Yes indeed, look, here it is," he said, handing her the letter. "As I have explained earlier, the late Mr Tate has asked that I be the principal trustee of his American estate. Well, Becky has agreed and asked us all down to Edgewater, which, she assures us, is perfect at this time of year."

"I think it might be fun—the boys would certainly enjoy it, and while you and Becky discuss matters of business, I would have the opportunity to see Catherine and Lilian again," said Anna cheerfully.

And so it was decided they would travel to Kent.

Becky had thought their visit would allow her to demonstrate to herself, and incidentally to her sister Catherine, that she was now able to deal with her youthful disappointment in a mature manner.

Much had happened in both her life and that of Jonathan Bingley in the intervening years. The sad disintegration of his marriage to Amelia-Jane, who had in time tired of her husband's seriousness and yearned for the fun of an active social life, had reached its disastrous conclusion when she and her companions had been killed in a dreadful accident on the road to Bath. Becky Tate, having lost the man she loved to her younger sister, had then seen him, a young widower, find consolation in a truly happy union with her cousin Anna Faulkner, recently returned from Europe, whose sweet disposition and artistic talents were far more conducive to contentment in marriage with Jonathan than the more willful vivacity of Amelia-Jane.

Despite her earlier reservations, Becky was determined not to allow the memories of her previous attachment to Jonathan to interfere with what was clearly an important enterprise.

"It is imperative that I make the very best use of this opportunity, Cathy," she had said, explaining her decision to invite Jonathan's entire family to Edgewater. "If Mr Tate believed that Jonathan Bingley was the best person to administer the trust fund and oversee the use of the money, then I must agree to work with him," she had said with resolution.

Catherine had not seen fit to question her decision, being herself convinced that Becky was now far calmer and more self-possessed than she had ever been.

"It is not only in my own interest to do so; it would also advantage those whom I wish to help with this money that my husband has so fortuitously made available to me. Were I to oppose Jonathan's role as trustee, it may delay the work I wish to embark upon and perhaps create some untoward embarrassment between us, which I would greatly regret. Do you not agree, Cathy?" Becky asked, clearly seeking her sister's approval.

Catherine was happy to agree. "I most certainly do, my dear Becky; I can see no reason why you and Mr Bingley cannot work together on the trust, as Mr Tate had envisaged. He is a gentleman of great integrity and sincerity, and since there has never been any ill-feeling between you, I cannot foresee any problems at all."

Becky smiled. "Indeed, and there may even be some advantage in it, since I, wishing to retain his good opinion, am unlikely to try his patience, whilst he, not wanting to appear disagreeable and contentious, may be more amenable than some fusty old lawyer might have been," she quipped, convincing Catherine that her sister had quite recovered her composure, even if she had not entirely forgotten her disappointment.

⌇

The Bingleys arrived and were welcomed at Edgewater with great warmth and courtesy and provided with every comfort. Jonathan had been here before, but Anna, who had a penchant for interior decoration and refurbishment, was enchanted by the tasteful work that had been carried out at Edgewater under Becky's supervision. Then, as her artist's eye caught sight of the lovely vistas the grounds afforded, she declared herself impatient to sketch and paint them.

"Do look at that group of poplars across the water; it is so appealing," she said as they went out to admire the prospect from the terrace, and Becky agreed.

"I do wish you would paint the poplars in the spinney; it is quite my favourite spot on the property," said Becky. "There is something truly enchanting about it. I was there yesterday gathering the last of the bluebells and forget-me-nots, which have been particularly profuse this year, and I was most reluctant to tear myself away and return to the house," she confessed.

"I can see why," said Anna. "It is indeed an intriguing place. The dappled effect of sunlight and shadows among the poplars creates an atmosphere of mystery; it would be a pleasure to paint the scene."

As Anna moved to admire the view from another part of the terrace, her son Simon had wandered away from them in the direction of an old gazebo beside the lake and caught sight of a little boy emerging from within.

Before any of the adults had seen him, Simon, believing he had found a new playmate, had begun to run across the grass towards the child, who, clad in an oversize blue smock and breeches, stood as if petrified beside a clump of wild irises by the lake's edge.

Hearing Simon's voice, laughing as he ran, Anna turned and, seeing him so close to the water, hitched up her skirts and raced over to him, obviously scaring the little boy, who ran stumbling through the long grass towards the gazebo and disappeared into its shadowy interior.

Simon had to be restrained by his mother from following his mysterious new friend, while Becky and Jonathan had only just become aware of the child's presence.

"Who is the boy?" asked Jonathan, and Becky, who was not as yet familiar with all of the servants and labourers she employed, assumed he was the child of one of the women who worked on the property.

The boy did not reappear, and they thought no more of him, when the maid arrived to say that tea was served and everyone repaired indoors to partake of it.

Later that evening, after the guests had rested and changed for dinner, they came downstairs to find that Catherine and Frank Burnett were to join them. The conversation was lively and varied all evening, ranging over their many interests. So much so, that there was no request for any musical entertainment until Frank Burnett mentioned that he had such excellent reports of Mrs Bingley's performance on the pianoforte, he would dearly like to hear her play. Becky hastened to open the instrument, which stood in an alcove, and Anna, who was truly an excellent pianist, was soon persuaded to take her place at the keyboard.

Her performance of a composition by Schubert was so compellingly lovely that no one moved or spoke, except to demand an encore, which Anna obligingly provided. Everyone in the room was enchanted.

Which is probably why no one saw the little boy outside peering in at the window behind the piano, until Anna, rising from the instrument at the conclusion of her piece, looked out into the darkening garden and exclaimed, "Good heavens! There he is again—it's the little boy by the lake; he was pressed right up against the window, looking in. Ooh! it made me jump!" she said as the others rushed to the window and peered out.

Jonathan made straight for the glass doors that opened onto the terrace and looked about, but there was no one in sight. The boy had vanished.

Becky sent for two of the servants and asked them to take a light and search the park around the house. "Mind you don't scare him; he may have wandered away from his mother," she warned, and the men went out to do her bidding.

While the guests turned their attention to tea, coffee, and sweets, the grounds were searched, but to no avail. No trace was found of the boy.

It was Jonathan Bingley, coming down early to breakfast on the morrow, who caught sight of his pinched little face pressed up against the cold glass of the bay window in the morning room. Hidden from the child's sight by an elegant chiffonier, Jonathan managed to steal out of the room and come up behind him without his being aware of it.

"Now, there you are," he said, placing a gentle hand on the boy's shoulder. "Who are you and what on earth are you doing out here?"

He said not a word, but the look of sheer terror on the boy's face as he struggled to get free of him surprised Jonathan.

Keeping a firm hold on him, Jonathan attempted to take him, still struggling, into the house, when the boy turned and attempted to bite his hand.

"Oh no, you don't! Come on now, all I want to know is who you are and what you are doing here. Who sent you?" he asked in a voice that was somewhat louder and which alerted Becky, who had come down into the morning room for breakfast.

Rushing outside, she was in time to see a young woman in worn work clothes running across the park towards Jonathan and the boy, crying out, "Oh, please, sir, please don't arrest him; he's only a child… He doesn't know what he's doing, sir. Please don't hand him over to the police."

As she reached the pair, she grabbed the child's arm and shook him. "Oh Tom, you naughty little boy! How often have I told you not to go near the big house? Whatever have you done?"

Then turning to Jonathan again, she begged, "I am very sorry, sir. If he has done any harm I'll make it good. Please don't send for the police."

"Send for the police? I had no intention of doing anything of the sort," said Jonathan, sounding quite offended at the suggestion that he would hand a child over to the police. "He has been seen around the house last evening and again today—I simply wanted to know who he was and what he was doing here. He wouldn't answer me; he struggled and tried to bite my hand! Now why on earth would he do that?"

The woman held a hand to her mouth. "I do beg your pardon, sir. He couldn't answer you; he cannot speak; it isn't that he is dumb or anything… he could speak even as a baby, but he just stopped about two years ago after the police came and took his father away. They say he had a bad fright then, sir, and never spoke again."

Becky, who had come right up to them, still believing the young woman was a labourer working the grounds, asked, "Who is he? Is he your brother?"

The girl smiled and, looking no older than eighteen years of age, answered, "No, ma'am; he's my son, Tom. I am sorry he's given you so much trouble, ma'am, he's never done it before. I did tell him he must not go near the big house or approach any of the ladies or gentlemen. He was to sit quietly in the gazebo until I came for him, but he doesn't always understand, ma'am; he gets a little excited and runs about, but he means no harm, ma'am."

"And where in the grounds do you work while Tom stays in the gazebo?" asked Becky.

To their amazement, she replied, "I don't work here, ma'am, I work in the hop fields over on the other side of the river. They don't let you bring young children along, not unless they can work as well, and he can't; he doesn't understand enough—he would make a mess and then I'd lose my job as well."

"And how long has Tom been sitting quietly in the gazebo while you went to work in the hop fields?" asked Jonathan.

"About two weeks, sir," she replied, adding, "I am very sorry, ma'am; I understand it was wrong, but I had no other way. I had to get work to feed him and myself, and the work in the hop fields is better than road work, ma'am."

"What is your name?" asked Becky, who had noticed a ring on the finger of her left hand.

She answered quickly—almost too quickly, Jonathan thought—"Alice, ma'am, Alice Grey," she said.

"And are you expected at work today, Alice?" asked Becky.

The young woman bit her lip and appeared somewhat tongue-tied before saying, "No, ma'am, I asked for an hour or two to take Tom to the apothecary in the village. He's been coughing a lot lately. He needs some medicine."

"And where do you live?" asked Jonathan, beginning to be concerned that the child's sickness was probably a consequence of his living conditions.

This time the answer came much more slowly. "Here and there, sir." She looked down at her feet, and Becky, following her eyes, saw her rather dainty boots were scuffed and dusty from walking.

"What do you mean, here and there?" she asked. "Do you mean you have no place to stay? Where do you and Tom sleep at night?"

Again, Alice looked down and away as she answered, almost reluctantly, "In one of the barns over there, on the other side of the lake, beyond the spinney." She pointed in the direction of the out buildings. "I am truly sorry, ma'am, I should have asked, but I was afraid I would be refused and then where would I have gone? I didn't think it would do any harm, ma'am; I didn't take anything. It was the small barn where they keep the empty sacks and things. We just kept our bundle of things there and slept overnight."

"And you have been sleeping there for two weeks?" asked Becky, astonished that no one had noticed.

"Yes, ma'am, just overnight. I spend many hours weeding and clearing up after they harvest the hops. We had a place in the village behind the fields, a farmer let us use his outhouse, but he wanted more rent, and there were other things... I couldn't afford it, ma'am, not on what they pay in the hop fields."

"And how did you find this place?" Becky asked.

"One of the lads in the village told me about it; he said he had slept there once or twice, when it was wet and he couldn't get home. I thought it would do just for a short time, until we found another place. It was clean and safe for Tom as well."

Jonathan was shaking his head, and Becky was finding it difficult to keep her own feelings under control. The young woman looked thin and weary, and the boy gazed longingly at a cloth bag in her hand, which looked as though it contained food. From the aroma emanating from it, it was probably stale bread and cheese, Becky thought.

Speaking very quickly, as if she had to act before she was persuaded to change her mind, Becky said, "Alice, I cannot have you and the boy sleeping in an open barn—it isn't safe. Besides, it might encourage others to do the same, and we cannot allow that. But, until we find somewhere more suitable, my housekeeper, Mrs Bates, will give you a room in the house. But first, you will go into the kitchen and have something to eat and drink. Tom looks hungry, and I am sure you could do with a good bowl of porridge, too. Come with me."

As Jonathan went in to join the others in the morning room, Becky took Alice and Tom into the kitchen and explained to Mrs Bates that they were to be fed and allowed to wash themselves and their clothes and found a place to sleep at night.

"The boy is sick, Mrs Bates, they've been sleeping in one of the barns and working in the hop fields. They will need some clean clothes, and, Alice, when you are ready, I should like to talk some more. But first, we will send for the apothecary Mr. Thomson to take a look at Tom's chest—that cough does sound bad," she said and left them in the kitchen, with the girl's expressions of gratitude in her ears and tears welling in her eyes.

As Becky walked out, two young chambermaids, having just come downstairs, stood at the door, looking askance at the young woman and her boy as they sat at the kitchen table eating their porridge. Their expressions said it all. Becky spoke sharply to them, "Stop staring at them; they're poor and homeless."

"They're dirty, ma'am," the girls protested, all starched and superior in their uniforms.

"So would you be if you had no proper place to sleep. They're no worse than you; they've fallen on hard times, that's all. It's only good luck that keeps you from going down the same path. Mind you treat them right," Becky said, and she sounded quite severe.

The maids did not look convinced, but they did know better than to disobey their mistress. Mrs Tate had a reputation for kindness; equally she could be very firm with anyone who defied her instructions.

Becky entered the morning room to find everyone agog to discover who the young woman was and what Becky intended to do with her. She had no definite answer to either of their questions.

Anna had heard some of the story from Jonathan. "Do you suppose, Becky, that the girl is alone?" she asked.

Becky could not be certain. "Do you mean does she have a husband? Well, she does wear a wedding ring and mentioned that the boy's father had been taken by the police some years ago. It seems the shock of that encounter has stopped his speech. The child does not say a word."

"Poor little thing," said Anna, thinking of her own two sons, "he looks thin and scared. He cannot be eating very well."

"Indeed, I doubt they pay them very much for working the hop fields—the poor woman must have struggled to find sufficient food for the two of them," said Jonathan, whose compassionate heart was already quite deeply affected by what he had heard. "It's unconscionable, but no one will do anything about it."

Becky nodded and said, "I know what you mean, but at least we have the chance to put that to right; once they have eaten and cleaned themselves up, perhaps we could begin to unravel the real story of Alice Grey."

Chapter Three

THE STORY OF ALICE Grey took a good deal of unravelling.

It was fortunate that Becky Tate was rather less impatient now than she had been at twenty, for the young woman was wary and unwilling to talk about personal matters, particularly those relating to her past.

When she and the boy had eaten and washed themselves, they were summoned to Becky's sitting room. Dressed in a motley collection of hand-me-downs supplied by Mrs Bates, they looked a rather comical pair: she in a faded scullery maid's uniform and apron, and the child in pantaloons and an overshirt so large, it could well have been his nightgown!

But at least they were clean, warm, and well fed.

One thing was more apparent now than it had been before. Alice, her face scrubbed, her hair washed and plaited, looked more respectable than she had appeared in her shabby work clothes. Her boots, which she had cleaned, though worn and scuffed, were well made. She could have been no more than twenty-three or -four at the most, Becky decided, noting the smooth complexion, fine slender neck, and slim brown arms.

The boy Tom seemed quieter now, more amenable, since he had eaten.

It must have been hunger that made him so restive, thought Becky, while his mother appeared nervous, probably anxious about her situation.

While Becky could understand her anxiety, she was determined to discover more about them. It had already occurred to her from aspects of the young woman's appearance as well as her speech, which was for the most part correct and without any trace of a country dialect, that Alice Grey (if that was her real name) was not some itinerant farmhand. In spite of her well-worn work clothes, she looked and sounded quite different to the young women who filled the fruit orchards and hop fields of the county every year.

There was something about her that had attracted Becky's attention—a quality of resilience and determination despite her obvious vulnerability that set her apart. Her features were small and delicate, as were her hands and feet. Her manner was neither arrogant nor obsequious, and there was a sense of self-sufficiency about her that was most intriguing.

When asked to sit, she looked around the room, drew out a stepping stool from beneath the bookshelves, and seated herself directly in front of Becky, with the boy by her side on the floor.

Becky, who had for years promoted the education of country girls and their emancipation from domestic or industrial servitude, was determined to discover who Alice Grey was and help her, if it was at all possible to do so.

"Now, Alice," Becky began, but she got no further, for the boy coughed long and hard, and his mother interrupted her.

"Please, ma'am, let me take him to the apothecary first, else he will be very sick. He's had no sleep; he's been coughing all night," she pleaded.

"There is no need, Alice, I have sent for Mr Thomson already. He should be here within the hour. Meanwhile, we will ask Mrs Bates to give Tom a spoonful of honey and a hot drink to soothe his throat," said Becky, rising to ring for the maid.

Having sent the boy to the kitchen, she returned to her seat.

"As I was about to say, Alice, I am inclined to let you stay here for some time, but if I am to do that, I need to know something about you. Where do you come from? Who are your parents? And the boy's father, who was he and where is he now?"

The girl looked very dubious about answering all these questions; it seemed when she had decided to take a chance and camp in an empty barn on the property, she had not counted on being found and quizzed in this way. When she remained silent, Becky began again, this time more gently.

"Alice, do you understand what I am trying to do? I should like to help you and Tom. I do not feel it is safe or seemly for a young woman like you and a little boy to be wandering the countryside working in the fields and sleeping rough, as you have been doing. You could be in grave danger, or you could be caught by the police for trespassing and thrown into prison, and young Tom would be sent to the poor house. Think on that."

At this the girl's eyes widened, and she looked most alarmed.

"They wouldn't?" she said, her voice barely audible.

Becky was quick to respond, "Oh yes, they would; but have no fear, I do not intend to call the police and hand you over to them. However, should you keep doing this for much longer, entering farms at night and sleeping in barns, you *will* be caught, and someone less charitable than I will do it."

The girl looked as though she had understood, and Becky took her chance to ask a different question.

"Tell me, before you came to work in these parts, what did you do and where did you live?"

This time Alice, having contemplated for a while, spoke very quietly. "We lived in Blessington, ma'am. It's a small village not far from Ramsgate. I used to work as a kitchen maid in one of the big houses up there. It was hard work—up at five and working all day until everyone else was in bed, but they fed us well and gave us a clean room to sleep in. The lady of the manor, Mrs Bancroft, was very kind—she let me keep Tom with me, so long as he got into no trouble."

"Why did you leave? Or were you sent away?" asked Becky suspiciously.

The girl looked horrified. "Oh no, ma'am, I was not. I did leave on my own account, ma'am, because it was not possible to go on working there."

"Why not? Was the work too hard? I thought you said your mistress was a kind woman."

"Indeed she was, ma'am, and it was not the hard work—I am quite used to hard work, and I have no complaints about the mistress or the work; it was…" She tried and failed to get the words out and had to be persuaded.

"You must tell me, Alice, what was it made you give up a place in a household where you and your son were comfortably lodged and you had paid work for as long as you wished. There must have been a reason. I could make enquiries and find out, of course. The Bancrofts must be well known in Kent, and my sister Mrs Burnett, who has lived in this county all her life, is certain to know the family or someone else who does. I could ask her to make enquiries..."

The girl reacted immediately. "Please, ma'am, don't do that. I do not wish to do or say anything that will make trouble for Mrs Bancroft. She was very kind to me—to both of us. But I could not stay, ma'am. It was impossible."

"Why?" Becky persisted, beginning to get a sense of what was to follow. "What was the problem?"

There was a long pause, and the answer when it came did not surprise her. "It was one of the gentlemen, ma'am, a good friend of the master's. He used to stay at the house whenever he came down to Kent, and he began to pester me. I think I escaped his attentions for a while, only because of Tom clinging to my skirts; he was scared and wouldn't leave me, not even when he was bribed with sweets or money. He even got a clip over the ear once for refusing to go away.

"But one night when Tom was asleep, he came down to the room I shared with the scullery maid, having waited until she had gone out. He was drunk and tried to force himself upon me. I fought him off, but I was very afraid; I screamed, and the cook heard me and came to my rescue, ma'am.

"On the very next morning, I told Mrs Bancroft I wanted to leave; I think the cook had already told the housekeeper, and Mrs Bancroft said she knew what had happened. She said she was sorry to lose me, but she didn't try to stop me. I think she knew she couldn't protect me, ma'am. The gentlemen had gone out very early that morning to shoot on a neighbouring manor, and I got away before they had returned."

Appalled though not shocked, for she had heard many such tales and not all of them had ended as well, either, Becky did not doubt her story. There were many men who thought that any young servant girl who took their fancy was fair game, and some hosts who were willing to turn a blind eye.

"How did you get away?" she asked.

"The hay cart, ma'am. Mrs Bancroft paid me my full wages for the month, even though it was a few days short, and she gave me some more money to pay the carter, and he took us all the way to Wingham."

"And when you got there, where did you live?"

"Nowhere, ma'am. We needed the money for food. I couldn't afford to pay for lodgings, so I had to work, and most places would not take you in with a child, unless he could work too. So we've been working the farms and hop fields, sleeping in barns and outhouses ever since," she said simply.

Alice sat with her hands in her lap, resignation written upon her face. Looking at her hands, neat and small, but coarsened and brown with exposure and hard work, Becky was amazed by her resilience. She did not wish to embarrass her further, but there was a question to which she had to have an answer.

"Alice, when we were out in the garden, I heard you tell the gentleman, Mr Bingley, that Tom could speak until the night the police took his father away. Is that true?"

"Yes, ma'am," she replied. "He could say little words like 'Papa' and 'Mama,' and he would sing to himself all day long. He was a happy little boy."

"And when did they take his father away?" asked Becky gently.

Alice looked down at her hands, which were clasped tight together.

"When Tom was two years old. It was not right, ma'am; he was accused of stealing from his employer… but he never did it… He was innocent, but the police would not listen. They took him away," and there were tears rolling down her face as she said, "Please believe me, ma'am, my husband was no thief; he never stole anything. He was a good, hardworking man."

Becky was deeply moved. "Where is he now, Alice?" she asked gently.

The girl wiped her tears away with her sleeve and said, "I do not know, ma'am. Some say he is in jail, and others say he was sent to Botany Bay. I don't rightly know what has happened to him, ma'am."

"And have you no parents? No other family?"

The girl replied quickly, "No, ma'am, they died when I was little."

Becky's heart went out to her, and she struggled to control her voice when she asked, "Does that mean you are alone, except for the boy?"

"Yes, ma'am," the girl replied.

They were interrupted by a knock on the door. The housekeeper came in to say Mr Thomson the apothecary had arrived to see Tom, and Alice went with her.

Later, after Mr Thomson had prescribed some medication for the boy, and he was put to bed in the room Mrs Bates found for them, Alice returned and Becky sent her with one of her older servants to inform the hop farmer that she would not be able to return to work in his fields. When Alice looked surprised, not understanding her instructions, Becky explained, "Tell him your boy is sick and needs looking after. Make sure you get all the wages due to you, mind. When you return, Mrs Bates will find you some work to do."

The girl thanked her, uncomprehending, as if in a dream; she was still unable to believe what was happening to her.

Becky had not yet decided what she would do about Alice; she wanted to know more and speak with Catherine before deciding how to proceed. However, of one thing she was quite certain—she was determined that the girl was not going to return to the hop fields.

~✦~

When Becky joined the others, they were enjoying the soft sunshine on the terrace. They were eager for information, and this time she had more to tell them.

Although she did not intend to reveal any of Alice's secrets, she was able at least to satisfy their curiosity to the extent that they accepted her judgment, that the girl could not be turned over to the police, nor could she be permitted to return to her hazardous, itinerant way of life—roaming the countryside looking for work and sleeping rough in barns and outhouses.

"It is only a matter of time before she will either be picked up by the police and thrown into prison or meet some even more dreadful fate," said Becky.

Anna agreed with her. "It is quite astonishing that she has survived this far; she seems so young."

"She certainly does, but she is also surprisingly strong and stubbornly independent," said Becky, and Catherine pointed out that many young women were compelled to do the same when they were either deserted or widowed.

"There is no help for them, except the workhouse or the streets. Many, especially if they have a child to support, try to keep body and soul together by working in the fields or factories, where they are often exploited; it really is a cruel and depressing world," said Catherine.

Later, when Becky and Jonathan met to discuss the matter of Mr Tate's American estate, he was not at all surprised when she raised the question of Alice Grey. In truth, he had been expecting it.

"Jonathan, before we even begin to discuss the subject of my husband's money, I wonder if I might ask your advice on another matter?" she asked, and Jonathan was quite agreeable.

"Of course, please ask, and if there is any way I can help, I should be happy to do so."

Becky smiled; quite clearly he was still as kind and obliging as ever.

"I wonder, is there some means by which we can discover what has become of a young man who was accused of stealing from his employer? Alice Grey's husband was taken away by the police some two or three years ago; she says she has had no information about him."

Jonathan looked disbelieving. "I find that very hard to believe, Becky," he said. "Even felons have some rights. In fact, those who were transported to Australia were usually allowed to take their wives and children with them, unless they had committed a capital offence, of course," he explained, and Becky looked confused as he went on.

"In the case you speak of, I would point out that stealing from one's employer is a serious offence, but it is no longer a capital crime; I am quite certain his wife would have been told what his punishment was."

"She claims he was innocent."

"Of course, and it is possible there has been some miscarriage of justice. It is not unusual to hear of such cases, but nevertheless, I would still be confident that Alice Grey knows what became of her husband."

"Is there some way we could discover officially what sentence was imposed upon him?" Becky asked.

"If you could persuade Alice to give you some details—his full name, place of residence, the assizes at which he was tried, the date of the case—yes, we could attempt to find out. Anne-Marie's husband, Colin Elliott, has some useful contacts in the Home Office; I am sure he would be happy to try."

Becky thanked him and promised to do her best to get all relevant information to him before long.

As to the disposition of the moneys from Mr Tate's bequest, Becky indicated that she was perfectly content to leave all administrative matters in Jonathan's capable hands, if she could be permitted to use some of the proceeds on a few pet projects.

"May I ask what projects you have in mind?" he asked, and Becky replied with some alacrity. "I should very much like to donate some of it to the Hunsford parish school," she said. "Catherine has said nothing to me, but I do know she needs more materials and would like to hire more staff in the New

Year. It would make a great difference to the work she is doing, and I should like very much to help."

Seeing that he appeared not to have any objection, she continued, "Then, there is the home for destitute women, which the church used to run until the money in Lady Catherine's benevolent fund ran out last year. Mr Jamison tells me it is likely to be closed, and there will be only the poorhouse for the women after years of work. They are mostly widows and older women with no children to support them. I should like to take it over."

Jonathan was silent, contemplating her proposition for a while. He could see she was very keen, but when he spoke, his words were measured and cautious. "I cannot see any difficulty with the school—it's an established institution, to which you can donate without any reservation. The home for destitute women, though it is a worthy enterprise, might require a good deal more work and planning before we know how much it is going to cost. I suggest we talk to the parson, Mr Jamison, and discover if he has any facts and figures for us. We may also need to see the local council."

That he was willing to accommodate her wishes and had not instantly turned down her requests seemed to bode well for their association, Becky thought. There were a few more matters to be discussed; none of them resulted in any controversy, and they were soon done.

Their business concluded, they went out to join the others.

Luncheon was served on the terrace, and afterwards, Becky and her guests walked about the grounds enjoying the pleasing ambience of Edgewater, where sky, woods, and water combined to create a most charming prospect. Anna Bingley was especially appreciative of the opportunities afforded her to sketch and paint; she was working on a watercolour of the poplars in the spinney across the lake.

Becky was delighted to have a picture of her favourite vista.

"Thank you, Anna, that will have pride of place in my study, and it will remind me of these delightful days we have had together. I do wish I had learnt to draw; I am quite hopeless at it," she confessed ruefully.

When Catherine and Frank Burnett thanked Becky for her hospitality and prepared to return to the Dower House, Becky could not resist giving her sister a hint of the good news she had in store for her.

"I am not able to tell you much more, dear Cathy, except that Jonathan has agreed that I may use some of the money from Mr Tate's estate to assist the work of the parish school. When we have agreed on amounts and other formalities, I shall tell you everything."

Catherine was elated; she knew there was a great deal to be done at the school, and any help would be most welcome. As they parted, she embraced her sister and thanked her for her generosity.

Over the next few days, Becky, with Jonathan's assistance, made further enquiries about Alice Grey and consolidated her plans for the refuge for destitute women. Mr Jamison proved helpful, having been involved in a similar project while serving in a parish in Southampton.

"There were many widowed or incapacitated women, who had no homes or families, nor anywhere to go to but the poor house, where the conditions were so wretched, many would rather die of exposure than enter there and subject themselves to the indignities that prevailed," he explained. "Families were often broken up when husbands and wives or male and female siblings were separated, while inmates were issued with regulation drab clothing and not permitted to keep any of their own property."

Mr Jamison painted a depressing picture. "While it claimed to dispense charity, it was no better than a prison," he said.

The city parish he had served had determined, together with other neighbouring parishes, to set up a refuge for destitute women and children, in order to get them off the streets, he said. It had provided a much better alternative.

Becky's enthusiasm was infectious, and Mr Jamison was soon expressing his complete support for her scheme to take over the old home, promising whatever help he could give. It was, he said, only the question of money that worried him, because there were sufficient volunteers from the two parishes of Hunsford and Lower Apsley to help him manage the place.

As they talked and Becky asked more questions, Jonathan Bingley took notes. Becky was gratified indeed; it meant he was taking the proposal seriously, and on further discussion, it became clear to her that he was genuinely interested.

"If it is a proposition that can be supported responsibly, I should be happy to recommend it. I understand your charitable motives, Becky, and I sympathise with them entirely," he had said, raising her hopes that he would agree to let her fund the project.

As they were leaving, Becky asked if Mr Jamison had heard of or had any knowledge of a family by the name of Grey, from the Ramsgate area, specifically a little village called Blessington.

"I am keen to trace a young couple by that name," said Becky. "I do not have much to go on except the girl's name is Alice and they had a son they called Tom."

Mr Jamison, who had some knowledge of the area, having been born and raised in the Lower Stour Valley of Kent, said he had no personal recollection of such a family, but would be happy to make enquiries on her behalf.

"A fellow clergyman, Reverend Higgins, whose parish includes Blessington, which lies in the Stour Valley, is a contemporary of mine. I could write to him," he offered, and Becky was pleased indeed.

"That would be much appreciated, Mr Jamison," she said and added, with a smile, "and I have not forgotten the kneelers, I know we must have them before Christmas."

With the promise of further donations to his parish, Becky was confident Mr Jamison would do his best to uncover the information she needed.

Back at Edgewater, with Anna Bingley's help, suitable work had been found to keep Alice Grey occupied. Anna had discovered that the girl was a good seamstress, and she was put to work to organise the sewing room, laundry, and linen store, which she appeared to take over quite readily, together with all their attendant tasks.

Clearly glad to be able to work indoors, in peace and free of harassment or fear, Alice was looking better already.

Mrs Bates was applied to for some material, and soon Alice had made up clothes for her son and a plain gown in blue-grey cotton cloth for herself, which improved her general appearance no end. Indeed, as Jonathan had remarked, she was well nigh unrecognisable.

She worked industriously and well, while her son seemed to benefit also from the change in their physical circumstances. Regular meals, a clean, secure place to sleep, and the constant presence of his mother must have made a difference, for the child became noticeably quieter and less nervous, not clinging, as he used to do, to his mother's skirts.

However, he still would not speak, only making occasional sounds, which Alice seemed to understand but no one else could comprehend. The servants thought he was both deaf and dumb; Mrs Bates and Becky had cause to speak quite severely to one or two of them who had tried to tease the child. While his mother seemed to accept his condition with some resignation, Becky was deeply concerned and wished with all her heart that there was something she could do to help restore the boy's speech.

Anna and Jonathan had both suggested that if it was true that the boy had stopped speaking as a consequence of the shock of losing his father, perhaps if he could be found and returned to his family, it might help unlock the child's speech again.

"Perhaps Richard Gardiner may be able to advise you," Jonathan suggested. "He will know of innumerable similar cases—it is not uncommon among soldiers or children who have witnessed terrifying or shocking events."

Becky agreed there was a possibility, and to this end, she returned one afternoon to question Alice Grey again. Promising to keep the information confidential, Becky asked if Alice would reveal the name of her husband and whom he had worked for when he was accused of stealing.

Taken aback by the question, Alice seemed very upset. She had sworn never to reveal any names, because she did not want any trouble, she declared, her eyes filling with tears.

But Becky persisted, arguing that it was probably the only chance she would have of tracing her child's father.

"For the boy's sake, Alice, if not your own, it would be best if he can be found. Do you not wish to see him again?" she asked.

The girl bit her lip and nodded.

"Well, then? Why do you not tell me his name? Mr Bingley, who is a kind and honourable gentleman, has offered to make some enquiries. We could discover if he is still in England," Becky said.

Still she got no response, other than tears. It was clear to Becky the girl was apprehensive because she feared those who had brought the complaint against her husband.

Two days before the Bingleys were due to leave for Standish Park, where they were visiting Jonathan's sister Emma and her husband, James Wilson, Becky had left Edgewater and was walking through the grounds of Rosings Park to the Dower House, where she hoped to meet and consult with her sister Catherine. She was in a dilemma with regard to Alice Grey.

Should she leave well alone as she had at first felt inclined to do? The girl seemed to be settling in well at Edgewater; she could foresee no problems.

Or was it her duty to try to discover the truth about the whereabouts of her husband and Tom's father, if only for the sake of the child?

She had not walked far when Catherine came into view, walking towards her. The sisters greeted one another warmly.

"Why, Cathy, were you coming to visit us?" Becky asked, and Catherine replied, "Indeed I was, I have a message for you."

Becky was curious, and as they walked on, Catherine explained that she had had a visit that morning from Mr Jamison.

"He said he had received some information that had to be passed on to you at the earliest opportunity. He has had to go to officiate at a funeral in the parish of Lower Apsley and could not come himself; however, he thought you ought to have this material as quickly as possible, which is why I was coming to Edgewater."

At this, she took from her bag a packet and handed it to Becky, adding, "I believe it concerns the girl Alice Grey."

Becky was excited and impatient to open the packet of papers. Instead of walking back to Edgewater, which lay some fifteen minutes away, she suggested they stop at the parish school.

"I would rather know what he has uncovered before I see Jonathan and Anna," she explained, "in case it is bad news. I cannot help feeling that Anna disapproves just a little of my taking Alice and Tom into my house, without any prior knowledge of their background or family—indeed we do not even know whether she is who says she is. But, Cathy, I had to do something. I could see she was not a tramp or a thief. She must be a decent young woman fallen on hard times, and then there was the boy; I could not turn them out, I had to help them. Do you not agree?"

Catherine, who was somewhat more circumspect than her sister, did agree, but was at pains to point out that since they knew so little about the young woman, they were entitled to be cautious, and Anna was probably just exercising some of her usually excellent judgment.

Becky went on, "I believe Anna feels I am taking a risk, but, Cathy, I could not have sent her back to work in the hop fields by day and sleep in empty barns by night and with the child as well? I should not have slept a wink myself for worrying about them. Why, Alice cannot be much older than my Josie was when she was married to Julian Darcy."

Catherine agreed that something had to be done.

"Well, let us hope Mr Jamison's papers contain good news, or at the very least, not bad news!" she said as they reached the empty school house and went within.

There were three or four sheets of paper in the packet: a letter to Mr Jamison from a fellow parish priest, a Reverend Higgins, whose parish included the village of Blessington; and two hand-copied entries from the parish register; as well as two old newspaper-cuttings from a local paper of some years back.

Before reading the letter, Becky looked quickly at the extracts from the parish register. The first was a copy of the registration of the marriage of one Annabel Grey, spinster, daughter of Mr Edward Grey and Mrs Grey of Maidstone, to a William Rickman, bachelor, of Ramsgate. The second entry, dated some twelve months later, was the registration of the birth and christening of their son, Thomas William.

The cuttings from the newspapers reported the arrest upon information laid, of William (alias Bill) Rickman, a stock clerk in a local brewery, for theft from his employer and of his being produced before a magistrate at Ramsgate.

As she read and passed them over to Catherine, Becky exclaimed, "I knew it, she was from a good family; she must be the daughter of a gentleman—Mr Edward Grey of Maidstone. It will not be difficult to discover his whereabouts. No doubt she was disowned or disinherited for marrying this man—William Rickman. But, Cathy, if she is Annabel Grey, why does she call herself Alice? And since she was quite clearly married to Rickman, why should she continue to use her maiden name? Why does she not say she is Mrs Rickman?"

"Could it be, Becky, that she did not wish it to be known that she was the wife of a convicted thief? It would not have been easy for her to get employment or lodging in any respectable house, if it was known," Catherine suggested. It was an entirely plausible idea.

"That is possible, of course, but she quite strenuously protests his innocence. I wish I knew more about the circumstances of this case; Jonathan says his son-in-law, Mr Elliott, could make enquiries, but he will need more facts—names, dates, places—in order to succeed. And there is another matter that puzzles me—why ever did she tell me that she had no family, that her parents had died when she was little?"

Catherine had no explanation and suggested that perhaps if they read the letter from the parish priest, Reverend Higgins, they might find a clue to the mystery. Becky turned eagerly to the two sheets of closely written paper, upon which Mr Higgins had detailed what he knew of the couple.

He remembered well their wedding; they had been married in Blessington because the girl's parents were set against the marriage and did not wish it to be solemnised in their own parish church in Maidstone, nor did either of them attend the wedding.

Mr Higgins recalled that the girl, Annabel Grey, was a devout and regular churchgoer until the arrest of her husband. Thereafter, he wrote, her attendance fell away and she came rarely to church.

Of the young man William Rickman, Mr Higgins said he knew very little, except he was from the North of England and worked at a local brewery. He was thought to be a quiet, industrious fellow, and it was said that information had been maliciously laid against him that he was stealing and selling kegs of beer to an innkeeper, who had a reputation for dubious dealings. Very few people who knew and worked with Rickman had believed the evidence given by the police at his trial, but the informer, being someone with influence with the authorities, had been believed above the accused, who had protested his innocence throughout.

Mr Higgins claimed that he knew only that Bill Rickman was tried and found guilty and his young wife was distraught with grief when he was sent down. She had told anyone who would listen, including Mr Higgins himself, that her husband was innocent and begged for assistance to clear his name. But it had been in vain. As far as Mr Higgins could ascertain, William Rickman had been sent to jail, and his unfortunate wife and son had nowhere to go but the workhouse.

Thereafter, Mr Higgins had been away from Blessington for some time, on account of family matters; but on his return, he had heard that Annabel Rickman had found employment at the manor, where Mrs Bancroft, a lady with a good reputation for charitable work in the parish, had taken pity on her and rescued her and the child from the workhouse. Mr Higgins had assumed then that the girl and her son would be cared for.

Of William Rickman, he said, he had heard nothing more.

Some time later, however, Annabel had disappeared from the village, and no one could tell him where she had gone. Not even Mrs Bancroft, who had expressed some genuine regret at losing her, but had given him no hint of her present whereabouts. Nor had he heard from the girl's parents, who appeared to have cut themselves off from their daughter completely.

Mr Higgins said he knew no more, beyond the information he had provided, but he hoped very much it would be of some assistance in tracing the couple and their son, whom he personally recalled with a good deal of affection, he concluded.

Despite the inconclusive nature of the information it contained, Becky was delighted with Mr Higgins' letter.

"Well done, Mr Jamison and Mr Higgins," she exclaimed, "that is very useful information indeed. Even though there are still some questions for which we needs must find answers, it will give Jonathan and Mr Elliott sufficient material with which to begin their enquiries," she said, adding with a satisfied smile, "Oh, Cathy, I *am* pleased, and I must make certain Mr Jamison gets those kneelers before Christmas! He has done very well indeed. Do you not agree?"

Catherine did agree, though she could not quite see the connection with the kneelers; but she knew her sister well enough not to argue. If Becky had promised to provide kneelers for the church, that was what she would do.

By such stratagems, Becky Tate had over many years given and received favours in the community, using her influence and persuasive charm to help many who couldn't help themselves.

Becky's curiosity had been greatly aroused by the riddles posed by the information contained in Mr Jamison's papers. They had opened up new pathways of enquiry, and she was more determined than ever to resolve the mystery of Annabel Grey.

END OF PART ONE

A Woman of Influence

Part Two

Chapter Four

THE NOT UNEXPECTED NEWS of the death of Reverend James Courtney interrupted all Becky's plans and drew her back to Derbyshire.

She was going to be at the side of Emily Courtney, a lifelong and loyal friend. Close enough to be sisters despite the difference in their ages, Emily, the younger daughter of the late Mr and Mrs Gardiner of Oakleigh, and Becky Collins had developed a warm and trusting friendship over many years.

Becky had visited her friend at Oakleigh before leaving Derbyshire for Kent earlier in the year; at that time, although Emily would not admit it, Becky had known Reverend Courtney was dying. Weakened by constant bouts of a persistent and debilitating disease, his condition exacerbated by long periods of arduous parish work, when he had paid scant attention to his own health, James Courtney was close to death. But neither he nor his wife would accept it, nor let other people believe it to be the case.

Emily had continued to run her household as though nothing was wrong and would explain her husband's frequent absence from the dinner table by saying he was tired and had his meals taken to his room. When Becky had asked her directly what the doctors had said of her husband's condition, Emily had been unable to reply, but her tears had given Becky her answer.

Later, Becky had learned from Emily's daughter Jessica, who was very close to being delivered of her first child, that Dr Richard Gardiner had warned them that the end was very near.

Amazingly, James Courtney had rallied in the Spring and appeared to be on the way to recovery, or so Emily had written only a month ago in a letter filled with hope. But then, in the midst of the quickening of new life, almost without warning, Death, like the proverbial thief in the night, had arrived.

An express from Jessica's husband, Julian Darcy, had brought the distressing news, and Becky, leaving her home in the charge of her housekeeper, Mrs Bates, had left with her maid Nelly to attend the funeral and support Emily in any way possible.

Before leaving, she had called on her sister and begged her to keep a watchful eye on Annabel Grey and young Tom.

"I do not expect to be away above a fortnight, Cathy, but I should hate to think that the girl might take fright and decide to leave Edgewater. I have made every effort to avoid alarming her, and to that end, I have given no hint of the information received from Mr Higgins to anyone except Anna and Jonathan Bingley.

"Indeed, I have written to Mr Jamison to thank him for his efforts, but I have urged him to speak of it to no one until I return," she explained.

Catherine agreed.

"You are quite right," she said. "He should avoid speaking of Annabel's presence at Edgewater to anyone who may make enquiries about her where-abouts while you are away. Depend upon it, Becky, I shall ensure that nothing untoward occurs and will speak to Mr Jamison myself, so he understands the need for caution."

Her sister was grateful.

"Thank you, Cathy. Mrs Bates has my instructions to send for you if there is any problem at all. I do hope the circumstances will not arise."

Privately, Catherine hoped so too.

She was not confident that her influence would suffice, in the absence of Becky's authority, to avert any possible calamity. Alice (or Annabel, whoever she was) seemed to be a young woman of some independence, and it was unlikely she would be persuaded by Catherine, if she had a mind to leave Edgewater, for whatever reason.

However, in order to set her sister's mind at rest, as she undertook her melancholy journey to Derbyshire, Catherine promised to do her best to ensure that all would be well in her absence.

Arriving in Derbyshire, Becky Tate went directly to the Tate family home at Matlock, where she confidently expected that she would be made welcome by her son Walter and his wife, Pauline. She had sent a message by electric telegraph to Walter advising him of her travel plans and had been somewhat put out when no one met them at the railway station. However, she put that down to his being a very busy man, now he was running his father's business.

To her surprise, on arrival at the house in a hired vehicle, she found no arrangements had been made; the new housekeeper, Mrs Stoker, advised that Mr and Mrs Tate were away at the coastal resort of Scarborough and were not expected back until the end of the month.

Astonished, Becky enquired who was running the business and the household in their absence.

"Mrs Tate's brother Mr Hartley Pratt is managing the business, ma'am," the woman replied, explaining that he had been appointed recently to the position. "And I am in charge here," she added, in a voice that suggested she resented being asked at all.

Becky knew better than to pursue the matter of Hartley Pratt, whom she remembered as a self-important young man with little talent, few achievements, and no style at all. How he had come to be appointed to manage the business was beyond her understanding. Clearly Walter's wife must wield a high degree of influence, Becky thought.

The revelation served only to increase her unease, but this being neither the time nor the occasion to comment upon such matters, she explained she was there for Dr Courtney's funeral and requested politely that the rooms she had occupied before the death of her husband should be made ready for her use over the next fortnight.

Whereupon Mrs Stoker informed her, with a degree of hauteur, that the rooms in that part of the house were no longer available to be used, since Mrs Walter Tate had decided to have them redecorated and refurbished for special guests.

Becky's patience was at an end.

Ignoring the housekeeper's shocked expression, she asked Nelly to take her bags up to the room and said quietly but firmly, "My dear woman, this happens to be the house in which Mr Tate and I lived for nigh on thirty years. My son lives here now under the terms of my husband's will, and by agreement with me.

"I am here to attend the funeral of Reverend Courtney, and I do not care if the rooms are to be refurbished for royalty; if they are vacant now, I am asking you to open them up and have them aired and readied for my use within the hour. I shall leave my things in the charge of my maid, Nelly, while I travel to Lambton to call on Mrs Courtney. When I return, I expect to see all the appropriate arrangements in place, including a room for my maid, and please do not pretend that you must have my daughter-in-law's permission to accommodate me in what was my home for thirty years."

So saying, Becky swept out of the house and down the steps into the waiting vehicle that was to take her to Lambton, confident that everything would be as she had asked, but unhappy at having had to ask at all.

~✥~

Arriving at Oakleigh, she found that several members of the family had gathered to support Emily Courtney.

Her brother Richard and his wife, Cassandra, greeted Becky and escorted her into the parlour, where Emily, her eyes red and her face pale with weariness, embraced her friend with warmth and gratitude.

"It is so good of you to come all this way, Becky; it is such a long journey," she said, and Becky hushed her at once.

"My dear Emily, did you think for one moment that I would not come?"

Their close friendship had meant a lot to Becky, but Emily had never presumed upon it. Her generous heart asked for very little in return for all she gave in affection and concern to anyone, family or friend.

Throughout the years when Becky had been *persona non grata* with Mrs Darcy and many in her family, Emily had persisted with their friendship, knowing full well that Elizabeth disapproved of it.

Later, they would sit together and speak of the difficult days and hours before her husband's death, and Becky would marvel at the calmness of this remarkable woman, who in one lifetime had loved and lost not one but two fine men, yet bore no signs of bitterness or self-pity.

The loss of Emily's first husband had left her deeply saddened, but with a determination to immerse herself in such a volume of work as to leave her little time for grieving.

Paul Antoine had been the love of Emily's young life; she had married him in the full knowledge that he was dying of tuberculosis, confounding her family and friends. She had travelled with him to Italy and nursed him devotedly until his death, following which she had spent much of her time supporting and comforting her cousin Mrs Darcy after the recent loss of her son William.

A young girl at the time, Becky had admired Emily's courage and single-minded devotion. Her mother, Charlotte Collins, had upheld Emily as an example of everything a woman could and should be, making Becky feel wholly inadequate. Yet as she grew older and confronted the vicissitudes of life herself, Becky had learned to value Emily's strength, and the two had become close friends.

Now, years later, here she was, once again bereft yet unembittered.

"I do not question God's will, Becky, but after all these years of shared dedication, I must admit to a terrible loneliness," she had said, and Becky had tried unsuccessfully to hide her tears, as Emily recalled her husband.

A modest, though distinguished, theologian, a scholar of repute and a hardworking parish priest, James Courtney had been loved most of all for his great compassion. He had worked all his days to help the poor, and Emily had supported him without question in all his endeavours.

"His sincerity and love for those who needed his help was an inspiration, which I shall miss most profoundly," she had said, "yet I must accept that my present sorrow, however dismal, would have been ten times greater had I been compelled to witness his painful lingering death. We have all been spared that anguish at least."

Becky could not help but recall her own dull response to the death of Mr Tate, whose every action had been motivated by his search for power or profit. She remembered feeling only a sense of resentful numbness on learning the news. Emily's honesty had left her feeling mortified.

Writing to her sister, Becky gave expression to her admiration of Emily as well as her frustration at the conduct of some of the Courtneys' children.

Eliza, her eldest girl, has arrived this very morning, with her husband Mr Harwood, who seems impatient to return to his business in London; but at least they are here. William, however, is still not here and no one, not even his mother, knows when he may be expected.

A message has been received by Dr Gardiner, in which he declares his intention to be present at his father's funeral and requests details of time and place, but I am reliably informed by Emily's sister, Caroline, that William is so busy with his career as a conductor, travelling often to Europe and America, that he has had little time to visit his parents and has seen them but once in the last year.

When one considers how much love and devotion Emily has invested in her children, Cathy, I confess I am quite unable to comprehend such behaviour.

Only Jessica and young Jude appear to have the loyalty and warmth of feeling one might have expected. Jessica, who is very close to being brought to bed with her first child, can do little more than comfort her mother, but young Jude ensures that all the chores are done on the farm, with the help of the ubiquitous Mr Mancini, an Italian flower farmer, who leases a part of the property. Without his help, for there is but the cook and a maid to assist Emily, I really do not know how she would manage at all.

Caroline also tells me that Elizabeth and Mr Darcy were disappointed that William did not visit his father at Christmas as he had been expected to do, even though word had been sent through Georgiana and Dr Grantley that Reverend Courtney was unlikely to live very long after. Indeed, at one stage it had seemed that he would not survive the Winter! But William did not come, having written to say he had committed to a series of concerts in Vienna and Berlin and would try to visit in the New Year.

I am sure Emily is hurt, but she will not say a word against William. She has been single-minded about ensuring that he had everything he needed to pursue his musical career; it is a pity he does not reciprocate with a similar devotion to her.

The Darcys, who were generous in their assistance to William when he was a student, are understandably dismayed, and Caroline believes that Lizzie will have her say directly to William Courtney, when he does arrive.

Becky's letter related also the circumstances of her stay at the Tate family home, declaring:

Nothing would persuade me to return here. Mr Tate would have been appalled by the meanness of the establishment maintained by Walter's dear wife, Pauline. While Mr Tate abhorred extravagance and ostentation, he was nevertheless generous and always hospitable. Pauline's hospitality appears to extend only to her family; her brother, appointed to manage the business with no qualifications to do so, now occupies my late husband's study and ante-room and orders the servants around as though he owned the place.

The new housekeeper, a Mrs Stoker, a rather haughty woman, obviously acting upon the instructions of her mistress, runs the household as though it were a boarding school, with a degree of severity that would have surprised even Mr Dickens, I think. The servants are uniformly cowed and meek; Nelly tells me they are frequently berated for all sorts of petty sins of commission and omission, with no allowance made for anything at all.

If it were not that I have no wish to inconvenience dear Emily, I would have accepted her kind offer to accommodate us at Oakleigh Manor, but I am loathe to add to her burden and have decided to stay on at Matlock for the moment, although it irks me to do so.

...she wrote, leaving Catherine in no doubt of her opinion of her daughter-in-law and her household arrangements.

Catherine had been aware that Walter Tate's marriage to Miss Pauline Pratt, the daughter of a wealthy manufacturer in the Midlands, had not met with his mother's approval, but she had not supposed it to be as bad as this.

"Poor Becky," she said, relating her sister's complaints to her husband, "it must be dreadful to return to her own house and find herself so unwelcome. How very fortunate we are to have this place, thanks to the generosity of Mr Darcy."

Frank Burnett could not but agree with his wife; however, he felt constrained to add, "But chiefly on account of your valuable work with the school, my dear, there is less obligation on your part than on your sisters; even though she may have some familial claim at Matlock, it *is* now legally her son's house."

Catherine had to accept the logic of his argument but felt her sister's grievance keenly. "I would have thought that Walter Tate would have ensured his mother would not have to endure such humiliation, don't you? What has become of the respect, if not the affection, that children gave their parents?

From Becky's account of the manner in which Emily's elder children have behaved, it seems that they have neither warmth of feeling nor a sense of family obligation; self-interest appears to be their only motivation."

Seeing she was clearly disturbed by these revelations, Mr Burnett sought to comfort her by reminding her that she could have no such concern about her daughter Lilian.

"Indeed no, Lilian is a great consolation to me. Forgive me, Frank, if I seem unduly distressed, but it grieves me to hear of such matters. We grew up in a very different world," she said with a sigh.

An invitation to spend a few days at Pemberley after the funeral brought Becky some welcome relief from Mrs Stoker's abstemious regime and afforded her another opportunity to enjoy her restored relationship with Mrs Darcy. Elizabeth, who for many years had held Becky Tate responsible for the ill-advised marriage of her daughter Josie to Julian Darcy, had begun to soften her attitude to Becky, chiefly influenced by her daughter-in-law, Jessica, whose sweetness of disposition could not accept the continuance of such a feud. There was also the fact that Becky was, after all, the daughter of Elizabeth's dearest and oldest friend, Charlotte Lucas.

They were meeting again for the first time since Charlotte's death, and Elizabeth was particular to treat Becky with a degree of gentleness and courtesy that took her quite by surprise. She had expected politeness at Pemberley, but found both Mr and Mrs Darcy as well as Jessica and Julian treating her with so much consideration and genuine warmth that she was astonished, albeit in the pleasantest way.

It was not difficult for Becky to understand the real reason behind Elizabeth's change of heart.

Her genuine pleasure at having her son Julian back, living at Pemberley with his second wife, Jessica, happily awaiting the birth of their first child, was plain to see. Her personal satisfaction seemed to increase her ability to treat Becky with greater consideration and respect.

Becky, to her credit, realising the truth of the situation, made every effort to enhance Elizabeth's contentment. Mr Darcy, who, while maintaining a degree of reserve, had never been overtly antagonistic towards Becky, even in the dark days leading up to Josie's death, was as hospitable and courteous as ever. All of which made her feel very much at home at Pemberley—more so, she told them frankly, than at the Tates' residence.

Elizabeth, learning of her experience, expressed her profound displeasure.

"Becky, that is unpardonable. Your tolerance is commendable indeed. I should not have had the patience to remain under that roof one night longer than necessary," she had said, on hearing of Mrs Stoker's rudeness.

Becky had responded lightly, "But, Lizzie, I do believe I shall have the last laugh, for I know now how very sensible was my decision to sell Mr Tate's London residence, despite Walter's objections, and acquire a property of my very own in Kent. To have done otherwise would have made my life quite intolerable."

Mrs Darcy agreed absolutely and went on to invite Becky to spend the remainder of her stay in Derbyshire at Pemberley, where she was assured she would be a welcome guest; a sentiment immediately echoed by her husband. Becky, genuinely surprised and exceedingly gratified, accepted and, having thanked her hosts, lost little time despatching her maid with a servant from Pemberley to pack her things and return with them forthwith.

Nelly was instructed privately to ensure that Mrs Stoker was made well aware of the invitation extended to her mistress by Mr and Mrs Darcy.

It was an instruction Nelly would take great pleasure in carrying out.

The rest of the week was filled with convivial activities, memories of which Becky would cherish for many years, as the Darcys extended to her the courtesy and hospitality for which Pemberley was renowned. It was, thought Becky, just like old times, when they had been friends together, as though the unhappiness that had come between them had never existed.

One evening, after a dinner party to which Richard and Cassy Gardiner had been invited, the ladies withdrew to the drawing room. Jessica had asked to be excused and retired upstairs; but Elizabeth and Cassy were both eager to talk of Emily Courtney's situation and in particular, the conduct of her two elder children, Eliza and William.

Eliza and her husband, whose desire to return to his business as expeditiously as possible had earned him the censure of most other members of the family, had left on the morning after the funeral.

William at least had stayed on for one more day, ostensibly to ensure that his mother was well and able to look after herself. It was not known to what extent he had satisfied himself on these questions, before deciding to depart a day after his sister and return to Europe, to resume a series of concerts.

Elizabeth, as ever, was not lost for words.

"I am astounded that both Emily's elder children could have so little concern and affection for their poor mother that they could so readily arrange to leave, knowing she is likely to be alone at Oakleigh, with only young Jude and the servants for company. I should have liked to have invited her to stay at Pemberley for a while, as she has done many times in the past, but Emily has made it quite clear to me and to both Julian and Jessica that it is her preference to remain at Oakleigh."

Becky had to concur. In her own conversations with Emily, her friend had said without any reservation that she had no intention of quitting her home.

On being asked if she would consider leaving Oakleigh, even temporarily, she had said with fervour, "Mama and Papa entrusted this place to me; I am not about to abandon it, Becky. Remember, this is Jude's home too. If I leave, what is to become of him? Would it not leave the door open for others to intervene in his life?"

Becky had assumed that Emily had meant her brother Robert and his wife, whose outrage at being left out of Mrs Gardiner's will was well known.

"But how will she live and support the farm and staff?" asked Cassy.

"Richard knows that Emily has used up most of the money that their father left her, chiefly in supporting charitable causes in the parish. She has very little cash to spare, except what comes in from the tenants and Mr Mancini's lease," Cassy said.

Becky was completely confounded.

While she had been aware of the charitable activities of the Courtneys, she had not known all of the details that Cassy and Elizabeth revealed. That Emily and her husband had used up most of their funds helping the poor in the parish and especially a number of impoverished Irish families living on the fringes of the common came as a considerable shock to her.

"And you say she does not receive any income apart from the rents?"

"No she does not, because many years ago, she transferred all her assets to William to enable him to establish himself in his career," said Cassy.

"And now that William is doing so well, does he not assist his mother?" Cassy and Elizabeth looked doubtful.

"We do not know if he does or does not, because Emily will not tell us, but there is little evidence that he sends her any money at all."

This revelation so perturbed Becky she rose hastily from her seat and walked quickly about the room, clearly distressed. In truth, she was thinking, playing with the possibility of making some money available to Emily, through Jessica perhaps, so as not to place her under obligation. She acknowledged it was a delicate situation indeed.

When she returned to join Elizabeth and Cassandra, she had the beginnings of a plan in mind. She would give Jessica a sum of money, with instructions that it be used to pay for the inevitable expenses that must come after Dr Courtney's funeral. Doubtless, her mother would be more inclined to accept such assistance from Jessica, she supposed.

"Do you not think so?" she asked, having outlined her plan, and both Elizabeth and her daughter agreed that it may be so.

They commended Becky's generous impulse, but it was Cassy who suggested that Jessica in her present condition would be unlikely to become involved, for purely practical reasons.

"With her child due within the next few days, Jessica's ability to assist her mother might be limited, she certainly cannot travel to Lambton," she explained. "Would it not be better to ask my son Darcy, who regularly visits his aunt Emily and may well be able to persuade her to accept the money? There is no doubt at all that she will need it."

"And would I be able to meet Mr Darcy Gardiner tomorrow?" asked Becky, knowing time was short. She had plans to return to Kent not long afterwards.

"Certainly," Cassy replied, "I shall send word to him and ask him to call on you here during the day."

"And will he agree to help, do you think?" Becky asked.

Cassandra was certain her son would be willing, but added a word of caution.

"Darcy is scrupulously honest and may feel he has to reveal to Emily the source of the money," then seeing the anxiety upon Becky's face, added, "but that will not matter a great deal if she will accept it and use it to pay her bills. I am confident Darcy will be happy to help; he is well aware of Emily's financial difficulties and has helped her on previous occasions.

"If anyone can persuade her to accept it, Darcy can."

The gentlemen entered the room, and the conversation changed to matters they had been discussing over port. Richard and Julian had almost succeeded in convincing Mr Darcy of the need to have the history of the Pemberley estate recorded for posterity.

"There is so much material scattered around the place, in the library, at the parish church, in diaries, notebooks, and personal letters and documents, which must be of great interest, yet no one has attempted to put it together for the future," said Julian, appealing to the ladies to use their persuasive powers to convince Mr Darcy it was a worthy and important task.

Richard Gardiner agreed. "It is absolutely imperative that the story of this great estate and its people should be documented," he declared, and Becky was happy to lend them her support, while Elizabeth rang the bell to order more coffee.

But all was forgotten when Jessica's maid appeared, breathless from having run all the way to say in an anguished voice, "Mrs Darcy, ma'am, it's Miss Jessica—I beg pardon, I mean Mrs Julian Darcy, ma'am, she says we must get the doctor at once—it's the baby, ma'am."

Everyone turned to Doctor Gardiner while Julian ran out of the room and up the stairs in seconds.

Cassandra had rushed to her husband's side, and he followed Julian immediately, giving instructions to the maid as he went.

Cassy went with him; she wanted to be with her young sister-in-law and brother at this moment, while Becky, Elizabeth, and Mr Darcy were left looking anxiously at one another, knowing there was little they could do but wait.

On the morrow, Becky wrote to her sister Catherine:

The birth of Julian and Jessica's daughter in the small hours of this morning, only days after the funeral of Reverend Courtney, has helped lift the melancholy mood that had descended over Pemberley and has given everyone a new and happier subject for conversation.

She is to be named Marianne, which is a pretty name and even better, one that has especially pleased Mr Darcy, because it includes within it his mother's name, Anne.

Lizzie is ecstatic, as might be expected; there has not been a child

*born at Pemberley since my dear grandson Anthony, who I must say is
growing into a very fine lad indeed. Cassy has spared no effort in her
care of the boy.*

*Meanwhile, Jessica and Julian seem truly devoted to one another and
I wish them every happiness in the future. It is an indication of Julian's
contentment that he appears not to miss his scientific work at all, while he
spends a great deal of his time around his wife and new baby daughter.*

*My business here is concluded, Cathy, and I hope to be back in Kent
before the end of the week. Much as I have enjoyed these days at Pemberley,
I do so look forward to returning home and taking up all those matters I
left behind at Edgewater.*

Having despatched her letter to the post, she went downstairs to meet
Darcy Gardiner, who had called to see her as arranged. She found him not only
agreeable but enthusiastic about assisting his aunt Emily Courtney and was
delighted to discover that he had no qualms at all about taking the money to
Emily and urging her to use it for all those bills, which he knew she would have
to pay with her quite meagre resources.

"It is very kind of you, Mrs Tate, and I should be honoured to be your
intermediary in this matter," he said, delighting Becky with that combination
of charm and responsibility for which young Darcy Gardiner was widely known
and loved.

"I know my aunt Emily needs help, and yet she will not ask and is reluctant
to accept it from my grandfather Mr Darcy, because she feels he and Mrs Darcy
have helped her too often. She is quite determined to struggle on alone, yet it
is an unequal struggle, and she must have help. I feel sure I can persuade her to
accept yours on this occasion.

"She has always spoken well of you and my wife, Kate, and I know that she
regards you with great affection. I am confident she will not feel any degree of
mortification in accepting your offer."

For Becky, his assurance was a source of great satisfaction.

It was with a much happier heart that she thanked young Darcy Gardiner,
his wife, Kate, and her generous host and hostess, as she bid farewell to
Pemberley and returned home to Kent.

Chapter Five

THROUGHOUT THE LONG JOURNEY, as the train carried her away from Derbyshire and back to her new home, Becky's sense of satisfaction in her present situation grew considerably.

Having endured, for however short a period, the indignity of being an unwelcome guest in her son's home, she was determined she would never again be so affronted. The purchase of Edgewater had given her the sense of security that she was sure her late husband had wanted her to have. Why else would he have agreed to transfer the title for the house in London to her and allow her the freedom to sell it if she chose to do so?

She smiled to herself as she recalled the dismay of her son Walter and his wife upon discovering that they would no longer have the convenience of a house in one of the best streets in London, maintained and paid for by someone else.

"But, Mother," Walter had protested, "surely there is no need to sell the place," and when she had quite justifiably asked, "How else would I acquire a home, a place of my own, Walter?" he had replied rather glibly, "You don't *need* a place of your own, Mother, you could live with us. Papa indicated in his will that if you chose to do so, we should accommodate your wishes. That way, we could all use the house in London."

Becky had laughed then, much to Walter's discomfort.

"I cannot believe that your father ever thought I would adopt that suggestion, which he was kind enough to put in his will. He was probably trying to remind you that the house in Matlock, which I agreed to relinquish to you, had been our home for almost thirty years; perhaps he hoped you would understand that it meant something to me."

"Do you not wish to live there anymore? We could come to a convenient arrangement, Pauline would have no objection I am sure," he had said rather lamely, but Becky had been adamant.

"No, Walter, I do not wish to enter into any such arrangement; you and your wife need have no fears that I will arrive on your doorstep and demand that you accommodate me for the rest of my life! I cannot imagine anything worse, for all of us. No, for several very good reasons, I must have my own place, and to that end, I shall sell the house in London and use the proceeds to acquire one elsewhere."

Becky recalled that Walter had been distraught.

"Pauline will be most upset; she had her heart set on spending some part of the season in town each year," he had said plaintively, and Becky had shrugged her shoulders gently and replied, "I am sorry to disappoint your wife, Walter, and I am confident you will find a way to comfort her. But you are both very welcome to come and visit me when I am settled into my place in Kent."

"In Kent?" Walter had exclaimed, as though she had named the Outer Hebrides as her chosen place of residence. Perhaps he had hoped she would choose to settle a little closer to London—in Richmond maybe, where he and his wife might still stay conveniently and inexpensively when in town. But not Kent! That would have been most inconvenient. Pauline would have been very vexed indeed.

But she had enjoyed telling him that she had already decided to purchase the picturesque property of Edgewater on the outskirts of the village of Hunsford, some two miles from Rosings Park and many miles from the noise and bustle of London.

"Why ever not?" she had argued. "It is without doubt one of the most salubrious and civilised counties in England, and besides, I shall be within walking distance of my sister Mrs Burnett. No, Walter, do not waste your breath, my mind is quite made up."

Walter Tate had not looked very pleased at all.

Becky had thought at the time that he must not have looked forward to telling his stylish wife Pauline that they would no longer have the use of a fine London residence for the season every year.

Now, as the train sped through the Kentish countryside, which she was coming to love, Becky savoured the memory of his disgruntled expression, even as she looked forward to returning to her home, confident in the knowledge that it was a good deal more elegant and comfortable than anything Walter and Pauline had to offer at the old Tate place in Matlock.

Above all, it was her very own.

~❦~

Back at Edgewater, Becky found to her relief that everything had proceeded as she had hoped, by which she meant that nothing of any real consequence had happened at all. Mrs Bates reported no problems.

The girl Alice (or Annabel) Grey had settled in and was continuing with her work satisfactorily; her son, Tom, was quieter and more amenable, often playing on his own, no longer clinging to his mother's skirts.

Becky could not have been more pleased.

Then, to her greater satisfaction, she found waiting for her a substantial communication from Jonathan Bingley.

Having extracted it from the bundle of mail on her desk, she retreated to her bedroom, ostensibly to rest awhile, but in truth, keen to discover what information it contained.

Opening the bulky packet, she found within it two letters, one from Jonathan Bingley to herself and the other some pages of carefully written notes, sent to Jonathan by his son-in-law, Mr Colin Elliott, MP.

Jonathan's letter was brief and to the point. He wrote:

Dear Becky,

I trust this finds you at home after a safe journey from Derbyshire.

With regard to the matter of Annabel (or Alice) Grey and her husband William Rickman, my son-in-law Mr Elliott has made some enquiries and through his contact at the Home Office has discovered some facts that may be of interest to you. I enclose his notes, which contain several useful details that may assist you in your quest for the truth in this matter. I

*certainly hope it will help the young woman and her son discover the fate
of William Rickman.*

*Should you wish to contact Mr Elliott regarding any of the material
in his notes, please feel free to write to him at his office in Whitehall. He
assures me he will be happy to answer any of your questions, if he is able
to do so.*

Jonathan concluded with felicitations and good wishes to her, her sister
Catherine, and Catherine's husband, Frank Burnett.

Turning to Colin Elliott's notes, Becky read them eagerly.

They comprised a number of paragraphs in which he outlined some of the
information he had gleaned from his contacts in the Home Office. It revealed
that a William Rickman had indeed been tried for stealing from his employer,
a brewer, and reselling the loot to a publican. Information had been laid, and
Rickman had been arrested, tried, and sent to prison.

Initially, he had been sentenced to be transported to Australia, but too late
it seemed, for the government had just decided that convicts would no longer
be sent twelve thousand miles across the world, but would be held on prison
hulks off the coast or incarcerated in remote jails on the moors. Out of sight
and out of mind was what the authorities desired, and to that end Dartmoor
would serve as well as Port Arthur. Becky read quickly, trying to discover what
had happened to Rickman, but could find nothing significant. She was keen
also to identify the brewer Rickman had worked for as well as the informer who
had accused him, but found no clues as to their identities in Mr Elliott's notes.
Colin Elliott had hinted that he might be able to get further information if he
had access to some detail of names and dates to which the girl alone would be
privy, and promised to maintain an interest in the case.

Becky suspected, because the girl had been unwilling to reveal anything at
all, that there was more to the matter than met the eye.

She determined to speak with Catherine first and try to persuade Annabel
Grey, in her own interest, to tell her more, chiefly in order that they may
attempt to discover the whereabouts of her husband and Tom's father. She
hoped it would provide the girl with a motive strong enough to overcome her
reluctance to name persons of whom she was very afraid.

Despite the fact that she was rather weary from her journey and should have enjoyed a bath and rest before dinner, Becky decided to call on her sister and show her the information she had received. Catherine had a capacity for clear thinking that Becky had previously relied upon, and she wished to sound her out about a plan she was developing in her mind.

When she set out alone and on foot, she did not immediately realise that she had not alerted anyone to the fact that she was going to visit her sister. Her mind concentrated upon her plan, and anxious to convince Catherine of its practicality, she had almost reached the boundary of Rosings Park when she saw, wandering through the trees, a woman, who on her approaching closer, turned out to be none other than Alice Grey.

Seeing Becky, she stopped in her tracks then approached with an expression that betrayed her astonishment. Clearly she had not expected Becky to be walking in the woods at this hour, and Becky made no secret of her own surprise at seeing her there.

"Alice! What are you doing here at this time of day?" she asked, and the girl, having initially looked rather sheepish, answered that she had been trying to rid herself of a headache by walking out in the fresh air.

"My head ached from working indoors all day, ma'am, and I thought the fresh air would clear it. The woods in these parts are very beautiful."

Becky agreed and, while she did not say it, wondered why the girl was this far out—there was similar woodland aplenty around the grounds of Edgewater.

"Does Mrs Bates know you are here? And Tom? Will he not fret if he finds you missing from the house?"

Alice's answer was plausible enough.

"I did tell Mrs Bates I was going out, ma'am, and Tom is asleep in our room. I wasn't going to be long, ma'am; I was just on my way back to the house."

Becky was not inclined to press the issue. Instead, she took the opportunity to send a message to Mrs Bates herself, ensuring thereby that Alice would have to return to the house promptly.

"All right then, but do have a care, Alice. When you return to the house, please tell Mrs Bates that I have gone to visit Mrs Burnett at the Dower House and expect to be back in time for dinner." Indicating the overcast sky, she added, "If it rains, she should send the carriage for me at seven. Now, do not delay; I am not happy that you should be in the woods alone at this hour. It may not be safe."

Alice nodded and looked relieved, "Yes, ma'am, I will return to the house at once, ma'am," she said and turned to go.

Becky waited a few minutes, watching the girl take the path out of the grounds of Rosings Park, before resuming her walk towards the Dower House. Being keen to see her sister as soon as possible, she took a shorter route, cutting across a meadow, rather than following the footpath through Rosings woods.

Arriving at her destination, she found Catherine and some members of her household in an unusual state of high anxiety.

Two of the maids, returning from a visit to Hunsford village, had taken the familiar path through the woods. Not far from the boundary of Rosings Park, they had encountered a man, a stranger whom they had never seen before, who in dress and general aspect had appeared quite frightening to them.

"His clothes were very odd, ma'am, ragged and foreign, like a gypsy, and his face, which was half covered by his hat, was very strange—pinched and desperate looking," said one of the maids, while the other, a quieter younger girl, was still shaking from the encounter.

"I was very afraid, ma'am," she said, and Catherine had to put her arms around her and reassure her that whoever he was, the stranger could not harm her now.

Both girls had been very distressed by the experience, Catherine explained to Becky, whose thoughts went immediately to Alice Grey, who had been walking alone in exactly that part of the woods. She determined, on returning to Edgewater, to draw the attention of all her servants, and especially the women, to the need for caution; alerting them to the presence of a stranger lurking in Rosings woods. It occurred to her that, had she not been in a hurry and decided to walk across the meadow rather than stroll through the woods, she may well have encountered the man herself.

Catherine, having pacified her maids, turned belatedly to her sister, embraced and welcomed her, inviting her into the parlour to partake of tea and cake, but Becky had more pressing matters on her mind.

Her unexpected arrival on the very day she had returned from Derbyshire had surprised Catherine, who had no idea that Becky had received more significant information about Alice Grey and her husband. When Becky produced the material received from Jonathan, Catherine was astonished by the amount of detail the notes contained.

Reading through them, she shook her head, unable to comprehend it all.

"Becky, this is very strange indeed. Why has Alice Grey been so reluctant to reveal the truth about what happened to her husband? If she is keen to find him or even to learn of his fate, would she not have spoken earlier and told you more about it? I cannot make it out," she said.

Becky nodded. "Indeed, in ordinary circumstances, one would have thought so, Cathy, unless of course, she fears that some other party may discover it too and may try to harm him in some way. Remember that William Rickman is still a convicted felon, and if it is true, as Alice swears it is, that he was indeed innocent, then should the man who informed against him discover his present whereabouts, is it not understandable that Alice would have fears that her husband may be in some danger from him?"

Catherine was not always inclined to accept her sister's more dramatic interpretations of situations; Becky's creative imagination could often eclipse her judgment of the facts of a case.

Catherine could recall occasions when Becky, with little material evidence to support her contention, had mounted a case that, when looked at more logically, did not stand up to scrutiny. She remembered teasing her sister and urging her to "go away and write a novella," but this time, she had to admit that Becky was being particularly persuasive.

She could not dismiss her arguments as exaggeration or flights of fancy, nor could she find some more mundane explanation to put in their place.

Both the behaviour of the girl, Alice Grey, and the information contained in Mr Elliott's notes did suggest that something quite extraordinary was afoot.

"I do wish Frank were here," she said. "I should have liked to have the benefit of his opinion on this matter. He has had much more experience of such matters and should be able to advise us. You would have no objection, would you, Becky, if we were to lay this information before him and ask his opinion?" asked Catherine, and Becky indicated immediately that she would not.

She had a good deal of respect for her brother-in-law's knowledge and understanding of legal matters, as well as his sound common sense.

"It is such a pity that he has had to go up to London and does not return until tomorrow. If you would leave these with me, I could let him read them, and perhaps we could bring them back to you at Edgewater," Catherine suggested, and Becky agreed, inviting both Catherine and her husband to dine with her on Sunday.

"I should very much like to hear Mr Burnett's opinion," she said, adding, "Meanwhile, I intend to question Alice Grey again; I am keen to discover more about the circumstances of Rickman's arrest and conviction, especially the identity of his employer and the informant upon whose evidence he was convicted. I cannot help thinking there must have been some connection between them."

"Do you mean they may have colluded to have him sent down?"

"It is possible, but I have no proof, nor will I have, unless Alice can give me more information. Oh Cathy, it is frustrating not to have the pieces of the puzzle, especially when I know she can give them to me. I cannot understand why she will not. I have given her my word that I will not reveal the information to anyone who can use it to harm her or her husband."

The sound of rolling thunder in the mountains and a bolt of lightning that lit up the sky alerted them to the lateness of the hour, and Becky rose from her seat. "It is time I was going," she said, but Catherine would not hear of it. "You cannot leave now; the rain is just minutes away, and you will be soaked through, long before you reach Edgewater. Besides, Becky, do you not think it unwise to walk home alone? I know I shall be worried sick."

Becky reassured her sister, recalling her instruction to Alice to ask Mrs Bates to send the carriage for her if it should rain. She was persuaded to take another cup of tea just as a drenching shower broke over the area.

Some half an hour later the carriage from Edgewater arrived, and Becky departed, leaving her packet of notes with Catherine, who could not entirely quell her anxiety as she watched her sister leave. Having led a quiet and mostly untroubled existence, free of contact with the sort of situation in which Becky was currently involved, Catherine Burnett could not help feeling apprehensive.

Becky's journey was for the most part uneventful, although she could not deny that her pulse raced as darkness fell and they had to make their way along winding, deserted roads. The fact that one could not see outside because of the heavy rain served only to heighten the feeling of unease, and she was glad indeed when they turned into the drive at Edgewater.

The housekeeper had been awaiting her return, and when Becky summoned her upstairs and urged her to warn the servants about the stranger in the woods, she was amazed to learn that Mrs Bates had a tale of her own to tell. Two of the servants had already reported seeing a strange man in the area around the property. A lad working in the lower meadow, binding up hay, had noticed someone lurking in the lane beyond the hedgerows and had gone to investigate, only to see a man clad in strange clothes and a large hat running away in the direction of the churchyard.

Another of the labourers had claimed to have been accosted on his way home the previous night, in the lane way behind the church, by a stranger who asked for food or money. Having neither in hand, he had offered him some fruit, green apples he had picked earlier in the day, and had watched as the man ate them greedily, as if he had not eaten in days. The lads believed the men were escaped convicts.

Both descriptions sounded very similar to that Becky had heard from the maids at the Dower House, and she had no doubt they had all seen the same man.

Disturbed, Becky asked Mrs Bates to call the servants together and went downstairs herself to impress upon them the need to take great care when they were outside the property.

"I would ask you especially to avoid going into the woods alone. Keep within the boundaries of Edgewater, where you are quite safe, and should you see any stranger at all, return to the house at once and report it to Mrs Bates or to me, and I shall send immediately for the constabulary. Indeed, I intend to inform them tomorrow of what has occurred already and ask that they keep a close watch on the area. If there is anyone up to mischief around here, they will soon be caught and locked up."

Becky sounded very serious, and most of the servants, particularly the women, looked anxious. Tales of escaped convicts troubled them. Trying to reassure them that there was no need to panic, she went on.

"Meanwhile, do try not to put yourselves in harm's way. We do not know who this man is—he may be just a harmless tramp or someone more dangerous. I shall rely on you to be watchful and report anything untoward to me immediately."

Later that night, after dinner, when most of the servants had retired to their rooms, Becky sent for Alice Grey.

She had noticed that the girl had been very quiet when she had addressed the servants warning them of the presence of the stranger in the woods. This time, she was quite determined to discover more about Alice's situation than she had revealed previously.

She had made up her mind to be frank.

"Tell me, Alice," she began as the girl entered the room, "why have you not been honest with me? All I have endeavoured to do is help you and your son, yet you have not been entirely truthful, Alice, or should I call you Annabel Grey?"

The astonishment upon the girl's countenance betrayed her total discomposure, even fear.

Becky went on, "I am informed that your husband William Rickman was convicted of stealing and reselling the stolen goods…"

The girl interrupted her, crying out, "Please, ma'am, I did say he was innocent, it was not true."

"Why should I believe you when you have not even told me truthfully who you are? You say your name is Alice Grey—my information is that before you married William Rickman you were Miss Annabel Grey, the daughter of a gentleman, a Mr Edward Grey of Maidstone. Is this true?"

The girl nodded and there were tears in her eyes.

Becky was touched, but, still determined to discover the truth, she persisted. "Why then did you lie to me, Alice? Why did you say your parents were dead?"

The girl spoke softly, "I am sorry, ma'am. It is not because I wished to deceive you—I am truly grateful for your help—but I was hoping to avoid trouble by keeping my past secret. I thought if I changed my name and moved away from Blessington, things would get easier for me. It seems I was wrong."

"What things? What trouble were you trying to avoid? Who were you trying to escape from when you left Blessington?"

The girl was silent. When she got no immediate answer, Becky pressed her further, though her tone was gentler.

"Was it the man who informed against your husband, or were you trying to get away from the man who pestered you at the Bancrofts' house?"

There was a long, uncomfortable pause. The girl blew her nose and looked up at Becky before answering, "Yes, ma'am."

Puzzled, Becky asked, "Which man was it?"

The girl replied in a low voice, as if she was afraid of being overheard, "It was the same man, ma'am; his name was Danby. He would not let me alone. His uncle managed the brewery at which my husband William worked. They were friends of Mr Bancroft, not Mrs Bancroft; she did not like them. She knew what they were after, and she protected me, and it was she helped me get away, else I might surely have been destroyed, ma'am."

This time it was Becky who said nothing, stunned into silence by what she had heard.

As the girl's story poured out, it seemed an incredible tale, yet Becky did not disbelieve her.

"Mr Danby's uncle, the manager at the brewery, gave William the job, ma'am, and it helped us to get married, even though my parents would not give us their blessing. We had a little place in the village, and Tom was born there. We were very happy together, ma'am. But after a while, Mr Danby arrived, and he was always picking on William. He thought there was something going on, but he did not want to be involved. He did nothing wrong, ma'am, but Mr Danby and his uncle, they wanted to be rid of him. Mr Danby had friends in the police, and they used them to make trouble for William."

"Do you mean he was falsely accused, and the police knew it was a false accusation but prosecuted him regardless?" asked Becky, horrified.

The girl insisted, "Yes, ma'am. No one who knew William believed he had done it. None of the men who worked with him would speak ill of him. The publican was bribed to give false evidence against him, and Mr Danby took it to the police. The police and the magistrate believed Mr Danby because they think he is a fine gentleman, always dressed up posh and with plenty of money to throw around; but in truth, he is no gentleman at all, ma'am. I reckon it was all done to get rid of William and get a hold of me."

Despite the shocking nature of her accusations, Becky found herself believing the girl's story. Nothing about it sounded false.

After a while, she asked, "And how much did Mrs Bancroft know of all this?"

"She did not know about the false witness, ma'am, I don't think. She found me when she came over to the workhouse looking to hire a kitchen maid. Seeing me with my boy, she took pity on us and gave me the job. She was very good to us, ma'am. I cannot tell what would have happened to us if she hadn't found us and taken us in. It's a dreadful place, the workhouse."

There was by now no doubt in Becky's mind that the girl was telling the truth. Clearly fear and lack of trust had prevented her speaking out before.

When Alice had finished, Becky felt enough had been said for the moment, and, reassuring her that she would speak of these matters to no one other than her own sister, Mrs Burnett, she sent the girl away, but not before cautioning her again about not wandering out into the woods alone.

"Alice, I shall continue to call you Alice if that is what you wish, and I will do all I can to help you. But you should be very careful. We do not know who this stranger might be. You may be in grave danger. Do remember what I have told you, and take great care."

The girl nodded and said, "Yes, ma'am, I will, and thank you, ma'am. May I ask how you came by this information, ma'am?"

Becky could give her no answer, except to say, "I cannot reveal that, Alice, but it is not anyone who will wish to harm you."

Alice nodded and went to her room, leaving Becky deeply troubled and confused.

In all her life, in all of her varied undertakings for the communities at Matlock, Becky had not become so intimately involved in the life of someone like Annabel Grey—a person wholly unconnected to herself or her family, yet for whom she was beginning to feel a particular affection.

While she had helped rehabilitate and educate many young women and, for their sakes, battled the councillors and parliamentarians who had stood in her way, it had been as part of her charitable activities, rather than a personal crusade.

What was it, she wondered, about the girl Annabel Grey that had been so different as to warrant such single-minded attention? How had she come to be drawn in so deeply, as though the girl and her child were her own flesh and blood?

The thought that Annabel (or Alice) brought back memories of Josie had pushed itself up once or twice, but she had swiftly thrust it away. She could not possibly be like Josie, she told herself. Josie had been young and independent, smart and ambitious, quite unlike poor Annabel Grey, clearly a victim of unhappy circumstances.

Yet, as she went upstairs to bed, it was the recollection of Josie that occupied her mind, recollections of a vivid and attractive young woman with a bright, promising future, who had been deceived and taken advantage of by callous and pitiless men.

These disturbing thoughts kept her awake into the small hours, until sheer weariness brought sleep.

Chapter Six

ON SUNDAY EVENING, CATHERINE and Frank Burnett arrived to dine at Edgewater. Becky had waited impatiently all day to see them, more particularly now she had learnt so much more from Alice Grey, which could throw some light on the situation. She was especially keen to have her brother-in-law's opinion, knowing he had a much wider knowledge of the ways of the world and matters pertaining to the law.

She had spent most of the day in a state of mind that ranged from bewilderment to agitation and anger. She hoped Catherine and more particularly Frank Burnett would help bring some clarity to her confused thoughts.

Assuming, as it happened correctly, that her sister would surely have apprised her husband of the salient facts of the matter and shown him Mr Elliot's notes, Becky waited until dinner was over and the servants had withdrawn downstairs to partake of their own meal to introduce the subject. She did so with not a little trepidation, for she was as yet uncertain of all the facts and had only the girl's word regarding the false accusation and conviction of William Rickman.

Becky could not be certain that Mr Burnett would be as willing as she had been to accept Alice Grey's story.

However, she was pleasantly surprised to discover that he was prepared to listen attentively, asking several pertinent questions, seeking to clarify a number of matters, before saying in a rather serious voice, "While it is impossible to vouch for the truth or otherwise of the young person's story, I have to admit that from your recital of it, it does ring true.

"I have seen many similar cases in the Midlands and the North Country where false witness was used against innocent men and women for quite malicious reasons. It is quite plausible that Rickman was a victim of the same pernicious practice, whereby the real criminals escape by having an innocent person convicted of their crime."

Becky expressed her disgust.

"Do you really mean to say that a perfectly innocent person would be convicted and punished while the real perpetrators got away?"

"Indeed, and often continued their careers of crime undeterred," Mr Burnett confirmed.

Both Catherine and Becky were outraged at such injustice. "And can nothing be done to protect these innocent people?" asked Catherine.

"Very little, my dear," her husband replied. "There have been a few instances where as a result of the intervention of some influential person or a charitable lawyer, who has taken up the cause of a particular prisoner, a pardon has been granted by the Crown."

"A pardon? But if he is innocent?" Catherine seemed confused.

"I fear it is generally far too difficult to *prove* that a miscarriage of justice had occurred, due to bribery or corruption or both. It is probably easier, just occasionally, to convince the Crown or a benevolent governor to grant a pardon on the grounds that the person maybe a victim of mistaken identity or malicious false witness."

"And would that help to get a prisoner pardoned and released?" asked Becky.

"It might do, in the right circumstances and if the prisoner has a record of good behaviour. However, I think it will be impossible to take any action to help Alice Grey and her husband, unless and until we can put together some material relating to the trial and conviction and, if it is at all possible, discover the present whereabouts of Rickman himself."

Turning to Becky, he said, "If the girl can be persuaded to give you some clue—and I venture to suggest that she may well know more than she is willing to reveal, probably out of fear of exposing him—then it should be easier to uncover some part of the truth at least."

Becky was delighted with Frank Burnett's response; not only had he taken her concerns seriously, but he had clearly thought about the possibility of discovering the truth, which was all Becky had aimed to do.

"And if we did find some useful information, how exactly would that help Rickman?" she asked. "If I could tell Alice how we might assist her husband, it may provide her with a strong motive to reveal more about his circumstances."

Frank Burnett shook his head as if puzzled by the question.

"What stronger motivation could she need than the prospect of seeing her husband free again? If she provides you with the information, it may well be possible to persuade someone in Parliament to take an appeal to the government; especially if sufficient evidence can be adduced to suggest that he *was* a victim of false witness. There are many honourable and ambitious young men in the Parliament today who are deeply concerned about such matters and are not afraid to speak out. However," and at this point, Frank Burnett looked exceedingly serious as he continued, "she should be made aware that only the truth and nothing but the truth will suffice. Were she to resort to lies, misleading rumours, or hearsay, she will not only jeopardise any chance of a successful appeal for a pardon, but she may well find herself in trouble too."

Becky nodded, realising the seriousness of this enterprise, but determined nevertheless to do whatever was necessary to achieve what had become something of a personal crusade. She thanked Mr Burnett for his sage advice.

"Thank you, Frank, I shall make that very clear to Alice," she promised.

When Catherine and Frank Burnett left Edgewater to return home, Becky went up to her room, feeling somewhat more hopeful than before.

Before retiring to bed, however, she composed a letter to Mrs Bancroft, introducing herself and requesting a meeting with her to discuss a charitable project concerning the rehabilitation of young women and their children.

I have recently become aware through my friend, Mrs Emma Wilson, of your work in helping these sad and unfortunate young persons, and while I hasten to say that I am not seeking any financial donations, I would very much appreciate your valuable advice in this regard,

...she wrote, hoping that Mrs Bancroft's kindly nature would be sufficiently moved to let her agree to a meeting.

If you are agreeable, we could arrange to meet at a place and time convenient to you. I would be prepared to travel to meet you wherever you propose.

Becky concluded with kind regards and expressed a hope they could meet soon.

Ideally, Becky would have liked to have discussed her plan with Catherine, but she had had no opportunity to do so. She was convinced that Mrs Bancroft must know something of what had occurred between the girl she had rescued from the workhouse and Mr Danby, her husband's friend.

It was, to her mind, not credible that Mrs Bancroft, who, if Alice was speaking the truth, had materially assisted the girl to get away from Danby, would not have known more of the circumstances under which Alice's husband had been convicted and sent to prison, when it was Danby and his uncle who had initiated the prosecution.

Becky did not think it likely that a woman of Mrs Bancroft's understanding would not have made it her business to discover the facts, unless she too had been deceived. If she had been the victim of such deception, then Becky was determined to disabuse her and ask for her help in uncovering the truth.

She was not without some reservations, in that she was concerned that Mrs Bancroft might rebuff her approach; however, the picture of the lady drawn by Alice Grey gave her reason to hope.

A woman as kind and generous as Mrs Bancroft had to be—to have taken a young girl and her child from the workhouse and afforded them protection—was unlikely to refuse to help them now, or so Becky argued. Even as she did so, she understood that she was indeed gambling on Mrs Bancroft's good nature. She could only hope that it would be justified.

Two letters arrived simultaneously at Edgewater a fortnight later.

The first, from Jonathan Bingley, was opened by Becky even before she reached her study.

It contained two short paragraphs.

Acknowledging hers, in which Becky had sent her compliments and thanks for his assistance with the case of William Rickman, Jonathan provided Becky with a piece of information that had been sent to him confidentially by his son-in-law, Mr Elliott.

It revealed the names of the complainant and witnesses, as well as the assizes at which a magistrate had tried and convicted William Rickman and sentenced him to be transported to Van Dieman's Land.

When it became apparent that this was no longer possible under the new law, the sentence had been changed to incarceration—temporarily upon a prison hulk in the estuary and subsequently in a jail somewhere on the Romney Marshes.

Mr Elliot stated briefly that despite his enquiries, he could find no further information about William Rickman on record.

I urge you, Becky, wrote Jonathan, *to use this information with great discretion; it may assist you to progress the investigation you have undertaken, but it must be remembered, those who have provided it have taken a very great risk in making it available, and Colin Elliott has asked that you pay particular attention to the need to keep secret his identity as the source of the material.*

Jonathan Bingley expressed his confidence that Becky would be responsible in her use of the information and offered her any further assistance it was in his power to provide.

Delighted, Becky turned quickly to her second letter.

Elegantly written on fine notepaper, in it, Mrs Bancroft thanked Becky for hers and expressed her pleasure at receiving it, before acceding to her request for a meeting. She wrote:

I should be happy to meet you to discuss the important subject of improving the lot of young women. Although it is not a matter on which I can claim any special knowledge, I have heard from Mrs Wilson, with whom I have been involved in some charitable work, that both you and the late Mr Tate have worked assiduously to persuade parish and local councils in the Midlands to educate and protect young persons. This must surely be most rewarding work, and I congratulate you on your achievements. While my experience in this field is not extensive, I would be pleased to discuss with you any scheme that helps these unfortunate women and their unhappy children.

I am aware of some cases of young women who, through foolishness or lack of knowledge, have been deceived and exploited by unscrupulous men, who will take advantage of them, and I would be interested to talk with you about them. If it were possible to find ways to rescue these unhappy women from what must be a dreadful fate, I should be most happy to assist.

There followed a most gracious invitation:

As to our meeting, should you wish to visit and stay to dinner, I would be delighted to see you at home, at the manor house in Blessington, Saturday week, if that would suit.

Becky could not believe her good fortune—this response was more than she had ever dreamed of. It would give her an excellent opportunity to discover how much Mrs Bancroft knew.

She set off immediately for the Dower House to acquaint her sister with her plans.

Catherine was as astonished as her sister had been, particularly because she had been ignorant of Becky's intention to approach Mrs Bancroft.

"Did you not tell me in case I advised against it, Becky?" she teased, but Becky was quick to deny this.

"Indeed no, my dear Catherine, how could you possibly think such a thing? I confess I had some doubts as to whether you would approve, but the letter was written on the spur of the moment—some time after Frank and you had left to return home—and sent away to the post the very next morning, before I had time to change my mind. I had spent so much time wondering how we might get some of the facts about this wretched matter, I could think of no other person to whom I might appeal.

"Mrs Bancroft, I thought, was bound to know something of what lay behind the conviction of William Rickman. Of course, I had not at that stage received Jonathan's letter with Mr Elliott's information, which means I am now even better placed to make the best of my meeting with Mrs Bancroft."

"You are indeed," replied her sister, adding with a smile, "Oh Becky, I can see why Mr Tate used to say you were like a terrier—you will not let go."

Becky smiled as she recalled the days when she had indeed played such a role for her husband, following up every lead that might spell success for one of his campaigns. They had made a good team then and had enjoyed some happy times.

But the nostalgic memory was quickly replaced by the urgent need to prepare for her meeting with Mrs Bancroft.

"Is it not a stroke of great good fortune that she already knows of my work through Emma Wilson?" she asked, and Catherine had to agree.

"Of course, I must say that was unexpected, though, Becky, it ought not be. After all, Standish Park is not far from Blessington, and the Wilsons are both well regarded in the county," said Catherine, who argued, "With James being a judge and Emma's long involvement in charitable activities, it is not at all surprising that the Bancrofts should know them."

"I daresay you are right, Cathy, but I do note that Mrs Bancroft does not mention her husband at all. Does that not strike you as unusual?" asked her sister, clearly implying she had some suspicions on that score.

Catherine shrugged her shoulders.

"Unusual perhaps, but then not all husbands become involved in their wives' charitable activities. Emma Wilson will tell you her first husband, David, had no interest whatsoever in hers."

Becky agreed, but could not entirely dismiss her misgivings.

Before her meeting with Mrs Bancroft, Becky decided she had to see Emma Wilson and, to that end, despatched a manservant with a letter, in which she asked if she might call on her on the Saturday following.

The letter arriving at Standish Park threw Emma Wilson into something of a quandary. She was much less intimately acquainted with Becky Tate than with her sister, Catherine, and was somewhat discomfited by the fact that she was not aware of the reason for Becky's request to see her.

But Emma Wilson was nothing if not polite and hospitable.

Her husband was in London and would not be home until Friday evening; but with the certainty that he could not possibly object to the visit, she responded immediately that she would be happy to have Becky visit, inviting her to dine with the family and stay overnight at Standish Park.

Emma could not help wondering, however, what it was that had caused Becky Tate to write with what was clearly an urgent request for a meeting.

They had met fairly often when Mr Wilson had been in Parliament and Mr Tate had been involved in a number of political campaigns, but most times it had been either at the Tates' residence or Mr Wilson's apartments in London. Emma could recall but one occasion, when the Tates had attended a celebratory dinner party at Standish Park, and that had been many years ago.

She had heard from her brother Jonathan that Becky had purchased a property in Kent after her husband's death and had assumed, that since they now lived in the same county, they would surely meet, but for a variety of reasons, a meeting had not come to pass.

Emma sighed and decided that perhaps it was better late than never.

When James Wilson returned from London, where the weather had been decidedly worse than it was in Kent, he found his beloved wife still puzzled by the request she had received from Becky Tate.

After they had dined and retired to their room, she brought out the note she had received and asked, "Dearest, do you suppose Becky is in some trouble? Could it be she is in need of some legal advice, perhaps?"

Mr Wilson, formerly an attorney at law and now a judge, smiled indulgently at his wife's anxious expression.

"If Mrs Tate was in need of legal advice, she could purchase the best in the land, my love. I understand from your brother Jonathan that Mr Tate has left her very well provided for. No, Emma, I do not believe it is a legal question that brings her to Standish Park; from my own knowledge of Mrs Tate, I would venture to suggest that she is probably seeking your support for some new scheme—a school for girls, a home for orphans, or some such worthy enterprise. Mrs Tate's enthusiasm for such activities does not seem to have abated at all," he said.

Happy indeed to have her dear husband home, for she missed his company when he was away, Emma had no wish to contradict him, but she was not so sure that he was entirely right.

❧

Becky Tate, arriving around mid-morning at Standish Park, noted even as she alighted from her vehicle that the grounds were some of the finest she had seen anywhere in England.

She had visited Standish Park on a previous occasion, together with Mr Tate, but that had been in Winter, when the park and its environs could not be seen at their best. She stood for a moment at the entrance, her eyes taking in the beauty of vivid green lawns and trees clothed in the soft hues of early Autumn, before Emma Wilson herself came out to greet her and take her indoors.

The house was as she recalled it, a gracious building, whose elegant furnishings and accessories spoke of the excellent taste of its owners.

Friendly and hospitable, Emma Wilson made Becky welcome and conveyed her husband's excuses; he was attending a council meeting at Cranbrook and would join them at dinner, she said, and was interested to note that Becky did not appear at all discomposed by this information.

It suggested to her that Mr Wilson was right and Becky's visit was not designed to seek his advice on a legal matter.

After the initial courtesies, Emma led the way to a private sitting room upstairs, where they were served a light luncheon and tea, before Becky was finally afforded the opportunity to speak with Emma alone.

She began by apologising for her letter requesting a meeting.

"Emma, I must ask you to forgive my seeming impertinence in writing to you as I did. It must have looked as though I was fishing for an invitation to your home... Please let me explain why I—"

But Emma Wilson, whose kindness of heart would not allow her to listen to such a recital, interrupted her.

"My dear Becky, there is no need to apologise. I most certainly did not regard your letter as an impertinence. Why would I? I confess I was a little puzzled as to the reason for such an urgent request, but I think I know you well enough to be certain that it would not have been made without a very good reason. Besides, we are neighbours now, since you have moved to live in Kent, and we ought be visiting one another. Indeed, I feel I have been remiss in not calling on you in your new home; Jonathan tells me you have acquired a most attractive property not far from Rosings Park."

Becky smiled.

"You are very kind, Emma. Yes, I am very happy with Edgewater, and you must visit me there soon, but it is a modest place, nothing when compared to the splendid estate you have here."

While Emma agreed that Standish Park *was* a beautiful estate, she was quick to point out that it was her husband's family property, refraining modestly from any boastful display, even as she acknowledged Becky's appreciation.

Happy that Emma had not resented her visit, Becky proceeded directly to its main purpose. But once again, she felt the need to ask for her forbearance, as she began her story, promising that while it may seem a long and complicated tale, all would soon be explained.

Through the afternoon, Emma listened quietly as Becky narrated the facts as she knew or had discovered them concerning the girl Alice Grey, her husband William Rickman, and their son Thomas.

She seemed shocked at some of the incidents and yet unsurprised by much of what Becky revealed. Emma Wilson had seen several instances of exploitation and betrayal before, and in her charitable activities had helped many young women like Alice Grey find work or homes for their children.

However, when Becky mentioned for the first time Mrs Bancroft and the manor house at Blessington, Emma sat up, alert and eager for information.

"Mrs Bancroft, how is she involved?"

Becky, whose intention in coming to Standish Park had been mainly to discover something of the background of the Bancrofts, was happy to oblige with a brief summary of Mrs Bancroft's connection with Alice Grey, including some detail of the persecution of the girl by one Mr Danby and her timely rescue from the workhouse by Mrs Bancroft.

She then asked, "Are you well acquainted with the Bancrofts, Emma?"

Emma's reply surprised Becky.

"No, not very well acquainted at all; indeed I have never met Mr Bancroft, but Mrs Bancroft has occasionally worked with my group of ladies, who have tried to help abandoned young women and their children.

"Some are left in dire circumstances, rejected by their families and ostracised by the communities in which they live, which is why I am not entirely surprised by your story. However, the matter of the girl's husband being convicted as a result of false testimony is new to me. I am shocked that the magistrate would have permitted such a thing to happen. Tell me, Becky, did you learn of this from Mrs Bancroft herself?"

"Indeed no; I am not at liberty to divulge the source of my information, but I can say it was certainly not Mrs Bancroft. But why do you ask, Emma?"

Becky was curious, and Emma's reply inflamed that curiosity to a much higher degree.

"Because," said Emma quietly, "the magistrate for the district which includes Blessington is Mr Bancroft. I may be wrong, but I don't think I am. James would certainly be able to confirm this when he returns this evening."

The expression of utter shock upon Becky's countenance convinced Emma that her guest knew little or nothing of the Bancrofts. An idea began to form in her mind then that Becky had come to Standish Park to seek information about Mr and Mrs Bancroft.

It was quickly confirmed when Becky said, "Emma, I should have been frank with you at the outset. I wish to help Alice Grey find her husband, who we are led to believe was falsely accused and convicted some years ago in Ramsgate, and to that end, I have approached Mrs Bancroft. Alice tells me Mrs Bancroft rescued her from the workhouse, gave her work and a place to stay, and then helped her escape the unwelcome advances of a certain Mr Danby, a friend of Mr. Bancroft.

"Mrs Bancroft has invited me to dinner on Saturday week and, in her letter to me, mentioned that she had heard of my work for charity from you. My intention in coming here today was chiefly to ask your advice on how best to deal with the Bancrofts. I had thought that you and Mr Wilson were probably acquainted with them, and I have to admit that I had no inkling at the time that Mr Bancroft was the magistrate for the district.

"Now, once more, let me apologise, Emma, for not revealing my intentions when I wrote, but I am very much in the debt of someone who has obtained this information for me and have promised to use it with the utmost discretion. I am not at liberty to say more."

Becky was very embarrassed, wondering what Emma would say if she knew it was her brother Jonathan Bingley and his son-in-law Colin Elliott who were her informants. Still, she had no other course open to her—she had given them her word. She hoped fervently that Emma Wilson would not persevere with her inquiries.

However, it seemed Emma, having been sufficiently astonished by Becky's revelations, did not seek to discover their source. She asked no more questions on the subject, but as was her wont, seemed more interested in the matter of the girl Alice Grey and the Bancrofts.

Admitting that she had not heard Mrs Bancroft mention the case at all, she said, "I am not entirely surprised, Becky, that Mrs Bancroft should be reserved about a matter that may have involved her husband and one of his friends. I do not wish to speak ill of anyone, but if the truth were known—and you do need to know the truth if you are to deal with them—the Bancrofts, and in particular Mr Bancroft and his friends, are not very well regarded in the community. Mr Bancroft, although he is a magistrate, has been known to indulge in rather riotous behaviour when he is in his cups—which is quite often, I understand, and as for his friends, the less said of them, the better.

"I had not heard of a Mr Danby, James may know of him, but I do know that two others—a notorious gambler called Knowles and a young tearaway from the militia, a Colonel Hackforth—were noted for their outrageous conduct in the town and have been before the court on more than one occasion, with very little consequence.

"They had become accustomed to getting away with it because the magistrate Mr Bancroft would send them off with a rap over the knuckles, but when they came before a judge of the County Court, they were taught a severe lesson and transported to Van Dieman's Land," said Emma with a deep sense of satisfaction.

"Transported to Van Dieman's Land?"

Becky was amazed.

But Emma was quite sanguine.

"Indeed, and I have to say there was not heard a single voice raised in support of them nor anyone who expressed any sympathy for them. Their crimes were so heinous and so frequent that it is said the villagers would lock and bar their houses and barns when they were known to be in the area, to secure their daughters and their livestock."

"And Mr Bancroft tolerated all of this?"

"He did, because they were his friends—Knowles had been at college with him, and Colonel Hackforth was his cousin."

"And Mrs Bancroft? How was she culpable?" Becky asked.

"Oh more by omission than commission, I believe," Emma explained. "She was for many years a rather timid woman, having married her husband when she was quite a young girl. I understand he was handsome and rich when they met, and she, having married him, remained loyal to him. I daresay, Becky, she would not be the first young woman to make such an error," said Emma, whose own life experience would not let her censure Mrs Bancroft or any other young woman for lacking judgment in her youth.

Becky concurred and listened as Emma continued.

"You would not believe it now, but James says Mr Bancroft read Classics at Oxford and graduated with honours before taking up the law. But greed and a total lack of self-discipline seem to have destroyed his character, and Mrs Bancroft has probably discovered to her cost that he was no longer the man she had married."

"Do they have any children?" Becky asked, beginning to feel some sympathy for the unfortunate Mrs Bancroft.

"Two daughters—Hermione and Diana—classical names as you can see, but, I am informed, both rather self-willed and more like their father than Mrs Bancroft. To the best of my knowledge, they have very little in common with their mother and are not inclined to participate in her charitable work. I understand they spend most of their time with their relations in London, enjoying the dubious delights of the city," said Emma, leaving Becky in no doubt of her opinion on the matter.

The arrival of the maid with news that Mr Wilson had returned brought their conversation to an end, but not before Emma had promised to ask her husband for more information about Mr Bancroft, if it would help.

Grateful and more surprised than she had expected to be, Becky retired to her room to rest awhile before preparing to dress for dinner.

Chapter Seven

B ECKY TATE'S DIARY WENT everywhere with her.

Each night, before she retired to bed, she made the entries for the day just gone. Her writer's instincts acted as an excellent discipline whenever she travelled, for she would make copious notes of everything, no matter how trivial, and record them together with her own observations and feelings.

Over the next few days, during her short but significant visits to Standish Park and later Blessington Manor, Becky's diary made engrossing reading.

This is such a delightful place, she wrote that night as she enthused over the hospitality and comforts she had enjoyed at Standish Park.

> *It is no wonder Emma seems so content. Yet there is so much more to her happiness than the elegance and comfort that marriage to Mr Wilson has brought; there is here real contentment, the kind that comes only with genuine love and deep satisfaction.*
>
> *That Emma and James love each other deeply is clear to anyone who observes them together. Their affection for one another is unambiguously expressed in everything they do.*
>
> *Going down to dinner, I entered the room and surprised them standing together by the windows overlooking the terrace, close together, talking softly, touching, like lovers, unwilling to move apart. Even when they knew I was there, as I very quickly apologised for having walked in upon*

them without knocking, there was not even a hint of discomposure. Emma smiled, and James came forward to greet me cordially and asked if I had had a comfortable journey.

Thereafter, having performed the usual courtesies as a good host should, he went back to sit on the sofa beside his loving wife, as though reluctant to leave her side.

At dinner, where we were joined by Emma's eldest daughter Victoria and her husband Mr Edward Fairfax, James and Emma sat, not at opposite ends of the long dining table, remote from one another as most couples do, but rather, she sat to his left, and I was invited to take the chair on his right, while Victoria and her husband sat one down from each of us.

Their two boys, Charles and Colin, are both at College, progressing well in their studies and expecting to go up to Cambridge, Emma says, with justifiable but not excessive pride. Her modesty is perhaps the best thing about her, though there is much to love and admire in Emma Wilson.

It was clearly difficult for Becky to conceal her feelings as she described the domestic bliss she sensed at Standish Park. Her own life had been very different. In Becky's marriage to Mr Tate, there had been little closeness of the kind she could sense between Emma and her husband, while the warmth of the Wilsons' bonds with their children contrasted with the sorry state of her own relationship with her son Walter and his wife, Pauline.

Becky wrote:

Emma's closeness to her children must be a source of great happiness, increasing surely the contentment she feels in her marriage.

Clearly Victoria enjoys an enviable affinity with her mother, and I understand from her that when the two boys are home, Emma dotes upon them. How fortunate must such a woman be.

I can truly say that apart from Richard Gardiner and Cassy, I have not seen such open affection between a married couple. There must be many who would long for such enviable intimacy.

Apart from noting with an understandable degree of benign envy the domestic bliss of the Wilsons, Becky also gathered some useful information of the sort she had come to Standish Park to find. Both Mr Wilson and Mr Fairfax had strong opinions on the conduct of the magistrate, Mr Bancroft, and the nature of his dealings with some of his friends.

She recorded the salient points for future reference.

James Wilson was the more discreet of the two men; being himself a judge, no doubt he was unwilling to speak ill of a fellow judicial officer, but even he did not deny that Bancroft had acquired a reputation for favouring his friends and relations. The fact that many of these people were heartily loathed by the general populace did not improve matters for him.

Mr Wilson was of the opinion that Bancroft's judgments were often affected by either friendship or alcohol or both.

Mr Edward Fairfax was much less restrained. Younger and more outspoken, he made it quite clear that he considered Mr Bancroft both ineffective and corrupt, to the point that his young wife felt constrained to intervene and caution him—but he was quite unapologetic

"The man's a blackguard, my dear," he said with brutal frankness, "it is common knowledge that he consorts with the lowest types—lazy rich men with no scruples, who get away with crimes that would see a working man hang!"

Becky had been amazed at the hostility expressed towards Mr Bancroft. She mused:

It does seem that the Bancrofts are not as well regarded as one might have expected them to be, largely on account of Mr Bancroft's reputation for nepotism and corruption. Unfortunately, his wife does not seem to get much credit for her charitable work, which Emma Wilson does vouch for, while her errant husband is roundly condemned for his misdeeds.

I wonder if I am to meet Mr Bancroft at Blessington Manor?

How then should I behave towards him, knowing as I do now that he is such a man? It would be impolite indeed to my hostess Mrs Bancroft, were I to show displeasure or aloofness towards her husband; yet how am

I to contain my feelings of abhorrence, since I am so well aware of his reprehensible conduct? Poor Mrs Bancroft, how must she feel knowing all this, as she surely must?

It is a matter that requires much more thought than I have time for now.

Becky could not decide how to deal with a situation that clearly she had not anticipated. She was determined, however, to be circumspect and diplomatic in her approach to Mrs Bancroft, as her main aim was to gain her confidence and assistance for the benefit of Alice Grey and her husband.

Awaking early on the following morning and looking out on the exquisite prospect that stretched across the river away into the distance, Becky felt an urge to be dressed quickly and walk in the garden before breakfast. The scents and colours of Autumn were all around her, filling her senses as she made her way through the grounds and out towards the orchard. Becky had never experienced such a delightful ambience in her life.

Returning to the house, she entered the breakfast room to find Emma Wilson already at the table. Greeting her cordially, Emma moved to offer Becky tea and toast and a range of delicacies, kept warm in silver dishes upon the sideboard. Becky was in the middle of her meal when James Wilson came into the room, a letter in his hand. Delivered very early that morning, he said, it had been sent from Pemberley by Mr Darcy.

He spoke gently to his wife. "Emma dearest, we have some grave news: Mr Darcy writes that Mrs Emily Courtney is unwell; she has apparently been sick for some considerable time…"

Emma rose from her seat at the table, clearly alarmed. "Mr Darcy has written? What does he say about Emily?"

"He does not give much detail, except to say that Jessica and Julian are gone to Oakleigh to see what needs to be done. He says also that Emily's brother Dr Richard Gardiner is attending upon her."

Emma, obviously distressed, tearful, and concerned, asked, "Does he say how she is progressing?"

"No, but she cannot be in any immediate danger, although it can be assumed that it is a serious condition, else Mr Darcy is not likely to have written with such urgency," her husband replied.

Emma moved to leave the table, asking to be excused. "James, I would very much wish to go to her. Jessica is unlikely to be able to do very much—she has only recently had a child... Do you think I could... Would you...?"

James Wilson did not wait for her to finish before putting an arm around her and reassuring her, "Of course, my dear, I will send for the steward and ask that the carriage be prepared to take us to Rochester. We had best take the train north from there."

Becky had been close to Emily Courtney for many years, but sadly could not offer to accompany them to Derbyshire. Reluctantly, she asked Emma to take her best wishes to Emily, her longtime friend, and promised she would see her very soon.

Later she would write of her sadness at the news.

For many years, when the family at Pemberley regarded me as the villain of the piece, because I had persuaded Josie to marry Julian Darcy, Emily never forsook our friendship. Indeed for a while she was, outside of my own family, my only friend. For that kindness I am ever grateful.

Yet twice in her life, when Emily has faced a crisis, I have not been able to go to her side. It is a matter of the deepest regret to me that this time too, I have another more pressing matter that keeps me from her.

As preparations for the Wilsons' departure proceeded apace, Becky made ready to return to Edgewater. Hers would be a much shorter journey, but she would leave with as heavy a heart as Emma Wilson's, with the added sorrow of being unable to see or assist her friend in any way at this time.

Shortly before leaving, she sought out Emma, who confessed that she had been concerned about Emily Courtney for some time.

"Things have not gone well for Emily ever since Reverend Courtney's illness," she explained. "It was only last month that I received from my mother, who had herself been poorly but thankfully is now on the mend, a most worrying letter, in which she wrote that Mr and Mrs Darcy had been made aware that the Courtneys had very little savings left and their youngest daughter Jessica was concerned, lest her mother should not have sufficient to live on, now she is a widow with no fixed income."

Becky understood Jessica's anxiety; she knew that despite her straitened circumstances, Emily would neither increase the rents paid by her tenants on Oakleigh Manor, nor would she consider retrenching any of her servants. When she pointed this out, Emma agreed and added, "And of course, she supports many of the poor families in the village as she has done for years. I do not mean to suggest that she should not, God bless her, she has the most generous heart in the world, but she will not consider that she must make some allowance for herself too."

Becky expressed her regrets once again at being unable to accompany the Wilsons on their journey, offering her assistance in any way that was necessary.

"If it is a question of money, Emma, please do not hesitate to call on me, because I should be honoured to assist. Emily is the closest friend I have in the family, and it would be my great pleasure to do anything to help. I find it very bewildering that things should have come to this unhappy pass."

It was a circumstance Becky was bound to ponder as she bade farewell to her friends and returned home to Edgewater that afternoon.

Chapter Eight

BECKY TATE, HAVING SPENT a week of nervous anxiety preparing for her visit to Blessington Manor, was within an hour of reaching her destination.

They had left Edgewater early and had made good time, travelling at an easy pace through some of the prettiest countryside in southern England; Becky had to remind herself that this friendly, welcoming county was now, once more, her home.

Having spent most of her adult life in Derbyshire, where the rugged magnificence of the landscape was of such a scale as to awe a young person who had been born and raised in the south, hearing its praises sung constantly by those who lived there, Becky had almost forgotten how engaging and attractive was her own home county, Kent.

With its gentle cultivated slopes bounded by friendly hedgerows, its wide swathes of thick but tidy woodland and verdant pasture surrounding prosperous farms and orchards, Kent had a uniquely pleasing quality that appealed to her present mood.

Much as she had enjoyed her earlier days at Matlock, where with Emily, Caroline, and Cassandra she had been eager to challenge the petty bureaucracies of the councils in order to improve the lives of people in their community, Becky had grown weary of public life, and more recently, she had found her interests centred upon more personal concerns. It was a mood that was more comfortably accommodated within the boundaries of the subtler, gentler environs of the southern counties than the rough-hewn contours of the North.

However, even here, Becky noted, not every prospect was equally pleasing.

As they approached the district in which the village of Blessington was situated, Becky noticed that the countryside had not the sense of spaciousness and prosperity that characterised the surroundings of Standish Park or Rosings. The roads on which they travelled, leaving the main highway, were rutted and uneven, while the lowly farm dwellings that could be seen across the fields were rough and deficient by any standard. They were nothing like the neat cottages of the tenants of Standish Park or Pemberley, and the women and children on the street and in the hedgerows looked much poorer than those she was accustomed to seeing. Clearly, not all landlords were equally concerned with the welfare of the rural poor, thought Becky as they journeyed closer to their destination.

The landscape around Blessington Manor was flat and uninspiring; it had just missed being situated at the point where the river, on its way to Canterbury, broke through the Downs, creating a graceful vista. Instead, it seemed to have been set down at random, without plan or purpose, a dull house in a broad featureless meadow, with neither woodland nor park to attract the eye or soften the aspect.

An orchard of mainly gnarled apple trees was all that clothed the bare surrounding grounds around the manor house. Compared with the simple elegance of Standish Park, Becky judged the building to be rather overdone, with too many windows glinting like pairs of spectacles on the plain brick façade and several nondescript farm buildings clustered around the main edifice.

Becky was disappointed; she had expected better.

"I hope the interior is rather more tasteful than its exterior," she thought as they drew up at the porch.

A manservant appeared and assisted her to alight, while a maid waited at the door to escort her into the house, along a large but unprepossessing hall, lined with trophies of several hunts, into the sitting room, where she was greeted by Mrs Bancroft.

A tall, lean woman with a dignified but kindly countenance, Mrs Bancroft was surprisingly friendly and agreeable. *At the very least*, Becky thought, *she is unlikely to throw me out when she discovers the chief purpose of my visit.*

Indeed, Mrs Bancroft's hospitality was unexceptionable; she had the fire stoked up to a comfortable blaze and ordered that tea be served at once, believing that her guest must be in need of refreshment after her journey across the county.

The two women talked easily of one thing and another and made general conversation ranging through sundry topics from the mild Autumn weather to the desirability of making public education compulsory for all children. On many of these matters they were happily agreed.

There was, however, no sign of Mr Bancroft and no mention of him through tea, which was odd, Becky thought. She assumed this was because he was out attending to business on the manor or presiding over the sittings of the County Court.

It turned out that neither was the case.

Mrs Bancroft, having refrained from making any reference to her husband for an hour or more, suddenly asked that his absence be excused and, by way of explanation, declared that he was from home, attending the assizes at Canterbury, where he had been summoned as a witness in a criminal matter. Becky, though thoroughly taken aback by this piece of unsolicited information, recovered quickly enough to smile and nod as though it was perfectly normal for gentlemen to be so engaged every day of the week. She could not help wondering though, after all she had heard from both Mr Wilson and Mr Edward Fairfax the previous week, what manner of criminal case Mr Bancroft had been summoned to attend.

As for Mrs Bancroft, she seemed completely unperturbed and continued to make conversation and dispense tea and cake until Becky felt compelled to introduce the subject that had been the main reason for her visit.

Almost an hour had elapsed since she had arrived and the servants had cleared away the tea tray before Becky first mentioned Alice Grey.

Seeing the astonished expression on Mrs Bancroft's face, she explained quickly how the girl and her son had been found camping in one of the barns on her property, furtively leaving the place at daybreak to work in the hop fields and returning at nightfall.

"She seemed fearful and timid; it took a great deal of time and effort to persuade her that she was safe from persecution in my household and would not be handed over to the police, of whom she appeared quite terrified," Becky explained.

Mrs Bancroft shook her head, and when she spoke, her voice was soft, as though she did not wish to be overheard. "That does not surprise me, Mrs Tate; she has reason enough to fear the police, poor girl. I am happy to hear she is safe—once she left here, I have had no idea where she might be hiding."

"Hiding?" cried Becky, confused. "Has Alice any reason to hide from the police? I had not thought she would be in any trouble with the law."

"Oh no, she is quite without guilt, but she may fear that the police would reveal her whereabouts to…" Her voice trailed away and she looked thoroughly discomfited as Becky asked, "To whom? Is there someone she particularly fears? Mrs Bancroft, I must appeal to you to be open with me, please. I have taken Alice Grey and her child into my home and given her work and a place to stay, free of worry and harassment. If there is anything I need to know, anything that might lead to involvement in matters outside the law, then I beg you to tell me, not just for my own protection but for the sake of the girl and her son."

Mrs Bancroft's countenance seemed to reflect both gravity and sadness.

Indeed, Becky could not help feeling sorry for her, as she struggled to explain with some degree of coherence that, while Alice Grey had done nothing to attract the wrath of the law, she was in danger of being harassed by others, whose status in society and influence with the officers of the constabulary could well pose a threat to her safety.

Becky grew impatient as her hostess talked around the subject, giving her little information. It seemed to her that Mrs Bancroft was reluctant to provide her with any facts. But as the evening wore on and they went in to dinner, she appeared to accept Becky's bonafides more readily and the disclosures came more quickly.

At first, Becky asked a few questions and received rather innocuous answers, but when she revealed that Alice was clearly afraid of someone and mentioned the name of the man Danby, Mrs Bancroft's face grew taut, and she said almost in a whisper, "Danby's a blackguard! I would not tolerate his presence in my house, but he is one of my husband's friends, and I have no control over *them*."

Becky, deciding to seize the moment, asked, "Was Mr Danby involved in the laying of information against Alice Grey's husband, William Rickman?" and was stunned by the angry response.

"Indeed he was, and so was his uncle the brewer. They were in it together, and I believe they suborned the police and plotted to get rid of Rickman. I am convinced it was a most unjust prosecution. No one in this village believes that Rickman was guilty."

Becky was eager to hear more, and having extracted a promise of secrecy, Mrs Bancroft revealed that Danby had become obsessed with the girl when she lived in the village and had begun to pester her long before she came to work at the manor house.

"I had picked her out at the workhouse after her unfortunate husband had been sent to prison; she wasn't a common village lass. I saw something decent and genuine in her and wished to help the girl," she said, explaining that she had known nothing of Danby's villainy nor the misfortunes of William Rickman at the time.

"But Alice told me soon enough. Although well able to cope with other duties in the house, when I offered the position of chamber maid, she refused and asked to be allowed to work in the kitchen, where she would never be left alone, rather than above stairs, fearing she would be importuned and would have no escape. I said nothing at the time, being unsure of her, but when Danby approached me with some far-fetched scheme about getting her well-paid work at his uncle's house in town, if she could be persuaded to give up her child for adoption, my suspicions were confirmed. Clearly he had not given up on her and was determined to have her one way or another."

"What did you say?" asked Becky, outraged.

"I refused, of course; I said I needed her to work for me and was certainly not prepared to suggest that Alice, having lost her husband, should now give up her son! Besides I was responsible for her, having removed her from the workhouse on my own warrant. I could see it was a preposterous ploy to get the girl out of my care and into their clutches. I decided I would not even tell her about it, even though Mr Bancroft thought it was a good idea. He thought the girl would benefit; I did not. In truth, I planned thereafter to help her get away from Blessington altogether. I gave her sufficient money and arranged to have her conveyed from the house, without anyone knowing but my housekeeper. The servants still think she ran away, and I have let them believe it for her own good."

Becky had been silent as she spoke but then decided to reveal that Alice Grey had told her of Mrs Bancroft's kindness to her. "I am sure you will be happy to hear that she speaks of you with great affection and gratitude," she said. "It was the reason I decided to approach you. I wanted to help Alice and her son, but I needed more information. I had to know the truth about William Rickman; Alice claims he was falsely accused…"

"He was," said Mrs Bancroft with conviction. "Sometime after Alice had left the village, I met with some of those who had worked with Rickman at the brewery; there was not one who had a bad word for him. They all knew William Rickman was not a thief; he'd been the victim of a malicious lie, a cruel, corrupt plot to get rid of him."

"And is Alice right when she claims Mr Danby used his influence with the police to have Rickman indicted?" asked Becky, wishing to discover how much Mrs Bancroft knew.

"I have no proof, but I believe it to be the case," Mrs Bancroft replied. "There can be no other explanation for Danby's behaviour. I understand also that he had attempted, on a previous occasion, to get her out of the workhouse, claiming his sister needed a housemaid and was willing to have her, if she would leave her child behind to be brought up as an orphan. Mrs Garbutt, whose husband was in charge of the workhouse, would not agree. She knew from seeing the marriage papers that Alice was really Annabel Grey, the daughter of a gentleman. She refused to allow it and told me later she did not trust Danby or his uncle; she was convinced they would take the girl and use her, and when they tired of her, they would get rid of her, as so many of them do."

Becky's face betrayed her horror; she had not imagined it could be as bad as this. Now, she could understand Alice's fears and her reluctance to reveal anything that might betray her whereabouts to Danby.

"Mr Danby must have been furious when she was released into your care," she remarked, and Mrs Bancroft smiled, for the first time, a rather contented smile.

"No doubt he was, and Mrs Garbutt has certainly heard some of his fury. He is not a pleasant man when he is crossed. But there was nothing he could do. I had signed the papers, and Alice came willingly to work for me," she said with some degree of satisfaction.

"She was with me for almost a year, and she could have done well here; she is an honest, decent girl and quite well educated—she reads and writes very well—but Danby kept visiting my husband and would not leave her alone. Finally, I had to get her away for her own protection."

Becky felt great sympathy for Mrs Bancroft; there was clearly a genuine, benevolent heart beneath her somewhat sedate exterior.

"Mrs Bancroft, knowing all you know, will you help me find William Rickman?" she asked.

"Find him? Is he not in prison? I had heard he was to be transported to Van Dieman's Land. I have heard no more of him," she said, and Becky, still cautious about giving too much away, said only that she had learned he was not transported but had been imprisoned somewhere in England instead.

"Alice Grey is desperate to find him, for her child's sake, even if he is still in jail, and I should like to help her, but to do so, we need to know all the facts of the case."

Mrs Bancroft was thoughtful at first, but seemed gradually to arrive at a point of understanding at which she agreed to help if she could, but said again that it would have to be done with great caution and secrecy.

"I shall have to approach the young lawyer Mr Nicholls, who was in court when Rickman was convicted. I understand he was so outraged, he wrote to his Member of Parliament about the case, describing it as a travesty of justice. He lives in town, and I am well acquainted with his wife, who attends the village church. I can appeal to her and through her to her husband. If I do discover some useful information, I shall contact you at once, but I have to be careful; Mr Bancroft will not be pleased should he find out that I am involved."

Becky was delighted. It was more than she had expected.

She thanked her hostess for her hospitality before preparing to leave, saying she wished to be back at Edgewater before dark.

Wishing her a safe journey, Mrs Bancroft expressed the hope that the parish school at Hunsford, of which they had spoken, should be the forerunner of many more in the county.

"I should have liked to establish just such a school here at Blessington; sadly, Mr Bancroft is unlikely to agree. He is of the opinion that the education of children, particularly girls, should be the province only of the church. I do not believe he will countenance our involvement in such a project."

There was no doubting the genuine regret in her voice.

The two women parted amicably; it seemed they had both acquired a degree of respect for one another. Each had begun their meeting with some reservations about the other, but their humanity and concern for young Alice Grey had helped them overcome their doubts and make common cause.

For Becky it had been a day well spent.

Chapter Nine

O N RETURNING TO EDGEWATER, Becky Tate made notes in her diary, documenting her impressions of Blessington Manor and its mistress, Mrs Bancroft.

She concluded her record:

I am in two minds about what might be done to help Alice Grey, but I am in no doubt whatsoever that Mrs Bancroft is genuine in her concern for the girl and will assist our efforts in any way she can. If only there were some way to ascertain the facts about the parties who gave false witness against William Rickman, we would be at least halfway to achieving our goal.

...she wrote, feeling a distinct sense of excitement about the prospect. She decided to go over to the Dower House on the morrow and acquaint her sister with all she had learned.

On Sunday morning, Becky visited Catherine only to be told that in her absence, the stranger had been seen again in the woods, and this time, it appeared he was trying to contact someone. He had attempted to approach one of the young servants, who, having been forewarned, had deliberately avoided the man.

On this occasion, it was reported that the stranger had not looked like a tramp or a villain; it was said he appeared more like a fugitive, furtive and wary, rather than threatening.

Becky was deeply worried. Could it be someone trying to find Alice Grey?

She was concerned but did not know exactly what to do. There was no way of knowing what stratagem they might employ; she knew Danby was wealthy enough to pay someone to do his dirty work for him and lure the girl away. She worried that Alice and Tom might both be in jeopardy.

Uneasy, she decided to return at once to Edgewater and warn Alice of the possible danger. The stranger could well be connected to Danby, who, if Mrs Bancroft was to be believed, was still obsessed with the girl and perhaps determined to find her. Of his persistence, there was no doubt.

Promising Catherine that she would return the following day to tell her all about her visit to Blessington Manor, Becky left hastily, making her way through the grounds of Rosings and the churchyard at Hunsford.

As she approached the church, she saw in the distance two figures, one somewhat familiar, the other quite peculiar in its dress and gait.

Becky was certain that one of them was the stranger who had been frequenting the woods. The other she could not make out, because of a heavy cloak he wore, although she felt quite strongly that she had encountered him before—there was something familiar about his figure.

Apprehensive, for she was alone and on foot, Becky hung back as the pair walked on and disappeared into the trees behind the church.

Keeping out of sight, Becky took a path through the trees into the lane that formed the boundary between the properties, and it was with immense relief that she reached the gates of Edgewater and passed within.

Hurrying up to her room, she sent immediately for her maid to help her change out of her walking gown and boots. After she had taken tea, she felt calmer and asked for Mrs Bates to come upstairs. Becky had intended to tell Mrs Bates of the two men she had seen in the woods and impress upon her the need to warn the rest of the staff, especially the young women, that they should not wander outside the property alone.

To her astonishment, Mrs Bates confirmed the fact that two men had been seen within the churchyard at Hunsford that very day. Earlier, one of the maids had claimed she had seen a figure, most likely a man with an old coat and a battered hat, skulking among the trees in the spinney, and Mrs Bates had despatched a servant to investigate but to no avail. He had found not a trace of the stranger in the grounds, and the girl had been roundly scolded for wasting their time with fanciful tales.

But Becky was troubled and anxious. Obviously, it had not been some fanciful tale for she had seen the man herself, she said.

She knew not what course of action to follow, never having faced such a situation before. Her desire not to alarm the household and especially Alice Grey conflicted with her wish to protect them from whoever was out there, for she was convinced that the stranger or strangers in the woods had some connection to the girl.

It was while she was in this state of perplexity that a visitor arrived, and on going downstairs, she found to her absolute delight that it was Mr Jonathan Bingley. He was, he said, staying at Rosings for a few days, attending to some business of the trust on behalf of Mr Darcy, and was meeting with Mrs Catherine Burnett regarding the parish school.

Becky's warm welcome surprised him a little, but when he heard more of the events of the day, he was less so and, on being invited to stay to dinner, accepted readily. He could see she was nervous and could do with the company.

They spent most of the evening talking seriously about the situation that Becky had described, including the circumstances of her visit to Blessington Manor and her meeting with Mrs Bancroft, which she narrated in great detail. Becky was a good storyteller, and Jonathan found her account of events both absorbing and entertaining.

He too had some further information to add, he said, revealing that it had been confirmed that William Rickman was never transported, nor was he incarcerated in a prison in England as they had supposed.

Rather, having been held for some time on one of the prison hulks in the estuary, he had been later pressed into service on a merchant vessel transporting goods and livestock to New South Wales. It was said that he had been away for some eighteen months in the colony, but now he was back in England, had left the ship, and was trying to find his wife and child, of whom he had had no information at all.

Becky was immediately seized of the notion that Rickman was in fact the stranger in the woods.

"Do you suppose it is him?" she asked, but Jonathan Bingley was not so certain.

"I doubt very much that it is," he replied. "Rickman is unlikely to be showing himself in this part of the country; he would surely be aware that were he to be apprehended and arraigned again, he would have no hope—he'd be back in prison for life."

"But why?" asked Becky, bewildered by this proposition. "Is he not a free man now?"

"Indeed no, as you see, he has not served the sentence passed on him for his original offence; he was forcibly taken on board a merchant ship and made to sail to Australia, where his crime and sentence would have been unknown except to his employers. It is quite likely that he worked well and made money and has returned to find his wife and child, but the law has not finished with him."

"Oh, that is so unfair!" cried Becky, and Jonathan agreed.

"Indeed, in this case perhaps, and it is evidence of the corruption of the system of justice that it happens; but if he were a man guilty of a much more horrific crime, murder perhaps, the same law would apply. Which is why I do not believe Rickman is the man whom you and others have seen in the woods. It is much more likely to be a friend or emissary of his, trying to discover the whereabouts of his wife. Unless, of course," and at this point his voice was serious, "unless it is a spy sent by the man Danby. One never can tell, and it pays to be exceedingly cautious in these matters. You must ensure that Alice Grey is never out in the woods alone. She is likely to be in grave danger."

Jonathan, Becky thought, was being his usual prudent self, circumspect and discreet as always.

After dinner, they withdrew to the drawing room and were taking coffee when he said, apropos of nothing at all, "Becky, I do apologise. With all of this excitement, I very nearly forgot the original reason for my visit; I have two messages for you. Anna would never have forgiven me had I returned to Netherfield without delivering hers. She was most particular that you should have it as soon as possible."

He was about to reach inside his coat when there came an urgent, loud, insistent knocking on the front door.

Becky was startled, for no other visitors were expected that evening; minutes later, a familiar voice was heard, and Mr Jamison, the parson, having divested himself of his coat and hat in the hall, entered the room.

So relieved was Becky that she looked as though she could have hugged him, but she restrained herself and invited him to take tea or coffee with them instead.

Mr Jamison accepted gladly. He had walked through a thin drizzle to get there and was grateful for the warm welcome he had received as well as the lively blaze in the fireplace.

Standing in front of it, he revealed that he had had a visit from a man, an ex-convict lately returned from New South Wales.

"Who is he?" asked Becky at once, eager and anxious.

Mr Jamison gravely refused to reveal the man's name; he had given him his word, but it would not signify anyway, because they would not know him, he said.

"Then it is not William Rickman?" asked Becky again, her anxiety written all over her face.

"Indeed no, it is not—but I could say that he is acting on behalf of Rickman and wishes to discover the whereabouts of his wife and child."

Becky gasped.

Terrified that Mr Jamison may have inadvertently betrayed Alice Grey's secret, she questioned him keenly on what he had said to the man.

But Mr Jamison reassured her.

"Mrs Tate, you may rest assured that being aware of the situation with the young woman Alice Grey, I was totally discreet, revealing nothing at all about her being in this neighbourhood. Indeed, the man was asking about a Mrs Rickman, so it was much less difficult for me to deny all knowledge of her.

"'I have met no one of that name,' I said, 'not in this parish.' He told me he was making enquiries for a shipmate, one William Rickman, whom he met and served with aboard a ship returning from New South Wales.

"I must say I judged him to be genuine, but the information was not mine to divulge, so I promised to make enquiries and sent him away, having given him some food and a little money. The reason for my visit to you, Mrs Tate, at this late hour, is because I felt the need to warn you of his presence in the area. He intends to travel around the county and has promised to return next week, in case I uncover some useful information. I thought you should know that he is looking for Alice Grey, even though he knows her as Mrs Rickman."

REBECCA ANN COLLINS

Mr Jamison was clearly convinced the man was not dangerous, but Jonathan Bingley was not so sanguine. He cautioned both the parson and Becky against trusting strangers asking questions about Alice or Annabel Grey. He urged them to be wary and watchful.

"There is no knowing what this man may be about or who he is working for. He may well be, as he has told you, a friend of Rickman, or he could be a paid agent of his enemies. As an ex-convict he may need the help and protection of men like Danby, who could use him to find Alice Grey.

"But," warned Jonathan, "he could then destroy Rickman by betraying him to the police. It is possible that no one in authority knows that Rickman is back in England—he may be living under an assumed name; all these things are possible. You must take nothing for granted and, above all, provide no information at all, none whatsoever, to a stranger. Remember at all times that he or she may be working for the police or Danby or others of his ilk."

The prospect horrified Becky, who wondered how she would have dealt with this situation had Jonathan not been present. Would Mr Jamison have taken her advice?

Following upon Jonathan's sage words, Mr Jamison agreed that it would be best to reveal nothing of the girl or her son if the stranger returned.

Becky intervened to beg him to try his best to elicit some information from the man, to discover, if possible, where William Rickman might be.

Jonathan agreed, suggesting that perhaps Mr Jamison might use his special position in the parish to discover the truth, offering to ask around the parish of Hunsford for a Mrs Rickman, but only if he could be certain that it was a genuine request from her husband.

"You should ask the man for proof that Rickman is in England," he advised. "That would help to ascertain the truth."

Mr Jamison, at first rather reluctant to become embroiled in the matter, later agreed that it was perhaps something he could consider in the next day or two; then, since it was well past his bedtime and he had to be awake early for matins, he declared he would take leave of them.

The rain outside was heavier, and Jonathan Bingley, who had risen to shake Mr Jamison's hand, offered him a ride in his vehicle, which Mr Jamison accepted with alacrity.

"That is uncommonly kind of you, Mr Bingley—I know it is only a short walk, but I shall be quite wet in this rain. I hope it will not take you too far out of your way," he said, and Jonathan assured him it would not.

Becky accompanied the two men into the hall, and there, when the manservant appeared with their coats and hats, she was quite taken aback by what she saw. As Mr Jamison put on his long cloak and weatherproof hat, seeing him from behind, Becky knew at once it was Mr Jamison she had seen that morning, walking in the churchyard with the stranger.

It was clear to her that there were not two strange men in the neighbourhood; just one—an ex-convict, who claimed to be a friend of William Rickman—and the parson Mr Jamison, whom he had approached.

She decided to say nothing more about it at this time, but relieved beyond measure, she bade both men a very good night and retired to her room.

She was determined to speak with Alice Grey on the morrow and, while counselling her to be careful, reassure her that there was now a good chance they could trace her husband.

Still pondering in her mind if she should reveal to the girl the information she had had from Jonathan Bingley, wondering if the knowledge that he was in England and free for the moment might lead Alice to take even more risks to find her husband, she regretted that she had not had time to ask Jonathan's opinion on the matter and decided she would try to do so before he left Rosings in a day or two.

This posed for her an unusual problem.

It would not be seemly for her to visit Mr Bingley at Rosings, she thought, and wondered if her sister might not be prevailed upon to invite him to dine at the Dower House, where they could meet and discuss the matter without undue concern. She was sure Catherine would have no objection at all and determined to pay her a visit on the morrow to suggest it.

She was right. Catherine was happy to ask Mr Bingley to dinner.

"Of course, he can come to dinner, Becky; indeed he does so frequently when he is visiting Rosings Park. Frank and I both enjoy his company. He is a regular visitor and a welcome one. I shall send him a note inviting him to dine with us on the evening before he returns to London. Will that suit?"

"It certainly will," said Becky, pleased that her sister had agreed to her request. It would give her an opportunity to obtain his advice.

When Becky had related all of the information she had gathered at Blessington on Saturday and back at Edgewater last night, Catherine's countenance betrayed her deep concern.

"My dear Becky, are you sure this is the right thing to do? If Alice Grey's husband is absconding from the law, will there not be a great deal of trouble if he were caught and you were found to be assisting him to evade the police?"

Becky was determined.

"Oh no, Cathy dearest, I shall certainly not become involved in such an exercise. I wish only to ascertain if he is in fact back in England and seeking to be reunited with his family. I shall then pass the matter over to Mr Colin Elliott, Jonathan's son-in-law, who will advise if there is any way in which his case may be reconsidered. He did earlier hint at the possibility of applying for a pardon, if it can be proved that the man was convicted upon false evidence. If Mrs Bancroft provides us with any credible information to support such a case, it would be a great help. I must at least try, Cathy, for Alice's sake. I have grown fond of her... she puts me so much in mind of what my Josie used to be, it breaks my heart," she said, and Catherine could see the tears that filled her eyes as she struggled to hold them back.

Her sister knew it was of little use to try to dissuade her, and after Becky had left, Catherine went to her room and penned a note to Jonathan Bingley inviting him to dine with them at the Dower House on the evening before he left for London.

She took the opportunity to remind him that it was a long-standing practice of his to do so and hoped he would accept. She added that her sister Becky would be one of the party too.

The note was despatched and the response came back very promptly—

Mr Bingley would be delighted, and yes, he did remember that it was a most pleasant practice, with which he was happy to comply.

Recalling as she read it some of her earlier conversations with her sister, regarding Becky's youthful fondness for Jonathan Bingley, Catherine could not help feeling a little pang of regret. If only it had been Becky and not Amelia-Jane he had fallen in love with all those years ago, how very different might all their lives have been, she thought with a little sigh.

But it was not to be, and practical as ever, Catherine sighed, shrugged off those futile thoughts, and went downstairs to consult her housekeeper about the menu for her forthcoming dinner party.

END OF PART TWO

A WOMAN OF INFLUENCE

Part Three

Chapter Ten

WALKING HOME THROUGH THE sunlit park at Rosings, Becky felt no fear, no sense of apprehension or concern for her own safety. It was a route she had taken on so many occasions, she scarcely needed to follow the footpath when she entered the woods, so familiar had she become with the trees, which were at their prettiest in Autumn.

She was almost within sight of Hunsford church, where the sturdy old oaks of Rosings Park gave way to darker yew trees, making cool pools of shade upon the grass, when a brisk breeze caused her to pull her cloak more closely around her. Winter, she thought, was definitely on its way.

At that moment, Becky heard, not far behind her, wary footsteps, then the sound of a cracking twig, which instantly told her she was being followed. That no one had passed her on her journey she was certain, which must mean that someone who did not wish to be seen was close behind her.

Suddenly, Becky felt inordinately cold and afraid.

Too terrified to turn around and confront whoever it was, she quickened her steps and, as she reached the lane between the properties, picked up her skirts and broke into a run, which carried her breathless and frightened into the arms of a gentleman who was just leaving Edgewater.

Jonathan Bingley took a step back to regain his balance and put out a hand to steady her as she ran into him. Still holding her, he exclaimed, "Good

God, Becky, what has happened? Have you been attacked? You look very upset indeed, and your hands are as cold as ice!" and Becky, unable to help herself, burst into tears with relief.

So terrified had she been, she had run as fast as she could to get away from she knew not what or whom. She had not waited to discover who it was had been following her.

She blurted out her story to Jonathan, who stopped to let her finish; then when she was calmer, gave her his arm to support her as they walked up the drive to the house.

He explained that he had been walking in the woods himself and, on finding he was in the vicinity of Edgewater, had remembered that he still had on him the two messages he had intended to deliver to her last evening, before they were interrupted by the arrival of Mr Jamison.

"I thought you would not mind if I called on you and handed them over," he said, "but your servant informed me that you had set out after breakfast to visit Mrs Burnett. I decided that rather than leave them with the servant, I would take them over to the Dower House myself, confidently expecting to see you there. You can well imagine my astonishment then, when I was almost bowled over by you, so obviously distressed."

Becky was by now beginning to feel a little embarrassed about her headlong flight. After all, she had seen no one and could give no description of the person who had supposedly followed her in the woods.

She had heard footsteps and the sound of a twig snapping underfoot and leapt immediately to the conclusion that Mr Jamison's convict had returned and was following her in the hope she would lead him to Alice Grey.

She said nothing for a while, still shaken by her experience and mortified at having cannoned into Jonathan Bingley at the gate.

Before they reached the house, she apologised and requested that he say nothing about it in front of the servants.

"I am sorry, Jonathan, I'm afraid I feel rather foolish. I have no proof that it was the convict, and I do not wish to alarm them. There have been many sightings of a stranger in the woods, and the staff have been instructed that they must be alert at all times for intruders. I should not like them to think that I had been thrown into a blind panic by a footfall and run through the woods like a scared schoolgirl."

Jonathan laughed but assured her that she need not be ashamed of being fearful in the circumstances; however, understanding her concerns, he said, "Of course I shall do as you ask. You can be sure I will say nothing to cause you any embarrassment. Please do not apologise; I am happy to have been here to be of some assistance to you. I quite understand your alarm, and I shall certainly look out for any signs of this man when I return through the woods to Rosings. I have to say, Becky, that while I am reluctant, in the circumstances, to advise that you call in the police, if this man, whoever he is, continues to trouble you or your staff in this way, you may have no alternative but to do so."

Becky was not in favour of bringing in the constabulary, remembering Mrs Bancroft's words on the subject of Alice Grey's fear of the police.

She suggested to Jonathan that she might have been mistaken: "Perhaps it wasn't the convict after all—it may well have been a poacher, which would account for his stealthy movements."

Jonathan agreed and when she invited him to stay and take tea with her before returning to Rosings, accepted gladly.

They went within and while they waited for tea to be brought in, he took from the inner pocket of his coat two letters.

"Well, here they are at last," he said, handing them to her.

Becky took them from him. One was on pale blue notepaper and the direction was in Anna Bingley's hand. Becky smiled and said, "Thank you for this; I have been expecting a letter from my cousin for a little while now."

Jonathan nodded.

"I do believe Anna feels she owes you an apology; she admits she has been tardy in responding to your last," he explained. "She has been kept busy with her mother being unwell and Dr Faulkner needing some help with caring for her, as I am sure she will relate in her letter," he said, as the servants brought in the tea and plates of cake.

As Jonathan helped himself to cake, Becky picked up the second letter. It was on unfamiliar notepaper and apart from her name, carried no other direction. Turning it over, she found no indication of the sender's identity and looked across at Jonathan as if for some explanation.

Seeing her look of bewilderment, he asked, "Do you not recognise the hand? I had thought you would know it."

Becky, looking even more puzzled, shook her head. "Should I? Is it someone I know well?" she asked.

Jonathan smiled and put down his cup and plate.

"Indeed, I believe you knew one another very well some years ago, although it is likely that you may not have been familiar with the handwriting," he said and returned to concentrate upon the cake.

Becky sat down opposite him and opened the sealed letter.

She looked quickly at the signature at the bottom of the page—*Aldo Contini*.

For one moment, her entire face flushed and her hand shook as she folded up the letter without even attempting to read it.

Then, looking up at Jonathan who was standing in front of her, she asked, "Mr Contini... is he... have you... I mean... are you two well acquainted?"

Jonathan appeared not to notice her confusion.

"Aldo Contini is the nephew of Mr and Mrs Roberto Contini, who have been close friends of my family as well as the Darcys and the Grantleys for many years. I have known him since our schooldays; we were at the same boarding school in London—he had come to live in London with his uncle and aunt to escape the troubles besetting Italy at the time," he answered.

"And this letter?"

"Mr Contini was briefly in London to attend a funeral last week, and we met for dinner at my club. He enquired after you and Mr Tate; he had not heard of your late husband's death last year, and when I told him, he was quite distressed and asked if I would deliver a note to you conveying his condolences. Of course, I said I would be glad to do so, and he went into the lounge, wrote it, and handed it to me before we parted that evening. I gathered that Mr Tate and you had met Mr Contini in Italy some years ago and become quite good friends?"

Becky nodded, acknowledging but adding nothing to his statement.

Jonathan continued in a quiet voice, "He seemed exceedingly concerned that he had not heard, saying more than once that he wished he had more time in England; he would have liked to have travelled with me to Kent to call on you and offer his condolences personally. He had to leave for Italy the following morning; I was very happy to be able to assist by conveying his letter to you," he said.

By the time Jonathan had finished, Becky was not as discomposed as she had been. Smiling, she nodded agreement at his explanation.

Yes, they had been acquainted with Mr Contini, she said, explaining that they had met in London and again in Florence, where he had been kind enough to act as their guide on several occasions, showing them some of the great treasures of that city.

She wished earnestly to convince Jonathan that there was nothing more than friendly courtesy in Mr Contini's interest, yet in truth, she could scarcely wait for him to be gone, so keen was she to retire to her room and read her letter.

Jonathan Bingley, unaware of the reaction that the note he had delivered had caused in the recipient, was enjoying the delicious tea-cake and appeared in no hurry to leave. He attributed Becky's unusually distracted demeanour and flushed countenance to her distressing experience in the woods that morning and stayed as long as he thought was necessary to let her recover from the shock.

When finally, he rose to leave, Becky held out her hand to him and once again thanked him for his kindness and concern.

He urged her gently to rest awhile and to avoid going out alone.

"At least until this matter is settled, it would be best if you avoided the woods and travelled by road in your carriage. While I doubt very much if the fellow, whoever he may be, would approach you or try to harm you in any way, it could be an unpleasant encounter for you and best avoided."

Touched by his concern, Becky thanked him again and when he expressed the hope that they might meet again before he left Rosings, she smiled and told him she would be dining at the Dower House on the Friday.

"Ah," said Jonathan, "then we shall meet again, and I hope you will have quite recovered from your little adventure by then."

"I am sure I shall have, and may I please ask that you do not speak of it before my sister; she is likely to be very concerned, and I do not wish to alarm her or my brother-in-law," she explained, and Jonathan agreed at once.

"Of course, you may be sure of that," he said as he bade her goodbye.

Waiting only until he had left the house and was striding swiftly down the drive, she went quickly to her room and shut the door before opening up Mr Contini's letter. As she read it, her mind slipped out of the present into a past she had thought was long forgotten. Everything, the problems of Alice Grey and William Rickman, Mrs Bancroft and Mr Danby, the stranger in the woods, indeed all those contentious matters that had so absorbed her for the past two weeks simply fled her mind.

Her thoughts became concentrated upon the letter in her hand and one other question—how much did Jonathan Bingley know of her past association with Aldo Contini?

The letter itself was innocuous enough, a simple, friendly note expressing in the sincerest terms his condolences on the death of her husband and his apologies for not having communicated with her earlier.

Please believe that I did not learn of your bereavement until Mr Bingley informed me just an hour ago, when we were dining at his club. If I had known, I would most certainly have written or called on you earlier, although it must be said, I had no knowledge of your moving to live in Kent.

I suppose it must have been good to be near your sister Mrs Harrison.

If it were not that I have to return to Italy tomorrow, I should have called on you personally. Please accept my sincerest sympathy and if I may be of any assistance, do not hesitate to call on me.

…he wrote. He concluded with the warmest of wishes for her future and expressed the hope that they may meet one day, perhaps when he was next in London.

It was as gentlemanly and kind in manner and sentiment as one could ask for, with not a hint of presumption.

Becky read it through once and over again, before folding it over and placing it inside her diary. The arrival of the letter had taken her by surprise; its contents had affected her feelings considerably.

That Aldo Contini had appeared in London was surprise enough; that he was apparently a close friend of Jonathan Bingley was a most amazing circumstance. It set up in Becky's mind the likelihood that the two men were perhaps intimate enough to have exchanged confidences, a possibility that caused in her such a tumult that every other concern was for the moment subsumed.

Becky now had a new source of disquiet. *If Jonathan Bingley should learn of her previous association with Mr Contini, how might he regard it?* she wondered.

She was concerned that there may be some disapproval, yet the fact that there had been no hint of this in his attitude to her when they met and he had handed over Mr Contini's letter gave her some hope that he knew little more than what had been said already.

Perhaps, she thought, Mr Contini had said nothing to Jonathan beyond his acknowledgement of his meetings in Italy with Mr Tate and herself, some years ago. That he had wanted to convey his condolences would add verisimilitude to this account, and Jonathan, himself an unsuspicious sort of person, was unlikely to have given the matter much thought.

Feeling confused and out of spirits, she decided she would remain in her room for the rest of the afternoon, sending a message to the housekeeper that she preferred not to be disturbed before dinner time.

She was tired, she told her maid, and wished not to be involved in any of the routine domestic matters that afternoon.

She did remember, however, to add a warning to all the young women in the household that they should stay well within the boundaries of Edgewater. She used the information given her by Catherine to urge them to avoid at all costs the woods around the Rosings estate.

Having secured her privacy, she looked only to concentrate upon Mr Contini's letter and what her response should be. She set to work to compose an appropriate reply.

However, when Nelly returned some hours later, her mistress had a blank page before her while several crumpled sheets of paper lay in the wastepaper basket. Becky had spent all afternoon on her answer, but every attempt had ended in frustration, if not failure.

Each time she had begun to write to Mr Contini, her mind had raced ahead of her pen, and she had difficulty in expressing even the simplest thoughts, without feeling that she was either being too familiar or offending him with too much formality.

When Nelly appeared to remind her it was almost time to dress for dinner, Becky was taken aback. So deeply had she been immersed in her seemingly fruitless task, she had not realised the lateness of the hour.

"Shall I prepare your bath, ma'am?" Nelly asked a little tentatively.

Becky rose from her couch, saying without much enthusiasm, "Yes please, Nelly. I think I would like that, but I doubt if I shall need much dinner tonight."

"Shall I bring a tray up for you, ma'am?" Nelly suggested. She knew her mistress was troubled, was anxious for her, and wished to help.

Becky turned to her as if to a savior.

"Would you, Nelly? That would be heaven, because I shan't have to dress for dinner and go downstairs and sit alone at table. I do hope Cook won't be upset."

Nelly smiled. "No, ma'am, I am sure she will be very happy to prepare a tray for you," she said and went away to give the necessary instructions.

Becky sighed, lay back on her couch, and gave thanks for Nelly, whose loyalty and kindness had sustained her through many dark days.

Chapter Eleven

WHEN BECKY RETIRED TO bed, she had hoped that the mood of melancholy she had suffered all evening would lift overnight. However, when she awoke the following morning to the same sense of distraction that had assailed her the previous night, she was disappointed.

Lying in bed would not cure her dejection, nor would it help her deal with her present predicament. She had to compose a suitable response to Mr Contini's letter. Courtesy demanded that she do so, yet she had no knowledge of his present situation and address and, were she to write, would need to ask Jonathan Bingley for this information.

How to do this, without revealing more than she wished to about her earlier association with Mr Contini, posed an almost insoluble problem.

By the time her maid appeared with tea, Becky had made a decision.

There was no other course to follow—she would have to seek her sister Catherine's advice.

She was expected to dine at the Dower House the following evening with Jonathan Bingley, Catherine's daughter Lilian, and her husband, Mr Adams. She had been looking forward to what would surely be a pleasant dinner party in excellent company. But now, she felt that she would enjoy it not at all while her mind was troubled by this new anxiety.

Taking advantage of her temporary indisposition to avoid the distraction of domestic routine, she rose from her bed, dressed, and wrote a short note, which she despatched to her sister, asking if she could spare a few hours to help her deal with a very particular private matter. She sent the carriage, with instructions that it should wait and return either with Mrs Burnett or her response.

Becky was aware that with Mr Frank Burnett in London on business and not expected back until that night, she could have every hope that Catherine would oblige her sister and come to her.

She was right. Shortly after midday, Mrs Burnett arrived at Edgewater, ready to help her sister deal with whatever troubled her. Becky remained in her room, and Catherine, fearing her sister was sicker than she had supposed, came swiftly upstairs.

As she entered the room, she looked uneasy. "Becky my dear, what is it? Have you been taken ill? I did warn you to take care, did I not? It must be all this tramping around the countryside that you delight in; you must have caught a cold or a chill, I think."

Catherine was her usual self, concerned and practical, eager to help.

Becky rose from her seat and the sisters embraced, as she thanked Catherine for coming so promptly and assured her she was not gravely ill, indeed she wasn't ill at all.

Having rung the bell and ordered that tea be brought up, Becky urged Catherine to be seated, indicating a place beside her on the chaise longue.

Catherine looked puzzled and could not understand what had caused her sister to send for her so urgently.

"Becky, your note suggested that you had a private matter that troubled you, which you wished to resolve. What is it that can have been so urgent that it could not wait until we met at dinner tomorrow? Is it something very important?" she asked.

"It is indeed, Cathy, and yes, it is a question I must resolve speedily, and I had hoped you would help me find a way to do so. But you must let me tell you about it in my own way, so you will understand my difficulty and advise me. I have great need of your cool head and perfect manners, Cathy; I am not very good at these matters; you must tell me what I ought to do."

Catherine certainly had a well-deserved reputation for good sense and exemplary manners. Like their mother, Charlotte, she had grown up with a strong sense of decorum and had a natural dignity, which stood her in good stead, but at this point she could not see how these attributes could help her sister.

"But what is the problem you must resolve? Is it to do with Alice Grey?" she asked, and Becky replied, "No, indeed it is not. In fact it has nothing at all to do with that matter."

Catherine was even more confused.

When they had last met, Becky had been eager to tell her all about Mrs Bancroft's revelations about the girl Alice Grey and her husband; she had left promising to return with an account of what she had learnt on her visit to Blessington, yet now, she was dismissing the subject as though it was of no significance. Catherine could not make it out at all.

The arrival of the maid bearing the tea tray interrupted their conversation, and they talked of inconsequential matters until the girl left the room.

But, even as she did so, Becky took from the pocket of her gown Mr Contini's letter and handed it to Catherine.

"There, read it, and when you have finished, I shall explain further," she said, as she proceeded to pour out the tea.

Still confused, Catherine took the note from her hand and began to read.

When she had read it through, she looked up at her sister, still unable to comprehend what problem it had caused.

"Becky, is this Mr Contini of the same Italian family who are friends of the Darcys?" she asked tentatively.

Becky nodded, and Catherine noted the particular smile on her face.

"Yes, he is; he is their nephew and has been a close friend of Jonathan Bingley for many years, although I had no knowledge whatsoever of that until this morning, when Jonathan called to deliver this letter. I understand they were at school together."

"And why has this note caused you a problem?" asked her sister.

Becky struggled to explain, wanting to convey her need to avoid undue awkwardness without further mortification, but succeeding only in confusing her sister even more.

After one or two futile attempts, she gave up and, as tears filled her eyes, turned to Catherine and said, "Cathy, I fear I have been very remiss. I have not been entirely honest with you; there are matters I should have told you of a long time ago. But in my own defence I have to say that I never believed it would be of any consequence. It was all so long ago."

"What do you mean, Becky? My dear, if you wish me to help you, I do need to understand the problem. Why does Mr Contini's note, which I have to say is a most unexceptionable communication, create such a difficulty for you? Was he not previously acquainted with Mr Tate and yourself?"

Becky nodded, looking away for a minute and then facing her sister, and said, "He was, when we first met in London, but you know what my husband was like, he collected acquaintances like a child collects shells at the seaside, but then he soon forgot them, unless they were useful to him."

"And Mr Contini was not?"

"Not particularly; not in the sense that he had useful business or political connections. But he was very helpful to us and exceedingly hospitable when we travelled to Italy, which Mr Tate appreciated, and he was a most attentive and helpful guide, especially in Florence, where his family lives. We spent a great deal of time together."

"There cannot have been any harm in that, surely?" said Catherine.

"There was not, except very often Mr Tate would spend most of the day with business associates, leaving me to wander around the city alone except for Mr Contini, who very kindly accompanied me and, I would think, protected me when I might have been putting myself in some danger, venturing into places that I shouldn't have, if only through ignorance or naiveté."

"Well, that was kind of him, and if Mr Tate had no objection to it, I can see nothing wrong in it, surely?"

When Becky was silent, Catherine seemed to realise there was more to this situation than met the eye and suddenly, as if simple understanding had dawned upon her, asked, "Becky, was there something more that you have omitted to tell me? Did Mr Contini flirt with you? And did you, perhaps, enjoy a little flirtation too?

"Was that it?" she teased her sister, and then noting a blush rising upon her cheek, she persisted, "And now, are you concerned that if he returns and sees you again, he may seek to renew the association? Is that what troubles you?"

Becky seized the chance afforded her by this remark.

"Yes, you are right; I fear I may have given him the impression that—"

Catherine interrupted her, "But, my dear Becky, that was years ago. How can it be that he would try to renew such an association when you have had no communication with him since? I do not believe it possible. Besides, Becky, Mr Contini may well be otherwise engaged himself; perhaps he is married and unlikely to be interested in pursuing the connection," she suggested.

This was a thought that had not as yet occurred to Becky, as she had searched around in her mind for a solution to her dilemma. She was as yet unready to reveal everything to her sister.

Suddenly, she smiled and said, "Yes, of course, you are quite right, Cathy, he may well be married, although Jonathan said nothing of that," adding thoughtfully, "I wonder if Jonathan does have an inkling of our previous association. I should be deeply mortified if that were the case."

Catherine attempted to reassure her sister.

"Oh I do doubt that, Becky," she said. "I think Mr Contini's note to you and the fact that he was so open about sending it through Jonathan Bingley must give you some confidence. As a friend of Mr Bingley, he is clearly a gentleman and an honourable one. Would you not say so?"

Becky agreed.

"Yes indeed, I should have no doubt of that."

Catherine was content.

"Well then, in such circumstances, I think you need have no concerns about his motives, nor need you worry about the possibility of his betraying a confidence. As it was so many years ago, when you were both much younger and Mr Tate was with you for most of the time, it is probably something he, like you, has long forgotten. Do you not agree?"

Becky nodded; she did not trust herself to speak.

"Well then, what is there to be concerned about?" asked her sister.

"I shall need to send a response—a letter acknowledging his kind sentiments. Would I not?" Becky asked tentatively.

"Of course, it would be the right thing to do after such a courteous message of condolence. But there need be no awkwardness about that," Catherine argued quite reasonably.

"Will you help me compose it, Cathy?" Becky's voice was low and Catherine appeared amazed at her request.

That Becky, whose chief talent was her ability to write lucidly and with conviction, should ask for her assistance was astonishing. Catherine stared at her in disbelief. Yet she said, "Of course, if you wish, but I cannot think it would be a difficult task. His note to you is couched in such genteel terms, it should be easy for you to respond in like manner."

"And if I were to compose such a response, and ask Jonathan Bingley for Mr Contini's address in Italy, do you think he would deem it to be an unusual request?"

"And why should he? Surely, Becky, having delivered Mr Contini's letter himself, Mr Bingley is hardly likely to be surprised that you should wish to respond. I cannot see it, honestly I cannot."

Reassured, Becky, with a little help from her sister, composed a brief, polite, and very acceptable response to be sent to Mr Contini.

In it, she thanked him for his kind sentiments and sent her regards and best wishes, while deftly ignoring his suggestion that they might meet when he was next in England. Catherine had been of the opinion that it was a formal suggestion best left unanswered at this stage.

When it was done, Becky thanked her sister for her kindness and her sensible counsel, apologising at the same time for bringing her out to Edgewater for what must have seemed to her a trivial reason.

Catherine dismissed her concerns. "Do not apologise, Becky dear, I am glad I could help. You must feel able to call on me, if you need me, at any time. We are sisters after all, and now, with Mama gone, you and I have only each other to confide in."

As Catherine prepared to leave and return home, Becky could not help wondering what her sister would have said had she been made aware of all the circumstances of her association with Mr Contini.

After Catherine had left, Becky returned to her room and read again both Mr Contini's note to her and her own response.

She was far from content, feeling there was something missing. His note had expressed genuine concern and a warm friendliness; hers seemed formal and cold.

On impulse, she tore it up and began again.

This time, she adopted a more informal, cordial tone, thanking him for his kind sentiments and saying she took great comfort from them and others she had received from family and friends since her husband's death.

She mentioned, in passing, that Mr Tate had died in America, where he had lived for the last two years of his life, but quite deliberately omitted to mention their separation. It was possible that Jonathan Bingley may have told him, she thought, seeing no reason to enlighten him herself.

However, she did, in agreeing that she had enjoyed moving to Kent and living very close to her sister Catherine, advise him that her sister was no longer Mrs Harrison as he had supposed. She explained that Dr Harrison had died some time ago from recurring heart disease, and Catherine had since married a Mr Frank Burnett, with whom she had been acquainted for many years when she lived at Rosings.

Noting that her letter was getting somewhat longer than she had intended, she decided to conclude it, which she did with a much friendlier salutation than before, wishing him health and happiness and then adding a significant postscript.

Regarding your suggestion, I think I should like very much to see you when you are next in London. It seems quite a while since we last met.

And she signed it—*Becky Tate.*

When it was complete, Becky read it through and proceeded to seal it, lest she should change her mind again.

No one, certainly not Catherine, would ever know that she had torn up the polite little note and sent a warm, convivial letter instead, she thought with a little pang of guilt at having misled her sister.

But at least, she was now content, especially as she contemplated how he would respond on receiving it. It was the certainty of his disappointment on opening her formal acknowledgment that had led her to tear it up and try again.

There was no need at all for Catherine to know, Becky decided.

The dinner at the Dower House on the following evening was wholly delightful. The food, the company, and the music provided afterwards by the hosts and guests alike were all of a standard of excellence as to gratify and enchant them all.

Becky was charmed as first Lilian and Mr Adams and then later Catherine and Frank Burnett played and sang for them. Only Jonathan stood apart, and when she took the opportunity to speak with him during a break in the entertainment, he confessed to her that he had often wished he too could sing or play as well as the rest of the family.

"My wife and daughters and all my sisters and their children are such proficient performers, I feel quite bereft of talent or skill when I see how wonderfully well they all do," he said, and Becky agreed that she too suffered the same sense of inadequacy in the face of such remarkable natural ability as they had enjoyed that evening.

Echoing his sentiments, she said, "Both Anna and your sister Emma are exceptional performers, but I do wish I had at least learnt how to entertain myself with music, if not others. I fear my time was spent mostly scribbling, as Mama used to say."

Surprised by her remarks, Jonathan urged her not to undervalue her own talents. "Well, Becky, your scribbling, as you call it, has opened up a quite remarkable world for you, has it not? I should not belittle your achievements; the literary world seems to be taking a lot of notice of women writers. They are at least assured of fame if not fortune."

He was clearly referring to Marianne Lawrence, the pen name she had used for her contributions to the *Matlock Review.* Surprised that he had noticed her work, Becky made light of his comments, assuring him that she would gladly exchange her small quantum of fame for the happiness her sister had found in life.

"Catherine is so happy and content, I envy her," she said, and the comment caused Mr Bingley to raise his eyebrows and look quickly at her face as if to check if she was being serious.

But, by then, Becky, taking advantage of a lull in the proceedings while everyone took more tea or coffee, had asked if he could provide her with an address for Mr Aldo Contini, in order that she might thank him for his kind note of condolence.

Jonathan provided it gladly, taking from his pocket book a card, which he gave to Becky.

"You may keep it; I have all his details in my diary at Netherfield," he said, and Becky was pleased that her request had raised no fuss at all.

On the morrow, she decided, she would take her letter to the post herself.

Chapter Twelve

WHEN BECKY RETURNED HOME, having despatched her letter and stopped to purchase some buttons from the haberdasher in the village, she was feeling especially elated. In her response to Mr Contini, she had accomplished something that she had not thought possible: she had, quite deliberately, set aside her sister's reasonable and proper advice and acted according to the dictates of her heart.

She arrived at the entrance with a lightness of step reflecting perhaps the lightness of spirit she felt, but sadly, it was not to last very long, for she was met by the housekeeper, Mrs Bates, who was in such a state of disquiet that Becky could scarcely comprehend a word she was saying.

The poor woman was simultaneously bewailing some misfortune and apologising for her own failure to prevent it, leaving Becky completely confused and quite alarmed. She had never seen Mrs Bates so agitated before.

Fearing that something serious had occurred, perhaps some dreadful accident had befallen one of the staff, Becky took Mrs Bates into the study and asked her directly for an explanation.

"Mrs Bates, would you please tell me what exactly has happened?" she asked, and Mrs Bates, by now a little calmer, began to speak more coherently, but what she said brought Becky no comfort at all.

It appeared that in the two hours that Becky had been away from the house, Alice Grey and her son, Tom, had disappeared.

Mrs Bates was determined to shoulder all the blame, even though Becky tried to console her by arguing that she could not have known what Alice planned to do.

"But, ma'am, it is my fault; I should have kept a closer watch on the girl, I am to blame, ma'am, I know I am." She wailed again, and nothing Becky could say would shake her resolve to be miserable.

Realising that it was a very serious state of affairs, Becky asked, "When did you discover they were gone?"

"Scarcely an hour ago, ma'am," said Mrs Bates. "Cook had baked a batch of biscuits and wished to give some to the boy—she is very partial to him, ma'am—but when Maggie went to find him, they were nowhere to be found. She told me, and I sent the maids to look for Alice in the rooms upstairs, but she was gone."

"And what have you done since? Has anyone tried to find them? Have you searched the grounds?"

"Oh yes, ma'am, the lads have looked in all the barns and outhouses, and we have searched the attics and the cellar as well, but they are gone, ma'am. I cannot think what can have happened to them, and I blame myself," she cried, about to start all over again.

Becky interrupted her to ask, "What about the woods? Has anyone been out to search the woods?"

Mrs Bates confessed that no one had thought to go into the woods.

Becky stood up and said, "I think you should have a look around the house again, Mrs Bates; send the maids into all the rooms, and I will take one of the men and search the grounds and the woods around the churchyard."

Becky believed they were exactly the places where Alice and her son might be found, unless they had been abducted, of course. It was a possibility she was not prepared to contemplate at this stage—it was too terrible, and she thrust it out of her mind.

She decided to take James, one of the older servants who'd been with her for many years, and her own maid, Nelly, who had made a friend of Alice Grey. Soon afterwards, the three of them set out, not knowing quite where to look and afraid that they may not find anything at all.

As they searched the grounds, Becky could not help wondering whether the convict who had approached Mr Jamison had returned and found Alice and the boy. The possibility that he may have succeeded in persuading her to go with him weighed upon her mind as they looked in all the available hiding places and drew a blank everywhere.

Once, Nelly thought she saw someone moving deep among the poplars in the spinney, and Becky immediately sent James to take a look, but when he returned shaking his head and saying it was probably just a trick of the light, she began to think the worst had happened.

Determined to discover whether the convict had been seen again, Becky decided to approach Mr Jamison. They went across the meadow and along the lane leading to the church, and as they entered the church yard, Mr Jamison came out to meet them.

"Mrs Tate, how very nice to see you," he began but soon realised from Becky's troubled countenance that something was amiss.

It did not take Becky long to explain the predicament in which they were placed, and Mr Jamison was completely sympathetic.

"My dear Mrs Tate," he said, clasping his hands together, "where on earth could the young woman have gone? One moment she is safe and well in your care, and the next she has disappeared and taken the boy too. I cannot make it out."

Becky wanted to know if he had seen the man, the convict who had approached him on behalf of William Rickman again.

"Do you know if he is still in these parts?" she asked, "Because I am beginning to fear that he may have abducted them… or…"

"Abducted them?" Mr Jamison appeared shaken to the core. "Oh no, Mrs Tate, not abducted, surely? He was seeking to discover if they were here; I do not believe he had the intention or the means to abduct them."

"Well then, has he persuaded her to go with him to meet Rickman, do you think?" she asked.

When Mr Jamison, still wearing a look of complete bewilderment, said nothing, she added reasonably, "It has to be one thing or the other, do you not agree, Mr Jamison? Alice Grey and young Thomas cannot have disappeared into thin air."

Realising that Mrs Tate was becoming somewhat distressed, Mr Jamison attempted to reassure her by offering to go into the village and ask if the girl had been seen there, at which suggestion Becky almost screamed.

"No, no, Mr Jamison, that will not do. We do not want to proclaim her presence here to the world, lest others, who may have even more malicious intentions towards her than your convict friend, should learn the truth. No, I beg you, please do nothing of the sort. It is possible, however, that either Alice or the convict may try to get in touch with you. If they do, would you bring us word directly please? You must not procrastinate, since any delay could be catastrophic. It could be a matter of life or death, so please remember that I am responsible for their welfare and I shall count on you to assist me in this," she pleaded, and he promised to do exactly as she asked.

It was getting dark, and Becky decided they should return to the house.

James offered to search the woods for a while longer, but there was general agreement that it would be of little use.

"Besides," said Becky, "it may not be safe to be wandering around in the woods after dark—I know Mr Jamison doesn't believe that his beloved convict is capable of violence, but desperate men may do reckless things, and an ex-convict may well be sufficiently desperate as to be dangerous."

Back at the house, they found everyone sunk into a state of despondency, which was deepened considerably by their return without Alice and the boy. Mrs Bates, who had recovered some of her customary composure, was anxious to know what, if anything, they had discovered and was only prevented from indulging in another bout of self-reproach by Becky, who told her the parson Mr Jamison had promised to help search for Alice and her son. A god-fearing, regular churchgoing woman, Mrs Bates took some comfort from that, although she was unable to explain even to herself what the source of that comfort was.

Mr Jamison, though a genuinely kind and good man of the cloth, had no heroic pretensions and certainly did not strike one as the type of man who might rescue damsels in distress, yet clearly he gave Mrs Bates some confidence, and for that Becky was grateful.

Going upstairs, she asked Nelly to prepare her bath and, as she went through her toilette, let her mind wander over the entire gamut of possibilities flowing from the disappearance of Alice Grey—bad, worse, and disastrous possibilities, for there could not have been any that were good.

If only Jonathan were here, she could have asked for his help, Becky thought as Nelly's voice broke in upon her musings.

"Ma'am, is it not possible that Alice may have gone to meet her husband?" she asked.

This remark jolted Becky back to reality. "What makes you think that, Nelly? Did Alice say anything that leads you to believe she would have done so?"

Nelly was innocently honest. "No, ma'am, but she did say how she had not seen him for a very long time and how much she wanted Tom to see his father, and when she said that she always sounded very sad, ma'am. I thought maybe if I felt that way, I should be wanting to see my husband—that is, if I was married and in the same trouble, which I thank God I am not, ma'am."

Becky smiled and, turning to let Nelly button up her gown, said, "I do understand, Nelly, and yet I wish I knew if Alice had indeed gone to meet her husband—that would not pose such a problem. It's the fact that we know nothing of her whereabouts or what her intentions were that makes me worry."

Nelly offered some further information, as she dressed her mistress's hair.

"I think Alice believed that he would send for them, when he had found a safe place for them to live, ma'am. She always swore he was innocent and believed he would return and prove it."

"Poor Alice, it is not as easy as she might think, Nelly," Becky said. "Her husband remains a convicted felon until he is acquitted or pardoned."

"But that isn't fair, ma'am!" Nelly complained, and Becky concurred.

"I know that, Nelly, but then, life is often not very fair, is it?" and reluctantly, Nelly agreed.

When they went downstairs, they noted that the weather had changed since early afternoon. There was a strong wind up, and clouds scudded across the sky. Rain was not far away.

As the candles were lit, the footman went to close the drapes across the large bay window, and in that moment, seeing a strange figure crossing the lawn, he called out, "Ma'am, there's someone out there coming towards the house."

Becky was up in a moment, and looking out on the darkening garden, she too saw a large figure, enveloped in a cloak, making its way towards the front porch. The manservant James went to the door and opened it cautiously, placing himself between those inside the house and whoever was approaching. No one was certain who this might be.

Becky stood to one side of the sitting room door, eager to discover who it was, but somewhat apprehensive that whoever it was may be the bearer of bad news. That it was not Alice Grey was obvious enough.

Moments later, James opened the door wide enough to let the burly figure into the hall, simultaneously exclaiming, "Why, Mr Jamison sir…" and then, as the boy emerged from inside Mr Jamison's cloak, "Tom! Where have you been, and where is your mother?"

On hearing his words, Becky rushed into the hall, and Mrs Bates, who had been alerted to what was afoot by Nelly, came forward and scooped the child up in her arms. He was wet and clearly scared. Mrs Bates and Nelly took him away to the kitchen; their priority was to get him dry, warm, and feed him well.

Mr Jamison was left to come into the sitting room and warm himself before the fire, while explaining his arrival with the boy.

He told a strange tale indeed.

About an hour ago, he said, he'd been reading in his study, when there had been a loud banging on the kitchen door. His housekeeper had opened the door to find Tom, cold and damp and probably hungry. She had taken him in and called Mr Jamison who, waiting until the child had been fed, had asked him where his mother was. It was then he had taken from inside his shirt a scrap of paper and handed it to Mr Jamison.

It was a note from Alice Grey, who had obviously sent the boy to the parsonage, knowing Mr Jamison would surely convey her message to Mrs Tate.

Not long afterwards, the storm that had been brewing all evening had broken over the district and forced him to wait until it had abated, before he could set out for Edgewater with the boy, he explained.

As he handed the paper to Becky, he apologised that he had not been able to reach her sooner, but Becky dismissed his concerns.

"Mr Jamison, there is no need for you to apologise; you have brought us the only good news we have had all day! I am in your debt and wish to say how very grateful I am." Mr Jamison beamed, looking very gratified at such fulsome praise, and continued to smile, although Becky, reading Alice's note, had begun to frown at its contents.

The note, though damp, was still quite legible. Clearly, Alice had had a good governess; she wrote well and in a neat round hand.

She apologised for her decision to leave the house while Mrs Tate was out and explained that she had received a message from her husband and had taken a chance to discover where he was and if it was possible for them to join him. It was what she had always wanted, she said, and begged Mrs Tate to trust her and to look after her son, Tom, until she returned. Plainly she had not wished to place the boy at risk.

Becky read the note a second time, with an increasing degree of anxiety.

Alice Grey had said nothing about who it was had brought her the message from her husband and where she intended to meet him. Becky was concerned that Alice may well have been lured away from Edgewater, where she was safe and secure, to some place where she may be exposed to danger without any protection. They had no proof that she had gone to meet her husband.

"Mr Jamison, I have to say that while I am exceedingly relieved to have Tom back with us, I cannot help being concerned about Alice Grey's safety.

"She claims she received a message from her husband; do you know who brought that message? Could it have been the man, the convict who approached you last week?"

Mr Jamison's smile disappeared, and he looked distinctly uncomfortable.

He shook his head and said he had no notion at all who could have brought Alice Grey a message; as far as he knew, the convict who had approached him in the churchyard had disappeared and never been seen again.

"He was probably frightened away when I mentioned the police," he said.

Becky wasn't willing to allow him such an easy exit.

"Are you sure, Mr Jamison? I understand that he has been seen on two or three occasions in the woods, near the church, and even in the spinney on my property! I am convinced he was trying to contact Alice."

At this, Mr Jamison's discomfort seemed to increase somewhat, and Becky had the impression that he was keen to leave. He put down his coffee cup, took out his watch and looked at the time, and put it away; then rose and walked to the window and looked out at the rain, which was falling much less heavily.

It was quite plain Mr Jamison was unwilling to talk about the convict, and Becky decided she would not press him at this stage. Better leave it for another time, she thought, but even as she rose to see him to the door, she added one significant line: "I cannot help thinking I ought call the police—were I not to do so and something untoward happens; if Alice comes to any harm, those of us who knew will be held responsible. I shall sleep on it and speak with my lawyer tomorrow before I decide," she said casually, and seeing Mr Jamison's eyes widen in surprise, Becky thought, "Good, clearly *that* has shaken you. Think on that, Mr Jamison, and let's see if you have anything more to tell me tomorrow."

He bade her good night and said he would pray that Alice would return safe and sound. Becky could not help smiling; she found that she was unable to believe entirely in the sincerity of Mr Jamison's sentiments, not because she suspected him of malicious intent; quite the contrary, she had no evidence that he was anything but a good and decent man. However, she had not forgotten that in every conversation they had had about Alice Grey, Mr Jamison had appeared exceedingly keen that Alice should be reunited with her husband. Was it possible, Becky wondered, that the parson could have connived with the convict to help get Alice Grey away from Edgewater to meet her husband?

Incredible as that might have seemed, she could not put out of her mind the niggling doubts that assailed her and kept her restless all night long.

Writing in her diary, Becky pondered her options and decided that she needed the advice of someone with a sound knowledge of the law. She wrote:

> *I am in no mood to put myself at variance with the law. Perhaps I should do as I said I would and see my lawyer—he could advise me; but would he then compel me to inform the police? If he did, how would that affect poor Alice Grey and her husband?*
>
> *It may well lead them to him, and if he was arrested, what would she do? Of one thing I can be quite certain: she will not thank me for interfering in her life.*

Recognising the dilemma she was in, Becky was deeply troubled and spent many sleepless hours agonising over Alice Grey.

What if she didn't return? How would they find her, and what of the boy? Becky felt sure she would have to carry the blame for any misfortune that befell his mother. It was not a circumstance she contemplated with any degree of equanimity.

As she turned the events over again in her mind, Becky wondered who she could apply to for some practical advice. She did not feel she could trouble her sister again; it was not a matter on which either Catherine or her husband could be expected to have much knowledge or experience. Yet it was imperative that she get some sound advice. Once again, her mind turned to Jonathan Bingley.

He was indeed the ideal person to help her, but despite this, on reflection, she decided against applying to him. She reminded herself that a female relative who calls upon a gentleman for help in other than the direst of circumstances may well be considered a nuisance by his family, and Becky had no wish to be so regarded.

Finally in desperation, she decided that on the morrow, she would write to Jonathan's son-in-law, Mr Colin Elliott, MP. He was already aware of some of the circumstances of the case of William Rickman, and Jonathan had said he had friends in the Home Office, which made it seem a sensible course to follow.

Using some of the information given her by Mrs Bancroft as well as her own observation, she wrote, laying all the known facts before him and asking if he had any advice for her.

> *While I must ask you to accept my apologies for troubling you at this time, which I know is a busy period in the Commons, I should appreciate very much your opinion. How is this situation to be untangled? Should I seek the help of a lawyer or apply to the police?*
>
> *If I did, what are they likely to do? I am exceedingly keen to recover Alice Grey and discover if indeed her husband is in England as we have been led to believe, but I am very afraid that any move on my part may lead others to her and so make matters worse for both of them. While we wish to see them reunited, it would be no comfort to have them torn apart again by the law.*

Having struggled with her dilemma for most of the night and a good part of the following day, Becky finally sealed and despatched her letter.

When it was done, feeling weary and longing for the soothing satisfaction of nature, she went out to walk around the grounds alone. She had decided she would say nothing to Mr Jamison about her approach to Mr Elliott. She did not feel she wanted to take him into her confidence on this matter.

She had begun to feel increasingly isolated, unable to confide in anyone.

Having written to Mr Elliott, she was impatient for an answer but knew there was no help for it, for wait she must for Colin Elliott's reply, however long it took. She was aware that he was a busy man, involved in much of the political machinations that were afoot at the time, but hoped desperately that he would find time to respond to her request.

The afternoon sun, already low in the west, cast long shadows over much of the grounds. As Becky walked towards the lake, her eyes were drawn to the poplars in the spinney, already deep in shadow. It had always attracted her, the sort of atmospheric scene she would have liked to paint if she had had the talent and skill.

She stood a while beside the water, looking across to the meadows beyond, lost in her troubled thoughts, when suddenly she thought she saw a figure in the spinney, moving swiftly in and out of the trees.

Glimpsed only for a moment, in fading light, Becky could not be sure who or what it might be and strained her eyes to see if she could make out anyone she might identify. But even as she looked, clouds moved over the setting sun, deepening the shade. It was almost dusk, and save for the slender trunks of the poplars, all else was vague and indistinct.

Becky waited; if whoever it was showed himself again, she thought, she would have to investigate.

Around the grounds, birds were returning to their nests in the trees as the light receded and then suddenly, just as she thought her eyes may have deceived her, a slim figure slipped for a moment out of the darkness of the spinney into the last of the evening light, stood there a moment, and then stepped back into the shelter of the trees again.

Becky did not stop to think; she knew only that whoever it was had to be a link with Alice Grey, and she intended to find out why he (or she) was there.

Without even a backward glance towards the house, she set out along the path that would take her around the lake, through the meadow, and into the spinney.

That the person had twice stepped out of the trees, quite deliberately, suggested to her that he or she had wanted to be seen.

Becky knew she must have been clearly visible to whoever it was, as she stood in the open at the lake's edge. She had not stopped to consider the risk she took in approaching the unknown figure.

Something, perhaps the fact that the person was slight and appeared to be clad in a long robe or gown, had allayed her fears.

As she approached the edge of the spinney, however, Becky, conscious of the darkness that surrounded her, wished she had a light. She stopped, wondering if it might not be sensible to return to the house for a lantern and a servant to accompany her; but then thought, "What if the person takes fright and flees?"

She stepped back only for a moment, considering how she should proceed, when there was a rustle in the bushes, and panicked by the sound, she asked quickly, "Who's there? What do you want?"

When the answer came, "Please, ma'am, it's me—Alice," her relief was indescribable.

"Are you alone?" Becky asked when she got her breath back.

"Yes, ma'am," said the girl, stepping out of the trees and moving towards her. "I had to come, ma'am; I had to know if my boy was safe. Is he with you, ma'am?" she asked, and though Becky could not see her face clearly, the strain in her voice was unmistakable.

Becky was momentarily stunned into silence, then in a rush she asked, "Good God, Alice, what have you done? Why did you not speak to me?"

"Yes, Tom is here, and he is well looked after, but he is restless and asks always for you. Where have you been?"

"Poor mite, he doesn't understand," said the girl softly.

"And neither do I. What has been happening, Alice? I must know," Becky insisted and added, "It's very cold out here, will you not come back to the house?"

Alice drew her shawl around her and shook her head.

"Not today, ma'am; I came only to see you if I could, to say I was sorry for the way I left you and to discover if my Tom was safe. I cannot stay."

Becky was bewildered. "Why ever not? What have you done? You are not in any trouble I hope?"

"Indeed no, ma'am," Alice replied. "It is only that it will cause too much talk among the servants and get around the village. It's best I avoid that for a little while."

Becky wanted to know more.

"Have you seen your husband?"

Alice replied softly as if afraid she might be overheard. "No, ma'am, but I have sent him a message through a friend, and he will come as soon as he can, I am sure of it."

"And where are you staying?"

"I am sorry, ma'am, but I cannot say. But please do not be anxious for me, I am in no danger; I am with a family in the village—they are good, kind folk."

"Are you sure?" With every answer Becky's astonishment grew.

"Yes, ma'am, and I promise to be very careful, as you instructed me. I do know there's folk who would like to get a hold of me, but I won't be tricked, ma'am. I know what I want, and I am determined to have it."

Becky urged her to return to the house, but without success. "I have been so anxious about you—last night I almost went to the police."

This brought the girl almost to her knees; she reached out and held on to Becky's hands as she pleaded, "Please, ma'am, not the police, I beg you. They will only take my husband away again and send me back to Blessington! You must not go to the police."

Becky gave her word, but added, "Then I need to know where you may be found. What do I do if Tom sickens for his mother and will not eat or sleep? How shall I find you?"

Alice responded quickly, "If you need to find me urgently because Tom is sick and only because Tom is sick, please leave a message at the parsonage. Mr Jamison will know how to find me. I will return later in the week, and if need be, I shall come to see my boy. Please, ma'am, trust me, as soon as I hear from William, I promise to return."

Becky was unable to decide what to think of this plan or how she might advise her. It seemed Alice Grey had made her own plans, and there was little anyone could do to change them.

Becky asked if she had enough money, and the girl replied that she had sufficient for now. "I don't need much, now Tom is with you, ma'am. Thank you for that thought, ma'am, and God bless you," she said as she held on to Becky's hand for a while longer.

Becky could not hold back her tears; she was glad of the darkness as she drew the girl to her in a swift embrace and let her go, urging her again to take care.

There was something about Alice Grey that went directly to her heart; a mixture of innocence and resilience that put her in mind of Josie.

She went, swiftly and quietly, taking the path through the churchyard into the village. There was by now only the light of the rising moon, and her slight figure in its dark garments was soon lost from sight among the trees. Becky prayed she would be safe.

Returning to the house, Becky found Mrs Bates and Nelly in a state of some anxiety because their mistress had gone out to walk around the grounds and not returned. With Alice's disappearance, their nervousness had increased and their relief when she walked in the door was palpable.

They were eager to know why she was late; it was almost dinnertime.

Becky gave some vague explanation about being entranced by the sunset and the early rising moon, then went directly upstairs to dress for dinner.

This time, she could confide in no one. Becky felt more alone than ever.

Chapter Thirteen

T WO THINGS HAPPENED UNEXPECTEDLY in the days following that significantly altered Becky's perception of the matter concerning Alice Grey and her husband William Rickman.

Mr Colin Elliott, MP, responded to her letter much earlier than she had expected. As a member of the recently elected government of Mr Gladstone, Becky had assumed he would be too busy with matters of state to pay close attention to her request.

But, as he was a courteous and discreet gentleman, she had anticipated a polite but brief reply would be forthcoming in a fortnight or so, which was why his swift response surprised and delighted her. In it, he acknowledged her own efforts in gathering the information she had sent him regarding the case of William Rickman. He wrote:

> *Dear Mrs Tate,*
>
> *Your persistence is admirable, and I do believe the material you have gathered suggests that Mr Rickman may well have been the victim of either connivance, corruption, or both. At the very least, there appears to have been a clear case of false witness.*
>
> *I should like to place all this information before a very good friend and colleague of mine, a lawyer and a Member of Parliament himself, with an*

abiding interest in cases of this type. Once he has seen the information, it is possible he will wish to meet with you. Were I to arrange an appointment, I wonder if you would be able to travel to London to meet him. It would give us an opportunity to hear at first hand the details of this strange, unhappy tale and for you to obtain the best available legal advice on the matter.

Meanwhile, dear Mrs Tate, please advise Alice Grey to lie low and not attract undue attention to herself or her husband, if he is in hiding. It would not do to let Mr Danby or any of his henchmen discover what is afoot. It would seriously jeopardise any hope of success and may even endanger Mr Rickman's life. Remember, these are desperate men.

He concluded with his best regards and expressed the hope that he would soon hear when she could arrange to come up to London.

Becky, already pleased by his prompt response, was elated by his opinion on the case of William Rickman, which had been clearly given after some serious consideration. It was now even more pressing that she should find Alice Grey and urge her to take great care not to be discovered.

How to do this was a question she was pondering with some concern, when without warning, her sister Catherine arrived looking very grave indeed. Surprised, Becky went to greet her, only to be asked in a hushed voice if they could speak in confidence, without being overheard.

Becky's surprise turned to astonishment, but she said, "Of course," and took Catherine up to her room directly, instructing Nelly to bring them tea and biscuits, but thereafter, to ensure they were not disturbed.

Catherine had never appeared so serious, and Becky was most anxious to discover what it was had caused her to look so solemn.

Once Nelly had brought in the tea tray and left the room, Becky could hardly wait to ask, "Cathy, what is it? I can see that you are distressed; what has happened?"

Catherine put down her cup and spoke softly, "Becky, my dear, I must ask you to prepare yourself for a shock. I had to come because it was important that you should not be left in ignorance."

"Left in ignorance of what?" Becky interrupted.

"Mr Jamison has been to see me," replied Catherine, who was clearly troubled and seemed to struggle to explain, "and he wished to confess…"

"Mr Jamison wished to confess? Confess what?" Consternation was written all over Becky's face.

"What indeed," said her sister. "Becky, he has admitted to deceiving you. He is ashamed of having done so and could not face you himself; I think he hoped, by telling me, to alleviate some of that shame, and he has asked me to convey his most profound apologies to you."

"In what way has he deceived me?" asked Becky, even more confused.

Catherine's voice was low as she explained that he had done so in a good cause, apparently to protect Alice Grey from discovery.

Catherine revealed that it *was* the ex-convict who had brought Alice a message from her husband, and Mr Jamison, who took it from him and delivered the note to Alice Grey, whom he had met secretly in the woods.

He had also agreed, when Alice had decided to go with the man to meet her husband, to look after her son, Tom, whom she had arranged to deliver to the parsonage. When Becky had asked him about Alice's disappearance, he had not been honest with her; he was sorry about that, but he had given Alice his word, Catherine explained.

"And does he know where she is?" Becky demanded to know. "Cathy, I am responsible for her safety. I must know."

"He says he does not know where she is, but he does have the means to contact her. He has promised to help her and wishes me to explain this to you. I believe he hopes you will forgive his actions—he tells me he is truly sorry, Becky, and I have no reason to doubt his word."

But Becky was not so easily placated. She said, "Why could he not have taken me into his confidence? He knew how anxious I was... I cannot understand why he felt he had to deceive me. He knows I have the girl's interest at heart."

"He does, and he is very contrite, Becky," said Catherine.

"So he should be. If he continues to help Alice Grey, I have no quarrel with him, but I must be able to trust him. You may tell him that, Cathy, but tell him also that I am deeply hurt. I have been through days of unnecessary anxiety. However, I am prepared to forget the matter, if he will promise to be honest with me in the future."

Catherine was certain that Mr Jamison, who was generally liked in the community he served, would have no difficulty with such a promise. She knew, too, that she feared Becky's disapproval.

The sisters, clearly relieved to have that part of their conversation finished and done with, proceeded to other, more congenial matters.

As Becky revealed more of the circumstances surrounding Alice Grey and her husband, including the interest taken in the case by Mr Colin Elliott, Catherine began to comprehend the gravity of the situation. Her initial inclination had been sympathetic, but clearly more was required in the face of recent developments, and she felt she had to support Becky in her efforts to obtain some justice for the couple, who were clearly victims of wicked, corrupt men, at the least.

When Becky mentioned Mr Elliott's request that she travel to London to meet his colleague the lawyer, who might be of help to them, she had not expected that her sister would welcome this suggestion. Not only did Catherine listen thoughtfully, she went so far as to encourage her to go.

"It can certainly do no harm, Becky, and it may well do much good. Your meeting with Mr Elliott and his friend may assist in their understanding of the young couple who are the innocent victims in this sorry business. Do you not agree?" Catherine asked.

Becky did agree that any opportunity to press their case should not be ignored. Moving to practical matters, she asked, "Do you suppose I should stay at the Bingleys' place in Grosvenor Street? I could ask Jonathan and Anna?"

Catherine had some doubts.

"You could, but I would not advise it. It may involve you in too many explanations. There is a very convenient hotel that Frank uses whenever he is in town on business; it should suit you well. It is a family business, very comfortable, and not expensive. I shall ask him for the address for you. I suppose you will take Nelly?"

"Of course," said Becky, and in that instant, a most audacious plan occurred to her, which she was not yet ready to discuss with Catherine.

She wanted time to think about it and make her plans. Nevertheless, the more she thought about it, the more determined she became to put it into action.

Not long afterwards, the sisters parted, with Catherine promising to help Becky in any way she could, but urging her sister to take great care.

"I know you must be aware that you are dealing with cruel, vindictive men, so you must promise me you will not place yourself in danger. Becky, I know your tenacious spirit well, but it does make me afraid for you sometimes," she said, and there was anxiety in every line of her face.

There were tears in Becky's eyes as they embraced and she said softly, "I thank you for your understanding, Cathy, and I promise I will bear in mind all you have said; I shall do nothing rash or stupid. I know I can ask for your help, but I had not done so only because I felt I had no right to trouble you and Frank with matters that had so little connection with yourselves."

Catherine looked hurt. "Becky dear, you cannot believe that. Anything that troubles you so profoundly must surely be of concern to us, and if we can help, we will. Both Frank and I think alike on this. You must know that."

Becky smiled and hugged her sister again and even as she saw her leave, began to make her plans.

Later, she set out to find Mr Jamison.

She found him at the parsonage, where he greeted her, looking rather dejected. Clearly, he feared she had come to berate him for his conduct. However, when she addressed him as though nothing untoward had occurred, he realised that Mrs Burnett had already been to see her sister and explained his actions far better than he could. He was very grateful indeed for Catherine's intervention and Becky's apparent forbearance.

Becky stated the reason for her visit directly; she wished, she said, for him to contact Alice Grey immediately and arrange for her to come to the parsonage, where Becky wished to meet with her. She said nothing of their encounter on the previous evening.

"I should prefer it to be here; I do not wish that the staff at Edgewater be made aware of this meeting. Besides, it could upset Tom, were she to arrive and disappear again," she said, and Mr Jamison agreed.

She told him no more, determined to teach him a lesson for not having trusted her, but left, asking that he send her a message when the meeting had been arranged.

It was late afternoon of the following day, when Mr Jamison came to Edgewater with the news that Alice would meet with her at the parsonage later that evening. He had seen the girl himself, he said, revealing for the first time that he did know where she was staying, with a farmer and his wife some distance from the village. He had told her of Becky's desire to see her, and she was willing and indeed eager for the meeting, he said, because she seemed to set great store by Mrs Tate's ability to help her and her husband.

"Well done, Mr Jamison," said Becky generously, "I am glad we are going to meet, but as to my ability to help Alice, a great deal will depend upon Alice and indeed her husband. But I shall do what I can, and we shall see what eventuates."

Mr Jamison, obviously contrite, appeared ready to offer his help, but Becky made it clear that she needed no one else at her meeting with Alice Grey. Disappointed, the parson left, leaving her smiling to herself.

Becky had no intention of revealing her plan to anyone else.

That evening, accompanied by her maid, Nelly, she went to the parsonage, where they waited for Alice Grey to arrive.

When she appeared, Becky was amazed at the calmness with which she greeted them and even more by the matter-of-fact manner in which she listened to what was proposed. It seemed as though Alice Grey, having once decided that she would take the first step to find her husband, had no reservations about what risks she would take to achieve her goal.

At the outset, Becky asked, "Alice, have you heard from him?"

The girl nodded and took a folded sheet of paper from inside her gown and handed it to Becky, who glanced at it and saw but a few sentences in what was clearly an educated hand.

The message was a deeply personal one from a man to his wife and son, from whom he had been forcibly and, he believed, unjustly separated. Becky did not wish to pry and so read it quickly before returning it to Alice, whose hand trembled as she took it and hid it away. It had been the first evidence she'd had in three years that he was alive.

Becky's voice reflected her own feelings. "I am sorry, Alice, that you and Tom have had to suffer for so long. I do hope we can get your husband back. We shall certainly do our best. But we need your help."

Alice nodded, indicating her willingness to assist.

Having listened without interruption to the information Becky had gathered and the plan she had devised, Alice asked but one or two questions, relating chiefly to the situation of her husband, before agreeing to participate. Assuring her that neither of them would be in any danger and that her son would be safely lodged and cared for, Becky had outlined a daring scheme, whereby she would travel to London, taking Alice with her as her maid, while Nelly would remain at the Dower House and look after Tom. No one, save the three of them and Mr and Mrs Burnett, would know of the plan, not even Mr Jamison or Mrs Bates, she promised, and Alice calmly agreed.

"It will give you a chance to tell everything you know about the conduct of Mr Danby and the rest to the gentlemen who hope to help William," Becky explained. "Once they know all the facts, they will be in the best position to do what is required to get William his pardon." It was plain from her response that Alice had no qualms about her part in the scheme.

Having sworn Nelly to secrecy and cautioned Alice about saying anything to anyone, Becky and the two girls entered the front room of the parsonage, where they waited for Mr Jamison to return.

Clearly, he had hoped to be taken into their confidence, but neither Becky nor Alice revealed anything of their plans before thanking him for his help and leaving to return, Becky and Nelly to Edgewater and Alice to her lodgings in the village.

As she walked away, towards the village, they noted a figure come out of the trees and join her, protectively shepherding her along the path. Becky wondered who it was, but said nothing, except to warn Nelly not to speak a word of this to anyone at Edgewater.

On the morrow, Becky went with Nelly to call on her sister.

When she revealed her plan, Catherine was understandably sceptical at first. "Becky, are you sure this is possible, let alone wise? Will not someone discover the truth and thwart your plan, probably placing both Alice and you in danger?"

But Becky was confident.

"What is there to discover? Nelly and Alice are the same size and can pass for one another quite easily, and since she is to be my personal maid, no one else will have access to her. It will give us the opportunity to let Mr Elliott and his lawyer friend get a firsthand account of what went on in Blessington with Danby and his uncle, and the manner in which William Rickman was falsely accused and unjustly convicted.

"Alice, you must remember, is a gentleman's daughter; she is educated and well spoken and makes a most credible witness. Her evidence together with the information I have from Mrs Bancroft will make a more powerful case than if I presented it alone. Remember, Alice was a witness to everything in this case, whilst I am only able to repeat what others have told me."

Catherine had to agree.

"I do see the point of your argument, Becky; it is only that I am rather apprehensive about your taking Alice to London. What does Mr Jamison think?" she asked.

To her surprise Becky replied, "Mr Jamison does not know, and I do not intend to tell him. Please, Cathy, I must rely on you not to give any hint of what I am going to do to him or anyone other than Frank."

Catherine was puzzled but did not question Becky's judgment. She knew her sister was far more experienced than she was in the machinations that were required in these matters. She agreed not to speak of it to anyone except her husband.

"And you will let me leave Nelly and Tom with you while I go to London?" Becky asked.

"Of course. Did you think I would not?" Catherine replied.

"Thank you, Cathy; I should have known you would help."

"I am happy to help, Becky, but you must promise me that you will take good care of yourself and Alice. You do realise you cannot afford to make a mistake in this matter?" she cautioned, and Becky nodded, understanding well the gravity of what she was intending to do.

"Dear Cathy, your good judgement and wise counsel have never failed us. I will be very careful and especially with Alice. You see, as she is to be my maid and travelling companion, she needs must go everywhere with me, and I have the best possible reason for keeping her at my side at all times. No one would expect me to leave a young girl alone in a hotel in London."

Catherine appeared to concede that this was the case, even though she retained some degree of nervousness about her sister's bold scheme. Accustomed as she was to Becky's impulsive nature, Catherine could not help being concerned that her plans may go awry. She knew she would pray daily that they would not.

Some days later, having secured their travel arrangements and fixed their appointments in London, Becky and Alice, the latter suitably attired in one of Nelly's gowns and looking every bit the perfect ladies' maid, travelled to London on the train.

Taking a hansom cab to the hotel, where a suite of rooms had been reserved for them, Becky asked for a light meal to be served to them, before sending a note round to Mr Colin Elliott's office at Westminster advising him of her arrival in London. He responded promptly with a message saying he would call for her at four o'clock and accompany her to the chambers of his friend and colleague the lawyer, Mr Harding, who was keen to assist in resolving this important case. He expressed the hope that they might achieve some benefit for the young couple who had been for too long the victims of malfeasance.

Alice, who was carrying out her duties as ladies' maid most assiduously, was laying out her mistress's clothes and accessories when the message arrived. Becky smiled as she read it, satisfied that the first step in securing the freedom of William Rickman had been successfully taken.

As Becky read it out aloud, Alice's eyes widened as if in disbelief and as the import of Mr Elliott's words dawned upon her, they filled with tears.

Chapter Fourteen

MR GLADSTONE'S VICTORY, WITH a substantial majority in the general election and his subsequent determination to initiate a number of important social reforms, had given Colin Elliott a whole new purpose as a member of the House of Commons.

The establishment of a system of primary schooling for all children had been an abiding interest for which he had striven for many years. It had for all of that time seemed a vain hope; now, it was a genuine possibility and the policy was absorbing much of his time and attention.

Becky was well aware of this, being herself an ardent advocate of the policy. Which was why, she explained in her letter to Catherine, that it was particularly generous of Mr Elliott to take the time to assist them in the difficult matter of Alice Grey and her husband. She described in some detail the events of that afternoon, when Mr Elliott had called at the hotel to take her to meet Mr Harding.

Colin Elliott had expected to find Becky Tate ready and waiting for him, but he had not expected that her maid would also be ready and waiting to accompany them. When Becky had greeted him and introduced her companion as Alice Grey (or Mrs William Rickman), he had been truly taken aback. Nevertheless, he had greeted the young woman politely, declaring that he was pleased to meet her. Alice had immediately thanked him for his kindness in offering to help her husband, which seemed to impress Mr Elliott, Becky wrote:

While there is no knowing what Mr Elliott had imagined Alice Grey would look like, it was quite clear he had not anticipated that she would turn out to be such a presentable young person, pleasant in manner, soberly attired, and well spoken. I think, Cathy my dear, that if Mr Elliott was surprised, then Mr Harding was likely to be quite astonished. He was probably expecting a simple country lass!

Becky had explained to Mr Elliott that she had brought Alice with her "because I felt that her evidence would be far more convincing, if presented directly to Mr Harding and you, than any recital of mine."

Colin Elliott had concurred, adding that his friend Harding, being an astute lawyer, would welcome the opportunity to hear her story at first hand and to question her about matters that required further elucidation, since she had been a witness to much of it.

And, wrote Becky, *this possibility did not appear to discompose young Alice at all. She nodded and, when I asked if she would mind, responded that she would be happy indeed to answer any questions that may help free her husband.*

Mr Elliott had accompanied them downstairs and helped them into the cab he had waiting, directing the driver to take them to Mr Harding's chambers.

When Catherine received her sister's letter, she was surprised at first by its lightness of tone. Becky's description of their arrival at Mr Harding's chambers was so entertaining as to make her sister forget the seriousness of their mission.

When we arrived, it had started to rain, and the roads were wet and dirty, and both Alice and I had to tread very carefully indeed to stay out of the mud and other unpleasant-looking matter that was running in the gutters! This is something I complain of constantly whenever I am in London. Of all these well-heeled ladies and gentlemen, does no one look down at what is under their feet and ask for some improvement to be made?

The lawyers' chambers in these parts of London are situated in some of the oldest and dingiest buildings you can imagine. Mr Dickens does not exaggerate. One cannot help but wonder that men who are said to make so much money in their profession should continue to occupy such inhospitable, dreary rooms.

Judging by the surroundings, I was confident that the astute Mr Harding would turn out to be a fusty old man, with his wig askew and a loud, booming voice. Imagine then my surprise, when his clerk admitted us into a room filled with books and papers and shortly afterwards a handsome, well-dressed gentleman entered and was introduced to us by Mr Elliott as "my friend Mr John Harding."

Cathy, my astonishment was so great, I do believe I stared for a few seconds at least before holding out my hand, over which he bowed in a most courtly fashion, before turning to do likewise with young Alice, who was introduced by Mr Elliott as Mrs Rickman. Mr Harding cannot be much more than forty, or perhaps just a little older, and he is by any standard a most personable gentleman. We are fortunate indeed that such a man should take an interest in our case.

Catherine read on, hoping to discover what had become of their mission to help free William Rickman, but found only continuing praise of Mr Harding.

He was courtesy itself, insisting that Alice and I should be seated beside the fire, without which we should have frozen in that room, and take tea and biscuits before proceeding to the business at hand. I have to say I was exceedingly impressed with his manners and subsequently his legal knowledge, which Mr Elliott had assured me was extensive.

He explained every particular of the possible application for a pardon, before asking Alice a number of very searching questions, which she, it must be said, answered without hesitation or equivocation. I believe both Mr Elliott and Mr Harding were mightily impressed with Alice.

At the end of our meeting, Mr Harding remarked that her statement and answers to questions had been remarkably consistent and credible, which, coming from a lawyer of his standing, is high praise indeed.

So you see, dear Cathy, it was certainly an advantage that I had brought Alice along to London with me. I am sure you will agree.

We are now safely lodged in this very comfortable little hotel, and tomorrow, if we are fortunate enough to have some fine weather, I hope to take Alice to Regent's Park and visit the London zoo! She is very keen to catch a glimpse of an elephant!

Mr Elliott did invite us to visit the Ladies Gallery in the Commons, but I think that may be a little unwise in the present circumstances. One never can tell who one might bump into in the lobbies at Westminster. Besides, Alice does not have a gown suitable for such an occasion.

We are to meet with Mr Harding again on Friday, and thereafter, we hope to return to Kent. God and the railways willing, you shall see us on Saturday afternoon.

Your loving sister,

Becky

In a hurried postscript, written just before sending her letter to the post, she had added:

Dearest Cathy, a note has just arrived from Mr Harding. He has made some enquiries and would like to acquaint us with the information he has received and has asked us to call on him this afternoon at half past four. I am hopeful this will be good news!

Catherine could scarcely wait until Saturday afternoon to discover what it was Mr Harding had found and if this would materially affect his ability to pursue the application for a pardon for William Rickman.

She showed Becky's letter to her husband, saying, "I do wish Becky had waited until after their meeting with Mr Harding to send this letter to the post; she could then have given me some indication of the way things had turned out."

Frank Burnett heard the frustration in his wife's voice and laughed gently as he read Becky's letter through.

"Dearest, you should know your sister well enough by now to be aware that she would never have considered holding her letter back once it was finished. It is so like a writer; having added a postscript that whets your appetite for more, she sends it off to the post!"

Catherine could see what he meant; he was right—it was exactly what Becky would have done. Yet Catherine was impatient to know what had happened; what had Mr Harding discovered, and why was he so keen to meet them?

"I do wish I knew," she said, and her husband could not but be amused at her impatience. Since being married to Catherine and having her sister Becky living at Edgewater, he had been frequently diverted by the divergence in their characters, yet they were so close and clearly devoted to one another. He knew Catherine would fret until Becky returned on Saturday, and then, he was certain, neither would be satisfied until all had been revealed.

"I fear there is no help for it, my love," he said gently. "You must wait until your sister returns. Meanwhile, can I interest you in a story that may be of some relevance to the situation your sister and Mr Harding are trying to resolve?"

Intrigued, Catherine came to sit beside him as he continued, "When I was at the British Museum last week, I discovered, by some assiduous searching, that there have been pardons granted to convicted men, not many, mind, and certainly not without a good deal of difficulty, but it has been done. One, I found, involved a man who had been transported to New South Wales, a certain William Robinson of Edinburgh, and another was a young man, one George Bates of Sussex. In the latter case, evidence was adduced of the exemplary conduct of the man Bates after his conviction and the possibility of false witness having been given at his trial by those who wished him out of the way."

"And were they both pardoned?" Catherine asked.

"They were, one by the Governor of New South Wales under the power granted to him by King George the Third, and the other was released much later, my recollection is that it was around 1850 or thereabouts."

Catherine was delighted.

"Does that mean William Rickman may be granted a pardon too?" she asked, but her husband was loathe to raise her hopes too high.

"Not necessarily, my dear, but to the lawyers, the existence of a precedent means there is a good chance of success. Well, these cases can certainly be termed precedents. I made a few notes, which Becky may wish to pass on to her friend Mr Harding," he explained.

So pleased was Catherine with the information her husband had uncovered that she was less inclined to spend the time until Becky's return in a state of anxiety. Instead she could now look forward to her sister's arrival with some hope, thanks mainly to Mr Burnett's discovery, and for this she felt particularly loving and appreciative of him.

"You are such a comfort to me, dearest," she said, settling in beside her husband, and for her subtle change of mood Frank Burnett was grateful indeed. Together, they had discovered the pleasures of love, which had been cruelly denied them in youth, and having done so, they cherished one another with singular warmth and devotion.

❦

Becky returned with Alice on the Saturday as advised and went directly to the Dower House. Alice was eager to be reunited with her son and Becky had some good news for Catherine and Frank. She revealed that Mr Harding's enquiries had confirmed that a credible case could indeed be made that William Rickman had been a victim of false witness and he intended to lodge an application for a pardon immediately. His hopes for a successful outcome were high, she said.

It was excellent news, and Catherine congratulated her sister on her success. "I am so proud of you, Becky; if Rickman is pardoned, it will be all due to you," she said.

But Becky would not accept all of the credit for it; she was careful to point out that success was not guaranteed by any means. "We shall have to wait awhile. Mr Harding has warned us it could take many months; if he does succeed, it will be due not to me but to his skill and persistence. Cathy, he is a truly remarkable gentleman. I have to confess that I have not met any person that I have admired so much in years. He is both principled and clever, a rare combination, I think you will admit," she continued, eyes bright with enthusiasm.

"Mr Elliott informs me that Mr Harding, though not much over forty, is so well thought of by the Prime Minister, he is to advise the government of Mr Gladstone on his new legislation."

Catherine and Frank exchanged glances; this was high praise indeed. They had no recollection of Becky being so exhilarated by meeting anyone else.

"And when will you know if he has been successful in obtaining a pardon for Rickman?" Mr Burnett asked.

"Not for a while, I fear, but he has promised to write and keep me informed of his progress in the case. Indeed, I may even have to go back to London; I shall not have to take Alice with me again though. She has made a full state-ment to Mr Harding with which he was very satisfied."

"Will you take Nelly then?" asked Catherine.

"I may," said Becky, sounding uncertain, and once again Catherine and Frank looked at one another. Becky's enthusiasm was certainly high, and they could not help wondering at the reason for it.

However, neither said anything at all.

After Becky had returned to Edgewater, taking Nelly, Alice, and Tom with her, Mr and Mrs Burnett went upstairs. After Catherine's maid had left the room, Frank Burnett entered their bedroom. Catherine, still seated before her mirror, was trying on a pair of earrings he had bought on his visit to London. Standing behind her, he admired them, but she seemed rather preoccupied.

"Do you not like them, my love? I thought they suited you rather well."

His voice interrupted her musing, and she was quick to reassure him.

"Of course I like them, Frank. I love them; they are beautiful. I am sorry, my dear, I think my mind was wandering… I cannot help worrying about Becky…"

"And her sudden enthusiasm for Mr Harding?" he concluded her sentence. Catherine turned to look up at him, disbelieving.

"Was it obvious to you too?"

He nodded, "One would have had to be very unobservant not to notice that she showed a certain partiality for the man; he must be a very personable fellow indeed."

"Perhaps he is, but to be so impressed on such short acquaintance, Frank, I cannot deny that I am somewhat apprehensive for her. After all, we know very little about this Mr Harding other than that he is a clever lawyer. Of his character, his family, we know nothing," said Catherine, and her voice told him that she was at least considerably perturbed by these latest developments in her sister's life.

"Frank, I should hate to think that Becky might make a mistake again, attracted to a man who is clever, handsome, and successful, just as she was to Anthony Tate," she said, and he was struck by the depth of her concern.

Their light-hearted banter had deepened in tone. There was no doubt that Catherine was anxious, and Frank felt he had to reassure his wife.

"You must not leap to conclusions, my love; your sister clearly admires him—perhaps he appeals to her sense of adventure—but she is not an impressionable young girl anymore, and I cannot believe she will allow her sound judgment to be overthrown by first impressions, however remarkable."

Catherine was not entirely convinced. "You are probably right, Frank, but Becky is impulsive and easily moved; if Mr Harding is as impressive as she says, and if he does succeed in getting Rickman a pardon, I fear her judgment will not stand in the way of her admiration for the man."

"Dearest, you are not suggesting that your sister is in danger of falling in love with him?" her husband seemed incredulous.

"No indeed," she replied and laughed as she did so. "If I thought that, my concerns would not be as serious. I do not believe my sister will fall in love so easily; my fear is that she will become entangled with a man she admires for his style and professional achievements, but does not love, just as she did with Mr Tate, and then she will be miserable all over again."

Once again, Frank Burnett tried to persuade his wife that she should not be too concerned, for not only was Becky unlikely to become so involved, it was equally improbable that Mr Harding would be available for such a liaison.

"A respected lawyer and a Member of Parliament, I doubt that he would be so inclined. He may even be committed already. No, my dearest, I do believe you are being too anxious; your sister will probably negotiate this situation quite successfully and avoid the obvious pitfalls."

His confidence did bring her some comfort, but Catherine knew enough of Becky's past life and general disposition not to be entirely reassured.

~᠅~

Some weeks later, Becky did travel to London, taking only her maid Nelly with her, ostensibly to attend another meeting with Mr John Harding and receive further information relating to the case of William Rickman.

On her return, she reported that an application for a pardon had been lodged and was being assiduously pursued. However, Catherine did note that while her sister was still hopeful of success, there was not as much fulsome praise for Mr Harding as before.

Trying to discover what had eventuated, without appearing to pry, Catherine found that Becky would say very little except that Mr Harding had promised the matter of William Rickman would be pursued most assiduously, but could give her no assurance of success at this stage.

"Did he indicate how long it might be before he would have an answer?" Catherine asked.

Becky answered in a voice that did not hide her disappointment. "No, Cathy, it does seem it will be many months, if not longer. Meanwhile, Alice and her husband must live apart. I feel for poor Alice and Tom and wish I could do something to help. It seems so cruel that they should be parted from Rickman, while lawyers and politicians argue about the merits of his case. It's so unfair."

Catherine could see that her sister was unhappy that matters had not moved faster. Becky was unused to procrastination and was impatient with the snail's pace at which the processes of the law seemed to move.

Later, Catherine was to discover from her own maid, whose friendship with Nelly was an advantage, that Mr Harding had called on Becky at the hotel and invited her to a dinner party at his town house in Mayfair, but Becky had declined the invitation.

Nelly's loyal version was that her mistress was "much too proper" to go to dinner at his house, but Catherine reckoned that it had less to do with propriety than with Becky's disappointment that Mr Harding had not been as successful as she had expected him to be.

She knew her sister well enough to understand that her frustration must have tarnished some of his brilliant reputation and probably diminished her enthusiasm for him.

Still, it was better that she should be disappointed than that her elation with his success should fire her admiration to the point where she believed herself in love with him, Catherine thought.

She had not suspected at the time it was announced that Becky's sudden acceptance of Anthony Tate's offer had been on the rebound, resulting from her disappointment when Jonathan Bingley became engaged to their sister Amelia-Jane. But she *had* wondered at the speed with which the pair had married a few months later. She hoped with all her heart that something similar wasn't happening all over again.

Unwilling to intrude upon her sister's privacy, Catherine maintained her silence, saying nothing for fear she might exacerbate the situation or, worse, distress Becky to the extent she might stop confiding in her altogether.

Meanwhile, it seemed that Alice Grey had accepted that she would have a long wait before she knew what fate was in store for her husband. She continued working at Edgewater, uncomplaining, grateful for the shelter and protection it offered her and her child, aware that her mistress and benefactor was determined to help them.

Neither the ex-convict nor any other stranger intruded upon their lives for some weeks, until one mild afternoon when Tom, who was playing in the yard, came racing in to his mother, crying out and pointing to a strange man coming up the drive.

His cries alerted Mrs Bates, who went outside to investigate, while Nelly rushed into Becky's study, where she found her mistress reading a book.

"Ma'am, please, ma'am, look, there's a man in the yard, and I think it's Tom's father..." she cried, and Becky going to the window, looked out in time to see Alice and little Tom rush out into the arms of a tall, gaunt man who gathered them up and held them both in a close embrace.

Lean and dark, his arms and neck brown with working out of doors, he looked older than his years. His clothes were old but clean, and on his head was a battered hat such as farm labourers wore. Becky had no doubt the stranger was indeed the husband and father that Alice Grey and her son had longed for. The warmth of their reunion was proof enough.

As they watched, both Becky and Nelly with tears in their eyes, the three sat down on a rough bench beside the stable door, in silence, as if unable to believe they were together at last. The man had one arm around his wife and hugged the boy to him with the other before releasing him to play.

Having waited awhile to allow the pair time alone, Becky sent Nelly out to ask Alice to invite her husband into the kitchen and to tell Mrs Bates to ensure he was given food and drink.

"He has probably walked miles to get here; he must be exhausted and hungry," she said, and Nelly raced away to do her bidding.

Later, Becky sent for Alice Grey and asked, "How did he get here?"

"He got a ride with a traveller, ma'am; there was no more work for him on the farm, and he decided to leave, but he wanted to see us before he moved elsewhere," Alice replied, quite unable to keep the delight out of her voice.

"What will he do now?" Becky asked, and Alice answered, "He means to look for work in the district, ma'am. He hopes to find lodgings in the village and maybe ask around the hop fields; there's always laboring work to be done after the harvest."

Becky thought a while and said, "There is work to be had on the Rosings estate; they are demolishing the burnt-out sections of the house and some of the old outbuildings. Will he do such work?"

Alice was sure he would. "I think he would do anything, ma'am. He works very hard."

Becky promised to ask her brother-in-law, Mr Burnett, who was in charge of the work at Rosings, if they had any suitable work for Rickman—but meanwhile, she urged Alice to be cautious about speaking too openly about their plans.

"And it is best that he stays out of the village for some time. There may be talk of a stranger seeking lodgings, and the police may become curious.

"It will not do to draw their attention to your husband, while Mr Harding is still trying to obtain a pardon for him."

Alice agreed at once. "Oh yes indeed, ma'am, I understand. I will tell him."

"Well, you may also tell him he can bed down in one of the unused stables. I shall ask Mrs Bates to provide him with some bedding and blankets. Now, Alice, I trust you to be very discreet and careful in everything you do. I know you are overjoyed to have him back, but it is important that both of you take very great care not to do anything that will draw undue attention to yourselves. You do not want people to be gossiping, do you?" Becky warned.

"Oh no, ma'am. I will be very careful, thank you, ma'am," said Alice, her eyes shining, and went away to break the news to her husband. If he could find work at Rosings and stay over at Edgewater, at least their family would be together.

It was almost impossible for her to comprehend what had transpired in the last few months to change her life, and though there were still many obstacles in their path and they had been warned not to be too optimistic, Alice Grey could not help humming to herself as she ran downstairs.

Watching her go, Becky's tears fell freely. Each time she saw the girl, she felt a sharp stab of pain, as she recalled the child she had lost. She was glad indeed that no one, not even her loyal Nelly, was there to see her weep.

Chapter Fifteen

I T WAS THE MIDDLE of Autumn, and Becky was becoming restive.

There had been no news from either Mr Harding or Colin Elliott about the progress of the application for a pardon for William Rickman. She had considered writing to Mr Elliott but had decided against it; he was a busy and diligent member of Parliament, and they were approaching the end of the sessions. He may not have welcomed an approach from her.

She wished desperately that she had the means to discover whether the appeal had travelled upward through the ranks of the bureaucracy or had stalled upon the desk of some procrastinating or pernickety official. More than once she had wondered if a letter to Colin Elliott's wife, Anne-Marie, might not help, but had decided against it, unwilling to draw more people into the small group who knew the details of the matter.

Rising from her desk, Becky walked restlessly about her study, playing first with one idea and then another but unable to fix upon any one of them. Looking out on the garden, she could see Tom playing on the lawn, while farther afield his father, wearing his battered old hat, was raking up the leaves and clearing away the debris left by the storm that had blown in from the northeast, keeping her awake most of the previous night.

Following her appeal to Mr Burnett, Rickman had been found some work at Rosings, but whenever he returned to Edgewater, he seemed to feel the need to make himself useful, working industriously at a variety of jobs around the grounds. Obliging and polite, he was generally well liked by the rest of the staff. Mrs Bates in particular could not praise him enough.

Becky smiled as she saw Alice come out of the kitchen and take him a mug of tea, which he drank, while she stood beside him and the boy raced back and forth between his parents. Having drained the mug, Rickman scooped the child up in his arms, and it seemed the boy whispered in his father's ear. Indeed, Nelly had already reported that the child had been trying to speak a few words again and that Alice was overjoyed. It was a picture of simple, warm affection that belied the anxiety they must feel about the future. It affected Becky deeply.

Recounting the incident, she wrote in her diary that night:

I would have given anything—all of the influence and comforts I have enjoyed these many years—to have felt such warmth and known such tenderness in my marriage.

I cannot tell for how long it will last, for much depends upon the pardon being granted. I can only pray that the appeal will succeed; if it does not and if the police come looking for him, I do not know what I will do. Perhaps, I should consult Frank and ask his advice so I may be prepared for such a situation.

I should not break the law, but it would certainly break my heart to hand him over to the police. Besides, Alice would never forgive me. It does not bear thinking about!

On the morrow, the post brought Becky some letters, one from Emily Courtney, thanking her for her concern and kind offers of help, and another from Jonathan Bingley's wife, Anna. The latter contained a surprise invitation to join them in London for an evening at the theatre. Anna wrote:

We are planning an evening at Covent Garden and a supper party after-wards at Grosvenor Street. Mr and Mrs Darcy are coming to London on one of their rare visits to the city, and so, I believe, are Colonel Fitzwilliam and Caroline, which should make for a very interesting party. We are expecting Anne-Marie and Mr Elliott, too. Becky, Jonathan and I were hoping you would join us.

Of course, you would be very welcome to stay at Grosvenor Street,
where we will be spending two weeks at least, before returning to
Netherfield. We should be delighted if you chose to stay on with us for some
days; it could be a lot of fun to spend some time in London at this time of
year, do you not think?

It certainly could, thought Becky, recalling previous visits to the opera in London; she had always been partial to the theatre. Besides, this visit would have the added benefit of affording her an opportunity to meet with Mr Elliott and enquire if he had any news of the progress of Rickman's pardon.

"Perhaps if I am very diplomatic," she said to Catherine, when she showed her Anna's letter, "he may not mind my asking."

Catherine encouraged her to accept the invitation. "Of course, you must go, Becky; write to Anna and say you will come. Just think, you could combine business with pleasure. I know you will enjoy yourself, you love the theatre, and will it not be fun to have both Lizzie and Caroline there?"

Becky agreed and, allowing herself to be persuaded, she wrote that night to Anna Bingley, thanking her for the kind invitation, which she was happy to accept. She had been in two minds, but Catherine's encouragement had made her decision easier.

She took the letter to the post herself, together with another, which she had written and kept awhile, re-reading and re-writing it many times before deciding to seal and send it.

It was a response to a letter that had arrived a fortnight ago from Mr Harding, which Becky had opened with much hope, expecting it to contain good news for the Rickmans. But disappointingly, it had contained no information at all about William Rickman's case; instead she had found within a formal proposal of marriage.

Becky had been completely taken aback.

Despite the fact that she had openly admired Mr Harding for his forensic skill and genuine dedication to the cause of justice for the poor and powerless, she had not supposed he had formed an attachment to her.

Certainly, she had become aware on their second and subsequent meetings, when he had greeted her with utmost cordiality, that he took pleasure in her company. Their conversations, when they had ranged beyond the unhappy fate of the Rickmans, had been interesting and agreeable. When he called on her at her hotel and invited her to a dinner party at his house, an invitation which, for very sound reasons, she had politely declined, she had no doubt of his being exceedingly disappointed.

Yet he had been very gentlemanly in his response, expressing the hope that perhaps he might be more fortunate on another occasion. Becky had been sensitive to his attentions and perceived some degree of partiality in his attitude towards her, but had assumed, too readily perhaps, that it was a mere transient attraction, a harmless fascination that would soon dissipate and most likely disappear when she returned home to Kent.

She had known similar circumstances before while working with her husband on political campaigns, but they had always amounted to little more than fleeting verbal dalliance.

That it might lead to a proposal of marriage, one couched in such serious terms, had never even entered her mind.

She could not deny that after the initial sense of shock, the realisation that a personable and prosperous young man some five years her junior had seriously contemplated the prospect of marrying her did bring some pleasure. It was certainly very flattering, but no more. Her own initial interest in him had lasted only a very little while, subsiding quickly into indifference, as other matters had demanded her attention, making it easier for her to reject his proposal.

The time taken to compose her letter of refusal was mainly on account of her wish to give as little offence as possible. She had no desire to hurt John Harding's feelings, not only because she was by nature kind and unwilling to upset someone she liked but also because she was conscious of his continuing role in obtaining a pardon for William Rickman. It would not do to jeopardise the success of something so important to Alice and her son, Becky decided.

How to reject an unwelcome proposal, from a man she admired but did not love, without appearing to affront the gentleman himself, had been the cause of several sleepless nights and many torn-up sheets of note paper. But finally it was done and in the post.

Returning from the village, she asked the driver to take the road through Rosings Park, intending to stop at the Dower House. When she got there, however, she found Catherine had gone out to the parish school.

Directing the driver to take the vehicle back by the main road to Edgewater, Becky decided to walk through the grounds to the school. It was not a long walk, and she had always enjoyed the crunch of Autumn leaves underfoot.

She was almost halfway there when she saw in the distance the figure of the local constable, Mr Hodges, unmistakable in his uniform, coming towards her through the trees.

Becky froze. What was he doing in Rosings woods?

Her thoughts flew instantly to William Rickman, who was working that day at Rosings, where the demolition of the burnt-out wing was proceeding apace. She was sure Constable Hodges was on his way there.

Turning around before he could see her, Becky walked swiftly back part of the way and then struck out through the old rose garden, taking a little used path and entering that part of the estate where work was in progress. There, she sought out Frank Burnett and warned him of the approach of the local constabulary and her fear that Rickman may be in danger of apprehension.

"If they were to find him here, Frank, they would take him away and lock him up, and who knows when his wife and son would see him again," she said, and Frank Burnett, practical as ever, asked no further questions but, going directly to where Rickman was working, had a word in his ear and despatched the young man on an errand into the east wing of the house.

As Mr Burnett returned to Becky's side, Constable Hodges was seen approaching them, but to her immense relief, he appeared to be just passing through. He greeted them, made a remark about the unseasonably mild weather, and went on his way, leaving her a little breathless.

As the constable passed out of sight, Frank Burnett asked, "You do realise you cannot hide him forever, do you not, Becky? If he does not get that pardon, he will be a wanted man, and if you conceal him, you will be breaking the law, too."

"But what can I do, Frank? I cannot refuse to help them. If they take him away, what will become of Alice and young Tom?" she said.

Frank Burnett looked very grave.

"Well, I should write to your friend Mr Harding and urge him to expedite the matter of Rickman's pardon. It is the only way to save him."

Becky groaned, realising that the letter she had posted an hour ago may well have destroyed William Rickman's chance of a pardon. After all, she knew very little of John Harding's character; although he had been amiable and friendly towards her, now she had rejected his offer of marriage, how would he respond?

What if he lost interest in the case altogether? What if he was a vindictive man and informed the police of Rickman's presence in the area?

Frank Burnett, seeing her obvious distress, urged her to step inside the building and rest awhile, but Becky was reluctant to do so and insisted on returning home, whereupon he insisted upon accompanying her, stopping *en route* at the schoolhouse to advise Catherine of the situation.

"My dear, I think your sister is unwell. It's nothing serious, probably just the exertion of a long walk and the shock of seeing Constable Hodges in Rosings woods," he explained and, not wishing to alarm her, added, "She was afraid he had come for young Rickman, but in fact he was just walking through the woods."

Catherine came out and, seeing Becky's pale, anxious countenance, decided to take her sister home to Edgewater, while her husband returned to Rosings.

There, sending for Nelly to help her mistress undress, Catherine urged her to rest awhile, promising not to leave her. She was in no doubt that Becky was feeling depressed. She sat with her while she rested and later took a cup of tea.

Then, without any prompting, Becky revealed what was troubling her, showing Catherine Mr Harding's letter and a copy of her response.

"I had no idea he had formed any attachment to me, Cathy; I certainly gave him no encouragement," she said, having explained the circumstances of his proposal and her rejection of it.

Catherine was not entirely convinced.

"Are you quite sure, Becky dear? I do recall you were very generous in your praise of Mr Harding after your first meeting. Is it possible he could have assumed that your quite understandable esteem could mean that you might welcome his proposal? It is, after all, a perfectly proper offer, and nothing in your circumstances or his own would stand in the way, if you were inclined to accept him."

Catherine had quite deliberately put a point of view, one contrary to her own inclinations, hoping that Becky's response would reveal her true feelings. And it certainly did, for Becky was adamant that there was no question of her ever accepting Mr Harding's offer of marriage.

"Why, Cathy, while he may be handsome and eligible as well as being a clever lawyer, I hardly know anything about him, his character, or family; above all I feel no deep emotional attachment to him at all. Oh I know I said he was personable and attentive, which I do not deny; he was very good company as well. But I do not love him, Cathy, and surely you, of all people, *must* know that another marriage without genuine love would be the very last thing I would contemplate."

Her outburst, sincere and passionate, did convince Catherine, and she put her arms around Becky as she continued.

"You do not believe I would make the same mistake again, do you, Cathy?" and Catherine did not have the heart to tell her that it was exactly what she had feared.

Instead, she did her best to comfort her.

"Of course not, Becky my dear, and in any event, I know how you love your life down here at Edgewater; I shouldn't think you would want to leave it all and go off to live in London, would you?"

Becky shook her head quite vigorously.

"Certainly not. It took me too long to acquire a place of my own; I am not inclined to leave it or share it, at least not unless it was with someone I could love very deeply indeed."

"And Mr Harding is not such a person?"

"Indeed he is not. You must believe me, Catherine; he is a clever and amiable gentleman, but I do not love him and could never marry him."

Catherine smiled and assured her sister she did believe her, but now a new anxiety assailed Becky.

"But, Cathy, what I fear is the nature of Mr Harding's response to my letter. What will he do about Rickman's pardon? Is it likely he would lose interest in the matter, or worse still, would he betray him to the police?"

Catherine could see she was genuinely troubled and was quick to reassure her, "Oh no, Becky, I do not believe that for one moment. Remember, he is also a friend and colleague of Mr Colin Elliott, as well as being a reputable lawyer. It would be unthinkable that he would, on some personal whim or because of his disappointment with your refusal, betray an innocent client, for that is what Mr Rickman is. If he did, how would he face his friends? No, Becky, I do not believe you need fear such a response at all."

She was very confident, and Becky appeared somewhat less distressed.

"Perhaps you are right, Cathy; I shall pray that you are," Becky said, and though she did not sound completely convinced, Catherine believed there was no further need for concern on that score.

Some days later, a letter arrived from Mr Harding, confirming Catherine's opinion. It was brief but served to set Becky's mind at rest. He wrote:

Dear Mrs Tate,

Thank you indeed for your letter. I am grateful for your generous remarks about me, although I am deeply disappointed that you feel unable to accept my offer. Had you done so, I should have been honoured indeed.

However, I do understand your reasons and do not question your right to respond as you have done. I cannot deny my regret, but your kind words of appreciation must be my consolation.

He followed with a paragraph explaining that the papers pertaining to William Rickman's appeal for a pardon had been sent to the office of the Lord Chamberlain. Two other Members of Parliament, one being Mr Colin Elliott, had allowed their names to go forward supporting the application. If approved, he explained, the pardon would be granted within a month or two, and he promised to advise her as soon as the outcome was known.

Concluding with his best regards and good wishes for her future happiness, he remained, he said,

Yours very sincerely,
John Harding.

Becky read the letter through twice, folded it and put it away, then unfolded it and read it again.

So great was her relief, she wept.

She could not have hoped for a better result. Mr Harding was, as her sister had predicted, a genuinely upright gentleman, and despite his disappointment, which he expressed without reservation, there was no hint of umbrage or spite in his words.

His attention to the matter of Rickman's pardon had been professional and effective, and his concluding salutation was generosity itself.

Becky was now ashamed at having suspected him of being capable of vindictiveness and even betrayal!

Contrite and chastened, she confided in her diary:

I am glad indeed to have been proved wrong in my fears. Thankfully, my first impressions of Mr H. as a decent and honourable man were right. I almost regret that I cannot bring myself to accept him; he will surely make some gentle, deserving young woman a most exemplary husband.

For my part, I am very happy to have made his acquaintance, for he is not only a clever lawyer but has both wit and understanding enough to be an excellent companion.

Yet, having learnt from my own unhappy experience that a marriage, to be truly happy, requires more than friendship and good conversation, I could not have agreed to his proposition.

Truly, I am so content as I am, that I doubt I shall ever wish to marry again; but if I do, it will only be for the deepest affection, and to a man with whom I could share the profound pleasures of my present existence and for whom I would be happy to surrender some of the independence I now enjoy.

Else, I shall stay happily single for the rest of my days.

Not long afterwards, she retired to bed in a more contented frame of mind than she had enjoyed for many a day.

End of Part Three

A Woman of Influence

Part Four

Chapter Sixteen

ARRIVING IN LONDON ON a cold, wet afternoon, Becky and her maid Nelly were met by Dickson, the young manservant sent by the Bingleys, to transport them from the railway station to the Bingleys' town house at Grosvenor Street.

Thanking him for attending to their luggage and protecting them as best he could from the rain, Becky asked if they were the only guests arriving that afternoon. She was wholly unprepared for his answer.

"Oh no, ma'am, we have been back and forth all day, Jack and I; there's many ladies and gentlemen arriving today and more tomorrow, but not all of them will be staying at Grosvenor Street, ma'am."

Though surprised, for Anna Bingley had not hinted that it was to be a very big party, Becky felt it would be unwise to pry, especially not to question Dickson about the Bingleys' guest list. She wondered if it could be a celebration of something—she knew it wasn't Jonathan's birthday; perhaps someone was receiving an Imperial honour of some sort. It was certainly possible and Becky was curious.

It was only after they had alighted at the house and Becky had been welcomed by Anna Bingley, who ushered her into a warm parlour, where tea and refreshments had been laid out before a comforting fire, that she discovered the reason for the festivities.

Anna confessed that she had been wheedled into hosting a combined celebration of two anniversaries in the family. Jonathan's daughter Anne-Marie and Colin Elliott had been married five years, while Anna's own marriage to Jonathan, which had taken place a few years earlier, was close enough in time to be conveniently linked to the family function.

"Jonathan and I had no wish to make much of our anniversary; we would have preferred to go away somewhere together rather than have a party, but Anne-Marie was keen, and its happy coincidence with a couple of other events, including the publication of Cathy's first little book of poems, persuaded us that we should agree," she explained.

The mention of young Catherine Bingley's book of poems brought an exclamation of delight from Becky, who knew all too well the difficulties a woman might encounter in trying to get into print. She knew that Catherine, Jonathan's younger daughter from his marriage to Amelia-Jane, had a talent for writing but had no idea that she had written anything that was ready for publication.

Anna revealed that the publication had been paid for by her father, as a gift to Cathy for her birthday. Becky could not help recalling with some poignancy her own daughter Josie's vain efforts to have her serious work accepted for publication.

Her proud father would surely have financed any number of privately published volumes; indeed he had urged her to write regularly for his journals, but Josie had not been satisfied. Her ambition to be published in the great metropolitan newspapers and journals had never been fulfilled; consequently her young life had been blighted by unfulfilled dreams. Becky hoped for Jonathan's sake that Catherine would be less demanding.

Considering her situation, that she should be invited to join in the celebration of the anniversary of Jonathan's wedding to her cousin Anna, seemed to Becky to be ironic indeed. Thankfully, she was confident that neither Jonathan nor Anna knew or would ever know what her own feelings had been. Feelings, she believed, she had at first concealed and then successfully subdued over the ensuing years.

Yet, each time she encountered him and saw his innate goodness and nobility of character, memories of her adolescent adoration returned, and she would catch herself wondering how things might have been if young

Amelia-Jane had not caught his eye and won his youthful heart. More recently, since her separation from Mr Tate, whenever she met Jonathan with Anna and saw the warmth of their mutual affection, she could not deny her feelings of simple envy. Not because she begrudged Anna her happiness with him, but because she longed to enjoy similar feelings of her own. And all this she had to conceal while maintaining an appearance of general bonhomie and familial friendliness.

It had not always been easy.

Although she would pride herself on being practical and resilient in most things, Becky remained at heart a hapless romantic, often reduced to tears at weddings by apparent manifestations of true love. Perhaps, she mused, it was because life had never afforded her the chance to inspire such love as she had seen between Mr Darcy and Elizabeth or Anna and Jonathan. Her marriage to Anthony Tate, though generally accepted to be a successful partnership, had left a void within her, which, after Josie's death, had become an abyss.

However, this was not the occasion to dwell on it, which was why she seized with some relief upon the publication of young Catherine's book of poems and declared that she must purchase at least six copies and hoped Cathy would sign one for her.

"I am quite sure she will be delighted to oblige," said Anna as they sat together taking tea.

"And are Mr Darcy and Lizzie coming to London for the celebrations?" Becky asked.

"Indeed, they are," Anna replied, "but they have quite another reason for being in London; their son-in-law Sir Richard Gardiner is being presented with an award from a distinguished body of scientists. It is a great honour, and Cassy writes that he has been overwhelmed by their recognition."

When Becky seemed interested, Anna explained, "Jonathan has told me that it is to do with Richard's contribution to the application of standards of hygiene and sanitation in our hospitals—a cause pioneered by Florence Nightingale and pursued by Dr Gardiner for many years. His study and application of antisepsis are to be recognized with this award. Jonathan's son, Charles, who is himself a physician at the hospital at Bell's Field outside Netherfield, declares that Richard's work has saved thousands of lives."

There was no doubt that this was going to be a significant family occasion, and Becky thanked Anna for inviting her to participate.

"It was very kind of you, my dear. I know we are cousins, but I have to confess that due to circumstances quite outside my control, we have not been as close as we should have been for some years. Mr Tate's business interests and my own work in the community at Matlock meant that we did not meet as often as we should have done. So it was very generous of you to include me in your party…"

Anna would have none of this.

"My dear Becky, it is not a question of generosity at all—your name was one of the first on our list. Indeed, Jonathan wrote it in himself, and as the only published author in the family, there was never any question regarding your invitation. I am glad you could come; Cathy and Anne-Marie too will be delighted I know—so let's have no more talk of generosity. Your place is here with us."

Anna's kind disposition and her sincerity reassured Becky. When they went upstairs to the room that had been prepared for her, she was overwhelmed by the efforts taken to ensure her comfort.

Nelly was already there preparing her mistress's bath and laying out her clothes. After Anna left them, Becky lay on the day bed by the window and sank into a pleasant reverie, determined she was going to enjoy this visit.

Dinner was at eight, and they were expected downstairs for drinks around half past seven; she was glad they had packed a few of her best gowns. Nelly had insisted, and Becky had agreed, albeit a little reluctantly.

A woman of excellent taste, Becky Tate always felt confident when she was well dressed and coiffured, and Nelly, who had been with her for many years, knew exactly what best suited her mistress.

Becky recalled with a wry smile that her late husband had always commented upon her appearance when they were due to entertain or meet people of influence in the community.

"You look just right tonight, my dear," he would say approvingly, as though she were part of a business presentation, and Becky remembered being pleased at first, even if he never complimented her upon her appearance at most other times. It had been much later that she had realised that she had indeed been part of his business, assisting him to win friends and extend his influence.

By the time Becky came downstairs, some of the guests had already arrived. Among them, she was pleased to see Anne-Marie and Colin Elliott in conversation with a couple of distinguished-looking men.

Seeing her enter the room, Anne-Marie came directly to her and, taking her across, introduced Becky to their friends, both members of Parliament and, like Mr Elliott, supporters of Mr Gladstone. To her enormous relief, both gentlemen were, unlike many MPs she had met, intelligent and quite knowledgeable about a subject that was dear to her heart—the Public Education Bill. Indeed, they confessed, it had been the subject of their discussion before she entered the room.

"I hope you will accept our apologies, ma'am," said one. "We Members of Parliament are often accused of discourtesy in company, because we do talk so much shop! It makes us dull companions for the ladies I'm afraid."

Anne-Marie laughed.

"You have no need to apologise to Mrs Tate; indeed she would probably be exceedingly disappointed were you not to discuss the Education Bill. It is a matter very dear to her heart."

On discovering that Becky was the widow of the late Anthony Tate, a publisher who had wielded remarkable power and influence, they seemed a good deal more interested to hear what she had to say, and Becky was especially glad of the distraction they provided. It had been some time since she had been so occupied with such weighty matters.

As she found herself engaged in a lively discourse, she discovered she was actually enjoying the experience. It was like old times, when the cut and thrust of political debate had been an important part of their lives and had given her marriage the excitement that had held it together as they strove to achieve a common goal. Sadly, after Josie's death, that excitement had all but evaporated as Mr Tate had lost interest in everything save his business.

Later, as other guests arrived, she moved away, albeit somewhat reluctantly, to join the ladies and participate in the social chatter that flowed around the room. Becky had very little interest in their trivial conversation but had no wish to upset her hostess, who was eager to introduce her to the others.

Some of the women had attended one of Mr Dickens's farewell readings, and one claimed to have been deeply affected—"moved to weep" she said, "by his rendition of passages from *Nicholas Nickleby*"—while another, somewhat younger lady declared she had been "petrified" by Mr Dickens's melodramatic reading of the murder of Nancy by Bill Sykes.

"It was too terrible to witness," she complained. "I thought someone in the audience of a more delicate sensibility than most may well have screamed or burst into tears! For my part, I vowed never to read *Oliver Twist*."

"Would not such an extreme response defeat the purpose of Mr Dickens's readings?" asked Becky, who had heard Mr Dickens read many times, and while she agreed his performances were occasionally melodramatic, she declared they could never have stopped her reading his books. Indeed, she would contend that they had whetted her appetite for the novels.

To this remark both ladies reacted with shock.

"Oh surely not, there are so many long and tiresome passages and such a deal of description in the books, I should be bored or tired or both. No, I do believe I am definitely partial to the readings, even if they do frighten me sometimes," said the younger of the two, and her friend agreed with her at once, giving her decided opinion: "Reading it all would be much too tedious," she declared in a languid tone, taking out her fan, as though that was the last word on the subject.

Becky did not bother to contradict them, and as they then proceeded to a discussion of Mr Dickens's private life and the inevitable speculation about his relationship with Miss Ellen Ternan, she grew bored and looked around for a means of escape.

Seeing that Emma and James Wilson had just arrived, she made her way across the room to the bay window, where they stood together with Jonathan and Anna Bingley.

Emma was apologising for their late arrival, caused, she explained, by her receipt of a letter from her mother, Mrs Jane Bingley, who had written to say they would not be coming to London because Mr Bingley had suffered another bout of bronchitis, which made travel in Winter very hazardous.

Emma's love for her parents was such that it would have been quite impossible for her to enjoy herself at the party, unless she could be reassured about her father's condition. To this end, she had persuaded her husband to despatch a message by electric telegraph to Mr Darcy, asking if her aunt Lizzie could ascertain the seriousness of Mr Bingley's indisposition before leaving Derbyshire for London.

She was naturally disappointed to hear from her brother Jonathan that Mr and Mrs Darcy would only arrive in London on the morrow and she would have to spend another anxious evening without the information she craved.

When Becky greeted her, Emma still wore a worried expression, but she was unfailingly courteous.

"Dear Becky, how good it is to see you here. I wish Mama and Papa could have come too, but it would appear that Papa is too ill to travel… Forgive me, but I cannot help worrying about him…" she said and looked close to tears.

Becky was not unaware of Mr Bingley's condition. The letter she had received from Emily Courtney had mentioned it, too. Emily, being unwell herself, had expressed her regret at being unable to go to Ashford Park to help her cousin Jane nurse her husband back to health.

However, seeing the extent of Emma's distress, Becky decided it would be best not to add to her present anxiety. She sought, instead, to console her with prospects of his recovery with medications and potions being much improved these days.

"I am sure, Emma, if a clever physician like Dr Gardiner were to see your father, he would recommend some treatment that would hasten his recovery. Why do you not ask Cassy when you see her tomorrow?" she suggested.

Emma thanked her for her concern and promised she would ask Dr Gardiner himself. "I do believe you are right, Becky. I cannot think why Mama has not approached him already. I know she relies on old Dr Robson, but a second opinion would not be a bad thing, would it? I shall speak to Richard myself and suggest it to my aunt Lizzie," she said, looking a little happier.

More guests had arrived, and the room, now quite full, was, with the candles and the fire, almost too warm for comfort. Becky went out into the vestibule and thence into the open morning room to get some air.

It was there that Jonathan followed her and said, "There you are, Becky. I have been meaning to speak with you privately; I have a message for you."

Wondering what message he could possibly have for her, Becky turned to face him, when he took from his inner pocket a sealed letter and presented it to her with the merest hint of a knowing smile. As she accepted it, he returned to the parlour, as though not wishing to stay and intrude upon her privacy as she read it.

Puzzled, Becky opened the letter and read it with increasing surprise.

It was brief but quite clear. After the customary salutation, the writer proceeded:

I expect to be in London on business for a fortnight at least, and I understand from Jonathan Bingley that you are to be in town also. I should like very much to see you, and as you indicated in your note that you would have no objection to our meeting, I hope you will not find it difficult to do so on this occasion.

If you are still of the same mind, would you be so kind as to send me word through Mr Bingley, and I will arrange to see you in the course of the week?

I hope I am not presuming upon your kindness in making this request with so little notice, but my journey to London was arranged in some haste.

I am,
Yours most sincerely,
Aldo Contini.

Becky's hand shook as she put the note in her reticule.

This was a most unexpected development; she had been caught completely unawares and did not know how she was going to respond.

When she went back into the parlour, feeling warmer than ever, having gained no relief at all from being away from the room, she sought to catch Jonathan's eye, but he was busy with some of his guests. She wondered how she was to convey the message, as Mr Contini had requested. She wondered also if Anna knew and hoped she did not.

For a moment she panicked and wished she had not come at all, but then dinner was announced and all the guests were moving towards the dining room. Jonathan appeared at her side, offered her his arm, and took her to her place at the long dining table, glittering with fine porcelain, silver, and crystal.

Becky noticed that ahead of her was Anna with young Dr Charles Bingley, Jonathan's eldest son, who had come up to London from Hertfordshire for the occasion.

As he helped her into her place, Jonathan asked softly, "And do you have an answer for my friend, Becky?"

Momentarily taken aback, she stammered and seemed uncertain but succeeded in indicating her consent. "Yes, the answer is yes, that is, if it can be arranged conveniently and without too much fuss..."

Jonathan smiled, clearly pleased. "Thank you, Becky; I shall send a note round in the morning, and may I say, I believe your answer will be received with much pleasure."

He moved away then to his usual seat at the head of the table, leaving Becky puzzled and unable to concentrate upon anything. Not the delectable array of food and wine presented for their pleasure, nor the witty speeches that followed, congratulating both couples on their felicitous unions; not even the excellent musical entertainment Anna had arranged when they withdrew to the drawing room could capture her attention for long.

Seated next to her, one of the MPs she'd been introduced to earlier in the evening tried once more to engage her in conversation on the subject of compulsory schooling for girls, but Becky was far too distracted to contribute more than a cursory comment or two, leaving the man puzzled.

When at last the guests began to leave, she escaped upstairs to her room, where she read and re-read her letter, and though she made every effort to quiet her mind and get some sleep, she could not, and lay awake into the small hours of the morning.

Chapter Seventeen

BECKY AWOKE THE FOLLOWING morning feeling much less well than she had been the previous night. Having slept only fitfully and for a very few hours, she had a dull headache. It provided her with an excuse to remain in her room until after breakfast, which she did, having asked Nelly to bring her a pot of tea. While the rest of the party planned to go out to the shops or drive in the park, Becky begged to be allowed to stay home.

Anna was concerned. "Are you sure you will not join us, Becky? The fresh air will do you good. I was afraid the rooms were too warm last night; we were such a big party."

Becky shook her head. "No, my dear, I think all I need is a quiet morning indoors. I am still a little tired from yesterday. Nelly will bring me more tea and some toast, and I shall read quietly and rest until you return from the shops. After all, we do have a busy evening ahead," she said and Anna agreed.

"We certainly do; I am sure we shall all enjoy *The Marriage of Figaro*. Jonathan has seen it before in Paris, but it's the first time for me," she confessed.

"It is for me, too, and I am looking forward to it very much. Now, don't let me keep you from your guests, my dear, believe me, I am perfectly happy staying in," said Becky.

Anna went, having urged her cousin to ask the servants for anything she needed and promising to be back in a couple of hours. But Becky knew better;

ladies shopping, especially in a group, never returned in a couple of hours. She expected to have most of the morning to herself, unless she had a caller, of course.

However, although she waited in all day, knowing that Jonathan had said he would send a note round in the morning, Aldo Contini neither came nor was there any written acknowledgement of her response. It was quite disconcerting.

By the time the ladies returned, it was afternoon, and Becky had begun to wonder if Mr Contini had changed his mind. She considered whether she should ask Jonathan in what manner he had conveyed her answer, but decided against it. She hoped she had not seemed too eager and worried that he may have misunderstood her answer.

But, if he had, there was little she could do to remedy it, which led her to shrug off her disappointment and decide to enjoy the rest of the evening.

After tea, which was served downstairs, Anna came upstairs to Becky's room to say that their party would leave for the theatre at seven.

The Darcys had arrived at Portman Square, Anna said, and would be joining them at the opera. Boxes had been reserved for the entire party, she explained. "Emma, James, and you will be seated with us, while Cassy and Richard will join Lizzie and Mr Darcy," said Anna, who then expressed a wish to see Becky's gown.

Nelly had already laid it out, together with the selected accessories and jewels for the evening.

"Will it suit?" Becky asked, a little tentatively. It was some time since she had been to Covent Garden.

"It most certainly will, Becky; it is very elegant indeed," Anna replied, "and the colour is just perfect for you."

Anna's good taste in just about everything was well known, and Becky was pleased to have her approval.

The gown was of a deep blue velvet, with an overskirt of lace, a design that had been very fashionable a year ago. Becky had not worn the gown in a long while and had brought it to London at Nelly's insistence, with the theatre party in mind.

She bathed and dressed slowly, and when Nelly arrived to help her with her hair, she too was full of praise for the gown.

"Oh ma'am, it's grand… and you do look lovely," she said, and Becky, although she knew Nelly's judgment was not entirely impartial, could not help feeling pleased.

When she went downstairs, the others were waiting.

Arriving at Covent Garden, they were escorted to the reserved boxes in the magnificent new theatre.

Becky had not been to the opera since the old theatre had been destroyed by fire some years ago. The new edifice was a superbly designed structure, where everyone who was anyone attended the opera, not always to see and hear, but quite often to be seen and heard.

Seeing the elaborate gowns and splendid jewelry of the ladies preening themselves under the chandeliers, Becky felt a little underdressed.

"Upon my word, I have not seen so many diamonds in one place in all my life," she declared as they took their seats, and Jonathan's riposte was apt.

"I believe it is claimed, by those who know something of these matters, that a lady's knowledge of the opera is usually in inverse proportion to the value of the gems she wears to the performance."

Both Anna and Becky protested that he was being unfair, but were glad indeed that neither of them were overly decked with jewels.

They were soon joined by Emma and Mr Wilson, and moments later, the conductor entered to begin the overture. It was a very special moment, and there was a hush in the theatre. As the curtain rose, Becky saw Anna Bingley whisper something to her husband and point with her fan in the direction of a box some distance from theirs and one tier above them.

Jonathan looked and whispered something very quickly to his wife, just as the first act was starting.

Becky could not hear what he said; she thought she had heard the name "Contini" but could not be sure. From her seat she could not see out across to the other side of the vast hall, and in any event, the intoxicating power of Mozart's music and the fine voices soon swamped her senses.

At the end of Act One, Becky joined with enthusiasm in the applause. She was enjoying this far more than she had anticipated.

Between the acts, Anna and Becky left their seats to walk in the long, richly furbished vestibule, where many other patrons of the opera were parading, some rather volubly giving their companions the benefit of their opinions on the performance so far.

One woman thought the tenor was superb; another disagreed, he was not handsome enough to be right for the part. Still others had already decided that the maid Susanna was the star of the show.

A little bemused, Becky accompanied Anna as she walked towards the stairs, while Jonathan, having left the ladies to their own devices, went swiftly up the stairs and was soon out of sight.

When it was time to return to their seats and he had not reappeared, Becky was concerned, but Anna was not.

"He has probably gone round to the Darcys' box or the Continis'—he will be back soon enough, but we had better not wait for him, or we shall miss the opening of Act Two," she warned.

Becky knew then she had heard right; the Continis were at the opera, and Jonathan had gone round to their box. When Act Two began, she could not concentrate on the performance, and each time the curtains moved behind them, she was distracted, until finally, Jonathan returned to his seat.

Puzzled, she wondered what had occurred. Had he met Mr Contini?

The others of the party were clearly enjoying the opera, but Becky wished Act Two would end. When it did, it was she who rose quickly and went outside first, wanting to get away from the closeness of the box, hoping her disappointment did not show on her face.

Neither Jonathan nor Anna made to follow her.

As she stepped out into the vestibule, standing just outside their box was a tall, familiar figure who moved forward to greet her.

"Mrs Tate, good evening," he said, and Becky almost jumped, but caught herself in time to avoid the clear embarrassment of looking either too shocked or too pleased to see him there.

She responded quickly, "Mr Contini? I did not expect to see you here."

He smiled, a self-deprecating smile, just the sort of smile she remembered well, and said softly, "My aunt is here. She is totally devoted to the opera. Unfortunately, my uncle was unwell and could not come tonight, so it was my privilege to accompany her."

When Becky said nothing, he continued, "But then, my friend Jonathan Bingley told me that you were here with their party, and I thought I must seize the opportunity, so to speak, and see you; so here I am."

Becky raised her eyebrows and asked, "You did not wish to wait until the performance was over? You must have missed quite a lot of Act Two?"

His answer was unequivocal. "No, because then there would be a great crowd of people in the vestibule… I wished most particularly to see you alone. As for Act Two, I am familiar with *Figaro*. I have seen him many times."

Becky felt her face flush as the blood rose in her cheeks. He was exactly as she remembered him—direct, charming, open—exasperatingly so. No pretensions, no idle flattery; Aldo Contini had not changed at all, except there was a little more grey in his hair than she could recall. She said nothing at first, just nodded and smiled.

Then she decided to ask, "Did you receive my answer?"

"Yes, most certainly, the very next morning, and I must thank you for it, I am very grateful. I would have called at the house today, but my aunt required me to escort her when she went to call on an artist in Chelsea. She wishes to buy a picture and asked for my opinion. So I had decided to call on you tomorrow, but when Jonathan informed me you were here, I had to see you. You do not object?"

"Of course not; I am very happy to see you," she replied lightly, and he smiled as though her answer had given him very special pleasure.

They had walked a fair way along the corridor, making light conversation, mostly about the opera and its complicated plot. When it was time to return to their seats, he walked back with her to their box, and as they entered, Jonathan rose, greeted his friend, and for the rest of the performance stood with Aldo Contini at the back of the box. Though she heard nothing of their whispered conversation, it became clear to Becky that the two men were firm friends. The intimacy and general ease of their association was unmistakable; she was quite certain they would have exchanged confidences.

Afterwards, when the audience had applauded until their ears were ringing with the sound and the final curtain call had been taken, they rose to leave, and Anna Bingley invited Mr Contini to join them at supper.

He would be delighted, he said, and thanked her, but he must first escort his aunt home. He was assured that would present no problem, whereupon he beamed with pleasure, kissed the hands of all the ladies, and left.

On the journey back to Grosvenor Street, neither Jonathan nor Anna made any comment on the unheralded appearance of Mr Contini at the opera.

However, Becky was certain they must have had some discussion of the matter; it was simply not credible that Anna knew nothing of it.

On reaching the house, Becky went directly to her room, attempting to avoid questions and trying to rest her feet and eyes as she lay on the couch. Nelly, ever anxious for her mistress, keen to ensure she had everything she needed, brought her a drink of water and, when she was ready to go downstairs, fussed around her, making certain her gown and hair were just as they should be.

Aldo Contini arrived at the house some half an hour later, apologising for his lateness, and was assured by his host and hostess that all would be forgiven, if he would promise to entertain them with a song after supper.

As he entered the room, Becky, sitting to one side of the doorway, saw him look around the company, his eyes searching until he found her. He then walked directly across to her, bowed over her hand, and seated himself beside her. Thereafter, there was so much to talk about, that it seemed to Becky they had hardly stopped speaking except to partake of supper, and even then, the food, though excellent, did not appear in any way to diminish their desire for conversation.

They had not met in more than two years, not since the year of Josie's death, when Becky, left to her own devices in London while her husband plunged deep into his business interests, had met Mr Contini again and found in him a companion who had offered her something more than the poor consolation of mourning her child while keeping a stiff upper lip.

With him, she had been able to express some of the deeply felt emotions she had hidden from most of her family and friends. He had been neither embarrassed nor uneasy when she, while speaking of Josie, had wept. Explaining gently that he too had known the heart-wrenching loss of a young sister some years ago, he had comforted her. At the time, it had made for a bond between them more intimate and precious, Becky felt, than if they had been lovers.

In his company, she had enjoyed also a level of intelligent discourse that had almost disappeared from her social life. Mr Contini's knowledge of matters artistic and his genuine interest in her views had combined to enhance her appreciation of the time they had spent together. She had looked back upon it as a period when every aspect of her existence had been enriched by his friendship.

She recalled their many conversations on subjects as arcane as Mr Darwin's theory of the origin of species and as ordinary as the closure of Hyde Park on account of public rioting in London. On every topic, they had debated, discussed, and resolved their respective views to their mutual satisfaction, all in the course of the Summer of 1866.

Becky remembered some conversations as though they had occurred a day or two ago. They had been chiefly about Josie and Becky's own feelings of guilt at having persuaded her daughter into what was to become an unhappy union, and he had understood and acknowledged them, like no one in her family would.

Since then, Mr Contini had returned to Italy, and back in Derbyshire, Becky had made a determined effort to put that exceptional Summer out of her mind, but without much success.

Meeting him again had resurrected every precious memory.

Clearly, he remembered too, she thought, but was being discreet, probably believing that she would not wish to be reminded of a time that, for all its passing pleasures, had been filled mostly with her grief at her daughter's death.

After a few moments silence, she, feeling the need to make conversation, said casually, "You have not changed much, Mr Contini."

His reply surprised her, "No? But you *have*, Becky, remarkably," and when she looked somewhat disconcerted, he added, "You look much younger today," and to her disbelief, continued, "You are a little happier now, yes? Or just a little less melancholy, perhaps?"

Becky found it difficult to respond to this suggestion; she had no swift answer to his question. Instead, seizing upon his earlier reference to the opera, she asked, "You said you were familiar with *Figaro*?"

"Indeed I am, very familiar. You see, I spent much time in Paris trying to study art, and *Figaro* was a great favourite with the French at the time."

"But it is a German opera!" she said.

"Ah, but the original story of Figaro, the play by Beaumarchais, was French and performed soon after the French Revolution," he countered. "It was used to ridicule the stupidity and pretensions of the old aristocrats—those they had sent to the guillotine! I think the French like to remind themselves of that period from time to time. As a student in Paris some fifty years after the revolution, I confess I enjoyed it too."

Becky was astonished that he knew so much, yet behaved with so little presumption or arrogance. He told it as though it were common or garden information, available to all and sundry.

Her own knowledge of music was slight, and while she had known he had an interest in art and music—indeed it had attracted her to him when they first met—he had never given any hint that he had been a student of art.

"And was your study of art successful?" she asked, and he laughed.

"Alas, not to the extent I might have wished, but it was fun, and I did learn to sketch quite well, so it was not a complete waste of my time."

She did recall that he seemed to like scratching at a drawing pad with a stick of charcoal, but she had not thought it a serious pastime.

"And do you continue your interest in art?" she asked.

"I do, I sketch and draw for my own pleasure, mostly slight pieces; I am unlikely to be invited to hang my work at the Uffizzi or the Louvre."

There it was again, that sardonic self-deprecation that he was wont to engage in and that she had found so diverting after the company of persons who took themselves so seriously.

She smiled. "Perhaps not, but may I see some of it?" she persisted.

"Certainly, if you wish it. I do not have any of my work here in London, but if you will let me, I shall demonstrate my efforts for you. I shall make a drawing of you, and then you can be the judge of my talent."

Becky laughed and said she didn't think there'd be enough time for that, but added that she would very much like to see his work one day.

They talked for a while about family matters until supper was over and the room was rearranged for the entertainment that was to follow.

Anna Bingley approached them.

"Now, Mr Contini, I must hold you to your promise," she said, and he, without fuss, begged that Becky would excuse him and went to join Anna at the pianoforte. And, with the kind of unaffected ease that was so typically Italian, he sang, taking Becky back to the time many years ago, when she and Mr Tate had visited Italy and heard the young boatmen sing at dusk, songs that seemed to come from the heart. She had not heard such spontaneous singing ever before. The song brought back memories, which she had thought were buried in the past.

Now, it was all returning, confronting her, demanding her attention.

There was a burst of applause and calls for more, but he bowed and smiled to acknowledge the gathered audience, graciously kissed the hand of his accompanist, then returned to Becky's side.

"That was very good indeed, Mr Contini; if your drawing is as acceptable as your singing, you are being far too modest about it," she said, and he looked genuinely pleased but said no more.

Coffee, tea, and chocolate were being served in the adjoining room, and Becky suggested that they go in and help themselves, but Mr Contini offered to go himself. He recalled that she took tea and brought her a cup of tea with no milk and two lumps of sugar, before helping himself to black coffee. Becky smiled and thanked him; it seemed there was not a lot he had forgotten.

As they moved to sit in an alcove overlooking a small, enclosed courtyard hung with pretty Chinese lanterns, he said, "I am very happy to see you looking so well, Becky. It seems your new life in Kent must suit you; there is contentment there for you I think, yes?"

When she didn't answer immediately and looked down at her cup, he stopped abruptly and apologised.

"I am sorry; I should not have said that. I know there have been some very difficult times for you; forgive me, please."

This time she smiled and reassured him. "There is nothing to forgive. I was miserable when we last met, but that was just a few months after Josie's death, and I was alone in London. I was so very grateful that you were…"

But he would not let her continue. "Please do not speak of it; it must hurt you deeply; I am sorry to have been so insensitive as to have upset you by mentioning these things…"

She had to tell him then, that he had not been insensitive at all; indeed she insisted, "Please do not apologise. You were not insensitive, and I am not upset; believe me, it is good to be able to speak again of those times. They were not all sad days—I have very good memories of those days."

They were alone in the room; most of the others had returned to the drawing room where Anna Bingley had persuaded two other guests to sing a duet. The music could be heard through the closed doors as they slipped out into the cool courtyard.

He placed a hand on Becky's arm, and as she turned to look at him, he said rather earnestly, "Becky, I should like very much to meet you again and talk as we used to do; please tell me, would you consider it an impertinence on my part if I invited you to join me for a drive into the country?"

Though his suggestion surprised her, she was not willing to admit it and, having considered it for a moment, said, "Of course not, I should like that. Thank you."

He was clearly pleased with her reply and was eager to set a time and date for their excursion.

"When shall it be? Are you very busy this week?" he asked.

"No, I do not have any fixed engagements except with the Bingleys, and I am not very fond of London," she replied. "A drive into the country would be very pleasant. Perhaps on Monday, if that is convenient."

She had recalled that on Monday, the Bingleys and Darcys were to attend the ceremony at which Dr Richard Gardiner was to receive his award. It was a day on which she could go out wherever and whenever she wished, and no one would miss her.

When she explained, he asked, "And you are not attending this ceremony for Dr Gardiner?"

She shook her head, pointing out that only the immediate family were invited. It was to be a very distinguished gathering, she told him.

He smiled and said, "Well, that is fortuitous, is it not?"

Becky agreed that it was, and they laughed together almost like they used to do those years ago, and so it was arranged.

When they returned to the drawing room, Emma Wilson was at the piano-forte, and they stood quietly at the back of the room until she had finished. Her performance, exquisite as always, brought applause and praise around the room.

As Emma left the instrument and joined her husband, James, his pride in her and the warmth of their affection was plain to see. Watching from a little distance, Becky could not hold back the deep sigh that escaped her lips.

Mr Contini looked quickly at her but this time tactfully said nothing.

It did seem to him, however, that despite appearances to the contrary, Becky Tate was not really as contented as he had thought.

As the entertainment drew to a close, several of the guests prepared to leave. Mr and Mrs Darcy were among the first to make their departure; Lizzie was tired, and she disliked long journeys.

Becky made a point of approaching her and asking after the health of her brother-in-law Mr Bingley. "I understand from Emma that he is unwell. Jane must be anxious; please be so kind as to convey my best wishes for his speedy recovery," she said.

Elizabeth smiled and thanked her.

"Thank you, Becky, I shall. It is kind of you to ask, and yes, Jane is very concerned, but I am assured by Cassy that Richard saw Mr Bingley shortly before leaving for London, and he is confident that the condition, while it is uncomfortable, is not serious."

When Becky smiled and looked relieved, she added, "Oh, if only Bingley could be persuaded to follow Mr Darcy's example and give up this insane habit of riding out every morning in all weathers. Jane is convinced it is the exposure to mist and damp that causes this condition; I do hope Richard will speak severely to him and advise against it, at least until the warmer weather returns."

Listening to her, Becky thought how confident Elizabeth sounded; how very well she had fitted into her role as the Mistress of Pemberley, expressing her opinions and giving advice without hesitation.

Poor Josie, she remembered, had always been a little intimidated by Mrs Darcy's elegance and self-assurance. As Mr Darcy joined them and the couple said their farewells and went out to their carriage, thoughts of Josie brought her back to reality.

Aldo Contini was standing a little apart from the family members in the hall.

He approached her and spoke softly, "Then it is arranged, I shall call for you on Monday? At what time will you be ready to leave?"

Suddenly, Becky became a little confused and said, "May I send you a note, once I know what arrangements the family have made? I should prefer it to be after they have left for the ceremony, only because I have no wish to answer too many questions."

He understood immediately.

"Of course, certainly. Send me a note on Sunday afternoon. I will be at my uncle's apartment in Belgrave Square, at this address," he said, handing her a card. Then, meeting her eyes, he said, "I am looking forward to it."

She thanked him and, as if to reassure, him said quickly, "I am too, very much."

She did not wish him to think that she had changed her mind and was trying to back away from the arrangement.

After he had said good night, Becky moved away and saw him standing in the doorway with Jonathan as she went upstairs to her room.

There, having completed her toilette, she took out her diary. She would not sleep until she had recorded the events of this evening. She did so, meticulously as always, noting Mr Contini's appearance at the opera.

It was difficult indeed to conceal my pleasure at seeing him there, for all the world as if he had just arrived, when he had in fact been outside, waiting for me through most of Act Two!

He looks so like himself two years ago that I, who have changed so much, could scarcely believe it. The face and head are as pleasing as ever, though not conventionally handsome, arresting and very agreeable, with perhaps just a new touch of maturity at the temples. I am always surprised at how well a little grey suits a man.

I am surprised at myself, too, for not being less forthcoming. But why should I be?

I suppose it could be argued that when he said he had wanted to meet me and had come round to our box at the opera, I should have been less flattered, more censorious. But I was not, and for good reason, because I did not wish to be. I confess I was pleased he had come especially to see me and delighted he had been prepared to miss most of Act Two to do so, even if he is familiar with Figaro!

Becky was not unaware of the delicacy of the situation in which she had placed herself. Equally, she had done so with a degree of deliberation from which she did not resile. She had wondered whether the Bingleys, Jonathan and her cousin Anna, would disapprove but had swiftly dismissed the idea as being rather jejeune.

Perhaps I should have been less accommodating when he suggested the drive into the country. Possibly, but I did not feel the need to do so. I am sure I shall enjoy it, though I did forget to ask where we would drive to!

But I am not a callow girl with some unreliable suitor. He is no Willoughby, nor am I Marianne Dashwood.

I do not feel the need to play hard to get. Surely, I can accept a gentleman's invitation to accompany him on a drive into the country if I choose, without endangering my reputation.

Besides, since he is such a good friend of Jonathan Bingley, there is unlikely to be any cause for concern.

Quite content with her own arguments in favour of what she had decided to do, Becky, for the first time in three days, went to bed and lost no sleep at all that night.

Chapter Eighteen

BY TEN O'CLOCK ON Monday morning, the Bingleys had left to join the Darcys and accompany Cassy and Richard Gardiner to the reception, where he would be presented with his award.

On the previous afternoon, Becky had sent a note to Mr Contini explaining that half past ten would be an appropriate time for their drive into the country. She was dressed and waiting upstairs, and he arrived promptly at half past the hour in the Continis' brougham. Becky went downstairs to meet him. Nelly, loyal and discreet, was the only person who knew of their intended journey.

It was a cool, pleasant morning redolent of late Summer rather than Autumn. After he had helped her into the vehicle, she asked, "And where exactly are we going today?"

He turned to look at her and smiled.

"Will you not trust me to take you somewhere and surprise you with my choice?" he asked.

Becky had no desire to make a fuss, nor was she inclined to be arch, so she shrugged her shoulders and said, "Very well then, I am perfectly happy to be surprised, just so long as it is a pleasant surprise."

"That I can certainly promise you," he said, and Becky nodded, aware only that they appeared to be travelling north out of London.

It transpired later that they were bound for the county of Essex, a distance of some fourteen miles and a part of the country with which Becky was not at all familiar. However, that information came much later, and in the meantime, contrary to her expectations, for she had felt some apprehension that this was the reason for his wishing to see her alone, he made no mention of any matters from the past. It was a subject she was certain must be in the forefront of his mind, as it was in hers.

Surprising her further, he talked chiefly of his present visit to England and some of the work he had undertaken in Italy during his time there, before asking her about her own plans for the future.

"I understand from Mr Bingley that you have invested much time and effort in setting up a parish school in Kent," he said.

"I have," she replied. "My main concern was to help my sister Catherine achieve her dearest ambition of establishing a school for the young women of the parish, who receive no instruction at all. They can neither read nor write. She had been frustrated in her original intention by her first husband's redoubtable patron, Lady Catherine de Bourgh, who had opposed any such proposal on the grounds that it would give the girls of the parish ideas above their humble station in life."

Mr Contini chuckled, "I have heard of this Lady Catherine de Bourgh. Jonathan Bingley has told me she was a most formidable woman, not to be crossed, on pain of death!" he said, and Becky agreed.

"Indeed, socially speaking at least! My sister's first husband was not the sort of man who would have wished to do so. Her Ladyship's patronage was very useful to him."

Mention of Catherine's first husband served to remind him of something he had been ignorant of until her letter had reached him in Italy.

"You did say in your letter that your sister is married again recently; I trust she is happily married?"

"Oh yes, very much so. She is married now to the man she fell in love with when she was a young girl and should have married twenty years ago. That she did not was yet another consequence of the arrogant meddling of Lady Catherine, who set out to prevent the match, with no respect for the feelings of the two people involved. But they are together now, and I have no doubt whatsoever of their complete happiness," she said with some satisfaction.

"A propitious conclusion then?" he remarked.

"Indeed, but sadly they were denied their felicity for too long," she said, and he glanced quickly at her, hearing a somewhat melancholy note in her voice.

He was silent awhile after that explanation, then asked without warning, "And what about yourself? Have you no similar plans?"

Becky, determined not to be disconcerted or coy, responded frankly, "If you mean matrimonial plans, I have not. But I do have plans of my own for the future; I mean to write and may venture into the publishing business if I can persuade Jonathan Bingley of the value of my project. There are too few good publishers who will accept a manuscript from a woman, however well written. If I could help more women have their work published, I should consider that I have done something truly worthwhile in my life."

He looked at her seriously and, as if taking her to task, said, "You cannot mean that? You have done many worthwhile things in your life. You have, for several years, been a woman of great influence."

"Only in my own small community and only because Mr Tate had the power of his newspapers, which he used to promote the causes we believed in. I very much doubt if he would have been as helpful if he did not agree with my aims, nor would I have been successful without his help. It was his position that enabled me to have my own work published in the *Review* and other journals. I do not flatter myself that another publisher would have been as willing. I am no Charlotte Bronte, Mr Contini; I do not write romantic tales that sell like hotcakes!

"But now, I should like to do something on my own, something that would help other women, who have very little chance of success as writers."

"Do you mean to establish a printery then?" he asked.

"I most certainly do. I know how hard it is for women to achieve some measure of success; my daughter Josie was destroyed by it. I should like very much to do something about it."

At the mention of Josie, he looked across at her quickly, recalling the circumstances of her daughter's death, and anxious not to say anything to rekindle her grief, he returned to an earlier question.

"And why must Mr Bingley be persuaded?" he asked.

"Ah, that is a long story..."

"Which you cannot divulge to me?"

"Oh no, there is nothing secret about it," she said, adding, "but it is a rather complex story, revealing something about my husband's opinion of my capacity to use the money he left me in a sensible way. He appointed Jonathan as a sort of 'guardian' over me. I shall tell you about it later if you wish; it is too dull a tale for such a pretty drive as this. I have never been in this part of England before and was not aware there was so much beauty here."

They were indeed traversing some very appealing country and fell silent as Becky sought to feast her eyes upon it. To the left of the road lay woodland as far as she could see, where age-old trees stood, still clothed in their Autumn hues of russet and gold, and the air was cold, smokeless, and sweet. They were passing through Epping Forest, the last remnants of the great Waltham Forest, within which stood the ruins of Waltham Abbey, where it was said King Harold had been buried after the Battle of Hastings in 1066. Although neither knew of its historic significance, both admitted to feeling a sense of awe as they regarded the ancient trees and marvelled at their great age.

Later, they talked again of matters of mutual interest; he asked about the parish school in Kent, and she enquired if he had been to the recent concert at the Albert Hall, where the performance of a young Italian maestro had received high praise from the critics and Anna Bingley.

He laughed and said, "High praise from the critics would not inspire me to attend—they are always so contrary, I cannot take them seriously. Praise from Mrs Bingley is quite another matter; she is an artist herself and understands the quality of inspiration."

Becky concurred, "Indeed she does, and because I know very little of the arts, I confess I do value her judgement on such matters."

"Ah, on that matter we are as one, then," he said, and they laughed together, as she protested that they had agreed on many things, before lapsing into silence again.

They had reached the crossroads, at which Mr Contini paid particular attention to their route, consulting a piece of paper he had taken from the inside pocket of his coat, which appeared to have on it some sort of map.

As he put it away and concentrated upon the road ahead, Becky said nothing, her thoughts in some confusion, as she realised how easily she could enjoy his company. It was no different now, she thought, from the way it had been before, and yet their lives had changed considerably in the intervening years.

They made good time, reaching their destination—a country estate on the fringes of Epping Forest—soon after midday.

The gates were open, giving access to the grounds, with woods, paths, and gardens that were quite beautiful with a wild, natural quality that was very different from anything Becky had seen in Kent.

Intrigued, she asked, "Whose estate is this?" and was informed that it belonged to a friend of Mr Contini and Jonathan Bingley, a gentleman and a Member of Parliament, by the name of Adrian Hart, who had invited them to drive there and take lunch with him at the house.

The mention of Jonathan Bingley caused Becky to wonder if he had known of their journey here today, but she was reluctant to ask and prepared instead to enjoy the pleasures this extraordinary place afforded them.

The drive to the house was long, twisting, and winding through stands of graceful beeches, silvery grey in the clear light of noon, their roots deep in dense clumps of fern and bracken that pushed out into the road, invading the path of their vehicle.

Becky was entranced, envisaging a scene from some Gothic tale of romance and intrigue being enacted here, when the house came into view quite suddenly, shattering completely the image in her mind. It was certainly not the edifice she had imagined at all, being neither old nor Victorian in character. Instead, it was quite deliberately modern, probably designed by one of the tribe of rising young architects everyone in London was talking about. It was said they were determined to drag British design into a new era.

They reached the wide front porch and alighted, to be met by a manservant, who apologised for his master, Mr Hart, who, he said, had been unavoidably delayed in London by some urgent business at Whitehall. However, he said, they were very welcome, and the master had asked that they stay to lunch.

Becky was surprised, even more so that Mr Contini seemed quite untroubled by this turn of events. She had expected him to be somewhat disconcerted at least, by the absence of their host, but clearly he was not.

Presently, they were shown into a spacious room full of light, with huge French windows opening out onto a terrace on one side and on the other, leading into an enclosed courtyard around which the house had been built. They partook of aperitifs and light refreshments before being invited to remove to a delightful outdoor space, where luncheon was served in a setting that could only enhance their enjoyment of an excellent meal.

Mr Contini, who had visited the house on previous occasions, explained the design, which he described as modern and one of the best examples he had seen in England.

"It is such a clean, light style, so different to the false Gothic structures one sees everywhere. I adore it," he said, and Becky could only agree.

Afterwards, they walked about the garden, which was, despite the lateness of the season, exceptionally verdant, being planted with a variety of trees and shrubs from the Mediterranean, which being evergreen helped alleviate the bleak appearance that heralded the onset of Winter in most English gardens. As they admired the beauty of the grounds, with their appearance of natural wilderness, Becky wished she could do likewise at Edgewater but, thinking aloud, supposed that it was probably too late to change things there, since the garden had been established many years ago.

"Becky, it is not like you to say that," Mr Contini said in a reproving tone that amused her somewhat. "Surely it is never too late to change things, if the change will make you happy, as your sister has shown by her remarkable example?"

She smiled and nodded, but said nothing, not trusting herself to speak. She was becoming increasingly aware that his previous knowledge of her had given him a singular advantage over her. While she was not uncomfortable, it did make her more wary.

When they returned to the house, tea was served in the sitting room, where a fire danced in a huge fireplace, banishing any invading chill. An attentive maid and footman were present to wait upon them. It was luxury like Becky had never known, and she could not but wonder at the generosity of their absent host, Mr Hart, whose hospitality they were enjoying.

The sun was sinking behind the great stands of trees that sheltered the house from both heat of Summer and the Winter winds, when Becky suggested that it was time to leave and Mr Contini rose immediately, ready to take her home.

Having ensured that she was warmly and comfortably ensconced in the vehicle, he thanked the butler and asked that their appreciation be conveyed to Mr Hart for his generous hospitality, before setting off for London.

Becky said nothing for a while, and her companion likewise kept his eyes on the road as he took the vehicle along the twisting drive and out onto the thoroughfare. Then he relaxed and asked, "You have enjoyed the day, Becky, yes?"

She had no other response to offer than, "I most certainly have, very much, thank you; but I now have a problem."

"A problem?" he seemed puzzled.

"Yes. However shall I thank Mr Hart for his kind hospitality when I do not even know him? It was such a splendid house and a delicious meal. The setting was superb; I have not enjoyed a visit anywhere so much in years. I feel I should write to thank him."

He smiled, clearly pleased the problem was not an insoluble one.

"I am glad you enjoyed it. I too have enjoyed being with you here. Do not concern yourself about Mr Hart; he is a good friend and I shall convey your thanks to him myself. He will be very pleased that you admired his house and grounds—it is an obsession with him."

"A most magnificent obsession indeed," said Becky and lapsed again into silence, contemplating the events of the day. She could not recall enjoying such a day as this in many a year.

Her companion's voice broke in gently upon her thoughts.

"Perhaps we could drive out again another day? We could go somewhere else; you could choose."

This time, she smiled and said, "Yes, that would be nice, but I do not have many more days in London. I return to Kent next Monday."

"That is six days away! Plenty of time for another excursion…" he said, but she was cautious.

"Let me think about it. Anna and Jonathan may have some plans of their own and may wish me to join them," she said, and he nodded and said, "Of course,"

Becky wondered at his reticence.

Why had he not once made mention of their past association? It bewildered her, even though she was grateful that he had not, for it could have caused her some embarrassment.

But the fact that he had said nothing at all was curious and concerning. Could it be that he did not wish to rake up memories from the past, when they had met in London at a time that she had been vulnerable and alone? Perhaps he was himself embarrassed by the recollection and was hoping she also wished to bury the memory. Yet he had sought her out and followed up their association, quite deliberately. It cannot have been simple kindness, she mused. These and other puzzling thoughts engrossed her mind as they drove into London, but she said nothing at all.

On reaching Grosvenor Street, Mr Contini escorted her indoors, and having thanked her and kissed her hand, he left, saying he had to get the vehicle back to his uncle and aunt, who were dining out that evening.

Becky felt no special sense of elation but could not deny the quiet pleasure that filled her as she retired to her room. Nelly waited for her, attentive as ever, anxious to see she was not too tired, bringing her tea and helping her change out of her clothes.

The Bingleys had not returned as yet, she reported. They were dining with the Darcys at Portman Square.

Becky was glad and asked that Nelly inform the kitchen staff that she would not require any dinner tonight.

Nelly was concerned; it had been a long day.

"Are you feeling poorly, ma'am?"

Becky, lying back against the cushions, smiled.

"Oh no, Nelly, on the contrary, I am very well. But I have had such an agreeable day and such a delicious luncheon, I really do not need any dinner. I think I shall take a bath, some more tea, and have an early night."

Relieved, Nelly said, "Yes, ma'am," and went away to prepare the bath for her mistress. She was content that Becky was indeed well and happy.

"If only," she thought, "if only she could be this way always."

But Becky had few such days and when they came she grasped them and enjoyed them, knowing how rare they were.

This particular day had been a curious one, she wrote in her diary:

It was a day full of anticipation and despite some disappointment, leaving me contented tonight. It is a strange sensation indeed, but an undeniably happy one.

It might well have been a perfect day had my companion been a little more forthcoming, but it did not signify, because he has been so charming and kind. I could not have asked for better company.

And there is a promise of more to come, if I choose!

Shall I? I confess it is an attractive prospect, but I have not decided if I should.

In the week that followed, Mr Contini arrived at Grosvenor Street almost daily, sometimes at the invitation of the Bingleys and at others, by appointment with Becky, who in the space of twenty-four hours, had overcome her reservations about further meetings with him.

Consequently, they visited, enjoyed, and talked of many more places and things than had first seemed possible in so short a time: the Tate Gallery in inclement weather, Kew Gardens when it was fine, and on one particularly happy day, a drive down to Richmond to watch a boat race on the Thames. Mr Contini was very excited about the contest on the river, while Becky drew her enjoyment chiefly from the pleasure of his company, which she had to admit had been enhanced on each occasion.

Yet one thing continued to perplex her.

In all of this time, while they had found so much to enjoy together, he had said nothing that gave her any hint of his feelings towards her, other than a general impression of warm friendliness and concern. It was as though, if he had any feelings of affection or attachment, he had determined not to permit her to see how he felt, concealing within a mantle of agreeable courtliness his real intentions.

This continued all week, until the Sunday before she was to return home.

They had dined with the Bingleys, and afterwards, while Anna played the pianoforte and Jonathan sat reading by the fire, Mr Contini had seated himself beside Becky on a sofa placed at some distance from the instrument. She had, in her own mind, concluded that they were to pass their last evening as they had all the others, when he said softly, "Becky, I have been meaning to ask you if I may call on you at your home in Kent, before I return to Italy."

The approach was so direct and so unexpected, she was taken aback and for a minute or two did not know quite how to respond.

This was not because she had any reservations about permitting him to visit her at Edgewater, more that she had prepared herself in advance to say farewell without any expectation of meeting him again in the near future, that she was thrown into some confusion by his request.

Her hesitation seemed to unsettle him, and he asked rather apprehensively, "I am sorry, have I offended you by asking?"

This she immediately denied. "Of course not. No, you must not think that; you are very welcome to visit Edgewater. There are, however, one or two unconnected matters, which I have to settle when I return home, that will keep me busy for some days. I have some obligations to attend to; thereafter, you may certainly come and visit, and I should like you to meet my sister Catherine and her husband, Mr Burnett, who live nearby," she said.

He looked delighted and agreed at once, pointing out that he was going to be in London awhile yet; his uncle and aunt wished him to assist them in settling some matters of business.

"I expect I shall spend the rest of this month with them before returning to Italy. So there will be plenty of time to pay you a visit, yes?"

"Oh yes indeed," said Becky, "I shall send you word as soon as it is convenient."

"Please do; I shall look forward to it, very much," he said, and after a few more minutes of casual conversation, he stood up and bowed, kissed her hand, thanked his host and hostess, and was gone, leaving Becky pondering what new direction her life was taking, and yet unsure what part Mr Contini would play.

Chapter Nineteen

BECKY AND HER MAID Nelly were packed and ready to leave on the
train the following day.

That night, she wrote in a rather melancholy mood of Mr Contini:

*If only I knew what he was thinking. Why does he not wish to let me see
if he feels anything for me at all, apart from an agreeable friendliness,
which I welcome, but am increasingly unsatisfied with? I would very
much like to know if he cares more deeply for me. He wishes to call on me
at Edgewater, but why would he, if he has no keener interest than sociable
companionship? It is a question I must resolve, even if only for my own
peace of mind.*

There were many other questions she would have wished to ask him, but he
had given her no opportunity. Why had he never married? Was there no lady
friend in Italy who awaited his return?

Other, less intimate questions had engaged her mind constantly since their
visit to the house of Mr Adrian Hart in Essex. Had Mr. Hart deliberately stayed
away to enable them to be alone together, she wondered. Had Jonathan Bingley
known of their visit, or did he have a part in arranging it? If he did, neither he
nor Anna had spoken of it to Becky, very properly respecting her privacy.

Apart from his role in bringing her Mr Contini's note, Jonathan had neither said nor done anything to encourage her interest in his friend except to agree enthusiastically each time Mr Contini had suggested some place of interest that Becky and he could visit. And she had noted an amused look in Jonathan's eyes on occasions when Mr Contini was with her.

Notwithstanding this, they had invited him to visit and to dine with them not once or twice, but three times during the week that followed, on each occasion ensuring that Becky and he were seated together at the dinner table and frequently left alone together in the drawing room.

All these machinations served to increase her suspicions that Jonathan must, at the very least, be aware of his friend's interest in her and may well wish to encourage it. That she could get no satisfactory answers to all these questions was vexing indeed.

I should have liked to be certain in my own mind whether he does or does not care for me. Many times during this week I have felt his interest not only in the warmth and courtesy of his manner but also in the questions he has asked.

They are certainly not the idle enquiries of an indifferent acquaintance; but why then does he not let me see behind the words and manners to the feelings he must surely entertain? Only then will I be able to understand my own.

She had hoped that her last evening in London would afford him the opportunity, but apart from an earnest request to visit her at Edgewater, which he had seemed genuinely keen to do, there was nothing more.

As for his desire to call on me at Edgewater, this is not a request a gentleman would make lightly, yet he has given me no indication whatsoever of anything more serious than a sightseeing visit.

Ah well, we shall have to wait and see how it turns out.

On the morrow, just as they had finished breakfast and Becky was about to ask that her trunk and bags be carried down to the hall in preparation for their journey to the railway station, the doorbell rang.

Becky was certain it had to be Mr Contini come to say farewell, and judging by Anna's anticipatory expression, it seemed she thought so too. But, disappointingly, it was only Mr Elliott who, knowing of Becky's imminent departure, had called to give her some very welcome news.

No sooner was he in the room with them, than he declared, "Mrs Tate, I am here to tell you that William Rickman's pardon has been signed and will be sent to the county magistrate next week."

Becky was delighted.

He continued, rather gravely, "Rickman must report, with a lawyer in attendance, to the magistrate, who will read him the conditions of his pardon, to which he must agree."

When Becky looked apprehensive at this, he reassured her that they were not very onerous conditions and involved mainly giving an undertaking that he would not seek out any of those involved in accusing, arraigning, and convicting him.

"This is excellent news," said Jonathan, and Becky was very grateful.

"Mr Elliott, I thank you from the bottom of my heart, on behalf of these young people, who have suffered so much through no fault of theirs."

Despite her initial disappointment on seeing him, Becky was particularly pleased with Colin Elliott's news. At least, she thought, one thing would now be settled. She thanked him again and asked that her appreciation be conveyed to Mr Harding for his part in obtaining the pardon for Rickman.

To her astonishment, Mr Elliott looked a little embarrassed and replied that he would do so, when he wrote to his colleague, but it may be a while before he received it, since Mr Harding had resigned from the practice in London and was preparing to move to Canada.

Becky was speechless as she heard Jonathan Bingley ask, "This is certainly very sudden, Colin. Has Harding said why he is going and when does he leave?"

Mr Elliott said he did not know, but agreed that it had been arranged very suddenly. "He is at present in Scotland, visiting his mother, who I believe is his only living relative."

Becky could not help wondering whether Mr Harding's sudden decision had anything to do with her rejection of his proposal; it was a most disturbing thought. She could not know if Mr Elliott had known of his friend's proposal and her response. If he had, he certainly did not give any indication of it, and

Becky was glad indeed of his discretion. She would prefer that the Bingleys did not discover it either.

Even as they were engaged in the discussion that followed Mr Elliott's announcement, the hansom cab arrived to take Becky and her maid to the station. As Becky thanked Jonathan and Anna with warm affection, the servants scurried to get her luggage stowed aboard the cab, while Nelly ran upstairs to fetch Becky's coat and bonnet.

The ten days of her visit had passed so pleasantly that they were all able to claim sincere disappointment that their parting had come too soon. Jonathan and Anna, always generous and considerate hosts, hoped she would return to them in the New Year, perhaps to Netherfield at Easter, and Becky could not conceal her sadness at leaving them.

But, this time at least, she was going home with some very good news and many happy memories.

On the journey from London to Kent, Nelly noticed that her mistress was exceedingly thoughtful. It was not unusual for her to spend many hours lost in contemplation, especially since the death of her daughter, but mostly during those times, Nelly had learnt to read her mood and understand her sorrow.

This time, however, it was different. She was clearly deep in thought, but Nelly could not detect the old sadness in her demeanour. Indeed she appeared to be in a rather volatile mood, moving without warning from apparent cheerfulness to melancholy. This puzzled Nelly greatly. She had been with her mistress for several years and seen her through many difficult and troubling times; it was frustrating not to know what lay behind her present disposition.

On reaching their destination in Kent, they took a hired carriage, which conveyed them to Rosings Park. There, Becky instructed their driver to take them to the Dower House and, finding her sister at home, alighted and went indoors to break the good news of Rickman's pardon.

Catherine, having embraced and greeted her sister, expressed her own satisfaction at the news. Her generous heart had been deeply moved by the story of the unfortunate Rickmans, and she was glad for their sakes as well as for Becky, who had expended so much time and effort on their behalf.

When she finally returned to Edgewater, Becky went to her room and sent for Alice. She told her the news about her husband's pardon, then watched with pleasure as the girl thanked her, then asked permission to leave, before racing out into the yard to find her husband. Rickman, who was chopping wood for the fire, saw her running towards him and put down his axe. He seemed uncertain and anxious at first, but as she spoke, threw his arms around his wife, holding her in a close embrace, while tears flowed down their cheeks.

Moved to tears as she watched them from her window, Becky felt a sharp stab of pain, not out of sadness, but because she envied their closeness and longed for some semblance of the affection they enjoyed. However, practicality soon took over and she was determined to make it her business to help them settle into a new life, free of the fear of the law.

First, she decided she would send for her lawyer, explain the case to him, and ask him to accompany William Rickman, his wife, and child when they went before the county magistrate.

Her next priority was to find Rickman a suitable job, one that would bring him a decent wage and enable them to live together as a family should, particularly one that had been unjustly parted for so long.

To this end, she determined to consult her brother-in-law, Frank Burnett, who had risen considerably in her esteem since his marriage to her sister.

A man of wide practical experience in the world, she was sure Mr Burnett could advise her on how best to secure a position for William Rickman, one that would be more appropriate for a young man of some education and good character.

On the day following, she went to the Dower House, where Catherine asked her to stay to dinner. Becky accepted gladly; it gave her an opportunity to discuss the matter with her sister. Catherine had always been sympathetic to the Rickmans, and Becky hoped to enlist her to their cause, when she approached her husband.

Before the meal, the sisters spent some time together, during which Catherine's enquiries if Becky had enjoyed her stay with the Bingleys in London brought an enthusiastic response, which left Catherine in no doubt. "Well, I did say that you would enjoy yourself, did I not?" she asked, and Becky admitted that she had, but apart from saying that she had spent many delightful days, many more than she had expected, she gave few details. Becky was as yet unready to confide in her sister.

Later, when they were seated at the dinner table, Becky asked Mr Burnett for his opinion on the possibility of William Rickman securing a job other than labouring work in the area.

"I would employ him myself, seeing that his wife works very satisfactorily for me, but Edgewater is only a small property and has no requirement for a man of the experience and learning that Rickman has. I am aware of it because both Alice and Mrs Bancroft have assured me that he was a very competent clerk and kept the books at the brewery very well, that is until he was falsely accused," she explained.

Turning to Mr Burnett, she asked, "Do you think there might be, in this part of the county, for I do not think they would wish to move away, a similar position for him? It would be a great pity were he to continue as a labourer, when he could do so much better."

Catherine turned to her husband.

"Frank, I recall that a few months ago, we were speaking of the need for someone to assist you with the books for the Rosings Estate. Have you given any further thought to the matter, my dear?" she asked, and Becky well nigh leapt at the suggestion.

"Now *that* would do very well indeed. It would be exactly the sort of useful occupation that Rickman could undertake."

Frank Burnett was more cautious.

"I would need to have some evidence of his ability and experience, as well as references as to his character, particularly in view of his recent incarceration, but it is a possibility. As to your question, my dear," he said, addressing his wife, "I have already written to Mr Darcy and Jonathan Bingley asking if they would approve such a position, if we could find the right man."

Becky was eager to know what response he had received.

"And what do they say?"

Mr Burnett was noncommittal.

"Mr Bingley has made no objection, if we can ensure that we appoint a man who is both honest and skilled in keeping the books. He understands that I have not the training to do the work myself. Mr Darcy, however, must be persuaded that it is not an unnecessary expense of the Trust's funds. As principal trustee, he is exceedingly careful of the way the money is spent."

"And so he should be," said Becky, adding, "but this cannot be seen to be a waste of money. A competent clerk can only assist and improve the management of the estate. Do you not agree, Cathy?"

Catherine nodded.

"I certainly do, and I think if Lizzie can be appealed to, then Mr Darcy may quite easily be persuaded by her."

"Do you think so? Oh dear, I wish I felt more confidence in my ability to appeal successfully to Mrs Darcy. She is so much the perfect Mistress of Pemberley now, I should be quite daunted by the prospect."

Catherine laughed, unwilling to let this pass.

"Oh come now, Becky, Lizzie was Mama's dearest friend; she is unlikely to wish to intimidate any of us. For my part, I will say that both Lizzie and Mr Darcy have been exceedingly kind and generous to us, most recently in appointing Frank to manage the Rosings Trust and permitting us to continue in this house."

Becky was not so easily persuaded.

"Ah, but you never did cross Lizzie in any way, did you, Cathy? You must remember that Lizzie held me responsible for all of Julian Darcy's misery because she believed that I persuaded my Josie to marry him. I do not deny that I did play some part in her decision, but in the end, Julian was the keener of the two. He was very much in love and determined that they should marry. Besides, I never could have foreseen their problems."

Catherine's voice softened as she acknowledged her sister's unhappy situation, but said with great sincerity, "Becky, I do not believe Lizzie bears you any ill will on that score, not now that Julian is married again and very happily to Jessica. I am confident that Lizzie is well pleased. Indeed, I had thought that both of you were quite reconciled last Christmas."

Becky sighed.

"Yes, you are probably right, but I do not believe I would have sufficient confidence to approach Lizzie and ask her for a favour, even if it would help the Rickmans. I would feel awkward and fear her refusal."

Catherine smiled, "Well, if that is how you feel, perhaps I could help. I should be happy to ask if she could put the idea to Mr Darcy. Since Frank has already written, it should not be too difficult for me to ask for Lizzie's support. I shall not mention William Rickman at all; my request will be on Frank's behalf. He needs a clerk to help him with this extra work."

Becky was surprised and delighted beyond words.

"Would you do that, Cathy?" she asked, incredulous. She had not expected this from Catherine.

"Why not? Frank, what is your opinion? Do you suppose it could be considered presumptuous on my part?"

Her husband took her hand and said, "No one would ever consider you guilty of presumption, my dear. If you were to approach Mrs Darcy, I think we can safely say the matter would soon be settled to everyone's satisfaction."

Which is how it came about that Catherine wrote to Elizabeth, who then approached her husband, and subsequently, William Rickman came to be appointed to the position of clerk, assisting Mr Frank Burnett in the management of the Rosings Estate.

When permission was granted and the position was offered, Alice and her husband were overwhelmed by the opportunity presented to them and the generosity of their benefactors. For them and their son, Thomas, whose speech had continued to improve, it was to be the end of a long nightmare and the beginning of a new, productive life.

And for all of this good fortune, they thanked most particularly Mrs Becky Tate, whose personal kindness to Alice and assiduous pursuit of William's case had brought them the happiness they now enjoyed. Happiness, which, a few months ago, had seemed completely out of their reach.

And after more than two years of concealment and gruelling hardship, Alice Grey was now free to be Annabel Rickman once more. When Catherine suggested that Annabel might enjoy helping the teacher at the parish school, her cup of joy flowed over.

❧

While all these matters were proceeding, Becky, who with characteristic keenness had become deeply involved in the arrangements, almost forgot her promise to write to Mr Contini.

She had undertaken to write when the "unrelated matters" that she had to settle were concluded, so he could visit her at Edgewater and meet her sister Catherine.

But as things had turned out, she had been unable to settle into a mood in which to write him a letter. Although she explained this lapse to herself by reasoning that there had been much work to be done and many arrangements to be made, in truth, the real reason lay elsewhere.

Since returning from London, Becky had begun to be concerned that perhaps she had allowed herself to be too easily beguiled by the charm of Aldo Contini. She could not deny the attraction of his engaging character, yet she was apprehensive that her feelings may be more deeply engaged than his were.

It was this, rather than any excess of work, that had prevented her from writing to him, as she had promised to do. Besides, she had not as yet told her sister of her renewed association with him and the extent to which their meeting had enhanced her enjoyment of her sojourn in London.

However, the arrival of a letter in the post changed all that. It was from Jonathan Bingley, informing her that he hoped to call on her when he attended the final meeting of the Rosings Trust for the year, adding that Mr Contini had unexpectedly returned to Italy two days ago, leaving with Jonathan a note and a keepsake for her. Jonathan promised to deliver these items when he visited the following week.

On reading the letter, Becky's emotions were thrown into a state of such confusion that she felt quite incapable of rational thought. Her feelings could scarcely be contained as she read on, and a sense of bewilderment overwhelmed her.

That Mr Contini had unexpectedly returned to Italy was sufficient surprise, but that he had done so without informing her, leaving a note and keepsake with Jonathan, was beyond comprehension. After all those days of close, almost intimate association, after sharing so many happy hours, how could he leave England so abruptly, without a word to her?

The fact that he had left a note with Jonathan seemed to indicate that it was probably not a very private communication.

Surely, she thought, if the note had contained anything like an expression of his feelings, he would have sent it directly to her.

After a day of mental tumult, followed by a sleepless night, she rose the following morning convinced it was all her fault. She had promised to write and invite him to visit, yet she had done nothing, made no real effort to communicate with him. It was no surprise, she surmised, that he had probably reached the conclusion that she had no further interest in their friendship, and Becky wondered how badly he would think of her, if that were the case.

Only now, with the prospect of meeting him again greatly diminished, if not lost altogether, did Becky realise the depth of her disappointment and understand that her feelings for Aldo Contini were much more intense than she had supposed. She could scarcely credit the discomposure that Jonathan Bingley's letter had caused. Unable to concentrate upon anything more serious than the most trivial of domestic matters, she found her mind returning incessantly to the implications of Mr Contini's departure and speculating upon the contents of the note he had left for her, not to mention the "keepsake" that Jonathan Bingley was to deliver.

What could it be, she wondered?

On re-reading Jonathan's letter for the tenth time, Becky could not help feeling some degree of guilt at the circumstances in which Mr Contini had returned to Italy, possibly following his disappointment at not receiving from her the promised invitation to visit Edgewater. Yet, knowing what she knew of his nature, she could not believe he would act in such a petulant manner, leaving without a word to her.

In an effort to assuage her feelings of guilt, she went over every occasion on which they had been together, endeavouring to discover if there had been one on which he had given some indication of his expectations.

She found none.

What then, she wondered, was she to think?

She knew very little of his life in Italy and whether some matter of family or business had called him away urgently. She supposed Jonathan Bingley may be able to enlighten her. She could not accept that he had departed in a fit of pique! It was not at all in his nature to do so. There had to be another reason.

In her heart, she hoped that there *was* some simple explanation; for in the course of revolving all these recollections and emotions through her mind, Becky had reached the conclusion that whatever Mr Contini's feelings might have been, her own were becoming very clear—she loved him.

END OF PART FOUR

A WOMAN OF INFLUENCE

Part Five

Chapter Twenty

A FEW DAYS AFTER Becky had received his letter, which had caused her such consternation and anguish, Jonathan Bingley himself arrived at Rosings Park to attend a meeting of the Trust.

He had decided to stay at Rosings, in the East Wing, which had survived the fire, where the accommodation, though not as comfortable as he could have enjoyed at the Dower House, afforded him complete privacy. Apart from the small staff employed to maintain the place, he would meet no one of any consequence, except Mr Adams, the curator, and he was generally a very discreet young man.

Jonathan was concerned because he had two missions to fulfill on this visit; one was the usual business of the Trust, and the other a combination of duty and pleasure. The latter, entailing a visit to Edgewater to deliver a letter from his friend Mr Contini, required some degree of confidentiality. He was unaware if Becky had taken her sister Catherine into her confidence on the matter of her friendship with Mr Contini, which was why Jonathan had determined that he would stay at the old house and avoid any awkward questions. He had, however, accepted an invitation to dine with Catherine and Frank Burnett at the Dower House, as he did whenever he was at Rosings, and looked forward to that occasion, as always.

Becky knew Jonathan was expected; Catherine had told her so and asked her to join them for dinner on the following day. Having accepted the invitation, she had hurried home to await some indication of when Jonathan would call on her, as promised in his letter.

Even as she waited, she was filled with foreboding.

Certain now that Aldo Contini had gone out of her life forever, Becky became increasingly miserable, castigating herself for having carelessly squandered a possible chance for happiness that may never come her way again. If this were true, she would have no one to blame but herself, she concluded, and became even more dejected at the thought.

Then again, she would consider the question and reach another, contrary conclusion. After all, she would argue, Mr Contini had never given her an indication of any serious intention; certainly, he had been attentive, charming, and kind, but there had been no declaration of feelings, and no hint of a proposal of marriage.

Why then was she feeling so dismal? Why did the future suddenly look so bleak? What had happened to the bright optimism that she had experienced when she had spent the best part of ten days in his company?

To these and other vexing questions she could find no answers.

Becky Tate was in a quandary largely of her own making.

Some little while after three o'clock that afternoon, Jonathan Bingley called on Becky at Edgewater. A note delivered earlier had asked if it would suit, and she had replied that it would; indeed, she had said, she was looking forward to seeing him.

Becky dressed with care for Jonathan's visit, keen to present an appearance of self-assurance, which she certainly did not feel.

Aware that he had a partiality for sweets, she had ensured that a variety of delicious refreshments were made ready, and received him not in the parlour, as she might have done at that hour, but in the more private and spacious drawing room, where they would not be overheard.

They greeted one another with affection and, as refreshments were served, exchanged the usual pleasantries, biding their time until the servants, their duties done, withdrew.

Almost as soon as they did, Becky looked across at Jonathan, and he came over to where she was seated, beside the fireplace.

Reaching into his pocket, he withdrew two items, a sealed letter and a small rectangular package, which he handed to her. As Becky took them from him, her hand shook slightly—not enough for him to notice, but sufficient to warn her that she had not quite got control of her feelings and must be careful not to betray herself.

At first she thought to put them aside and proceed with dispensing more tea, but Jonathan had other ideas. Speaking quite casually, he said, "Of course, you wish to read your letter and open your package in private, Becky. I should very much like to take a look at some of the books in your library; I quite envy your fine collection of the work of Mr Dickens, so if you will permit me, I shall repair to the library now and will return in a little while."

Becky, astonished at his sensitivity, could say very little except, "Yes, of course, please feel free to look at anything you wish. I was fortunate to inherit most of my mother-in-law's excellent collection; Walter had little interest in it…"

Whereupon, he smiled and left the room, crossed the corridor, and entered the library. She heard the door shut behind him.

Left alone, Becky opened her letter.

She had expected it to be no more than a brief note, probably saying farewell, explaining that he had been urgently and unavoidably recalled to Italy and expressing his regrets at not seeing her again.

She had steeled herself for just such a message.

It was nothing of the sort.

Indeed, whatever her expectations may have been, they were overthrown completely as she opened up the sealed envelope and read the two pages of carefully penned writing contained therein.

She scanned them swiftly, reading eagerly and impatiently to the end, before returning to the beginning and reading it over again, more slowly and with greater attention to the sentiments expressed.

It was on perusing it a second time that the full import of the letter became apparent to her, which the rather old-fashioned courtliness of the writer's style had initially obscured.

Having made it clear that he was returning only temporarily to Italy and expected to be back in London quite soon, Mr Contini had proceeded to describe in some detail his current circumstances, his own family responsibilities—he had, he said, an aged mother who expected regular visits, and his business required travel back and forth from Europe some two or three times a year.

At first, all this information had Becky rather puzzled. But as she read on, it became clear that in the manner of some European gentlemen, Mr Contini was setting out his credentials as a suitor, placing before her the pros and cons of his case.

Becky could not suppress a smile, as she recalled the somewhat matter-of-fact manner in which Mr Tate had proposed to her. There had been no need to tell her of his circumstances or his family; these were well known in the Matlock district; indeed, Anthony Tate would surely have been regarded as the best "catch" in the county, and Becky had been universally considered a very fortunate young woman to have "caught" him.

Mr Contini, on the other hand, had no pretensions to great wealth or a family dynasty, although he did in his description of his family's estate in Italy reveal that he would one day inherit a share in a well-run business as well as a villa outside Florence, where his mother now lived.

His own financial circumstances were comfortable enough though modest, he said, but he considered them adequate to his needs.

Having provided her with all of these mundane details, he then proceeded to the main purpose of his letter.

> *I had hoped, dear Becky, to have an opportunity to call on you at your home in Kent and speak with you on this subject, but clearly your circumstances did not permit it at this time. You did explain that there were some domestic matters that required your attention, and I understood and accepted that.*
>
> *Therefore, I have had to resort to writing to you in a manner that you might find awkward. If this is the case, I beg you to forgive any gaucheness on my part, as I am at a disadvantage expressing myself on a subject as delicate and important as this, not having the same felicitous ease of expression in the English language as I would have in my own.*

…he wrote modestly. Becky could scarcely credit this in the light of his letter; there was certainly nothing gauche or awkward there. She read on; knowing her own heart, she sought eagerly for some evidence of his feelings for her. He continued:

Nevertheless, I ask you to believe that I have, for all of the last few weeks, thought only of how to convince you of the sincerity and depth of my feelings for you. These feelings had their origins some years ago, during a time, that I hope you will recall with the same degree of pleasure as I do.

While I was not at liberty to express them then, in the circumstances of that time, which was why I sought to quench them, they were rekindled when we met again in London last month and spent so many delightful hours together. Consequently, I am convinced that my feelings are both true and strong. My hesitation to speak to you in London arose only from my uncertainty about your response. Ever since you left London to return to your home in Kent, I have thought unceasingly of you and, realising how much I missed you, have reached finally the inescapable conclusion that I love you too well to remain silent.

Dearest Becky, if, as I hope, you have similar feelings and are willing to consider my proposal, you will make me a very happy man, and I promise most solemnly to do all in my power to ensure your happiness. Please permit me to say that I would be deeply honoured if you would consent to be my wife.

I have no wish to rush you into a decision, but ask only that you send me word through my friend Mr Jonathan Bingley, in whom I have confided, if I may hope for a favourable answer or not. I am content to wait for your answer, and dependent upon it; I shall arrange to call on you at a time of your choosing and meet with your sister and brother-in-law, Mr and Mrs Burnett. Afterwards, if you agree, I would like us to visit Signor and Signora Contini—my uncle and aunt in Richmond. They know of my feelings and have indicated to me that they would welcome you into our family with the warmest affection.

Should Mr Bingley bring me a negative reply—and I am not so presumptuous as to assume that this is unlikely—I shall accept your decision without rancour and endure my disappointment as best I can, wishing you every happiness in the future. But, I must confess, in such a case, my anguish will be great.

If you would be so kind as to say yes, dearest Becky, it will be the happiest day of my life so far. I only say so far because I hope in the future to enjoy much greater happiness with you as my beloved wife.

I await your answer,
Yours very sincerely,
Aldo Contini.

A brief postscript mentioned that he had enclosed also a keepsake, which he had made especially for her, in fulfillment of a promise given when they were in London, and expressed the hope that she would like it.

Becky folded the letter and placed it in its envelope, before reaching for the package, which lay on the tea table before her. When she tried to open it, her hands were still shaking, for she was as yet unable to assimilate completely the feelings his letter had aroused in her; so unexpected had it been, so open and direct in its appeal.

The package contained an object wrapped in several sheets of soft paper, which she parted impatiently to reveal in a simple silver frame a portrait of herself.

It took her only a few seconds to realise that it was his own work, a fine charcoal drawing of the type she had seen him make on occasions, deftly sketching objects and scenes that caught his eye. She had admired some of them then but had never believed he had made one of her, even though he had once suggested that he would.

This one, clearly drawn from memory, showed Becky in a pensive mood, her fine features highlighted by the simplicity of her gown and hair, both suggesting that she had been "captured" by the artist at home.

She was still gazing at it with some amazement when Jonathan returned to the room and, seeing it in her hand, remarked casually, "It is an excellent likeness, is it not?"

Becky was taken aback.

She was disconcerted because she did not know what Jonathan knew. Mr Contini had admitted to having confided in his friend, but Becky wondered how much he had told him.

To begin with, she was surprised that Jonathan had obviously seen the portrait. She responded to his comment, a little belatedly. "Do you think so?"

"Certainly," he said, "Contini does very good portraits; he has made excellent sketches of my daughters. You shall see them when you visit Netherfield and tell me if they are not remarkably like the girls."

Becky nodded politely and turned to pour out his tea.

Jonathan took his cup and seated himself across from her. It was for Becky a most awkward moment; "Surely," she thought, "he cannot expect that I could give him an answer for his friend now?" Her mind kept returning to the question of what Mr Contini had told him. Was it possible he knew of their previous association?

In order to make some ordinary conversation, she asked if he would like a slice of cake. Jonathan chose the fruit cake and as she handed him the plate, said very gently, "Becky, I want to assure you that while Mr Contini has confided in me and asked me to help him, I do not intend to make any effort to influence your decision one way or the other. He is a friend, a loyal and dear friend of mine, and while it would give me great satisfaction to see him happily married, I would not presume to persuade you to accept him."

When she looked at him in some confusion, he continued, "I have made that clear to him, before I agreed to act as an intermediary on this occasion. I did so because he was so desperately unhappy that he had not taken the opportunity to speak with you whilst you were in London. He had not anticipated being recalled to Italy over an urgent family matter and had hoped to see you here at Edgewater in more propitious circumstances. Sadly, that did not eventuate, and when he did not hear from you, I believe he feared he had missed his chance with you. He spoke with me an hour before his departure, and I will say that I have rarely seen a man more deeply in love and more distraught."

Becky was too distressed to say more than, "It was my fault; I should have kept my word and written him as I said I would; but I became confused… when I was back here, I did not feel as certain of him or my own feelings as I had been in London."

Jonathan was puzzled. "Why?"

"I cannot explain it, Jonathan; I have been busy and there was a lot to do here with the business of Alice Grey, and yet I know I should have written and I do feel guilty at not having done so and probably distressed him unduly."

Her voice was low and she seemed so harrowed, Jonathan rose and went to sit beside her. "Come now, Becky, you must not blame yourself; there is no real harm done. Aldo Contini has loved you for a very long time—it is almost two years since he first confided in me. He knew then there was no future in it, and now he has renewed hope. When you did not write, he was disappointed of course, but he has not gone off in a huff; indeed, he was reluctant to write for fear of offending you—it was my idea that he should."

Becky was astonished. "Offending me? Why?" she asked.

Jonathan explained patiently, "Because, my dear Becky, he feared that you were unprepared for his declaration or that you may have felt he was presuming upon your friendship on too short an acquaintance. He is not an arrogant man; it is likely that he thought you did not know him well enough to make such a commitment."

"Too short an acquaintance? Why, Jonathan, he knows me better than I know myself... in those dismal days after Josie's death, when I was so much alone in London... were it not for him I might well have..." She stopped abruptly, a hand to her mouth as if to hold back the words that had already escaped.

Jonathan, looking at her directly, spoke quietly, "I know."

"You do?" she looked up at his face, disbelieving.

"Yes, I have known for some time," he said. "He confided in me at a time when he sincerely believed there was no hope at all. Mr Tate was still living, albeit in the United States, and you had returned to your place in Matlock.

"He knew how deeply you had been hurt, both by Josie's death and your husband's abrupt departure for America; indeed, he was most unhappy that he could do so very little to comfort you."

"Did he tell you then, that he loved me?" she asked, incredulous.

Jonathan nodded, "Indeed he did, and he appealed to me for help, but what could I do? I had no way to influence your circumstances; I could only advise him to return to Italy for a while."

Becky met his eyes as she spoke.

"But, Jonathan, he did comfort me, at a time when I had no one but my maid Nelly to turn to. I was very grateful for his presence... I had felt so alone and friendless. He was kind and understanding; I have thought of it often... a lesser man may well have taken advantage of my vulnerable state of mind, but he was both compassionate and honorable in every way."

Jonathan was silent, letting her speak, guessing she had not confided in anyone else and had long concealed the intensity of her feelings, "At the time, it seemed to me that he was the only person who understood how I felt; everyone else, especially members of Julian's family, appeared to blame me. I was grateful for his generosity, but I had no idea how much his kindness had meant to me until we met again in London last month. Then, I discovered how easy it was to be happy in his company, how much I could learn from him about coping with life's misfortunes."

Jonathan nodded, "He has admitted to very similar feelings; he is not a stranger to the sorrow of bereavement, his family lost a beloved daughter, too— Aldo's youngest sister, Rosetta, died of tuberculosis at the age of fourteen. I am not at all surprised that he could offer you the understanding and sympathy you needed at the time. It must have been a grievous time for both of you. And yet, he recalls only the pleasure of being with you and none of the pain, and hopes that the affinity you have shared will sustain you both. He loves you, Becky; he swears he has never cared as well for any other woman, and I know him to be a man of his word."

"And you do not condemn me?" she asked.

Her question surprised him. "Condemn you? For what offence? For reaching out for comfort when you were left to grieve alone after the death of a beloved child? For accepting some affection when your husband had virtually deserted you? Would that not make me a hard man and a hypocrite to boot?"

Becky was confused.

She would never have called him a hard man; Jonathan was renowned for his gentleness and consideration of others.

"Why a hypocrite?"

"Why indeed? When Amelia-Jane died in that dreadful accident, I too felt alone and distraught, I sought comfort, and when Anna reached out to me, I took her hand with gratitude. It was simple kindness on her part. I enjoyed her company, her delightful nature, and sweet disposition, believing it to be part of an innocent friendship. But later, I realised that I had fallen in love with Anna, even before the death of my wife," he said.

Becky could see clearly the strain upon his face as he spoke.

"As you would know, Becky, your sister and I had some unresolved problems at that time. We had lost two little boys in infancy, I was bored with working for Lady Catherine, Amelia-Jane was impatient with my political interests and had no desire to move to Netherfield; it had not been the happiest period of our marriage.

"I had met Anna at Pemberley after many years, and she, quite unwittingly, had let me see how easy it was to love someone with her warmth and generosity of spirit. We are all only human and respond to acts of kindness when we are hurt. Of course, I did not seek it—perhaps I was not even aware it was happening—but I was very shocked when I discovered the truth about my feelings for her, although I did not admit them even to myself until well after my wife's death. So, tell me, how then should I condemn you, Becky?"

She had listened, stunned by his admission, amazed that he had chosen to reveal it to her. He continued gravely, "I have disclosed this to no one but yourself, and I have done it only to reassure you that I am no hypocrite. When I learned from Aldo Contini that some intimacy of feeling had developed between you, I made no judgment. I knew that as an honourable man he would wish to take it to its proper conclusion. Indeed, he asked me if Mr Tate could be persuaded to divorce you, so he could ask you to marry him. He loved you very much, Becky, I have no doubt of that."

Seeing the effect of this on Becky's countenance, he said very quickly, "At the time, it did not seem likely, and I told him so. I knew also that your situation in the family was such; you would suffer intolerable damage if such a proposition were even contemplated. He understood and, though he was deeply dejected, accepted that nothing would come of it in the circumstances that existed at the time. You may ask why I acted as I did. It was chiefly to protect you from criticism by my family and others. Reluctantly, Contini returned to Italy, where he appeared to recover some of his spirits, becoming involved in work over there, and when we met again last year, he enquired after you but seemed resigned to his fate. However, as you can see, that is all in the past—the circumstances of your life have changed; he still loves you and the future is now yours to grasp."

Becky had one more question.

"Jonathan, forgive me, but I must ask you, does Anna know?"

He smiled.

"That Aldo Contini loves you? She must know. One would have to be blind not to see it. Whilst you were with us in London, he was the life and soul of every occasion. Since you left to return to Kent, he has been impossible to please, speaking of you often with much pleasure, clearly missing you and growing melancholy because you were not there. I doubt that Anna could have avoided drawing the obvious conclusion."

Becky persisted.

"I meant, does Anna know of our previous friendship… while Mr Tate was in America and I was in London following Josie's death?"

She was very anxious, and he, understanding her anxiety, moved swiftly to reassure her.

"She does not, nor will she hear of it from me. On that subject, Becky, I can give you my solemn word. Your secret is safe with me."

"Thank you," said Becky, and her face showed the relief she clearly felt.

Anna Bingley was her cousin, and it would have been mortifying to discover that she had known of her previous association with Mr Contini and perhaps talked of it with others in the family, who might not be as sanguine or understanding as Jonathan had been. But, he reassured her, "It was a confidence, and I should never breach a trust and reveal such matters, Becky, not even to my wife. It is not a matter of concern to her, nor to anyone else other than Mr Contini and yourself," he said, and she believed him implicitly. She was immensely grateful and said so again.

It was almost dark outside, and the servants entered to light the lamps.

Jonathan rose and, waiting until they had left the room, took her hand.

"Think carefully before you send him your answer, Becky; he is a good man and loves you dearly. That is all I will say."

Taking his leave of her, Jonathan left, and as Becky turned to go upstairs, she heard his footsteps striding down the gravel drive.

On reaching her room, Becky lay on the couch, exhausted but strangely elated, too. Her mind was filled with a plethora of competing thoughts, all swirling around demanding attention.

She could not help wondering at the irony of her circumstances.

Jonathan Bingley, whom she had loved hopelessly as a young girl and lost first to her younger sister Amelia-Jane and then to her cousin Anna, was he to be the one who would show her how she might find the happiness that had eluded her for so long?

It was a circumstance she never could have imagined.

Then, there was Mr Contini's appeal that she send him an answer—if not an immediate acceptance of his proposal, at least one that offered him hope of future success.

How was this request to be fulfilled? How was she to respond with the kind of honesty that he had shown in his letter to her?

She longed to do so, yet held back from such an open acknowledgement of her feelings. Becky found herself in a state of such perplexity as she had never experienced before. She knew exactly what she wanted to say. She had consulted her heart; her feelings were strong and consistent.

But how to say it?

She was not unaware of the incongruity of her situation; that she, a writer, who could weave together evocative words to express thoughts and ideas, should struggle to convey what was nearest to her heart.

She tried writing in her diary:

How shall I tell him that I have waited to hear such sentiments all my life and feared that I would perhaps never have such pleasure?

What reason shall I give if I were to refuse him? How shall I explain it? Not just to him, but to myself?

And if I do, will I then forever wonder if I had done the right thing, or shall I live to rue the day I made such a stupid decision?

Who shall I please by such a decision? Not myself, surely, for if I were to think only of my own affections, of which I am now so certain, I should not lose a minute before sending my answer. Yet I must not be precipitate as I have been before. I cannot afford another mistake.

How shall I know that I am doing what is right for both of us?

An hour later, Nelly came to ask if Becky would change for dinner. She found her asleep, with her diary fallen from her hands. She picked it up and put it away before leaving the room.

Nelly seemed to know intuitively that her mistress would not be dining downstairs that night.

Chapter Twenty-One

A S THE TIME APPROACHED to prepare for the dinner party at the Dower House, Becky began to feel increasingly nervous. The confidence and *savoir-faire* she had cultivated over several years of dealing with many people in high places had all but disappeared.

She knew Jonathan Bingley was leaving Rosings Park on the following morning, which meant he had to have her response to Mr Contini's letter that night. Becky had spent most of the morning scribbling numerous brief notes, then tearing them up. When Nelly enquired if she wished to have her gown pressed in readiness for the evening, she had been so distracted, she could not decide which gown to wear.

Shortly after noon, a note had arrived from Catherine advising that the weather appeared to be turning for the worse and inviting Becky to stay overnight at the Dower House to avoid a hazardous journey home.

Becky was touched by her concern. "My dear sister, she thinks of everything," she said and instructed Nelly to pack a bag for their overnight stay.

Although that may have solved one problem of a purely practical nature, it did not make it any easier for her to compose her reply to Mr Contini.

She had tried a number of responses—one adopted a collected and calm approach, another appreciative but cautious; she even tried a dignified and noncommittal tone, but none of them seemed right.

There was an impression of contrivance about the words, which she abhorred, and her present feelings were such that she had no wish to torment him with more uncertainty.

In the end, she wrote with simple sincerity that she hoped would convey both her appreciation of his sentiments and the need she felt for some discretion in her answer and hoped he would understand.

Having thanked him for his letter and expressed her gratitude for his kind words, she asked for some little time to consider his proposal.

I would like to think about it for a while before I give you my response, she wrote:

> *...not because I am unappreciative of your feelings or wary of them, but only to give myself time to reflect upon my own. I do not for one moment doubt your intentions, but wish to be entirely confident of mine.*

Then, as if prompted by a tug upon her heart strings, she added:

> *When you are returned from Italy, I should be very happy for you to visit me at Edgewater and shall look forward to seeing you here.*

It was brief, but it was done, and she signed it:

> *Yours very sincerely,*
> *Becky Tate.*

At dinner that night, they were six.

Lilian and John Adams had also been invited, for which Becky was grateful because both young people had a great deal to say, having been recently in France, visiting Mr Adams's family.

Lilian, no more the shy young girl Becky had known before her marriage, had many interesting stories to tell of the rustic charm of the French countryside, while Mr Adams regaled them with his accounts of the battle raging between the artists of the new Impressionist movement and the old school of *realisme* in art.

Jonathan Bingley, whose wife Anna was herself an artist of some talent, was acquainted with the subject and listened with interest, but Becky, whose knowledge of art was somewhat perfunctory, found her mind wandering to other more pressing matters.

She knew she had to tell her sister of Mr Contini's proposal; she would not be forgiven if she neglected to do so. Yet she had already decided that she was not going to reveal anything of her previous relationship with him.

"If Jonathan has not felt the need to tell his wife about it, why need I tell my sister?" she argued quite reasonably and reached the conveniently logical conclusion that she need not, because it was of little significance now. Through dinner, she had pondered the question of how much she was going to tell Catherine.

The opportunity afforded by the invitation to stay overnight at the Dower House was worth seizing, she decided. When they retired upstairs, she would tell her sister of his proposal, though she could not predict what Catherine's response might be.

After dinner, when the ladies left the table and withdrew to the drawing room, Lilian, who was feeling tired, went to rest awhile on a sofa in the library, until the gentlemen were ready to join them. Becky saw her chance and whispered to Catherine that she had some important news for her, eliciting an immediate demand to be told what it was. But Becky was able to persuade her sister that there was not sufficient time to tell her, and besides, if the gentlemen arrived in the middle of her narration, it would all be spoilt.

Catherine was a little puzzled at the secrecy, but she agreed, countering with her own little mystery.

"Well, I have some news for you too—I have only just heard and have been planning to tell you tonight. So I shall come to your room after the others have gone home. It will be like old times, when we were little girls and would tell each other secrets! You can tell me everything!"

Becky nodded, thinking to herself, "Not quite everything, Cathy, but that does not signify, for you shall know the essential truth of the matter."

Presently, the gentlemen entered the drawing room, and while Catherine went to get Lilian, Jonathan approached Becky. She knew he would come and had her letter ready for him, which he put away in his pocket. Discreet and proper as usual, he asked nothing about its contents, and Becky said nothing, except to thank him once more for his kindness. "It is very kind of you, Jonathan, and I thank you for it and for your understanding," she said, only to be assured that it was an errand he undertook with pleasure.

His hope, he said, was that he could in this way help two people, for whom he had a great deal of affection, to find the happiness they both deserved.

Becky reddened at his words and smiled but said nothing more. She did not believe it was expected that she would reveal any part of her answer.

No doubt, she assumed, Mr Contini, on receiving her letter, would enlighten him. Theirs was clearly an intimate friendship.

Later that evening, after Jonathan had left, followed by Lilian and Mr Adams, Becky retired to the spare room. She had changed into her nightgown and despatched her maid, when there was a light knock on her door and Catherine entered.

"Now, Becky," she said, seating herself on the bed, "what is this piece of important news you have for me? I am all excited; I must know everything."

"Will you not tell me yours first?" Becky asked, and Catherine obliged.

It was just as Becky had suspected. Lilian was expecting a child.

She had noticed that her niece was looking pale and had complained of tiredness after dinner.

"The doctor thinks the baby will probably be born in the late Spring," said Catherine, and Becky embraced and congratulated her sister.

"You will enjoy having a grandson or daughter to spoil, will you not?" she said, and Catherine agreed she would, saying with some sadness, "I suppose it will make up for the fact that I may never see the others, if their father continues his work in India. Oh Becky, I had no idea they would be away so long; the children will hardly know me."

She was speaking of the children of her elder daughter, who had married the chaplain to a regiment stationed in India. They had been away almost five years, and there had been no sign of their returning soon.

Becky was sympathetic; she had grown accustomed to missing her own grandson, Josie's child—Anthony Darcy. He lived with Cassy and Richard Gardiner, being educated and trained to be the future Master of Pemberley. Sadly, Becky saw very little of Anthony, a fine young boy, who was growing up very much under the influence of his grandfather Mr Darcy and his aunt Cassandra Gardiner.

Becky regretted the circumstances of their separation, but, as things had turned out, she could do nothing to alter them.

But this was no time for melancholy, and Catherine claimed she would soon have her hands full preparing for the arrival of Lilian's child.

Turning eagerly to her sister, she said, "Now, Becky, you've heard my news, I must hear yours."

Becky had brought along Mr Contini's letter, which she now placed in her sister's hands.

Catherine read it carefully, taking in everything and occasionally going back to re-read some part of the text. She made no comment until the end, when she said in the most matter-of-fact tone, "Becky, this is a proposal of marriage."

When Becky nodded, Catherine pointed to a line in the letter, which referred to times past when, Mr Contini claimed, his affection for her had been first aroused.

"There, I knew it; you did flirt with him then? Oh Becky, you naughty thing, whatever would Mama have said or Cousin Lizzie?" she teased her sister, pretending to be shocked and laughing at her supposed discomfiture.

In truth, however, Catherine's mock outrage suited Becky well, allowing her to let her sister believe that she and Mr Contini had indulged in a minor flirtation in the past, which had turned serious when they had met again, more recently in London after the death of Mr Tate.

It also helped confirm Becky in her determination not to reveal any more details about her previous association with him. Catherine, she decided, need never know of the brief but impassioned encounter that had created such turmoil in her life that she, unable to contain her feelings, had fled London and returned to Matlock, where the emotions that had been awakened continued to smoulder for many unhappy months, when she had swung between moods of euphoric recollection and guilt.

Catherine's voice broke in upon her thoughts.

"Do you mean to accept him?"

"I don't know yet," she replied. "I would like to, but I have to be sure it is right this time. I must not make another mistake, Cathy; I must know that this time it is the right decision, or I would rather remain single to the end of my days."

"Of course you must, but surely, Becky, there cannot be any doubt. He loves you and says so very clearly. Do you not love him?"

"I believe I do," said Becky, "but, Cathy, I am determined to be quite certain that what I feel *is* love, not fondness or friendliness or regard. I have known all these before, and they are good, honourable feelings, but love is quite a different matter, and I must be sure that I love him as deeply and as passionately as he claims he loves me. Else we might as well remain good friends, as we are now, and neither of us will be hurt. Do you not understand my feelings, Cathy?"

Catherine, whose life had been significantly altered by the return of Frank Burnett, understood exactly. "Of course I do, my dear Becky; never would I expect you to marry him without the certainty of love. I know it can change our lives as nothing else can. Of course, you must be certain, but how will you know? Do you intend to meet him?"

Becky nodded. "I do. I have sent him a brief reply; I have said I would be happy to see him at Edgewater, when he returns to England. I think, Cathy, that when we do meet, I will know," she replied.

Catherine rose and embraced her sister.

"Of course you will, and you will tell me, when you decide?"

"Most certainly, you shall be the first to know, apart from Mr Contini himself," she assured her.

As they parted, Becky knew she had been right.

There was no need to burden her sister with further information about matters from the past. She feared Catherine's exemplary goodness may be outraged without the benefit of all of the facts, and there were some things she was not prepared to reveal, even to a beloved sister.

After Catherine had left her, Becky had tried to sleep, but she could not; her mind was filled with thoughts and images she could not evade. She recalled vividly the day when, not long after Josie's death, Mr Tate had returned from Europe and announced soon afterwards that he would be travelling to the United States on business, leaving her at the house in London.

Grieving alone, unwilling to return to Derbyshire, where she had felt shunned by Julian's family, Becky had suffered many days and nights of anguish, with only Nelly for company. One afternoon, unable to find any consolation, afflicted with a headache, she had wandered out wearing only a light coat over her Summer gown, walking aimlessly until she had lost her way in the park. Drenched by a sudden Summer shower, she had sought shelter in an arcade across the road, where Mr Contini, coming out of a bookshop, had found her, clearly distressed and very wet.

Becky recalled the kindness and gentleness with which he had wrapped his overcoat around her, helped her into a hansom cab, and taken her home. There, he had urged Nelly to get her dry and warm and put her to bed while he went for a doctor. Becky had caught a chill, and the doctor had warned of the danger of pneumonia, but being both healthy and resilient, she had recovered more quickly than expected.

That week, Mr Contini had called at the house every day to ask after her progress, bringing books and flowers for her comfort. When she was well enough to come downstairs, he had sat with her, and when she was quite recovered, invited her to drive out with him in the park. The fresh air, he had said, would do her good, and Nelly had persuaded her he was right.

Thus had begun a brief interlude in the Summer of 1866, when Becky had found friendship and consolation that had pulled her back from the abyss of self-pity and remorse, which may well have destroyed her mind.

At his urging, she had let him take her out for drives in the countryside, at times spending all day out of doors in some little village or coastal town, and delaying their homeward journey until light had faded from the sky.

Always he had been careful not just of her comfort but of the need to maintain a degree of decorum, treating her with gentlemanly courtesy at all times and making allowance for her situation without ever referring to it.

Becky recalled how easily they had exchanged confidences as their friendship deepened. In him she had confided, as in no one else, her feelings of guilt over Josie's ill-fated marriage and subsequent death. She appreciated his understanding and his ability to share her feelings.

"I thought I was doing what was best for Josie, I was not just being ambitious for her; Julian Darcy loved her, and he was a fine young man as well as the heir to Pemberley. It never was my intention to push Josie into marrying him because of his heritage, and I did not. I did advise her, and she made her decision; yet when it all went so wrong and they were clearly miserable, I could not help feeling guilty. It was as if I had persuaded my own daughter into making an unsuitable marriage that finally destroyed her life. What was worse, everyone else seemed to blame me too."

Aldo Contini had said he had known of her loss but not the detail of the circumstances. He had begged her not to speak of it if it hurt her to do so, but when she had wept and told him some more, he had simply gathered her into his arms and held her, letting her weep until she had no more tears to shed. Thereafter, he had told her of his own loss—a young sister, Rosetta, taken by a dreaded disease at fourteen—his mother's last and most beloved child.

"So you see, Becky, I share your feelings because I too know what it is to lose someone much loved, someone young and beautiful. Nothing can compare with the sorrow of such a loss. For many years my mother could not look upon another little girl without weeping for Rosetta. She was jealous of every other mother she met who had a daughter, because she had lost hers. Which is why I understand exactly how you feel," he said.

That day, a special bond had been wrought between them, and Becky had known that, even if she never saw him again, she would not forget the kindness of Aldo Contini.

Thereafter, unhindered by family scrutiny, they had spent many delightful days together in an increasingly intimate mood, which had made it seem quite natural that they would fall in love. When it happened, nothing Becky had known before had prepared her for the emotions aroused by the discovery that, for the first time in her life, she was loved and desired by a man for whom her own feelings were as deeply and passionately engaged.

Like Summer sunshine, it had poured new warmth and energy into her cold life and illuminated every dreary corner of her existence. It had filled her days with such delight as she had never believed possible. If this was love, Becky had decided, she had never loved any man before.

But, at the moment of discovery, when after pretending to be just good friends, they had finally admitted their love to one another, the realisation of the impossibility of their situation had startled her as much as had the passion they felt for one another.

Despite her deepest feelings, despite longing for its continuance, she had pulled back from the relationship. Afraid of scandalising her family and friends, Becky had ended the association and retreated to her house in Derbyshire, while Mr Contini, bereft and despairing, unable to understand her flight, had returned to Italy.

Neither had denied their love, and both had taken with them exquisite memories of a time that had brought them great happiness but had ended in tears. Both had endured great anguish—Jonathan Bingley had vouched for his friend's distress—but Becky's had been the greater, for she had no close confidante to talk to, no sympathetic shoulder to cry on, indeed no one but Nelly, her loyal maid, who knew the truth but could offer little more than simple compassion.

For many months thereafter, Becky had agonised over her decision, and while there were days and nights when she had regretted having made it, never had she contemplated the possibility that there may come a day when life would present her with another chance to revive the relationship that had promised such felicity.

Now that such an opportunity was at hand, Becky knew she had to discover if that promise was as real today as it had been before. Only then would she know if she could marry Mr Contini. For his sake as much as for hers, Becky was determined to make the right decision.

Chapter Twenty-Two

T HE WEEK FOLLOWING THE dinner party provided few distractions for Becky Tate from her concentration upon the dilemma she faced. With the weather consistently bad, she could neither walk nor drive out anywhere during the day, nor could she sleep well at night, as the sounds of wind and incessant rain kept her awake.

To make matters worse, there had been not a word from either Mr Contini or Jonathan Bingley. She had no means of knowing even if he had received her letter, except she was certain that Jonathan was unlikely to have delayed the delivery of a message he knew his friend awaited with some impatience.

Occasionally, without any logical reason for doing so, she would take out her copy of the letter and brood over the words she had written, concerned that they may have sounded too distant and given him no encouragement to come to her; then at other times, she would torment herself with worrying that she might have seemed too eager to see him and so compromised herself.

After a week of miserable weather, on the Sunday following, Becky awoke to a morning miraculously transformed, as the sun shone out of a sky that had cleared to an almost cloudless blue. It was warmer too, quite unlike the depressing chill of the past week.

Becky decided she would go to church and had Nelly prepare her clothes.

Feeling the need for some fresh air, she walked to church, taking the route across the grounds and along the lane that lay between Edgewater and the church at Hunsford.

The service was dull, including a tedious sermon on the value of good neighbourliness, and Mr Jamison's eagerness to greet and chat with his parishioners afterwards delayed her departure, further adding to her vexation. As she made her way out of the church, she saw, to her surprise, Nelly standing outside the gate, clearly waiting for her mistress. The girl looked anxious enough to cause Becky to worry, and when she reached the gate, she asked, "Nelly, what is it? Why are you here? What has happened? Has there been bad news at the house?"

Nelly behaved oddly, as though she had been struck dumb, and stammered, "Yes, ma'am, I mean, no, ma'am... it's not bad news, but yes, something has happened."

Becky, her anxiety rising by the minute, was so exasperated, she seized her arm.

"Nelly, tell me at once, has there been an accident? Is anyone injured?" she demanded.

Nelly's voice was deliberately low, conscious of the departing congregation around them.

"No, ma'am, it's not an accident."

"Then what is it?" asked Becky, even more confused.

"He's here, ma'am; he has come," said Nelly softly.

"Who has come?"

"The gentleman from Italy, ma'am, Mr Contini. He has arrived; he is waiting for you. I told him you were gone to church, and he said he would wait."

Becky almost reeled back in surprise. This she had not expected. "When did he arrive?"

"About half an hour ago, ma'am, in a hired vehicle; I thought I should come and tell you, so you would be prepared, ma'am..."

By this time Becky was walking rather briskly, and Nelly was trotting fast to keep up with her.

"You did right to come, Nelly, thank you," said Becky, and as they approached the gates of Edgewater, she stopped and asked, "Nelly, is my gown all right and my hat? How do I look?"

Nelly looked at her mistress; her face was slightly flushed with the exertion of a brisk walk and the cold air, but her eyes were bright, her skin glowed, and her blue silk gown had been Nelly's choice that morning.

"You look lovely, ma'am; that blue gown really suits you, and the hat is very pretty," she replied and was rewarded with a special smile.

"Thank you, Nelly," she said, and they resumed walking.

Once within the gates of Edgewater, Becky asked, "And did you order some tea for Mr Contini? He must have been in need of refreshment after his long journey."

Nelly's reply was a further surprise.

"No, ma'am, he did not wish to come into the house; he said he would like to walk about the grounds while he waited for you to return."

Becky shook her head. She could not understand why he would wish to walk about the grounds. Admittedly, it was a fine day, but it seemed an odd thing to do, she thought.

As they approached the house, she looked around the front lawn but could not see him.

"Which way did he go, Nelly?" she asked, and Nelly, looking past her mistress, caught sight of a tall figure walking at some distance from them through the grove of trees on the far side of the lake. She pointed in the direction of the spinney; the poplars were bare, and one could see through them into the woods beyond. He had his back to them and could not have seen them as they came up the drive.

"Shall I go and tell him you are here, ma'am?" Nelly offered.

"No, Nelly, I will go to him, but do go in and ask Cook to have tea and refreshments made ready. You can bring them into the parlour later."

"Yes, ma'am," said Nelly, and as Becky turned to go, she added softly, "Please, ma'am, begging your pardon for saying this, but he's such a lovely gentleman; don't send him away again."

Leaving her mistress speechless, she rushed indoors as Becky walked around the lake and towards the figure, now moving even farther into the woods.

She hurried forward, and as she approached, hearing her footsteps, he turned and, seeing her, quickened his steps as he came towards her.

They met within a grove of elms whose leafless branches let the Winter sun through. He held out his hand to her, and she took it, letting him draw her into his arms. Neither said a word for several minutes as he held her very close. As they stood together, Becky felt the rising excitement of her own heart and knew he must surely feel it, too.

When he spoke, it was to say, "My dearest Becky, I love you so much, will you marry me, please?" and when she replied, "Yes, yes, I will, and I love you too, very dearly," his joy was so profound, impossible to contain, he held her in his arms and kissed her, quite oblivious of the curious glances of two young farmhands who had appeared behind them, making their way through the woods to the village, with a barrow-load of kindling.

Becky saw them as they passed and said softly, "There, now it will be all over the village that I have been seen kissing a stranger in the woods."

He threw back his head, and his laughter filled the air as he said, "Ah, that is very good; then they will all know that I love you, and when we tell them that we are to be married soon, they will be very happy for us."

Becky laughed too, and for the first time in weeks, her heart was filled with the same joy she had known two years ago, but with none of the guilt.

"Are we to be married soon?" she asked, a teasing note in her voice.

"As soon as you wish, my dearest; I feel as if I have waited for you for years. It has been too long."

Though she did not say it then, Becky's feelings were no different.

It was as though she had waited for him all her life.

As they returned to the house, her arm through his, Nelly came to the door, and seeing them thus, she smiled and ran back in again, confident that this time her mistress would not be sending Mr Contini away.

The rest of the day was spent in the sort of conversation that occupies most lovers who, having become engaged, find themselves released from the restraints previously placed upon them by demands of decorum.

Seated together on the sofa in the parlour, they found there were many questions to be asked and answers to be given. Some were lighthearted, others more serious.

Becky wanted to know why he had not written before leaving England for Italy. "I was very surprised and a little hurt; I had soon convinced myself that you had returned to Italy without a word to me, because you had decided our friendship was no longer worth pursuing," she said, and he was most apologetic, explaining his reasons.

He insisted she was mistaken.

"Not so, my love; in fact, I was recalled very suddenly because my mother, who is very old, had become ill and was asking for me," he said, adding with a distinct twinkle in his eye, "Of course, it was not serious; each time she becomes ill, they call the priest first and then send for me. Most often, neither of us is required to do more than hold her hand and recite a prayer, but I had not the time to call on you as I had hoped. I am sorry if I caused you pain, but I did leave a letter with my friend Mr Bingley, who gave me his word that he would deliver it on the earliest possible occasion."

Becky was reassured. "Which he did very well, and despite his protestations to the contrary, Jonathan was a most eloquent advocate for you. He began by insisting that he was a disinterested intermediary, merely conveying your message, but before long, he left me in no doubt of the value he placed upon your character and the sincerity of your feelings for me," she said.

"Dear Jonathan, he is a good friend; I have many reasons to be grateful to him," he said. "He persuaded me to write. I was very afraid you would consider it impertinent of me, presumptuous even. After all, you had given me no indication that you had any particular feelings for me when we were in London, and besides, I am not a very clever letter writer, especially in a foreign language. My English friends are amused by what they consider my 'bookish' style. You, Becky, are a real writer—I was afraid you would laugh at me, too."

Becky was determined to make it plain that she did not share the opinion of his friends.

"Laugh at you? You need not have feared any such thing. Your friends may laugh, but I certainly did not. I may not have said this before, but now we are decided upon our future, I can assure you it was one of the most charming letters I have ever received. It was certainly not impertinent or presumptuous— indeed it was so well argued, so pleasing without being at all excessive, I think I shall preserve it forever."

He looked delighted.

"Forever? That is a very long time. I am flattered and relieved to hear you say so. I wished very much to see you and tell you how deeply I felt. It would have been easier than writing but, as I explained…"

She interrupted him with another question, "May I ask why, when we were in London, you did not give me any sign that you cared for me? You could have let me see that there were deeper feelings involved, could you not?" she asked, adding, "It would have spared me much heartache, when I thought you would not come."

He was immediately contrite.

"My dearest love, I am sorry to have hurt you; it was not my intention to do so, but I was reluctant to intrude upon you without knowing how you were likely to respond. Perhaps I was being too cautious. Forgive me, but you had lost your husband not very long ago, and in Italy, a widow and her family would be outraged if a man attempts too soon to woo her. I did not know if you would consider an approach by me indelicate. I decided to ask my friend Mr Bingley's advice on the matter before approaching you."

"Indeed? And what was his advice?" asked Becky, curious to know what guidance Jonathan may have given him.

Mr Contini smiled, "He assured me that widows in England, unless they were the Queen, did not generally go into deep mourning for many years and that in any event, Mr Tate and you had lived apart by mutual consent for some time before his death. It was something I was unaware of. He told me you were unlikely to be offended and wished me success."

Becky looked quite solemn, and he asked, "Forgive me, am I causing you more pain by speaking of this?"

"No, no indeed, you have answered my question exactly; I was puzzled that you had not spoken earlier, when we were so happy together in London, but now I do understand. And you are not to apologise, because there is nothing to apologise for and nothing to forgive," she said, realizing as she spoke that she too owed Jonathan Bingley a debt of gratitude.

Becky was very much moved by what she saw as his genuine modesty.

There were few men in her circle of acquaintants, whom she could credit with similar sensibility and integrity of character.

Her serious expression troubled him a little, and fearing he had reawakened painful memories, he sought to change the subject and, adopting a lighter tone, asked, "And the keepsake I sent you, you liked it a little, yes?"

"Oh yes, I did," she said, smiling. "More than a little; it was a delightful surprise. I must ask you now, was it all done from memory? I cannot recall a time when you could have caught me in that mood for long enough to make a sketch."

He looked somewhat abashed as he admitted that he had covertly made a little pencil sketch of her as she had sat with Anna Bingley in the sitting room on the afternoon before her return to Kent.

"You seemed deep in contemplation, listening, as Mrs Bingley read from a book of poems. It made such a perfect picture, I had to make a quick sketch. Later, I worked on it from memory, and I was not sure I had caught your expression, but I am glad you like it," he explained, clearly keen to have her approval.

"I like it very well; it has pride of place on my dressing table. Nelly thinks it is an excellent likeness, and so does Jonathan. Would you like to know what I was thinking on that afternoon?"

He was eager to know, and she told him, this time without any reservation, that she had been contemplating the possibility that perhaps he would give her some hint of his feelings, before she left London for Kent.

"By then I had begun to realise that my own feelings were much deeper than I had believed them to be, but I was afraid to acknowledge them even to myself, lest yours were not similarly engaged; I was afraid of being hurt," she said.

This admission brought such expressions of contrition and warm affection that Becky could no longer have any doubt at all of being deeply loved. Both acknowledged that they owed much to the generosity and wise counsel of Jonathan Bingley.

"He is an exceptional man, Becky; I have known him since our schooldays, and I can say quite truthfully that I do not know a better man."

Becky had to agree, aware once again of the ironic circumstances by which the man she had once loved and lost to her younger sister Amelia-Jane had been instrumental in bringing them together.

Mr Contini was keen to talk about their plans for the future, but Becky had a few more questions for him, and like most lovers, he was at that stage of their relationship when he was happy to indulge her.

"Will you tell me something about our visit to the house of Mr Adrian Hart?" she asked.

"Of course, what is it you wish to know?"

"Was it prearranged with Mr Hart that he would not be present, perhaps to let us have the place to ourselves that afternoon? Did you know before we reached the house that he would not be there?"

His countenance betrayed his surprise at her question.

"Becky, there are two matters in your question. Let me answer them thus— first, no, it was not prearranged that Adrian Hart should not be there, not by me at any rate. I was very surprised. But, second, I did learn later from Jonathan Bingley that he had suggested to Mr Hart that they meet for lunch at Whitehall on that very day to discuss urgent political matters."

"And he did not warn you?" she asked.

"He did not; indeed he confessed to me only after I expressed some concern that you may have been embarrassed by the absence of our host. Doubtless, Jonathan decided to let us have the afternoon together and arranged it, but I was afraid you might have suspected me of conniving at it, which I see now you did. Did you not?" he asked, challenging her playfully, and Becky smiled.

"The thought did cross my mind, but I am happy to believe you were quite innocent. I asked not because I was annoyed or embarrassed but only out of curiosity; I had never thought of Jonathan Bingley as a matchmaker!"

He laughed again and she remembered how she had enjoyed his big, unin- hibited laugh when they had first met in Italy many years ago. It had filled the room like music, as it did now, and she loved hearing it again.

"Have you any more questions for me?" he asked patiently, and she, thinking to tease him a little, replied, "Not now, but there may be others later; will you answer them as willingly?"

"But of course, my love, it will be my pleasure. You must feel free to ask me anything you wish. It will mean that we are both open and trusting with each other," he said and, wishing to reassure her, continued earnestly. "My dear Becky, there is nothing in my life I wish to conceal from you."

There was no doubting his sincerity, and almost in spite of herself, she said, aware even as she spoke that it was not the whole truth, "Nor I from you," which led to an exchange of loving reassurances between them that brought an end to questions and answers for some considerable time as they reaffirmed their love.

It was late, and Mr Contini had to return to the village, where he had taken a room at the local inn, which, he assured her, was clean and comfortable, if not particularly luxurious. There being no other means of transport available, Becky asked for her modest carriage to be brought round, to convey him thither. They parted reluctantly; he would return on the morrow, when she would take him to meet her sister and brother-in-law.

After he had left, Becky retired to her study to write a note to Catherine, which she despatched almost immediately, asking if she may bring a visitor to tea at the Dower House around mid-morning of the following day.

When the servant returned with the reply, it was clear Catherine had guessed who the favoured visitor might be.

She wrote:

> Dearest Becky,
>
> Of course you may bring your visitor to tea. If it is who I think it is, you are both very welcome to stay to dinner, unless you prefer to dine alone together at Edgewater. I shall tell Frank and warn him whom to expect—I hope you will not mind. Becky dear, I do hope this means good news; I look forward to seeing you both and meeting your Mr Contini. Afterwards, you must tell me everything.

That night, when Nelly came to assist her mistress in preparing for bed, she found her seated at her dressing table, solemnly regarding her face in the mirror.

Having laid out her nightclothes and warmed the bed, Nelly stood behind her, ready to take down her hair as she always did. Becky favoured a somewhat old-fashioned style and had resisted her maid's attempts to change it.

She caught Nelly's eye in the mirror and said, "What do you think, Nelly? It's not such a bad face, is it?"

Taken aback by the question, Nelly said, "No, ma'am; I mean, it's a very handsome face, ma'am. I do believe if you would let me do your hair a little differently, like Mrs Bingley's perhaps, it would look even nicer, ma'am."

Anna Bingley was not just beautiful, she was always tastefully dressed and coiffured. Her hair was always elegantly styled.

Becky smiled. "Do you really think so?"

"Yes, ma'am," Nelly replied and, for good measure, revealed that when they had been in London with the Bingleys, she had learnt exactly how Mrs

Bingley's maid dressed her mistress's hair and, having practised on the parlour maid, was quite ready to try it out on Becky.

"I think it will suit very well, ma'am," she said, persuasively.

Becky nodded and, having looked critically at her hair in the mirror, said, "Very well then, perhaps I shall let you try it out before the wedding."

Nelly, her eyes wide, bit her lip to keep from exclaiming too loudly. Eyes glistening, she clasped her hands in front of her and asked, "Oh ma'am, is there to be a wedding then?"

"Yes, Nelly, I think there is," Becky replied softly.

The girl held her mistress's hands and wept. "I knew it, ma'am; I told you he was a lovely gentleman, and I think he loves you very much. Oh ma'am, I am so happy."

Nelly knew more than anyone else what Becky's life had been, having shared her home and much of her life for many years. She had seen both the success and the sorrow, the disillusion and hurt, and had longed to see her mistress happy again.

Becky patted her hands. "There now, see what you have done! You've made me break my promise to my dear sister! I gave her my word that she would be the first to know, and now I have told you. Never mind, Nelly my dear, don't you fret; I do believe you've been through so much with me, you deserve to know, but you must not speak of it to anyone else yet, and remember, Mrs Burnett must never learn of this conversation," she cautioned.

Nelly nodded, thrilled to have the responsibility of keeping such a secret; she smiled like the sun breaking through a cloud and declared, "Oh yes, ma'am, certainly not, ma'am, my lips are sealed."

When the sisters met the following day, their meeting turned out exactly as Becky had hoped it would. She had had some misgivings, wondering how Catherine and her husband would respond to Mr Contini, but she need not have worried.

With Frank Burnett's extensive knowledge of Europe, his travels and studies in France and Italy, the two men had plenty to talk about and there was never an awkward moment between them.

The dinner proved to be so delectable and the company so convivial that they hardly noticed the passage of time. Indeed, afterwards, when Mr Burnett discovered that their guest was staying at the local inn, he applied immediately to his wife to ask if they might not accommodate him under their own roof more agreeably.

Catherine agreed they could.

"There are two empty rooms, and you are very welcome to stay. It will not be luxurious, but I am sure it will be more comfortable and convenient than the inn," she said, and Mr Contini, after a little hesitation, for he was reluctant to impose upon them, was happy to be persuaded.

They arranged to send a servant for his things and had a room prepared for him, for which favour he was most grateful, recalling the rather cold accommodation at the inn.

Becky, seeing the generosity and warmth with which her sister and brother-in-law had accepted Mr Contini, was close to tears. Their hospitality and general friendliness towards him had exceeded all her expectations and convinced her that she had indeed made the right decision.

Later, as the gentlemen, both of whom had an abiding interest in Italian politics, settled down to drink port and talk of the Risorgimento and Mr Garibaldi's heroic struggle to unite Italy, the two sisters slipped away to Catherine's room to enjoy their own share of the happiness that Becky had finally found. Cognisant of the doubts that Becky had previously suffered, Catherine was determined to assure her sister of her pleasure at seeing her so happy, for it had become very clear to her that afternoon that the presence of Mr Contini had transformed Becky's life.

Becky had no reserve from her sister, knowing well that Catherine would set her happiness above any other consideration; she told her of the manner in which they had met again in London and of the part she suspected Jonathan Bingley had played in bringing them together.

Catherine was incredulous.

"Jonathan did that? Becky, I cannot believe it, he is such a proper gentleman, I cannot see him becoming involved in such a stratagem!"

"Well, neither could I," said Becky, "and while I did have my suspicions about his prior knowledge of the arrangement, I could not be certain until yesterday, when Mr Contini informed me himself. It seems Jonathan kept him in the dark as well! I was as surprised as you are."

Having heard all of the story, Catherine offered another view.

"It is possible of course, to see his actions in another light—not frivolous matchmaking at all, but as something done with the best of intentions—to help a friend, whom he knew to be in love with you, and give him the best opportunity to approach you," she argued.

"It might also be that Jonathan, aware of Mr Tate's conduct towards you, may have seen this as another chance for happiness for you too. Do you not think so, Becky?" she asked.

Becky laughed merrily.

"Indeed, Cathy, I am perfectly willing now, in my present state of felicity, to believe the very best of Jonathan Bingley and anyone else you care to name. Of course he wished to help his friend, who had confided in him and asked for his advice. Perhaps you are right that he also thought I deserved another chance at happiness. Whichever it was, and I am sure either or both were motivated only by the goodness of his heart, I have forgiven him completely for the tiny deception he practised, now that Mr Contini and I are so happily agreed upon our future."

She smiled and then was solemn again, as she took her sister's hand.

"Cathy, I can scarcely believe it. Can it really be that I am at last to be truly happy?"

Catherine was quick to respond.

"Of course it is, why must you be so dubious, so lacking in confidence, Becky? This is not like you at all; of all of us, you were the one with the most assurance, you were determined and bold."

"I was, and yet that self-assurance has deserted me often in the last few years," Becky admitted.

"Why, Becky? I know things have been difficult for you recently, but you have had courage and influence and have achieved so much in public life."

Catherine could not comprehend her sister's attitude, which seemed almost to suggest that she was undeserving of the happiness she was now offered. Determined to be direct, she asked, "Becky, you do love him? You are sure of that?"

Becky spoke candidly, with a degree of openness she could use with her sister, without the fear of being misconstrued.

"Yes, Cathy, I love him dearly and I want very much to marry him, but I am afraid. I know it must sound strange, but I cannot help being uneasy; you see, each time I took a chance or grasped some opportunity that life offered, hoping it would bring success or happiness for me or my family, it has turned to dust."

She was looking down at her hands; her voice was low, and Cathy strained to hear her.

"With Mr Tate, we had much in common; I had hoped we could help one another. I wanted to write, he sought success in business and politics, and I thought if I worked hard at promoting all his favourite causes, we would be successful and happy together. But, in the end, although I did work very hard for him, there was little happiness for either of us and even less love between us."

Catherine was in no doubt of her sister's anguish as she continued.

"Then there was Josie. I doted on her, Cathy, and so did her father; we would have given our lives for her. All I wanted was the best for her; yet, when things went awry and we lost her, my husband, like Mrs Darcy, blamed me and turned away from me altogether. At the time I most needed him, he left me to grieve alone."

Her voice broke and Catherine embraced her, comforting her. "Dearest Becky, please do not upset yourself all over again. I know how hard it has been, but it is going to be different now, you must believe that. Mr Contini loves you very much, I can see it. He wants to make you happy and you must let him."

Becky dabbed at her eyes.

"He does, but do I deserve it, Cathy?" she cried, and it took all of her sister's powers of persuasion to restore her spirits and convince her that her present chance of happiness was not undeserved.

Catherine was quite firm.

"Becky, I cannot understand how you, who have helped so many people over the years, why even so recently as last week, with the Rickmans for whom you have done so much, how can you believe that you alone do not deserve happiness? Do not judge your past actions too harshly, my dear; you were very young and had no one to counsel you. I know that you respected and liked Mr Tate; it was not as if you had married him for money or position. You cannot carry all the blame for what went wrong; others too were culpable, and though I have no wish to speak ill of your late husband, his conduct after Josie's death was selfish and reprehensible. I said so at the time to Mother and she agreed with me."

As Becky listened to her increasingly passionate words, Catherine went on,

"You have a future now, Becky, and the past is no longer important. If you and Mr Contini love one another, and it is clear to me that you do, then you both deserve the happiness it can bring you. There, that is all I am going to say on the matter.

"Now, promise me that you are going to let him make you as happy as I am with Frank, for that is the best I can wish for you."

Becky was deeply grateful for her sister's gentle kindness and sound common sense. She assured her she intended to enjoy the happiness that Mr Contini had brought into her life, because, as she explained, "I love him dearly, Cathy, and I have never known such joy as I feel when I am with him."

When the sisters went downstairs, the gentlemen were engrossed in a discussion of Frank Burnett's work at Rosings, and arrangements had been made to show Mr Contini around the Rosings Estate on the morrow.

He was particularly interested in some of the treasures that had been rescued from the fire, and Frank Burnett was eager to have his opinion of some of the fine old paintings that had been recently restored.

Becky's greatest satisfaction came from seeing the man she loved welcomed so readily into the circle of her sister's family. With her mother gone, there was only Catherine, and had she expressed some reservations about Mr Contini, it would have hurt Becky deeply. With the Tates, despite her mother-in-law's kindness, she had always felt an outsider, just as Josie had been at Pemberley. This time it was quite the opposite.

The week that Mr Contini had planned to spend in Kent was soon deemed to be far too short a time, and he required little persuasion to extend his stay by a further week, during which time, they made their plans and wrote many letters to friends and family. There was time, too, to explore and enjoy the depth of their love in an environment of quiet tranquility.

Over many hours spent together not only did they discover the many matters on which they were in complete agreement, but were able also to resolve without rancour other subjects on which they were not.

For Becky there were but a few simple questions, little niggling worries about which she quizzed him.

"Do you suppose your family in Italy will approve of me?" she asked, to be met with laughter.

"Approve of you? My love, they will adore you," he had declared with great conviction, and when she followed it with another tentative enquiry, "And will they not expect us to make our home in Italy?" he had looked serious and responded confidently, "Becky my love, I have lived most of my adult life in France and England, fleeing our political enemies; now I know this is where I am happiest and where I wish to live with you. My family will not expect me to do otherwise."

Content with his responses, Becky was then faced with a question from Mr Contini; one she had long dreaded even as she knew that one day, it would be asked and she would have to give him an answer.

It reached right back into the Summer of 1866, when after months of great anguish following Josie's death, Mr Tate announced without warning that he was leaving England to travel to America on business. Alone in London, Becky had found in Aldo Contini a friend and confidante, whose generosity and kindness had opened up for her a Summer of warm friendship, filled with happy companionship and many innocent pleasures. It had helped staunch her grieving and heal her wounds, and Becky, enjoying the delights it brought, had not recognized the peril they were in, until the day they had stumbled into an intensely passionate intimacy, during which they had both admitted to being in love. Becky had never known such a transforming moment before. Yet, soon afterwards, riven with guilt, she had ended the association and fled.

Ever since they had met again at the opera in London and at the Bingleys' house, she had wondered when he would broach the subject with her.

When he had not done so, she had been at first surprised, then puzzled, and finally relieved, hoping he had decided to put the episode out of his mind.

Which is why she was startled when, on a tranquil afternoon at Edgewater, as they sat together beside the lake, he threw a pebble into the water and asked quietly, directly, and with no preamble, "My love, I have not asked this before, and if you do not wish to answer, I will not ask again, but I wish very much to know why it was that at the very moment we knew how dearly we loved each other, how much we needed each other, you chose to abandon everything we had and run away from me without a word of explanation?"

He was holding her hand when he asked, and Becky was so discomposed, she almost withdrew it, but he held on to it and drew her towards him as if to reassure her that his question was not meant to wound.

Sensing her distress, he added quickly, "You need not answer, if it is too painful. Perhaps I should not have asked..."

But Becky, seeing the bewilderment in his eyes, said firmly, "No, you have every right to ask; you had been my friend and confidante all Summer, you had helped me bear what was an unbearable sorrow; of course, you are entitled to ask why I behaved as I did. And I will answer you honestly."

Stopping to let him kiss her gently, she continued, in a quiet steady voice. "I left London then, because I felt guilty, not because we loved each other—I felt no guilt at all on that score—but because I thought if I stayed and went on seeing you, as I longed to do, people would inevitably find out and gossip about us and blame me, and I was afraid my guilt would taint and destroy what was the most beautiful experience of my life. I was terrified that it would be exposed and talked of and ruined for us forever. Better, I thought, to hold on to the memory than allow that."

She looked at him and continued, "That was why I left London and you. I know it seemed cruel, and perhaps I should have tried to explain, but I did not have the courage to face you. I was afraid you would persuade me to stay. I have suffered much, thinking of what I did, and more recently, I have learnt from Jonathan how deeply I had hurt you, but please believe me, it was not because I did not care..." and as her tears fell, he took her in his arms and comforted her, promising that the question would never be asked again.

"I asked only because I wondered if you had doubted the sincerity of my feelings..." And on this she was quick to reassure him that she had never doubted his feelings, and her only motive had been to hold fast and protect the memory of their love.

There was, however, one more question she needed to ask.

"When you wrote and asked to meet me in London, what were your feelings? Were you not resentful or angry at me?"

He was adamant, "No, Becky, never angry—puzzled and sad perhaps, but Jonathan had explained that it was a hopeless situation; your husband was living in the United States, your family would not have welcomed my attentions—they may have used it to discredit you; it made a lot of grief for me, but I was not angry with you."

"Then you did not blame me?" she asked.

"Blame you? No, certainly not. I was confused until Jonathan helped me understand how impossible your situation was. He was determined to protect you and ensure that you should not be persecuted by gossip and further criticism by the Darcy family. I understood then, and all I wanted was to hear from your lips the reason why you had left me."

Becky was genuinely contrite.

"I am very sorry, if it had been at all possible I should have stayed—"

But this time, he interrupted her gently.

"I know that now, but let us not waste time on the past, my love; we are together, and there is so much happiness to look forward to."

With reassurances given and warmly received, restoring them to their previous state of mutual tenderness and trust, they had reached once more a complete convergence of their expectations of felicity.

So plain was this, that when they returned to the house, Nelly, who had been Becky's only confidante for many years and had seen her mistress suffer much anguish in the past, was content that her future happiness was assured.

By the time Mr Contini was ready to leave, they had also, in consultation with Catherine and Mr Jamison, reached general agreement on the arrangements for their wedding.

For Becky it was a period of exceptional pleasure, for while she had hoped, she had never quite believed that she would ever find the kind of love that they shared. Based as it was upon understanding, deep affection, and trust, their love was in her experience unique. Her tender feelings were engaged as never before, and she looked forward to their marriage with the deepest conviction of happiness.

Chapter Twenty-Three

ARRANGEMENTS FOR A QUIET family wedding sometime after Christmas, followed by travel to Italy in the New Year, proceeded apace, and Becky suggested to Catherine that she would teach Annabel Rickman to keep the books and assist at the school while she was away in Europe with Mr Contini.

"It will do her a great deal of good to work at something worthwhile; she is educated and intelligent and should do well," Becky had said, and Catherine, though a little surprised, was not averse to the plan. Always of a practical inclination, she could see its value both to the school and the girl.

Annabel, needless to say, was overjoyed. At long last she could see a way to improve her own situation and use those skills she had almost forgotten over the years of privation. Her gratitude and loyalty to Becky and her sister were incalculable.

Catherine had taken the opportunity provided by Mr Burnett's absence in town to visit her sister. They were in the middle of compiling a list of the possible wedding guests when Becky mentioned her intention to offer the Rickmans accommodation in a vacant cottage on her property.

"It has lain empty for almost a year and needs some repairs, but I am sure William will be able to get it ready for them to move into in the New Year," she said, and Catherine agreed that it would provide a convenient solution for the young couple.

"If Annabel is to work at the school and her husband continues at Rosings, it should suit them very well," she said and was about to continue when Nelly brought in the post.

There were several letters, and Becky was of a mind to set them aside for later, when one caught her eye.

"Oh look, this is from Jessica; no doubt she writes to thank me for the gift I sent her daughter on her christening," she said, opening it at once.

Of all Emily Courtney's children, Jessica was Becky's favourite, possibly because of her resemblance to her mother in both appearance and disposition, and though they did not correspond as often as Becky and Emily used to do, her letters, full of news and good humour, were always welcome.

However, as she began to read it, Becky was struck by the urgency of Jessica's tone and language. There was but a cursory mention of Becky's gift and little news of her daughter, which was puzzling indeed.

The second paragraph revealed the reason for this seemingly inexplicable omission. Jessica's mother, Emily, was ill and wished to see Becky urgently. Jessica, who seemed convinced of the seriousness of her mother's illness, was writing to ask if Becky could possibly travel to Derbyshire at once.

She wrote:

> We are all very anxious about my dear mama. Although she insists she is "perfectly well able to manage," my uncle Dr Gardiner does not agree. As you know, I have been at Pemberley since my little girl was born, chiefly because Mrs Darcy insists upon it.
>
> She believes it is more convenient and comfortable for the baby, and of course, it affords her easier access to her little granddaughter, whom she loves dearly. Nevertheless, Julian and I intend to move to Oakleigh if Mama's condition does not improve.
>
> Mama wishes most particularly to see you before Christmas, if that is at all possible. She has asked me to say that you are welcome to stay at Oakleigh.
>
> Mr Mancini's granddaughter Teresa comes in daily to help Mama and my brother Jude, who does most of the work around the farm; it will, therefore, be no inconvenience at all to have you stay with her, especially if your maid Nelly can help out, too.

If I may add my voice to hers, dear Becky, to persuade you, I shall have to say that Mama is far sicker than she will admit, and I beg you to come if you possibly can, if only because it will be a source of great comfort and encouragement to her.

I do know also that she is very attached to you and speaks often of the days when you lived at Matlock and she would see you two or three times a week, when together, you ran several of the charities in the area.

Sadly, Mama is now too weak to go out to do the work she loves and wishes very much that you were here to help her...

As she read the letter out loud, Becky could not restrain her tears.

Clearly, Jessica's appeal was couched in words that would touch her heart, and she must have had hopes that Becky would come, since she and Emily were both unaware of Becky's own plans. She had not, as yet, revealed her intended marriage to Mr Contini to any person outside of her immediate family. She had assumed that Mr Contini would acquaint his friend Jonathan Bingley with the news, and of *his* discretion she was equally certain. Jonathan would not reveal the information to anyone other than his wife.

Emily was a very dear friend, and Becky was eager to go to her, but with Christmas and her own wedding approaching and a cold Winter in prospect, she wondered how such a journey might be accomplished.

Her sister had some sage advice, recommending that Becky should travel by train rather than by road. "Frank assures me the trains are far safer in Winter than coaches on icy roads and they are faster," she explained, and Becky decided she would await the return of Mr Contini from London before responding to Jessica's letter. She would not have long to wait; he was due back on the morrow.

Catherine was curious to discover if Emily's elder children had visited their sick mother recently. "Does Jessica mention Elizabeth or William Courtney?" she asked.

Becky looked again at the letter and shook her head. "No, and I cannot pretend that I am surprised, Cathy; it is not something I would ever say to Emily—she does so dote upon her children—but it is a sad fact that both Elizabeth and William have shown little concern for their parents' welfare. Not when their father was alive, nor when they attended his funeral did they seem at all perturbed by the prospect of their mother being left to manage on her own with only young Jude and the servants for company," she replied.

Catherine was shocked. "I do recall you saying that both of them seemed in a great hurry to leave Oakleigh after the funeral and get back to their busy lives," she said. "It seems hard to believe, when Emily has devoted so much of her life to her family."

"And spent every spare penny of the money her father Mr Gardiner left her on William and Elizabeth, when they needed her help," said Becky. "It is not generally known, but she used most of her savings setting William up when he went to live in Oxford with the Grantleys in order to study music seriously. Mr Darcy paid for his education, it is true, and the Grantleys invited him to stay, but all his sundry expenses came out of Emily's inheritance. She wished to ensure that he would want for nothing when he decided to pursue a musical career. Cathy, I believe I must be the only person who knew. Emily certainly did not reveal any of this to Mrs Darcy or Caroline, nor did she trouble Reverend Courtney with it. He was often too engrossed in his parish work to ask.

"Yet, there appears to be little gratitude from them, and were it not for Jude, she would be entirely alone at Oakleigh. I do wish I could go to her, Cathy—Jessica is unlikely to have written in such urgent terms if Emily were not seriously ill."

Catherine understood her sister's feelings but felt the need to ask a practical question, "If you do go now, what about arrangements for the wedding?"

Becky shrugged her shoulders.

"I don't think I should be very happy making wedding plans while Emily was lying sick, possibly dying in Derbyshire," she said, and Catherine was truly shaken.

"Come now, my dear, you cannot think that? It is not possible that we would not have heard from Lizzie if things were so bad. She and Mr Darcy take a very special interest in Emily's situation. Perhaps you should write to Jessica and say that you will come after the wedding…"

Even as she spoke, Catherine knew this would not satisfy Becky.

She could see her sister was both distressed and determined; on such matters as these, she would not change her mind.

Catherine moved to look out of the window. The leaden sky gave her no comfort at all, merely mirroring their disconsolate mood.

Meanwhile Becky, picking up another letter, said in a rather strained voice, "I wonder what *he* wants."

Catherine swung round and saw her sister ripping open a sealed letter.

"It's Walter," said Becky. "He never writes unless he wants something. I cannot think what has provoked him to put pen to paper. Perhaps he too has heard of Emily's illness and is writing to inform me…" she mused.

But, when she had it open, her surprise was far greater and the news it brought much more disconcerting than Jessica's had been.

Becky's son Walter was writing, he said, to acquaint his mother with the fact that he and his wife, Pauline, viewed with some alarm a recent report that had reached them, concerning herself.

Astonished, Becky read on, while Catherine looked over her sister's shoulder. Walter Tate's letter continued:

My dear wife, Pauline, has recently received from a friend in London a letter containing a somewhat disturbing piece of information relating to you, which naturally, she has communicated to me.

Of course, I need not say that I do not believe a word of it and have told her so.

But Pauline did insist that I should write to you at once, to alert you to this clearly mischievous rumour, so you may be given an opportunity to deny it.

I have agreed with her that this is a sensible and fair course of action, hence this letter, which I trust you will receive in the same spirit.

Clearly, Walter was very agitated about something, but as he had not as yet indicated *what* specific piece of news his wife had recently received, Becky was quite bewildered as to the reason for his agitation.

She was not kept in ignorance long. Turning over the page, she read on:

It is said, dear Mother, that you are about to marry again, scarcely a year after the death of my late father, and to a certain foreign gentleman, who lives in London and travels regularly between England and his native Italy. We hear that his family did champion the cause of Mr Garibaldi and are therefore now in his favour. Be that as it may, I cannot credit such an outrageous report as I have heard connecting you with this person and wish to deny it forthwith.

Doubtless it is a fabrication, which ought be promptly demolished, and I would be assisted greatly in this endeavour if you would write to confirm my belief that this story is wholly untrue or the result of a misunderstanding, perhaps?

Pauline suggests that you should place such a denial in writing, in order to give the lie to the rumours, which may originate from those who seek to impugn your reputation and damage my family's prospects as well.

By the time she had read both pages of the letter, Becky was no longer confused; rather, she was incensed, not at the rumours that Walter believed would impugn her character, but at the presumptuous nature of his letter and his demand that she deny the "rumour" forthwith.

"Cathy, can you believe this?" she cried, turning to her sister. "My son writes to demand that I deny in writing my intention to marry again because it will damage the prospects of his family if I do so. This is preposterous! What does he mean, it will damage his prospects?" she asked, handing over the offending document.

Catherine, who had been deeply shocked by her nephew's arrogant and insensitive letter to his mother, could scarcely speak. After a moment's hesitation, she said, "I am as dismayed as you are, Becky; I cannot imagine what possessed him to write such a letter. It is very strange indeed. Could it be that Walter fears that if you marry again, he will lose some part of the family inheritance he hopes for?"

Becky's indignation was almost explosive. "He cannot be serious! Walter inherited all of Mr Tate's business interests in England and Wales, including the Tates' house and estate in Matlock. As you know, Walter and Pauline objected most strenuously when I sold the house in London to buy this property, and subsequently, I set aside a certain sum of money from the proceeds of the sale to be held in trust for their children. What more does he want from me?" she demanded.

"No, Cathy, it is greed that makes them do it. It grieves me to say this of my son, but Walter has always been selfish, even as a little boy, and since his marriage to Pauline, who is not averse to some self-aggrandisement, he has become even more so. He is weak too and will do as she asks in these matters. But, I admit, I had not thought he could be as callous as this."

Catherine could see she was hurt, more than ever before. "Perhaps," she said, trying to assuage her pain, "perhaps it is just the shock of hearing from some stranger of your intention to marry. Should you not write to him, confirm the story, and explain your reasons? It may help him understand…"

Catherine was conciliatory, but Becky would have none of it. "I shall do no such thing. Why should I have to explain to my son and daughter-in-law, who have hitherto shown no interest in my happiness whatsoever, why I wish to marry Mr Contini? What reason must I give, except that I love him dearly and hope to be happy with him? Even if I were to ignore the rudeness of his reference to Mr Contini as 'a certain foreign gentleman,' by what right does he ask such a thing of me?"

Becky's words betrayed both her indignation and hurt. "No, Cathy, I shall not explain, but I will confirm that his wife's informant, whoever she might be, is right. I do indeed intend to marry again and expect him to be pleased for me, because I am going to be happy at last.

"As for his fears that my reputation or his prospects are in jeopardy as a consequence, I shall disabuse him by pointing out that not only has the late Mr Tate been dead above a year, he had lived apart from me in the United States, by his own choice, for almost a year before his death. Furthermore, I shall take pleasure in advising him that I have nothing now that he can expect to inherit, so he need have no fears on that score."

Catherine could understand her sister's outrage and did not try to restrain her anger, hoping that, when she had time to reflect, Becky would write a calmer response to Walter's insensitive letter.

While she had no doubt Walter Tate deserved all of the opprobrium Becky was about to heap upon him, Catherine's nature was such that she would at all times prefer to tread a more peaceable path than the one her sister appeared set upon. Apart from herself, Walter was her sister's only living relative, and it would be hard for her to be estranged from him, too.

Before leaving to return home, she did try to advise some degree of restraint.

"Do not let Walter's thoughtlessness goad you into bitterness, Becky dear; it is not worthwhile, especially when you are preparing for such a happy occasion. Why do you not speak to Mr Contini before you write?" she suggested.

Becky smiled; she knew her sister well and thought to humour her, saying, "Thank you, Cathy, I wish I had your sweetness of disposition, but Walter's gratuitous provocation has offended and grieved me, and I do not wish to draw Mr Contini into this matter. He is not responsible for any of it, and I will not have him insulted and distressed on my account. No, Cathy, you can trust me, I shall write to Walter and tell him what I think, but I promise not to be abusive or rude. You can count on it."

Shortly after her sister had left, still somewhat anxious about her intentions, Becky retired to her study and composed a letter to her son that, by its tone and language, could leave him in no doubt of her opinion of his conduct.

Scrupulous not to lay herself open to a charge of discourtesy, but equally careful to be entirely candid, she informed him that it was neither his right nor his duty to demand statements or explanations of her intention to marry again or not as she pleased. She wrote:

In view of the circumstances of the last years of my marriage to your father, I am unable to share your sense of shock that, as a widow, I should decide to marry again. Nor do I feel it should concern you that the person I choose to marry is a "foreign gentleman." Had I not received your letter when I did, I would have written to you in the course of this week to inform you of my plans; as it happens, you have made that unnecessary. I can now confirm that I do intend to marry Mr Contini, with whom I have been acquainted for several years, and hope that you will not find it too difficult to wish me happiness.

The letter was concluded appropriately, read over, sealed, and despatched to the post before she could change her mind.

That should have been an end of the matter, but it was not.

Walter's extraordinary letter continued to trouble Becky for many hours, and as she contemplated its possible consequences, the effect it had upon her spirits was one of serious discomposure. She could not avoid some unease as she wondered if Walter and his wife might not, by their interference, make mischief. The gossip and rumour they could generate about her and Mr Contini may well reach the ears of Mr and Mrs Darcy at Pemberley or Caroline, even Emily, she thought.

Because she had not informed them herself, she worried that it could set their minds against her and wished with all her heart that some means might be found to set it all to right. Yet how to achieve this was an insoluble conundrum.

For the next step in her plan she had to await the return of Mr Contini from London.

Aldo Contini returned to Kent, expecting to make arrangements to travel with his wife-to-be to visit his uncle and aunt at their villa in Richmond, where she was assured of a warm welcome. His host and hostess at the Dower House were not surprised, therefore, when, not long after he had arrived, he announced his intention to visit Edgewater.

There, he was surprised to find Becky in unusually low spirits.

Concerned, he asked for an explanation and was presented with Jessica's letter. Reading it through, he was at first puzzled that Mrs Courtney, who had four children, a sister, and two brothers, should find herself so bereft of help at a time in her life when she needed support. Raised in an Italian tradition, where family ties were paramount, no matter what disagreements existed between individual members, he was at a loss to understand her situation.

Becky had to explain. "I know it seems difficult to understand, my dear, but Emily has always resisted asking her children for help, and while her brother Dr Gardiner cares for her very well, he is also a busy medical practitioner, and she does not wish to trouble him too often. As for Robert, he might as well not be there at all—he is not a particularly useful or loving brother, caring mainly for himself and his self-indulgent wife."

"Mrs Courtney and you are close friends?" he asked.

"Indeed we are, and I owe a great deal to Emily, who alone among the members of the Pemberley family remained my friend through those dismal days after Josie's death."

"And of course you wish to go to her now, yes?"

Becky could not deny it; she wanted very much to go to Emily,

"Yes, I do, especially now, because she is gravely ill and has asked to see me," she replied. She could not believe her ears when he said, "Then you shall go, and I will take you there. When do you wish to leave?"

Becky looked at him, her eyes wide in astonishment.

"What do you mean?"

"Just what I said, my love, you must go and I shall not let you travel alone, not even with your maid, so I shall accompany you. I shall need perhaps a day to change my plans and send a message to my aunt and uncle; thereafter, we can leave as soon as you are ready."

Becky put her arms around him and hugged him to her warmly. "Thank you, my dearest, from the bottom of my heart, and God bless you," she said and did not even try to hide her tears.

She wrote to Jessica that night, advising her of their intention to travel, saying only that she would be accompanied by a friend and would be happy to stay at Oakleigh, if that was convenient.

Two days later, they left for London and thence by train for Derbyshire.

Nelly attended upon her mistress, and Sam, a trusted manservant from Edgewater, joined them, chiefly to assist with their luggage and ensure their safety and comfort on the journey north.

Although Becky had written to inform Jessica of the date of their arrival, aware of the difficulties the family faced at the time, she had not asked that they meet the train. Instead, they took a hired vehicle from the railway station to Oakleigh, arriving at the house in the middle of the afternoon.

It was clear they were expected, and to judge by the manner in which they were received, they were very welcome. Julian Darcy and Jessica appeared at the front door, without fuss or formality, to greet them and following introductions, Becky and Mr Contini were ushered into the sitting room.

The housekeeper, a kindly woman who had worked for the Gardiners at Oakleigh since Emily was a girl, assured Becky that rooms had been made ready for everyone, before taking Nelly and Sam into the kitchen for a cup of tea.

Entering the sitting room, Becky saw Emily sitting up on the couch by the large bay window, a warm rug over her knees and several cushions supporting her back. Never before had Becky seen her dear friend looking so frail. She went to her at once and knelt beside the couch.

Jessica sat on a footstool beside her mother, while Mr Contini and Julian stood to one side, beside the fire.

Emily's eyes brightened with pleasure as she smiled and took Becky's hand. "Becky my dear, I am so happy to see you. I did not know you were coming until Jessica told me this morning... I could scarcely believe it. It is very kind of you to make the journey at this time of year. Tell me, was it very uncomfortable? I have never made such a long journey by train."

Her voice was quiet but steady, and the hand holding Becky's was warm and firm. Becky took a little time to tell Emily some details of their journey, but then, looking into her friend's eyes, she said quietly, "Emily, there is someone I wish you to meet," and turning, she beckoned to Mr Contini to come forward.

As Jessica and Julian looked on, Becky said, "Emily, this is Mr Contini, who accompanied us on our journey from Kent. He has been a friend for many years. He is a close friend of Jonathan Bingley, and his family is known also to Mr and Mrs Darcy."

As Emily smiled and extended her hand to the visitor, Becky added, "Mr Contini and I are to be married soon after Christmas."

Mr Contini had taken Emily's hand and kissed it as Becky spoke, and to the astonishment of almost everyone in the room, Emily said, "Are you? Well then, let me be the first to wish you both every happiness and say how very welcome you are, Mr Contini. I am delighted to meet you."

The door opened to admit the maid with the tea tray, interrupting the flow of conversation and providing Jessica and Julian with an opportunity to catch breath after Becky's unexpected announcement. Having had no inkling of Mr Contini's status in the party, they had been amazed, not just by the revelation that he was to marry Becky Tate but even more by the calm manner in which Emily had received the news. They looked at one another, unable to comprehend how this had come about.

Tea was served and while Jessica busied herself dispensing cake and biscuits, Julian poured Mr Contini a glass of sherry.

Emily, her face now aglow with satisfaction, spoke softly to Becky. "Becky my dear, your Mr Contini is a fine-looking man—you must tell me all about him later. Is he the son of Mr Darcy's friends, the Continis?" she asked. Becky explained that he was their nephew, had been at school with Jonathan Bingley, and was intimately acquainted with the Grantleys, all of which seemed to please Emily very much.

Emily's delight at having her friend with her once more was plain to see, while Becky's pleasure was somewhat diluted by her sadness at seeing Emily so frail and unlike her usual self.

After tea, Jessica retired upstairs to attend to the demands of her baby daughter, while it was clear that Emily and Becky wanted to be alone to talk together, leaving Julian to entertain Mr Contini.

A somewhat reserved and shy young man at the best of times, Julian Darcy had struggled to make conversation with a complete stranger until Mr Contini himself came unexpectedly to his rescue.

"I understand, Mr Darcy, that the late Mr Gardiner had a unique collection of travel books and memorabilia in his library. I should very much like to see it, if I may."

Scarcely able to suppress a sigh of relief, Julian's face lit up with a new enthusiasm. "Yes indeed, Mr Contini, I should be most happy, come this way," he said and led the way to the library across the hall, where he left Mr Contini ensconced for the next hour, whilst he escaped upstairs to join his wife.

Meanwhile, Emily, not wishing in any way to pry, but eager to hear more of Becky's news, learnt of the circumstances in which she and Mr Contini had met and become engaged.

With her intimate knowledge of the distress and embarrassment Becky had endured when Mr Tate had abandoned her to move to the United States, Emily had always had far more sympathy and understanding for Becky than had many other members of the Pemberley clan. With their judgment distorted by the shock of Julian and Josie's shattered marriage and Josie's subsequent death, for which they had inexplicably blamed only Becky, none of them, save perhaps Cassandra, had understood Becky's grief. Emily alone had witnessed the pain she had suffered at the death of a beloved daughter in such dishonourable circumstances and had enfolded her with friendship and affection.

Consequently, she appreciated the particular partiality Becky had felt for Mr Contini, who by his warmth and sincerity had won first Becky's friendship and then her heart.

"He is, without exception, the kindest man I have ever met, Emily," Becky had said. "He loves me, and when I tell you that I feel fortunate and deeply happy at the prospect of being his wife, I know you will believe me."

Emily patted the hand that she held in hers.

"You do not have to convince me of that, my dear, I can recognise true affection when I see it, and I am in no doubt whatsoever that he loves you. If you love him just as well…"

"Oh I do," said Becky softly, "passionately."

"Well then, what more is there to say, except be happy together. You deserve some happiness, Becky, I know how long you have waited for it."

Becky knew this was no idle remark, for Emily in her youth had known deep love and happiness when she had married her brother's friend, Paul Antoine; happiness she had enjoyed but briefly. So sincere had been that love that not even the certainty of his early death had shaken her resolve.

Becky thanked her friend. "Thank you, Emily; I knew in my heart that you would understand and approve," she said, and the two friends embraced.

"You have no need of my approval, Becky; if you have made your choice because he is a good man and you love him, you *will* be happy. Nothing is more certain," said Emily.

Emily's maid entered the room; it was time to dress for dinner, and she had to assist her mistress to the room prepared for her downstairs.

Becky realised with a shock that Emily was too weak to walk up and down the stairs any longer, and as she went to her own room, she was filled with sadness for her friend. It was plain to her that Emily was very ill indeed.

Nelly, who had prepared Becky's bath and waited to assist her, revealed what she had learned from the servants.

"They are all very sad, ma'am; they love Mrs Courtney dearly, but they fear she is past saving. It seems she has been sick for a while, but as she nursed Mr Courtney, she hid her own illness from her family," she said.

"They say that one afternoon, Mr Mancini brought in some logs for the fire in the sitting room and found Mrs Courtney collapsed on the floor. It was he raised the alarm, called her maid, and carried Mrs Courtney to her room. Had he not found her, she may well have died, ma'am."

Nelly's eyes were wide and tearful as she told how young Jude Courtney had ridden hard to fetch Dr Gardiner, who had come at once to attend upon Emily, and when he had heard the tale, he had gone out to the farm to seek out Mr Mancini and thank him for saving his sister's life.

Becky was badly shaken. Mr Mancini was an Italian flower farmer who leased a part of the farm at Oakleigh; to think that Emily owed her life to his fortuitous intervention was truly appalling and indicated to Becky a serious dereliction of familial duty on the part of Emily's older children. Jude alone remained to care for his mother, with the help of a few loyal servants and Mr Mancini.

When they all met for dinner, which was a simple, wholesome meal, it was the company rather than the food that provided the greatest pleasure; it was clear to everyone that both Jessica and her mother were happier that night than they had been for many weeks. Becky's arrival and the delight it had brought Emily had lifted all their spirits.

Afterwards, Emily was tired and retired early to her room. The gentlemen continued with their discussions, assisted by the appearance of port and cheese, while Becky and Jessica repaired to the privacy of the sitting room upstairs.

They had a great deal to talk about. There was much Becky wanted to know, and Jessica had no desire to conceal anything from her mother's dearest friend. As they talked into the night, Becky learned much of what had gone before and could scarce believe what she heard. Emily, it seemed, had developed a form of tuberculosis, which had been slow to manifest itself but was no less deadly. No doctor could say for certain, but she had probably not many more months to live and needed constant care and medication, which clearly Jessica, in her present condition, nursing a new baby, was unable to provide.

"Julian and I wanted to move to Oakleigh, because it means that I can at least be aware of her condition and see she is cared for, but both Dr Gardiner and Mrs Darcy advise against it, and Julian is inclined to agree with them. They believe that my little daughter and I are at risk if we stay.

"I am very disappointed. The servants are devoted to her, but they are not able to give her the care she needs, and Mama will not move to Pemberley, as Mrs Darcy has suggested. She could be well looked after there, but Mama fears it will mean abandoning Oakleigh and the staff here. She will not do it."

As Becky shook her head sadly, Jessica added, "Mama is more concerned with the staff and what will happen to them once she is gone than with her own health."

"She has spoken of it to me, too. She is anxious that they should not be abandoned by the family," said Becky.

"Indeed, many of them have been here for most of her life, and she is determined that they will not be deserted. She has made Julian promise not to retrench any of them and has personally assured them of this," said Jessica.

"And what about your older brother and sister? Have you any expectation of assistance from them?" asked Becky.

Jessica looked down at her hands, clearly unwilling to blame her siblings, who, by all reports, had shown little inclination to help their parents.

"I have no knowledge of what they may have said to Mama, but I do know Mrs Darcy has spoken to William when he was here for Papa's funeral, and she was not satisfied with his response. Mama will not ask them for help, yet there is little enough money left to keep her in comfort. Julian has been very helpful, and my uncle Dr Gardiner is exceedingly generous with his time and money," she explained.

"But Elizabeth and William?"

"We have had no word from them since Papa's funeral," Jessica replied softly, "though I do know that William writes to Mama occasionally."

Becky was astounded; it was the future she was most concerned with, and even as she listened, her mind was working on a plan that might help her friend. That Emily had little money left and no prospect of increased income from the farm was her greatest concern, and having sworn Jessica to secrecy, she revealed her intention to use some of her own inheritance to alleviate the problem.

"I shall write to Jonathan Bingley tomorrow and propose that a fund be set up in Josie's memory, which may be used to help Emily and others like her who suffer from this dreadful affliction. To begin with, I want you to engage a good nurse with proper training, who will live at Oakleigh and look after your mama for as long as she needs her care. I shall pay her wages; I will give you a sum of money in advance and send you more later, but you must ask Cassy or Caroline to help you find the right person. She must be a kind and amiable woman as well as a good nurse."

Jessica, astonished at her generosity, was somewhat reluctant to accept without question everything Becky had offered.

She asked, "Are you quite certain, Becky? Mama may not wish me to take your money."

But Becky insisted. "My dear Jessica, your mama is the dearest friend I have. There is no need at all to be concerned about accepting this money. I am certainly not likely to go hungry without it," she said lightly and then proceeded to explain.

"My late husband, Mr Tate, left me the entire proceeds of his American business, held in trust and administered for me by Jonathan Bingley. I am permitted to use it for special purposes, if I am able to convince Mr Bingley of their value. I do not, even for a moment, anticipate any difficulty on that score. If helping to care for Emily is not a deserving cause, I do not know what is. So you must have no qualms about this at all. I shall write to Jonathan tomorrow and have it all arranged before we leave for Italy."

Jessica, somewhat reassured by this explanation, turned eagerly to the subject of Becky's wedding.

"Are you to be married in Italy?" she asked, expecting that Mr Contini would wish to be married in his native country.

"Oh no," Becky replied, "it is to be only a very simple ceremony—at the little church in Hunsford, which is my parish church. I had my big wedding many years ago, Jessica, when I married Mr Tate—there were hundreds of guests. I am sorry to disappoint you, my dear, but this will be a very different wedding."

Jessica smiled; she had learned from her mother, some years ago, of the circumstances of Becky's marriage to Mr Tate and her consequent life of considerable influence but little felicity.

"But it will be a happier marriage, I think?" she asked simply, and Becky put her arms around her. "My dear Jessica, that I can absolutely promise you. Now, I think I must get some sleep, and so must you. Julian will be worried that I am keeping you awake too long. Tomorrow, I shall want to meet your daughter. Your mama assures me she is very beautiful."

A few days later, when they were taking tea in the parlour, a message arrived from Mr and Mrs Darcy, inviting everyone at Oakleigh, and in particular Becky and Mr Contini, to a dinner party at Pemberley on the Saturday following. The invitation was accepted with pleasure.

Jessica, with Becky's permission, had informed Elizabeth of the engagement between Becky Tate and Mr Contini.

"Of course you may tell Mrs Darcy," Becky had said. "I was intending to write to her before the wedding, but the arrival of your letter, with news of your mama's illness, threw all my plans into disarray," and when Jessica had carried the news to Pemberley, it had been received with some surprise and a good deal of curiosity.

At first, Mr Darcy had said very little, except to remark that he remembered Mr Aldo Contini well.

"He was Jonathan's friend—a very handsome and accomplished young fellow as I recall. I understand he had to leave Italy in something of a hurry, because his family had supported Mr Garibaldi."

Jessica replied that Becky had said the Contini family were back in favour, now that Mr Garibaldi had won the day.

"Indeed," Mr Darcy had said, nodding sagely, "but I believe Aldo Contini prefers to reside in England."

Elizabeth was curious to know more; the Continis had been good friends of the Darcys and Grantleys for many years, but she had little knowledge of this particular member of the family and even less of his connection with the Tates.

"And how did Becky Tate meet Mr Contini? I was not aware she was intimate with the family, were you?" she asked. Her husband replied, "I confess I was not; but I understand Anthony Tate did some business in Italy some years ago, and they met in Florence and then again in London more recently. Jonathan Bingley knew that they were rather well acquainted, I think."

"Clearly, they must have made quite an impression upon one another at their previous meeting. Darcy, have you known about this romance and kept it from me?" asked his wife, feigning outrage at the extent of his knowledge and her own ignorance.

Her husband laughed and ignored the implication of her question.

"No, my dear, I have not. I will admit, however, that when we were in London, his aunt, Signora Contini, did ask rather a lot of questions about Mrs Tate; I thought she appeared unusually interested in her, and of course, I did see Aldo Contini with Becky at the opera and again at the Bingleys' dinner party; they did appear to be well acquainted, but I had no idea there was romance in the air."

"Jonathan must have known; did he not mention anything to you?" his wife persisted.

Mr Darcy shook his head, "He did not and I would not expect him to. Contini is an intimate friend of his; he may have confided in him, and Jonathan is unlikely to betray such a trust."

Elizabeth looked sceptical, but Jessica ventured to suggest that it was not entirely surprising that they should have become engaged, since the pair had been friends for some years now.

"Have they?" said Elizabeth. "Well, I suppose it is not an unsuitable match."

"No indeed," said Mr Darcy. "They are both persons of independent means and, I daresay, mature enough to know their own minds."

"Which is certainly more than could be said for Becky when she married Anthony Tate in such a precipitate fashion," Elizabeth remarked, recalling the day she had heard the news from her sister Jane.

"Why, Becky was scarcely seventeen. When Jane told me of their engagement, you could have knocked me down with a feather. It had all happened so suddenly, I was afraid it would end in tears, and it did. Tate was only interested in business and politics, and poor Becky, for all her hard work, was treated rather shabbily when he left everything to Walter and that dreadful wife of his. Everybody knows she is a grasping, unpleasant sort of person."

Mr Darcy then reminded his wife that Mr Tate had also left the entire proceeds of his American estate in trust for Becky's use and she did get the house in London. To which Elizabeth had to add that it was no more than she deserved, considering all the hard work Becky had done, lobbying for her husband's favourite causes and promoting his business ventures.

"It beggars belief that he could be so unfeeling as to leave their family home to Walter, suggesting that he reach some accommodation with his mother. It was a callous, heartless thing to do, and I am sure Becky was very hurt," she said.

Amidst all this discussion of marriage and money, Jessica felt compelled to offer the opinion that it had appeared to her and her mother that in Mr Contini, Becky had at last found someone who genuinely loved her.

"Mama is confident they will be happy together and what is even more hopeful for their future felicity, they seem like good friends, too," she said, to which her mother-in-law, feeling a little chastened, replied, "Now that is certainly an advantage, Jessica. No one could pretend that Anthony Tate had many friends; business partners and political allies, yes, but genuine friends were few and far between, I think. No, I am truly pleased that Becky is happy with her Mr Contini. I know Emily will be delighted for her; they were always particular friends."

Jessica was perplexed by Elizabeth's attitude to Becky Tate. She wished that Mrs Darcy, who had herself known the desolation of losing a much loved child, could feel more empathy for Becky. It had always puzzled her that Elizabeth, a woman of intelligence and strong feelings, had seemed incapable of sharing that particular emotion with Becky, as though she saw her loss of William as being different in depth and quality to the death of Becky's daughter Josie.

Jessica, whose heart was easily moved, found that difficult to reconcile with Elizabeth's kind and generous nature. Naturally, it was not a subject she could discuss with Julian; his anguish at the death of Josie had been plain to see. When she had asked her own mother, Emily had said lightly that it was Lizzie's "blind spot."

"Cousin Lizzie is loving and kind, but I am afraid it does seem she has no understanding of Becky's situation," Emily had said. "It has puzzled me, but I love them both dearly and do not have to choose between them."

❧

The Pemberley dinner party was a fortnight before Christmas. Becky and Mr Contini were to leave for Kent on the following day.

Becky dressed with care for the occasion, glad that Nelly had packed a new silk gown and fur-lined cape, in which she could grace the halls of Pemberley with confidence. As for Mr Contini, she noted that he looked his usual distinguished self; indeed, she thought, they made a rather handsome couple.

Sadly, Emily could not travel to Pemberley—she hardly left the house at all these days. Becky was loathe to leave her on their last evening, but Emily had insisted.

"You must go, Becky, I insist. I know how very important it is to you that you maintain your friendship with Lizzie. Besides, Pemberley dinner parties are always superb—I have been at many of them. You must go and enjoy yourselves. I think I need an early night; we shall talk after breakfast tomorrow, and you can tell me all about it."

The dinner party, as Emily had predicted, was a triumph; fine food and wine, excellent company, and music provided by a small chamber orchestra combined to produce a perfect evening.

The Darcys, excellent hosts as always, greeted Becky and Mr Contini and made them very welcome. They were joined by Mr Bingley and Jane, Elizabeth's daughter Cassandra and her husband Dr Richard Gardiner, Colonel Fitzwilliam and Caroline, all of whom congratulated Becky and Mr Contini and wished them every happiness.

Jane was particularly kind, seeking Becky out and expressing her good wishes in the sincerest way, assuring her that everything she had ever heard from her son Jonathan about Aldo Contini had been in his favour.

"I have told Lizzie that Mr Contini and Jonathan have been friends since they were at school together, and my son speaks so highly of Mr Contini, I am in no doubt he is an exceptionally fine man and you will both be very happy."

Becky blushed at this fulsome praise and thanked her; Jane had always had the capacity to see the very best in everyone she met, even if it meant turning a blind eye to some of their faults; with Mr Contini, however, Becky was happy to let her sing his praise, especially to Elizabeth.

She was even more gratified by the utmost courtesy and appreciation with which both she and Mr Contini had been received at Pemberley, as well as the interest evinced by Mr Darcy and the other gentlemen in Mr Contini's opinions on a range of subjects, from the success of Mr Garibaldi to the immense popularity of Italian opera in England.

As for her own relations with Mrs Darcy, about which Emily had expressed such concern, Becky could not fault Elizabeth's conduct on this occasion.

At dinner, she had placed Mr Contini between herself and Dr Gardiner, and Becky had noted that he appeared to carry on conversations with both of them with equal ease. Watching them from across the table, she had been pleased to see that Elizabeth listened attentively to her guest. Becky knew from observing her that Elizabeth was not just being a courteous hostess; her manner and engagement in the conversation suggested she was genuinely interested.

Later, when they were seated together after dinner, listening to the musicians, Becky had remarked upon the pleasure of being at Pemberley again, and once more, Elizabeth's response had surprised her.

"Well, Becky, I know you will forgive us if we do not travel to Kent for your wedding," she had said. "Neither Mr Darcy nor I do much travelling in Winter, but I hope that when you have returned from Italy, Mr Contini and you will return to Pemberley and spend some time with us, perhaps in the Spring? It is very pretty here in May, and it will be our great pleasure to welcome you back as husband and wife."

Delighted, Becky thanked her sincerely and said she was sure Mr Contini would like very much to return to Pemberley in the Spring.

"He has a great love of the English countryside, and Pemberley has within its boundaries and in its environs so much beautiful country, I know he will enjoy it very much. For my part, there is nothing I would like more. It is a most peaceful place. Mama always loved Pemberley and spoke often of the many happy days she had spent here with you."

Elizabeth, remembering her dear friend Charlotte, could not conceal her feelings, and impulsively, the two women embraced.

Elizabeth's voice was gentle as she said, "Life has not always been kind to either of us, Becky, though I count myself more fortunate, in that I still have my dear husband with me; but I do want you to know that I am glad you are happy now. Jessica has told me what you intend to do for Emily—I must thank you very much; it is very generous of you. Mr Darcy and I want to help her, yet she will not accept any more help from us. We have tried to persuade her to return to live at Pemberley, where we can look after her, but she has refused, insisting she must stay on at Oakleigh. Your plan will mean she can continue to live there comfortably, and I thank you for your kindness with all my heart."

Becky hardly knew what to say; she had not expected such praise from Elizabeth. Yet she was so touched, she had to fight back tears and was relieved when Jessica came to say it was time to leave. She was glad they had accepted the invitation to dinner. It had been the best possible end to what had been a bittersweet week.

Promising to write, she thanked Elizabeth and embraced her again, and when Mr Contini said farewell and kissed her hand, Mrs Darcy appeared to be particularly pleased.

"Becky seems to have made a sensible choice this time," Elizabeth said to her husband as they went upstairs, as the servants cleared away the debris of the dinner party. "Mr Contini seems a most acceptable person, and his affection for her is undeniable. Do you not think so, dearest?"

Mr Darcy did not even bother to suppress a smile. "Indeed, my dear, I noticed you were having what appeared to be a most lively and entertaining conversation at dinner. I was sorry to be too far away from you to eavesdrop on any of it."

"I assure you it was more than entertaining, much more," Elizabeth declared. "Mr Contini was regaling us—Richard and myself—with wonderful tales from the Italian campaigns of the Risorgimento. I had no idea Mr Garibaldi's followers had such fun."

"Hmm… between bouts of killing and being killed themselves, no doubt!" Darcy retorted and added, "Confess it, Lizzie, he is a charming fellow and you liked him very much, but, I agree with you absolutely, Becky does seem to have made a happy choice this time. From my limited knowledge of him, I believe Mr Contini is a man of integrity. Jonathan speaks very highly of him—they have been friends for years. He is amiable enough, and if, as you have found, he also has a sense of humour, he will suit her well. It is quite plain she seems happier already than she has been in a very long while."

Elizabeth agreed.

"Yes, I believe you are right, my dear, and anyone Jonathan calls a friend must be particularly acceptable," she conceded, and Mr Darcy had no wish to contradict her.

Before leaving Oakleigh on the following day, Becky told Emily of her conversation with Elizabeth.

Her satisfaction was clear. "Oh my dear Becky, I cannot tell you how happy that makes me. I never felt it was my place to lecture Lizzie or you about it, but I have been saddened by the coldness that existed between you. You have both shared so much of life's experience, it was such a waste that you could not talk to one another," she said with such obvious pleasure that Becky had to warn her not to be too optimistic.

"I do not know how far this feeling goes, but I am happy too, and I promise I shall try my very best to maintain good relations with Elizabeth. But, Emily, I owe all of it to your goodness and kindness of heart, and I shall not forget that, as long as I live."

Emily characteristically refused to accept the credit for the rapprochement between Elizabeth and Becky, which did not surprise Becky at all; what did continue to amaze her was her friend's uncomplaining acceptance of life's afflictions.

Emily had loved and lost twice over good, loving husbands, yet never had she been heard to bemoan her misfortune or curse her fate. Indeed, she would, at every opportunity, speak of the great happiness she had enjoyed in both her marriages and extol the wonderful qualities of the two men she had loved.

Becky could not help but wonder at her resilient spirit, having not loved as passionately at all, except for Josie, whom she had probably loved too well and indulged too often. With her untimely death, Becky had felt every happy person in the world was her enemy and her life had become tainted with bitterness, until Aldo Contini had shown her that it could be different.

When it was time to leave, Becky could not dispel her feelings of apprehension as they drove away from the house, leaving behind Emily, Jude, Jessica, and Julian. They appeared cheerful, smiling and promising to write, but Becky had felt a shiver pass through her body, and Mr Contini, sensing it, took her hands in his. They were cold and trembling, and he held them firmly, drawing the folds of her cape over them to keep them warm, calming her unspoken fear and grief.

Becky was grateful for his presence in her life; now, as she coped with her anxiety about Emily, and later, as she would have to face the vexation and woes that life would undoubtedly bring, she knew he would be there, loving her, understanding her fears, and making everything easier to bear.

Slowly, her hands stopped trembling as she felt his strength. Most of all she was deeply and happily aware of his warm, comforting love. Their wedding was a week away. Soon there would be time to speak of their deepest feelings; Becky had never felt more certain of anything in her life.

END OF PART FIVE

An Epilogue...

RETURNING TO EDGEWATER, with Christmas only days away, Becky was eager to tell Catherine of her conversations with Mrs Darcy. "I must confess to being somewhat surprised; I had not expected such a cordial welcome from Elizabeth," she said, but Catherine responded differently.

"Why, Becky, I do believe you are too sensitive about Lizzie's opinions; as I have said before, she is no longer upset with you. She has no reason to be, with Julian happily married again; even if Lizzie did harbour some kind of grievance about Josie, I do not believe she does so any longer. Besides, I am convinced that Mr Darcy would have counselled her against it, and Mama used to say, Lizzie always heeds his advice."

At this, Becky had to laugh.

"Cathy, I doubt that Elizabeth would agree with you on that last matter. She does pride herself upon her independence, you know. However, I am prepared to accept that she has at least ceased to blame me for everything that went wrong with Julian and Josie's marriage and genuinely wishes us to be reconciled."

"I have no doubt at all on that score," said Catherine and rang to ask for more tea.

The maid who answered brought in the mail, which was chiefly for Mr Burnett, with the exception of two letters, one of which was from Emma Wilson. Catherine opened it, not expecting to find within it any startling news.

The two women had carried on a casual correspondence for some years, and their letters had dealt mainly with family matters.

It was therefore with some surprise that she turned over the first page and read the reference to a Mr Danby, who had been brought before Emma's husband, Mr Justice Wilson, at the county assizes.

Emma recalled Becky's interest in the case of one William Rickman of Blessington and advised that Mr Danby and a co-conspirator had been charged with perjury, conspiracy, and several other offences in relation to a case of false witness.

She wrote:

I am sure Becky will be very pleased to hear of this.

Becky, who had been reclining on the sofa, her thoughts miles away, was wrenched back to reality when her sister cried out, "Oh well done! Look, Becky, Emma writes that a Mr Danby has been brought to court and charged. Is that not good news?"

Becky sat up, disbelieving. She reached for the letter, and as she read it, her elation knew no bounds.

"Oh Cathy, this is wonderful news!" she cried. "It means Mr Danby has been brought to justice at last and is likely to be punished for his crimes."

"I thought that would please you," said Catherine.

"It certainly does," Becky replied, "but it will also come as a relief to Annabel, who never believed that Danby would give up. She feared that his evil mind would conjure up some other means of persecution to wreak his revenge upon Rickman. She will be truly grateful for this news."

"Well, Emma will be pleased to know that her information has brought such universal joy—I shall tell her all about it when I next write," Catherine promised, and Becky could not resist some self-congratulation at the result.

"You may certainly convey my thanks and my feelings of utter satisfaction," she declared, adding that she could not wait to give Annabel the good news.

꩜

The journey to Derbyshire to visit Emily Courtney had taken almost ten days from Becky's wedding preparations, which, therefore, had been seriously set back. She now faced the fact that there was very little time left and, save for her family and a few close friends, no one had been invited. Having considered the matter overnight, she had reached a decision, which she put to Mr Contini the following day. It was a somewhat radical plan, and she was not entirely sure he would approve. He had arrived at Edgewater after breakfast, and they were seated in Becky's study, where her desk was littered with lists and notes that lay exactly as she had left them before departing so hurriedly for Derbyshire a fortnight ago.

Mr Contini had expected to receive a catalogue of tasks that had to be done and letters that must be written and despatched forthwith. To his amazement, his bride-to-be proposed no such thing.

Instead, Becky said simply, "Dearest, would you mind very much if we had just a simple ceremony at the church and a wedding breakfast for our families and closest friends, here at Edgewater? I very much doubt there will be time to prepare for anything grander."

So surprised was he by her suggestion, he took a minute or two to respond, during which time she, fearing he was disappointed, tried to explain. "I am sorry, I know I should have asked your opinion earlier; it is only that I have just realised we would need to spend a great deal of precious time in all these preparations, when what I really wish for is for us to spend as much time together as possible."

By the time she had completed her sentence, Mr Contini had understood that Becky was seriously suggesting something he had always wanted but had not dared to ask, believing all ladies wished for elaborate weddings.

It was certainly true in Italy, and he had not supposed it would be any different in England.

But now, in view of what she had said, so delighted was he, he could do no less than rise and take her in his arms.

"Becky my love, that is precisely what I would wish for us to do—a simple ceremony and a wedding breakfast just for the family would be perfect!" he said.

When she expressed her surprise, he went further, saying with a smile, "How very clever you are to have discovered exactly what my feelings were on this matter. I cannot imagine anything more congenial to my present mood, especially if you will let me suggest that we have only our most favourite family members and friends to join us on the day, yes?"

Becky could scarcely believe her ears. She was happy to comply, she said, but felt compelled to warn him that some folk may not be pleased at being left out.

She reminded him that he had aunts and uncles in Italy who may well expect to be asked to attend.

"Will they not be unhappy about being left out?" she said, only to have him laugh merrily, and say, "Of course, and they are just the folk we do not need to see at our wedding, for they will only make long faces and criticise your gown or my coat or the length of the sermon and perhaps fall asleep in church and snore in the middle of the ceremony. Can you not see it, my dear? Besides, many of them will probably attend the wedding party in Florence."

Becky was pleased that they had agreed upon this very first question in their marriage with such good humour.

"I agree entirely; if only we could settle all matters that we may have to confront in the future in such a harmonious fashion, we should never quarrel at all," she said.

This drew from him a light riposte about a lesson learnt at his father's knee.

"My father was a wise man; whenever he had lost an argument with my mother or my grandmother, he would say to me, 'Remember, Aldo, my son, never begin an argument with a woman, unless you mean to surrender in the end. It is far less painful that way and may even be pleasurable.'"

"It is a lesson well worth learning. Clearly, your father was not just a wise man, but a witty one as well," said Becky.

On Christmas Eve, Mr Contini was to return to London to spend Christmas with his aunt and uncle, planning to return in time for the wedding with them and a gentleman, Mr Antonio Pieri, who was to be his best man.

"Antonio and I have been friends all our lives. His father was killed in the early struggles of Garibaldi, and my family took him in. We are as close as brothers, maybe even closer, for there is no petty rivalry between us as there often is between siblings. I have long wished to introduce him to you, and he will be honoured if you were to meet him," he explained, and Becky was quick to respond.

"I should be very happy to make his acquaintance, and so will Catherine and Frank. Any friend of yours must soon be one of ours, too," she said.

Before leaving for London, Mr Contini presented his bride to be with a necklace, fashioned in Florence of silver and polished turquoise, which brought exclamations of envy and admiration from the entire family. It was the first gift he had given her, and Becky was overwhelmed by its beauty.

"You will wear it on our wedding day?" he asked, and she said without hesitation, "Of course, it is very beautiful; thank you."

When he left, having taken long and loving leave of her, she was dismayed at how lonely she felt without him. She missed him within the first hour of their parting and was glad she had made him promise to take great care on his journey and return to her as soon as ever he could.

Becky spent Christmas Day at the Dower House with her sister and Mr Burnett, hoping that with Catherine's help, she could prepare for her wedding without needless bustle or panic.

Recalling the extravagant celebrations of her first marriage, where all of the arrangements had been taken over by the staff of the Tate household and most of the guests were friends and business associates of her husband's family, Becky delighted in the thought that this time, everything would be as she and Mr Contini wished it to be.

They had promised each other there would be no fuss, no formality, and above all no speeches.

"I do not think we need speeches, my love," he had said when they had talked of their plans. "Politicians make speeches, not lovers. In Italy, they drink wine and sing love songs at the wedding feast; I do not understand this desire for speeches. It is not a political occasion; is it not sufficient that we promise to love and care for one another for the rest of our lives?"

Becky agreed wholeheartedly, saying she could not recall a single wedding at which anyone had made a speech she cared to remember.

"You are quite right; what need is there for speeches? I would much prefer that someone sang love songs at our wedding breakfast; sadly, I know of no one who could be persuaded to oblige," she had said, and he had promised there would be love songs sung at their wedding feast in Italy.

❦

On a cold, bright morning, a few days after Christmas, with their chosen friends and family around them, Becky and Mr Contini were married in the church at Hunsford, where as a child, she had sat with her mother and sisters in the front pew on the left of the aisle, below the pulpit, while her father, Reverend Collins, had preached dreary sermons to his captive audience of parishioners, under the stern, judgmental gaze of the formidable Lady Catherine de Bourgh. Their mother, Charlotte, had ensured that none of her daughters fidgeted or yawned, for fear of bringing down the wrath of Her Ladyship upon them.

On this special day, there was no intimidating presence and no boring homily. Mr Jamison concentrated with peculiar earnestness upon the hymns and readings they had chosen, while the small congregation of family, friends, and staff gathered to wish them happiness.

Jonathan and Anna had arrived at Rosings on Boxing Day together, with James and Emma Wilson representing the Pemberley families. At the wedding breakfast, there were no tiresome speeches, but Jonathan Bingley did rise to propose a toast to the couple.

"They are very dear friends of mine, and I have known them both for most of my life. It is my greatest pleasure to ask you to join me in wishing them every happiness in the future," he said, and Becky could not have been more pleased.

~❧~

Some days later, the newly wed Mr and Mrs Contini travelled to Italy, where they attended a ceremony at an ancient village church, situated above the villa that his family had owned for several generations.

There, a rotund and jovial priest, who remembered Aldo Contini's First Communion, blessed their marriage according to the Catholic rite.

After a traditional wedding feast, at which Becky was welcomed with all the warmth and enthusiasm for which Italian families are renowned, Mr Contini's mother had given them her own special blessing. That she had included a prayer to the Blessed Virgin, asking that they be blessed with many children, was clearly a tribute to Becky's youthful appearance.

Becky concealed her amusement well but made a mental note to tell her sister about it when they met. Then, three fine-looking young men sang traditional Italian love songs, as Mr Contini had promised they would, moving her to tears.

They had hired a vehicle to take them on their wedding journey to a place in the hills above the town, and the winding road required careful negotiation.

Becky's heart was too full to let her make casual conversation, and she was glad her husband was kept busy giving the driver instructions on the route.

Her thoughts were all about him; how in so short a time, her life had become inextricably entwined with his and, by that means, transformed from one of cold anxiety to a life of passionate feeling and vigour.

Becky had no doubt about the rightness of her decision to marry him. In the days following their wedding, when they had returned to spend some time at Edgewater, each hour of every day had brought confirmation of her hopes for happiness as they explored with increasing delight their love for one another.

It was during this time that Becky had begun to contemplate how very alike she and her daughter Josie had been.

They had both wanted more than the dreariness of ordinary life in a country village. Becky had experienced at first hand the humdrum routines of her mother's life at Hunsford parsonage, and later she had seen the privation of her dear friend Emily's household at Kympton; no matter that neither her mother, Charlotte, nor Emily had ever complained, indeed Emily and her husband had seemed to rejoice in their poverty while spending their meagre savings on charity. Becky had determined that she would never be trapped in such a situation.

With youth, energy, and a talent for persuasive speech and writing, she had grasped the chance when Mrs Therese Tate had offered her work on the *Matlock Review*. Young Josie too had hoped that her writing would open doors for her to a new and more exhilarating world, when she had married Julian Darcy and moved to Cambridge. But, eager to succeed, though without the strength to last the course, she had lost her way and destroyed both her marriage and her life.

Becky knew she had married Anthony Tate, not loving him but determined nevertheless to make a success of their marriage, contributing all her skill and enthusiasm to his causes, until his final betrayal following Josie's death had left her bereft and empty of all feeling except pain.

All this passed through her mind in a kaleidoscopic array of images and feelings, as the carter instructed by her husband took their vehicle up the winding road into the hills, leaving the clatter and colour of the town behind. It was much cooler than it had been all afternoon, and as the vehicle stopped and a stiff breeze blew in, her silk shawl provided little protection, and Becky shivered.

Mr Contini leapt out and came round to help her alight and, as he lifted her out, exclaimed, "My love, you are so cold; here let me," he said, taking off his warm coat and placing it over her shoulders, before turning to settle with the carter.

Two servants, a man and a woman, appeared and, having greeted them, carried their luggage indoors. Becky turned to look at the house where they would spend the next few weeks together and, as she did so, heard her husband ask, "Do you like it, Becky?"

She turned to answer him and felt his arms encircle her, keeping her warm.

"It used to belong to my family once; it was a hunting lodge; now, it is a sort of *pensione* for travelers and those like us, who wish to get away out of the bustle of the town. This Winter, we shall have it to ourselves, and we can come and go as we please. Would you like that, my love?"

"I love it already; it's perfect," she replied, looking up at the house set into the hillside, with the forest rising above it. Becky found it completely seductive. "I cannot think of any place I should prefer to be at this moment."

He took her indoors then, assuring her that it would be both warm and comfortable, and the caretaker and his family who would look after them were excellent cooks.

Becky laughed. "Indeed, what more could one want?" She believed, as they went up the stairs, that perhaps she had finally atoned for the mistakes of her past and would be given the chance of a more fulfilling and passionate life with a man who had proved, long before they were lovers, that he could give her the tenderness and comfort that would be at the core of their marriage. It was what Becky had longed for all her life.

❧

Some three weeks later, Catherine received a letter from her sister, which puzzled her just a little. She had expected to find in it descriptions of the sights they had seen—the beauty of the countryside, the wonders of the art and architecture of an ancient city. Catherine knew Becky was deeply aware and appreciative of all these things, and Mr Contini would surely wish to show her more of the rich heritage of his native country.

They had talked together often of the many treasures of Florence—the Palazzo Vecchio, the Uffizi, and the chapel of the Medici—all of which

Catherine had visited on her own wedding journey, and Becky had appeared enthusiastic about the prospect of seeing them herself.

However, astonishingly, Catherine noted there was no mention of any of it, save for a brief reference to the ancient village church, with its monastery dating back to the middle ages, where their marriage had been blessed.

For the rest, Becky wrote chiefly of her husband, of their love and the delight of being together. She wrote:

> *It is, my dearest Cathy, as though I have sloughed off every vestige of my old, unhappy self and learned in these few weeks to begin a new life, seeing and understanding new things, discovering and enjoying new feelings, and, above all, learning that nothing in my life has been worth more than the love we share.*
>
> *I know that you, above all others, will understand how I feel, because you have been so close to me in recent times and know how my life has been.*

Catherine smiled as she read these words. In her heart, she understood exactly how her sister must feel.

Becky had found, in her middle years, the kind of love she had foregone when, as a young woman, she had married for practical reasons a man she could not love with the same ardour. In accepting Anthony Tate, her youthful yearnings for affection had been exchanged for influence, status, and financial independence.

Catherine could not know for certain if her sister had regretted altogether her earlier marriage; what she knew with absolute conviction was that this time, her chances of happiness were far greater, for there had been no compromise on love.

She was about to put the letter away when her husband entered the room. "A letter at last, from Becky," she said and handed it to him with a smile.

Frank Burnett read it carefully through and, as he returned it to his wife, said gently, "It seems to me, my love, that your sister is a fortunate woman indeed. She has learned, in the happiest possible way, the important difference between a loving marriage and a shared bed."

Postscript

THEY RETURNED TO ENGLAND in the Spring, and the countryside was at its best, when Becky and her husband arrived at Edgewater. The house, which had looked its age in the dark of Winter, had taken on a new lightness with the trees in bloom and daffodils pushing up all over the park.

Across the lake, the poplars in the spinney wore new subtle green scarves, which moved lightly in the breeze, and everywhere birdcalls resounded in the soft air. Nelly came out ahead of Mrs Bates to greet them, and so excited was she at seeing her mistress return home, she quite forgot the little speech she had prepared, and simply grasped Becky's hands and said, with tears in her eyes, "Welcome home, ma'am."

Catherine and Mr Burnett had come over from the Dower House to welcome them home, and the two sisters had so much to say to one another, they disappeared upstairs for a while. Catherine did not need to ask, nor her sister to say in so many words, what they both knew well.

Clearly, Becky's happiness was complete.

Catherine had more good news for her sister, which she was impatient to impart.

During the weeks after the wedding, while Becky and her husband had been in Italy, Catherine had been visited by Annabel Rickman, who had brought with her a letter she had received from Mrs Bancroft. It had contained an invitation to Annabel, her husband, and son to visit Blessington Manor, with the permission of her present employer, of course.

In the absence of her mistress, the young woman had pleaded with Catherine for permission to accept the invitation.

"I decided to let her go; I did not think you would have any objection. They were away for a week, and, Becky dear, what do you think? When they returned, we heard that Mrs Bancroft had also invited Annabel's mother, who is now, sadly, a widow. Annabel was so happy to have seen her mother again; I do hope, Becky, that you agree I did right?"

"Of course you did right, Cathy; I am truly pleased that Annabel and her mother are reconciled. The poor girl has suffered enough. It seems such a pity that her father remained intransigent to the end," Becky replied and added, "Doubtless, Mrs Grey must have enjoyed seeing her grandson, too. I think, Cathy, that Mrs Bancroft is a genuinely good woman. I must write to thank her for her kindness to both Annabel and her mother."

Catherine concurred, then referring lightly to Becky's letter, she asked in a teasing tone of voice if they had not found time to visit any of the great attractions of Florence.

Becky laughed and admitted that indeed they had.

"On two or three afternoons, when most of the population of the town was taking its siesta and there were not too many visitors around."

She did, however, explain.

"But I did not wish to fill my letters to you with descriptions of statues, palaces, and fountains; I knew you had seen them too, and they would have meant little to me had I not been with someone who had so completely transformed my life. I wanted you to understand that. Oh Cathy, I am happier than I have ever been, more than I had ever hoped to be," Becky said softly.

"Of course you are," Catherine replied, taking her hand, "and you deserve to be, for I know no one more generous or more compassionate than you. Yet, life has been hard for you; you have had so few rewards, Becky. It seems so unfair—it has troubled me often."

Seeing the sadness on her sister's face, Becky leaned forward and placed her finger on Catherine's lips.

"Let it trouble you no longer, my dear, for I am so well rewarded now, so completely content, unused as I am to happiness, I can scarcely believe it myself."

Catherine was smiling, but there were tears in her eyes.

※

When they came downstairs, a table had been laid in the garden in the dappled shade of a flowering peach tree. Soon, tea was served and the conversation flowed easily, being mainly about Italy and their mutual enjoyment of its treasures and, conversely, the pleasure of returning home to England.

Later, the gentlemen elected to take a tour of the grounds, and they walked out towards the lake, delighting both sisters, who noted how well they seemed to get on together, auguring well for their future as brothers-in-law and good neighbours.

Nelly brought out a basket of letters, which had arrived during their absence in Italy, placing it upon a stool beside the tea table.

Becky reached for a few and began to open them.

"Oh look, this one's from Cassy," she said.

It contained a brief but sincere message.

Cassandra and Richard Gardiner apologised for not attending the wedding. Their young daughter, Laura-Ann, always a delicate child, had been ill with bronchitis again, Cassy explained, preventing their attendance, but they wished Becky and her husband every happiness and invited them to stay at Camden Park, when they were next in Derbyshire.

There was a note from Anna Bingley inviting the couple to visit Netherfield in June, and yet another from Emma Wilson reminding Becky that she and her husband would always be welcome at Standish Park.

Becky seemed surprised by the many offers of hospitality from members of the family.

"It is very kind of them to invite us," said Becky. "I shall write to thank them all, of course, but I do not believe we shall do much more travelling until midsummer, unless it is to Netherfield; I have already accepted an invitation to visit." Then turning over a letter, which carried no indication of the writer's identity, she said, "Now who could this be? I do not know the writing at all, and, it must be said, it is a very poor hand."

When she opened it, Becky exclaimed, "Good heavens! It's from Lydia Wickham! Why ever would she be writing to me?" she asked as she handed the letter to Catherine.

Catherine read it through, with some difficulty, for the handwriting within was even worse than that of the direction outside and deteriorated as the writer rambled on.

"What does she say?" asked Becky.

"Well, she congratulates you on your second marriage—she underlines 'second'—and proceeds to grumble that she has not been able to find anyone suitable to marry her only daughter."

"That does not surprise me at all, for who would want Lydia Wickham for a mother-in-law?" asked Becky.

"Who indeed?" said Catherine, before continuing.

"She complains also that she was offended at not receiving an invitation to your wedding. Oh poor Lydia, she is such a silly woman—Mama used to say that she has changed not at all since she was fifteen and eloped with Mr Wickham, to the chagrin of poor Jane and Lizzie. She believes you have deliberately slighted her."

Becky was astonished; what could she possibly say in reply? Inviting Lydia had never even been contemplated. They had not met in years until she had turned up at Mrs Collins' funeral in full formal mourning!

"Must I respond?" she asked, a little bewildered by this unexpected intrusion of Lydia Wickham into their lives.

"Not unless you wish to, since she does not actually ask anything of you. I suppose she merely wished to grumble about not being invited to the wedding," said Catherine, and Becky made an instant decision.

"Well then, since nothing I can say is likely to satisfy any of Lydia's concerns, and as I have no suggestions for a suitor for her daughter, I had best ignore it," she said, putting the letter back in the basket.

As she opened the rest of her letters, Becky was struck by the amount of comment that her wedding to Mr Contini had aroused among their general acquaintance, some of whom had not corresponded with her for years. Clearly, there were those who felt that marriage to a handsome "foreign gentleman" was a matter for congratulations, while others expressed surprise and, presuming that he spoke only Italian, wondered if Becky intended to learn the language herself!

That their ignorance amused rather than angered her was an indication of the lightness of her present disposition.

"I have to say, Cathy, I am astonished at all these people taking the time to write and express such strange concerns. I should not have thought my marriage warranted such interest," she said as she picked up the last letter left in the basket.

It was from Jonathan Bingley, and to judge by the date, had been written only a few days ago.

As she opened it up, Catherine heard a quick intake of breath and, not wishing to pry into her sister's affairs, said nothing, while Becky's exclamations grew ever more excited. Then, turning to Catherine with a look of absolute delight upon her face, she handed her the letter.

Intrigued, Catherine began to read.

After a paragraph of casual pleasantries, expressing his hope that they had enjoyed a pleasant holiday in Italy, Jonathan Bingley wrote:

My main purpose in writing is to acquaint you with two matters that will be of interest to you.

First, there is the matter of a letter I received from your daughter-in-law, Mrs Pauline Tate.

She assured me she was writing unbeknownst to her husband, but because she felt he, despite her pleas, had not been willing to do so. She claims she decided to approach me on the grounds that I was the trustee of the late Mr Tate's American estate. Mrs Tate contends that since you have remarried, you no longer need all of the money in the Trust, and it is unfair that her husband and children should be denied some benefit from it.

I have written to Mrs Walter Tate, stating my opinion that neither she nor her husband Walter are entitled to any benefit from the Trust, because it has been sequestered for your use alone under the terms of Mr Tate's will. Besides, I have pointed out that I have no power at all to make any changes to the dispersal of the benefits, only to carry out exactly the intention expressed in your late husband's will.

I sincerely hope that will be the end of the matter. I do not expect that you will be troubled in any way by another such attempt. The fact that your son Walter did not agree to make the approach suggests that we will hear no more from that quarter.

Catherine looked stunned. "Becky, I cannot believe what I am reading here; it is hard to imagine that even Pauline, who is not averse to pushing her own interest, would stoop to such a devious device as this and without her husband's knowledge."

Becky seemed untroubled. "Neither could I, but nothing Pauline does surprises me anymore. However, Jonathan has dealt with her in a most satisfactory way, I think. At least, I can be grateful that Walter did not lend his name to her clumsy, mercenary effort."

Then, with a smile, Becky urged Catherine to return to the letter. "But read on, Cathy, there is far more interesting news on page two."

Catherine did as she advised.

On another matter, which is likely to be of much greater interest to you at this time, Jonathan wrote:

I have given some time to considering your proposition for purchasing a small printing business, and while I have not had an accountant look at the figures, I am not set against the idea, if it can be sensibly managed.

My enquiries have revealed a considerable demand for the kind of service such a printery would provide, and I do not mean only the publication of novels by ladies.

I am informed, by those who are better acquainted with the business of printing than I am, that there are several other possibilities—catalogues, invitations, posters, pamphlets, and similar items. It will require some careful planning and accounting, which is why I believe I should like to discuss some of these matters with you and Mr Contini when we meet later this year, before making a final decision.

If a business may be purchased for the right price and a suitable person be found to manage it, you may well look forward to the day when you will have your own personal imprint. Then, perhaps, Becky, in a few years, the name of Rebecca Collins will be as well known in literary circles as that of Miss Charlotte Bronte, whom you admire so much.

He concluded with the customary salutations and good wishes, but Catherine could scarcely contain her delight.

"Oh Becky, this is excellent news." She rose and the two sisters embraced.

"Indeed it is, Cathy; it is such good news, I could not have asked for a better homecoming present," said Becky.

Then, seeing Mr Contini and Frank Burnett returning from their tour of the property, she added, "Come, we must tell them at once," and they walked out across the lawn, towards the lake, to meet their husbands.

Appendix

A list of the main characters in *A Woman of Influence:*

Becky Tate (neé Collins)—daughter of Charlotte Collins and widow of Mr
    Anthony Tate, publisher, of Matlock in Derbyshire
Josie (deceased)—Becky's daughter and first wife of Julian Darcy
Anthony Darcy—young son of Julian and Josie and the next Master of Pemberley
Catherine Burnett—Becky's elder sister
Frank Burnett—Catherine's husband
Jonathan Bingley—son of Jane and Charles Bingley
Anna Bingley—Jonathan's wife
Signor and Signora Contini—friends of the Darcys and Bingleys
Mr Aldo Contini—their nephew and a friend of Jonathan Bingley
Emily Courtney—cousin of Jane and Elizabeth, daughter of Mr and Mrs
    Gardiner and wife of Reverend Courtney of Kympton
Dr Richard Gardiner—brother of Emily, husband of Cassandra Darcy
Cassandra Gardiner—daughter of Mr and Mrs Darcy
Julian Darcy—son of Mr and Mrs Darcy of Pemberley
Jessica—his second wife and daughter of Emily Courtney
Emma Wilson—daughter of Jane and Charles Bingley, sister of Jonathan
Mr James Wilson—her husband, a judge of the County Court

From the pages of *Pride and Prejudice:*
   Mr and Mrs Darcy of Pemberley
   Mr and Mrs Bingley of Ashford Park
   Mrs Charlotte Collins (née Lucas)

Acknowledgements

The author wishes to thank her many friends who have helped with information for this book and especially Ms Claudia Taylor, librarian, for her specialised research.

Thanks are due also to Marissa O'Donnell for the artwork, Anthony for technical assistance with her computer, and Beverly Kleinjan Wong for her excellent work on the website. So also to the many readers who have sent their comments, which are greatly appreciated.

To Miss Jane Austen, as always, heartfelt thanks for her inspiration.

—Rebecca Ann Collins
www.rebeccaanncollins.com

About the Author

A lifelong fan of Jane Austen, Rebecca Ann Collins first read *Pride and Prejudice* at the tender age of twelve. She fell in love with the characters and since then has devoted years of research and study to the life and works of her favorite author. As a teacher of literature and a librarian, she has gathered a wealth of information about Miss Austen and the period in which she lived and wrote, which became the basis of her books about the Pemberley families. The popularity of The Pemberley Chronicles series with Jane Austen fans has been her reward.

With a love of reading, music, art, and gardening, Ms. Collins claims she is very comfortable in the period about which she writes, and feels great empathy with the characters she portrays. While she enjoys the convenience of modern life, she finds much to admire in the values and world view of Jane Austen.

The Pemberley Chronicles

A Companion Volume to Jane Austen's Pride and Prejudice
The Pemberley Chronicles: Book 1
REBECCA ANN COLLINS

"A lovely complementary novel to Jane Austen's *Pride and Prejudice*.
Austen would surely give her smile of approval."
—BEVERLY WONG, AUTHOR OF *Pride & Prejudice Prudence*

The weddings are over, the saga begins

The guests (including millions of readers and viewers) wish the two happy couples health and happiness. As the music swells and the credits roll, two things are certain: Jane and Bingley will want for nothing, while Elizabeth and Darcy are to be the happiest couple in the world!

Elizabeth and Darcy's personal stories of love, marriage, money, and children are woven together with the threads of social and political history of England in the nineteenth century. As changes in industry and agriculture affect the people of Pemberley and the surrounding countryside, the Darcys strive to be progressive and forward-looking while upholding beloved traditions.

"Those with a taste for the balance and humour of Austen will find a worthy companion volume."
—*Book News*

978-1-4022-1153-9 • $14.95 US/ $17.95 CAN/ £7.99 UK

The Women of Pemberley

The acclaimed **Pride and Prejudice** *sequel series*

The Pemberley Chronicles: Book 2

REBECCA ANN COLLINS

"Yet another wonderful work by Ms. Collins."
—BEVERLY WONG, AUTHOR OF *Pride & Prejudice Prudence*

A new age is dawning

Five women—strong, intelligent, independent of mind, and in the tradition of many Jane Austen heroines—continue the legacy of Pemberley into a dynamic new era at the start of the Victorian Age. Events unfold as the real and fictional worlds intertwine, linked by the relationship of the characters to each other and to the great estate of Pemberley, the heart of their community.

With some characters from the beloved works of Jane Austen, and some new from the author's imagination, the central themes of love, friendship, marriage, and a sense of social obligation remain, showcased in the context of the sweeping political and social changes of the age.

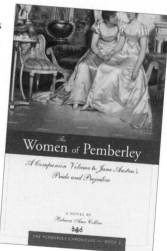

"The stories are so well told one would enjoy them even if they were not sequels to any other novel."
—*Book News*

978-1-4022-1154-6 • $14.95 US/ $17.95 CAN/ £7.99 UK

Netherfield Park Revisited

The acclaimed **Pride and Prejudice** *sequel series*

The Pemberley Chronicles: Book 3

REBECCA ANN COLLINS

"A very readable and believable tale for readers
who like their romance with a historical flavor." —*Book News*

Love, betrayal, and changing times for the Darcys and the Bingleys

Three generations of the Darcy and the Bingley families evolve against a backdrop of the political ideals and social reforms of the mid-Victorian era.

Jonathan Bingley, the handsome, distinguished son of Charles and Jane Bingley, takes center stage, returning to Hertfordshire as master of Netherfield Park. A deeply passionate and committed man, Jonathan is immersed in the joys and heartbreaks of his friends and family and his own challenging marriage. At the same time, he is swept up in the changes of the world around him.

Netherfield Park Revisited combines captivating details of life in mid-Victorian England with the ongoing saga of Jane Austen's beloved *Pride and Prejudice* characters.

"Ms. Collins has done it again!" —BEVERLY WONG,
AUTHOR OF *Pride & Prejudice Prudence*

978-1-4022-1155-3 • $14.95 US/ $15.99 CAN/ £7.99 UK

The Ladies of Longbourn

The acclaimed **Pride and Prejudice** *sequel series*

The Pemberley Chronicles: Book 4

REBECCA ANN COLLINS

"Interesting stories, enduring themes, gentle humour, and lively dialogue." —*Book News*

A complex and charming young woman of the Victorian age, tested to the limits of her endurance

The bestselling *Pemberley Chronicles* series continues the saga of the Darcys and Bingleys from Jane Austen's *Pride and Prejudice* and introduces imaginative new characters.

Anne-Marie Bradshaw is the granddaughter of Charles and Jane Bingley. Her father now owns Longbourn, the Bennet's estate in Hertfordshire. A young widow after a loveless marriage, Anne-Marie and her stepmother Anna, together with Charlotte Collins, widow of the unctuous Mr. Collins, are the Ladies of Longbourn. These smart, independent women challenge the conventional roles of women in the Victorian era, while they search for ways to build their own lasting legacies in an ever-changing world.

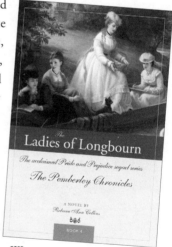

Jane Austen's original characters—Darcy, Elizabeth, Bingley, and Jane—anchor a dramatic story full of wit and compassion.

"A masterpiece that reaches the heart." —BEVERLEY WONG, AUTHOR OF *Pride & Prejudice Prudence*

978-1-4022-1219-2 • $14.95 US/ $15.99 CAN/ £7.99 UK

Mr. Darcy's Diary
AMANDA GRANGE

"A gift to a new generation of Darcy fans
and a treat for existing fans as well." —AUSTENBLOG

The only place Darcy could share his innermost feelings...

...was in the private pages of his diary. Torn between his sense of duty to his family name and his growing passion for Elizabeth Bennet, all he can do is struggle not to fall in love. A skillful and graceful imagining of the hero's point of view in one of the most beloved and enduring love stories of all time.

What readers are saying:

"A delicious treat for all Austen addicts."

"Amanda Grange knows her subject...I ended up reading the entire book in one sitting."

"Brilliant, you could almost hear Darcy's voice...I was so sad when it came to an end. I loved the visions she gave us of their married life."

"Amanda Grange has perfectly captured all of Jane Austen's clever wit and social observations to make *Mr. Darcy's Diary* a must read for any fan."

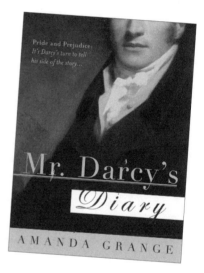

978-1-4022-0876-8 • $14.95 US/ $19.95 CAN/ £7.99 UK

Mr. and Mrs. Fitzwilliam Darcy: Two Shall Become One

SHARON LATHAN

"Highly entertaining... I felt fully immersed in the time period. Well done!" —*Romance Reader at Heart*

A fascinating portrait of a timeless, consuming love

It's Darcy and Elizabeth's wedding day, and the journey is just beginning as Jane Austen's beloved *Pride and Prejudice* characters embark on the greatest adventure of all: marriage and a life together filled with surprising passion, tender self-discovery, and the simple joys of every day.

As their love story unfolds in this most romantic of Jane Austen sequels, Darcy and Elizabeth each reveal to the other how their relationship blossomed from misunderstanding to perfect understanding and harmony, and a marriage filled with romance, sensuality, and the beauty of a deep, abiding love.

What readers are saying:

"This journey is truly amazing."

"What a wonderful beginning to this truly beautiful marriage."

"Could not stop reading."

"So beautifully written...making me feel as though I was in the room with Lizzy and Darcy...and sharing in all of the touching moments between."

978-1-4022-1523-0 • $14.99 US/ $15.99 CAN/ £7.99 UK

Loving Mr. Darcy: Journeys Beyond Pemberley
SHARON LATHAN

"A romance that transcends time." —*The Romance Studio*

Darcy and Elizabeth embark on the journey of a lifetime

Six months into his marriage to Elizabeth Bennet, Darcy is still head over heels in love, and each day offers more opportunities to surprise and delight his beloved bride. Elizabeth has adapted to being the Mistress of Pemberley, charming everyone she meets and handling her duties with grace and poise. Just when it seems life can't get any better, Elizabeth gets the most wonderful news. The lovers leave the serenity of Pemberley, traveling through the sumptuous landscape of Regency England, experiencing the lavish sights, sounds, and tastes around them. With each day come new discoveries as they become further entwined, body and soul.

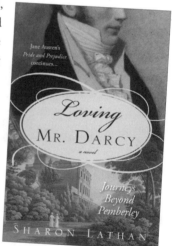

What readers are saying:

"Darcy's passion for love and life with Lizzy is brought to the forefront and captured beautifully."

"Sharon Lathan is a wonderful writer… I believe that Jane Austen herself would love this story as much as I did."

"The historical backdrop of the book is unbelievable—I actually felt like I could see all the places where the Darcys traveled."

"Truly captures the heart of Darcy & Elizabeth! Very well written and totally hot!"

978-1-4022-1741-8 • $14.99 US/ $18.99 CAN/ £7.99 UK